Between The Sheets

Dear Reader:

Cairo fans and new readers alike will love this latest erotic adventure in his true off-the-chain fashion. *Between the Sheets* is simply an ongoing sexfest carried out by a married couple, Marcel and Marika, who have an extremely open mind when it comes to who's doing who and where.

Both explore same-sex relations as much as with each other, and the rules are firmly laid down. Each one selects their next conquest and must be present or participate in the action. They bring new meaning to threesomes and heat up the sheets with their never-ending fantasies. Truly combining business with pleasure, their sizzling, no-holds-barred lifestyle is balanced with their professional personas. Marcel, president of a record label, dishes the heat on his late-night radio show, and Marika runs her own publishing company.

Tune in and discover how Cairo brings the heat once again in this crafty tale and what happens when an unexpected encounter adds mayhem to the mix.

As always, thanks for the love and support shown toward myself and the authors that I publish under Strebor Books. We appreciate each and every one of you and will continue to strive to bring you cutting-edge, exciting books in the future. For more information, please join my Facebook page @AuthorZane, Twitter @AuthorZane, or Instagram@ AuthorZane. You can also find my "toys" at Zanespleasureproducts. com and my main web site remains Eroticanoir.com.

Blessings,

Zane

Publisher
Strebor Books
www.simonandschuster.com

ZANE PRESENTS

Between The Sheets

A NOVEL BY

CAIRO

SBI

STREBOR BOOKS

NEW YORK LONDON TORONTO SYDNEY

SBI

Strebor Books
P.O. Box 6505
Largo, MD 20792
http://www.streborbooks.com

ISBN 978-1-59309-594-9
ISBN 978-1-4767-7580-7 (ebook)
LCCN 2014943295

First Strebor Books trade paperback edition February 2015

Cover design: www.mariondesigns.com
Cover photograph: © Keith Saunders/Keith Saunders Photos

10 9 8 7 6 5 4 3 2 1

Manufactured in the United States of America

For information regarding special discounts for bulk purchases, please contact Simon & Schuster Special Sales at 1-866-506-1949 or business@simonandschuster.com

The Simon & Schuster Speakers Bureau can bring authors to your live event. For more information or to book an event, contact the Simon & Schuster Speakers Bureau at 1-866-248-3049 or visit our website at www.simonspeakers.com.

ACKNOWLEDGMENTS

Eleven titles in, with me currently finishing up my twelfth, and, still, it feels like my first release. I'm always like a virgin in heat tryna get that first nut, waiting with baited breath for the book to drop. Then after the clock strikes midnight and all the iPads & Kindles are downloaded with their books, and my joints are snatched off the bookstores' shelves, I'm always on pins 'n' needles—cupping my balls, hoping that those who've dropped their paper on me enjoy the heat as much as I enjoyed writing it. With each joint, I breathe fire onto those pages. And I am thankful to be able to share my love of hotness in the sheets with those open-minded enough; those bold enough, those adventurous enough, to wanna step into the light. On some realness, I am forever grateful for having Juice Lovas who show me mad luv, spread the word, and wave their freak flags proudly! I say all this to say, THANK YOU! Here's to *Between the Sheets* & every other hot joint I drop. All that I do is for you! Fuck what ya heard. The Cairo movement is here to stay!

As always, special shout-out to all the Facebook beauties 'n' cuties and cool-ass bruhs who make this journey mad fun: Real rap. Y'all my muthaeffen peeps! Too many of you to name, but YOU know who you are, godddammit!

To Zane, Charmaine, Yona and the rest of the Strebor/Simon & Schuster team: As always, I hope you all know how much ya boy appreciates the never-ending luv!

To the members of *Cairo's World*: Thanks for the mad luv!

And, as always, to the naysayers: You still mad or nah? Ha! Lick balls, baby! What would the movement be without you? On some realness, I am all that I am because of you. Thanks for the inspiration for me to continue to do what I do, how I do it, just so I can fuck with you. Here's another dose of heat for you to choke on. Gag on the flames, muhfuckas!

One luv—

Cairo

ONE

Marika

I have a confession. I'm a slut. Yes. That's right. I'm a smutty, dick-sucking, ball-slurping, ass-licking, toe-sucking, pussy-eating, cum-loving whore. For my husband, that is…*always* for him.

The man of my most sweetest, wettest dreams.

My lover.

My soul mate.

My freak in the sheets.

The man I *love* getting filthy with.

Marcel.

Mmmm…yes! He's my addiction. And Lord knows he's sinfully fine.

Dark chocolate-coated perfection with long lashes wrapped around smoldering dark chocolate eyes and soft, full, luscious lips.

Everything on him is long…*and* thick.

His fingers.

His dick.

His feet.

Oooh, did I mention his tongue? Yes, yes, yes…his wet, pussy-pleasing tongue.

"Mmm," he moans. "This wet pussy…" His tongue dips inside my cunt, then glides over my clit. "You taste sooo fuckin' good…"

His voice, rich and deep, vibrates over my swollen lips, oozes its way through my slit, resonating inside my entire body.

I let out a gasp and claw at the sheets. "Mmmmm, oooooh, yes-ssss…"

God, I, uh, mmm, love…this…mmm…man.

He's six feet eight, 245 pounds of chiseled bliss.

A delicious mix of hood swag and sophistication, he is as rough, raw, and rugged as he is seductive and sensual. Combine all of that with an overactive libido and an extremely creative imagination and you have the recipe for long nights of toe-curling, lip-biting, hot, sweaty fucking or nights of slow, passionate, steamy love-making; or an all-night oral-fest with him feasting on my pussy until I am dazed and confused.

Take your pick.

Marcel closes his warm mouth around my clit and gently sucks.

"Oh, God, oh, God, oh, God…fuck, fuck, fuck…yes, yes, yes, yes…oooh, oooh, oooh…"

Floetry floats around us low in the background. "Say Yes" plays. And all I can think is, *yes, yes, yes, yes!!!* Marcel pauses just long enough to ask, "You like this tongue all in your sweet, tangy cunt?" He doesn't wait for a response. He goes back to sucking my clit in sync to the beat, grinding himself into the mattress.

My eyes flutter closed, then open all unfocused. Blurry. Teary-eyed. It takes several seconds to stop them from rolling up in my head before I can blink my lover back into view. His head is bob-bing up and down between my splayed legs, his tongue working feverishly over my clit, along the mouth of my pussy. My hips lift slightly off the bed as his big hands cup my ass and squeeze.

"Mmmmm…yessss…"

I eye Marcel through a haze of passion as he closes his mouth, his lips puckering around my clit, and suckles as he licks into me. I gasp and shiver. The heat of his tongue causing me to slip in and out of consciousness as my clit is being sucked into his mouth, pulled at, and nibbled.

The more Marcel licks, the more his tongue flicks, then dips, then feathers over my clit, my pussy gets wetter and hotter. Slick juices pool out of my slit, bringing me closer to another climax. I arch my back and willingly, lovingly, offer him more of me—my gift, my love offering, to him.

He moans into my sex again, causing my cum-coated walls to pulsate.

"Yesssss, yessss, yesssss…"

Marcel tongues my pussy, pinches my clit, and causes a whimper to hitch in the back of my throat. He knows what he's doing to me. He's pushing me to the edge of an orgasm, tongue-fucking me…speechless. My wet cunt stains his mouth, his lips, his tongue. His chin is slick from my boiling juices.

I buck my hips. "Oh, yes, right there, right there, right there… oh, yes, oh, yes, ohhh, ohhh, ohhh, yes, yes, yes, yessss…"

My eyeballs roll up and around in their sockets a few times before I am finally able to open them again. I blink. Blink again until my eyes swim back into focus. Then slowly take in the heavenly sight before me. My man looks so fucking good between my legs, his face drenched, his tongue swimming in my juices as he alternately licks and sucks at me, alternating from suck to lick, then doing both at the same time, then alternating quick up-and-down strokes with swirling tongue circles that makes hot wet greed swell inside my pussy, causing my sweet musky scent to thicken the air. It fills my nostrils as I inhale, deeply, intoxicating me.

I love the smell of my wet pussy.

Love the *click-click* sound of Marcel's tongue. Its melody playing against the low sounds of Marsha Ambrosius' "With You" easing through the surround sound.

"Oh, God...ohhhhh, God, yes," I mewl. "Eat my pussy. Oh... oooh..."

"That's right, baby," Marcel whispers, looking up from between my thighs; his dreamy, bedroom eyes full of lust and love and a hint of mischief; his cum-slick lips glistening, "give me that sweet pussy..." He licks his lips, then dips his head back in between my quivering legs, sucking my clit into his mouth like an oyster as he slides a thick finger into my slit and pumps inside me in a steady rhythm. He swirls his finger into my wetness, pulls out, then slides two fingers in, then three, until I feel everything inside of me start to throb and ache. My pussy clenches around his fingers, greedily sucking them in. He is skillfully stretching my walls and stroking my spot, stoking the fire.

Oh, God! I want, need, his huge dick filling me.

"Please," I whisper.

"Please, what?" he taunts, lapping at my juicy pussy, sinking his tongue between the plump folds of my throbbing lips, then swirling it back over my clit.

My heartbeat quickens. My body trembles. Drool settles at the corner of my mouth. I moan his name and cum hard, the hot pulse of my need spews out and drenches his fingers, his hand, as I get lost into a knot of swirling, throbbing ecstasy. I grind my pelvis into the blaze—his thick, sticky fingers still pumping into the flames—and beg him over and over and over.

"Please, please, please...oh, Marcel, baby...pleeeeeease..."

"Please, what? Tell me what you want, baby." He looks up and grins that lopsided grin; his deep dimples creasing each side of his face. "Tell daddy what you want..."

Daddy. Oooh, daddy, daddy, daddy…

"I w-want t-that b-big d-dick, d-daddy…mmm…f-fuuuck m-meeee…"

He leaves me breathless and begging.

"Your Hands" floats around the room and Marcel's face disappears again. He hums the tune into my pussy. And tears spring from my eyes.

I know most people don't believe in love at first sight. But I do. And I knew the first time I spotted Marcel—fall semester of my freshman year at Howard—coming out of the student center with three of his frat brothers that he would be my everything. And I knew the first time he slid my black-laced panties down over the swell of my hips—at the end of fall semester the following year—spread open my thighs and licked my clit, then slid his long, delicious dick into me, slow-fucking my pussy and stretching open the inside of my silky walls—causing wave after wave of wet blazing heat to flood my body, that he was the man I'd spend the rest of my life with.

And here we are sixteen years later, and nothing's changed. I am still in love with my husband, more so now than ever before. With him, there are no sexual limits. He has pushed and tested and tried every one over the years, taking me to places beyond my own imagination. And there is *nothing* I will not do to pleasure him. There is *nothing* he will not do to pleasure me. My fantasies are his. And his deepest desires are mine. All within reason, of course.

And, together, we are a never-ending inferno. A wild, thrashing river of hot sensations, forbidden desires, and fulfilled fantasies.

I gasp as Marcel sucks on my labia like it's a juicy peach and my heart nearly stops beating as my nipples pebble and my pussy floods with more liquid warmth. "Oh, yes, baby," I whimper, grinding into his mouth. "I love you, I love you, I looove you…"

I fight to keep my eyes open, fight through the glaze of encroaching pleasure slowly blinding me. I don't know how much longer I can hold on. I am hanging on the edge of the cliff, losing myself, my mind falling deeper into the haze as he pulls his fingers from between my slick heat and brings them up to my lips.

"Taste your pussy," he murmurs, sliding two fingers into my drooling mouth. I flick my tongue over his fingers, tasting the sweet thickness of my cunt cream, sucking him into me, pretending it is his thick dick in my mouth. Wishing it was.

Oh how I wish, yearn, for him to inch up over my body, hoist my legs up over my head and aim the thick, bulbous head of his dark, veiny dick at the opening of my slit, then fuck his way into the scorching heat. But he doesn't.

Instead, he pulls his fingers out of my mouth and sucks them into his own, sliding them in and out, then flicking his tongue over each finger.

"I want you to come for me, Marika. Give me that sweet, juice, baby. Squirt it all over my face…" His gaze shimmers with heat and want—and determination. Then his face disappears, again, his tongue circling over my clit, then plunging back into my hot pussy, darting in and out, in and out, hard, fast.

Marcel slides a wet finger along the crack of my ass—my asshole is juicy and slick from my pussy and his spit—then pushes it inside of me. In synchronized motion, his finger and tongue work in harmony with Jill Scott's "He Loves Me." He tongue-fucks my pussy. Finger-fucks my ass.

And now I am gasping for breath. Sweet torture. That's what this is.

I open my mouth to speak, to murmur, to moan, to babble…anything, but nothing comes out. Mouth agape, my eyes float around in their sockets as a jolt, the tingles, a surge of rippling fire, coils through my body and causes my pussy to spasm uncontrollably.

I am overwhelmed.

Powerless.

The searing heat completely takes over.

And I come. And come. And come. Clasping my thighs around my lover's head, I squirt and soak him, wetting the sheets beneath me.

TWO

Marcel

"Yo, what's good, my beauties, cuties, hookers, hoes, pimps, and playboys…this is ya boy, Mar*Sell*, coming at you live with another steamy segment of *Creepin' 'n' Freakin' After Dark*. All of my peeps who get down with me know how I like to serve it up: Hot, raw 'n' ohhhh so nasty. So if you're just tuning in to the Tri-State area's hottest radio station, 93.3 *The Heat*, sit back…relax…light a candle… pour yourself a glass of your favorite wine…pull out your favorite lube…your favorite toy…or hit up that special someone…and prepare to be stimulated beyond your own imagination as we get into tonight's topic of putting in that tongue 'n' neck work.

"That's right, my freaky peeps. Oral sex. It's not an option. It's a requirement. And tonight it's going down. But before we get it poppin', we're gonna slowly heat you up with this sexy Janet Jackson joint, 'Warmth.' I don't know 'bout you, but I like it when it's real wet 'n' nasty…"

I adjust my microphone as Janet whispers over the air about nothing comparing to the warmth of her mouth. I'm looking forward to tonight's segment, already anticipating the freak-nasty comments callers would make about their dick-sucking-and pussy-eating sexapades. All things real, I love getting my dick sucked. Love fucking it down into a wet, tight throat. Hearing them juicy smack-suck sounds coming out of a mouth while I'm sliding this dick in 'n' out turns me the fuck on.

Shit.

I slip my hand down into my sweats and stroke myself on the sly underneath my desk; the urgent need to bust this nut deep inside a wet mouth slowly swells up in my balls.

I reach for my buzzing cell with my free hand. I smile, opening the text message. OOH I LOVE HEARING UR VOICE OVER THE AIRWAVES. CAN'T WAIT TO HEAR TONIGHT'S HOT TOPIC. I BET UR ALREADY PLAYING W/THAT JUICY DICK ☺

I grin, removing my hand from my sweats, temporarily leaving my thick, aching dick stretching along my thigh. I text back, U KNO ME SO WELL, BABY. CAN'T WAIT 2 STRETCH DAT WET PUSSY N FEEL ALL THIS DICK DEEP UP N U

Less than three seconds, another text comes through. HMMM! THIS PUSSY MISSES U! U TEASED N TONGUED ME REAL GOOD 2NIGHT. I CAN STILL FEEL UR TONGUE INSIDE OF ME. U LEFT ME SO WET N HORNY 4 MORE OF U

I smile, sliding my hand back down into my sweats, then quickly glance over into the control room at my producer, Nina, who is staring back at me licking her succulent lips. I wink at her. She smiles, shaking her head.

Janet Jackson fades out and Marsha Ambrosius' "69" eases over the airwaves as I squeeze the head of my dick. I'm ready to fuck. Ready to gut a throat and beat some pussy up. I glance down at my watch. *Two more hours to go.* I've been working the 8 p.m. to 12 a.m. slot on Thursday nights at the radio station for the past seven years. It was supposed to be a temp thing, but when the ratings shot through the fuckin' roof and peeps started calling in begging for me to come through and hit 'em with that nasty heat, that sealed the deal.

And here I am one night a week, keeping the heat cranked up and the freaks *turnt* up. Not because I need the paper. Nah, I'm paid out the ass. I'm on the air doing what I do because—despite having built my own empire—my first love has, and will always be, radio broadcasting. Being on the air as a radio personality is all I ever dreamed of as a kid. And it's what I went to school for.

I look over and eye Nina, who gives me the signal that we're back on the air in five…four…three…two…one…

"What's good, my peeps. We're back on the air ready to turn up. And tonight we're talking about putting your mouth on it. That's right, my freaky peeps. Sucking. Licking. Slurping. Tonguing it down. Fellatio. Top. Dome. Head. Neck. Becky. Brain. Pole Smoke. Knob Slob. Whatever lil' term you wanna call it, I wanna hear from the ladies, first. Where are all my bobble heads 'n' deep throat divas at? Holla at ya boy. 212-FreakMe."

Instantly the lines light up.

I grin. *Aiight. Let's see how many cock swabbers are callin' in.*

"Hello?"

"What's good, beautiful? You're on the air." There's a bunch of unnecessary feedback. "Yo, do me a favor, love. Turn ya radio down or *off* for me." *Why the fuck I gotta keep telling these dumb hoes this shit?* I shake my head.

"Oh. I'm sorry. Is that better?"

"True. What's good…whom am I speaking to?"

"Oh, hi. This is Ciara."

"Uh, ohhkay, Ciara; you giving out them deep throat specials or what? Talk to me, ma-ma."

She giggles. "Umm, not really. I mean, I've tried it a few times, but I'm not that good at it. I'm hoping someone will call in, so I can get some tips to help me get better at it."

"Aiight, baby. Hold tight. In the meantime, ma-ma, the best

way to get them skills up is practice, practice, practice. The more dingdong you suck, the better you'll get. So drop down 'n' get ya suck on, baby. And remember: No teeth. And use lots of spit. Next caller."

"Hey, Mar*Sell*." She smacks in my ear. I frown. "This Quita aka Head Nurse aka Bobble Head aka Slurpy aka Prime Time Neck Work aka Deep Throat Diva, straight from Brownsville."

Damn, this dick-suckin' ho gotta lot of nicknames. "Aiight, Quita. What's good, baby…?"

"This head game, boo. That's all I like to do. I can suck a whole block 'n' still want more."

"Damn, baby. What, you gotta motor in ya neck?"

She laughs. "Nonstop, no-gag, neck action. East New York! We go hard! Make a niggah nut quick. And *what?*"

"Oh, aiight, aiight, baby. I ain't mad atcha. How often you puttin' in that neck work?"

"If not every day, then at least three, four, times a week. And all weekend long. I like to throw head parties." I blink. Ask her what that entails. She smacks and chews in my ear. "Oh, it's where I rent a room 'n' invite like five to ten niggahs to come through 'n' we drink 'n' smoke, then I give 'em all the business."

Goddam! This freaky broad's sucking dick all willy-nilly. "Oh, word? Aiight, aiight. You the neighborhood cock-washer then."

She smacks in my ear again. "Somethin' like that. I just love suckin' di—*bleep*."

"You swallow?"

"*Swallow?*" she says indignantly as if I've offended her. "I'm a *guzzler*. Don't get it twisted, bae. I'ma guzzler, baby. And *what?*"

"Then suck on, suck on, ma-ma. Just know you can't draw a pension down on ya knees. Next caller. You're on the air with ya boy, Mar*Sell*."

"Yeah, this is Trixie, from Hillside."

"Oh, aiight. What's good, Trixie. You givin' head, baby?"

She sucks her teeth. "No. I'm not doin' none'a that nasty shit. And all y'all hoes out there drankin' 'n' sloshin' watermelon all around in your filthy mouths are all a buncha nasty-asses. Ratchet-ass tramps. Dic—*bleep*—suckin' tricks. I hope you nasty bitches get throat cancer. All of you nasty whores going to hell in a gasoline hand basket."

"Whoa, whoa…slow down, *mami*. Yo, you gotta man?"

"Yeah, why?" she says defensively. I ask her how long they've been rocking. She says three months. "What my man got to do with all them nasty dic—*bleep*—suckin' hoes out there? He ain't goin' nowhere."

"Oh, you think? Well, good luck with that," I say, rolling my eyes and shaking my head. It's mind-boggling how there are many whack muhfuckas out there who *still* don't/won't suck dick or eat pussy. "Know this Trixie, baby. If you plan on keepin' him, you had better learn to do some tongue tricks 'cause if you ain't toppin' him off, he's eventually gonna be out getting it somewhere else. A wet mouth is a wet mouth. And you better hope it's with another chick. Be well."

I hang up.

"Yo, my freaky peeps, I'ma say this. Lonely has a face 'n' it's a chick who ain't suckin' a dic—*bleep*. Next caller. You're on the air."

"This is Wanda from Jersey City. I don't know where you're getting your callers from, but they definitely can't be black." I frown. Ask her why she says that. "Because no *real* black woman is sucking no *dic*—*bleep* all willy-nilly and reckless like that. I'm sorry. I don't know not one black woman who loves giving head like that or who just goes around putting her mouth on some random man's penis."

"Well, baby. Dingaling sucking is real. Sorry to hear you're not surrounded by head doctors. Or maybe you are but they do what they do 'n' just ain't telling *you* because they know how judgmental you are."

"I'm *not* judgmental. Trust. I just know that black women don't suck unless they're getting something out of it."

"Oh, but they are. They're getting a hot juicy nut. But thanks for the Public Service Announcement, baby. Let's keep hope alive. Next caller, you're on the air…"

"Hi, boo. My name is Sabrina, from Irvington."

"What's good, Sabrina from Irvington…please tell me, you puttin' in that throat work?"

"All day every day, boo. My man stays sucked. And I'm a proud black sistah who loves cock 'n' cum. Mmph. You don't know? You betta ask somebody. Them uptight bitches who ain't sucking need to get up off them pedestals 'n' drop down on them knees 'n' get their bobble on. Sucking dic—*bleep* does the body good!"

I chuckle. "I heard that, baby. So tell us. What is it about puttin' in that mouth work that turns you on?"

She moans. "Mmm. Everything about it turns me on. The way it tastes. The way it stretches in my mouth 'n' hits the back of my throat. I swear I love sucking my man. It ain't even gotta be hard. If I see it, my mouth automatically starts watering. My man is real freaky like me. He loves his balls 'n' ass licked, too. And, trust. I do it *all* for my man. If I don't satisfy him, somebody else will. And ain't no other ho getting up on my man's dic—*bleep*. All I'ma say is, I'm in love with making him come. It gets me soaked every time. And that hot, gooey nut oozing down my horny throat." She makes smacking sounds as if she's licking her fingers. "Hmph, hmph, hmmph. My man's baby batter is finger-licking good, boo. Right down to the last hot drop."

I press my legs shut, licking my lips. "Yo, I heard that. That's what it is. Sounds like you know how'ta suck the chrome off a tail pipe. Thanks for sharing, baby. Keep wavin' that freak flag. Next caller."

"Lawd God, listen to the hooligan from Brownsville!" my next caller cries out in her thick West Indian accent. "No class! She brite to come on radio a chat like some kinda downtown sketel bam. Just pure unattractiveness. She just come sprawl out her likkle black self like ole stinking pussy jezebel mother of harlot, prostitute hog! Lawd God! She mud up fi dat." *Click.*

"Alrighty then, ma-ma. Tell us how you really feel. Next caller."

"Yo, I ain't no chick. But I suck a mean dic—*bleep.*"

This dumb muhfucka. I shake my head, leaning up in my seat. *I said chicks call in.* "Oh, aiigh, aiight. Where you callin' from, bruh?"

"Yo, this Thug Throat. I bet I can suck a dic—*bleep*—better than any chick out there. DL masculine freak niggah out in Paterson tryna link up wit' them DL thug bulls to blow a Dutch wit' 'n' suck da shit outta his dic—*bleep*—'n' lick up on them balls. Yo, you want dat wet sloppy head, *come* holla at ya boy!"

"Yo, Hol'up, hol'up, Thug Throat. Drop the flag, bruh." I smirk. "Next time you wanna place an Ad, go hit up Nastyfreaks4u.com, or the classifieds. Next caller."

The next chick that calls in, Precious, says she's been with her man for almost two years and he hasn't eaten her pussy once. Won't even lick it. But she sucks his dick on-call. And she's getting frustrated with him always making excuses as to why he won't chow down on her cunt.

"Damn, ma," I say, shaking my head. "Sounds like you need a replacement, baby. Cat should be feastin' on the cookie. His tongue, mouth, fingers working in sync to cause heat to flare all through ya body, baby. He should have you soaking them sheets 'n' the room should be flooded with moans 'n' the wet smacking sounds coming from his mouth as he tongues, slurps 'n' gulps in all them sweet juices."

She grunts. "Mmph. Well, there sure isn't any *slurping* or *gulping* going on over here. And these sheets are drier than a sandstorm."

"I feel for you, ma-ma. My advice. Get you a *real* man. Real men eat the cookie. Next caller. You're on the air with ya boy, Mar*Sell*."

"Ooooh, daddy," the caller seductively coos into the receiver, "you sound like you really know how to please a woman. Can I borrow you for the night?"

I chuckle. "Nah, beautiful. I'm flattered. But I don't think my wife would approve of that."

"Ooh, as sexy as you are, she's more than welcome to come along for the show, if you need a chaperone."

My dick jumps. I lick my lips, opening and closing my legs. Her voice is like honey, thick 'n' sweet. "Oh, word? What's ya name, baby?"

"Anonymous," she says. "And I have a question."

"Oh, aiight, Miss Anonymous. What's your question, baby?"

"I wanna know how can I get a taste of *you?* I bet you got that good nut. I'll come up to the radio station 'n' suck your dic— *bleep*—and swallow your nut under the table. I'm playing in my kitty now imagining you sliding your tongue all up in it. I love hearing your voice on the radio. I tune in *every* Thursday night. But this is the first time I got up the nerve to call in. You keep my *coño* wet."

"That's what it is. Keep that thing soaked, baby. Thanks for the luv." I disconnect the call. We go into a quick commercial break, then Kelly Rowland's "Kisses Down Low" plays over the airwaves. Nina struts her fine-ass over to me, sliding her hips on the edge of my desk.

"You have so many callers on hold, you might have to split the segment," she says, licking her lips. My gaze locks on the way her pink tongue slides over her full, glossy lips. I lick my lips and grin. Nina's fine as fuck. Although I've never given her a dose of this dick, I know she wants it. And she *knows* I know she wants. I've caught her eyeing it on many occasions. But, as sexy as she is, as enticing as her plump 'n' juicy made-for-dick-sucking lips are, I'd never stretch her neck out or beat the box up. One, I love my wife too much to ever cheat on her. Two, I don't believe in shitting where I eat. And, three, Nina isn't Marika's type. So, nah, I'm good.

"Oh, aiight. I'll take a few more calls, then we can call it a wrap. We can do"—I slowly lick my lips, dropping my gaze down between her legs—"pussy eating next week. Is that cool with you?"

She smirks, getting up and heading back to the booth. "Whatever *you* want, Mar*Sell*."

I grin. "Yeah. Daddy likes the sound of that."

She laughs, flicking a dismissive wave at me. "Whatever."

We're back on the air in five…four…three…two…one…

"Aiight, my freaky peeps. We're back." I tell 'em we only have time for two more callers and will pick up the other portion of this segment when I'm back on the air next week. "Next caller. What's poppin'…"

"Ooh, yessss, gawtdammit! Is this my sugah-boo, Mar*Sell*? Am I on the radio?"

"True indeed. Turn down ya radio, love." I shake my head.

"Fuquan, turn down that radio, boo!" There's a bunch of yelling in the background. "Fuquan! Don't do me, gawtdammit! I said turn down that gawtdamn radio before I punch ya eye sockets in." There's more yelling, then she's back on. "Okay. I'm back. Oooh, these bad-ass kids stay tryna do me. Is that better, sugah-boo?"

I frown. "Yeah, you good. Who are you 'n' where you callin' from, baby?"

"Yes, Fahvergawd! This Cassandra Simms from Brick City, boo. Oooh, you do me right, *gawt*dammit! Every time I hear ya voice on the radio, you get my drawz real gooey. Yes, Fahvergawd! But y'all need to get y'all a new system 'cause I've been on hold for almost thirty damn minutes tryna get to you, sugah-boo. You coons done made me miss half the male revue down at The Crack House tonight."

I chuckle. "Whoa, whoa…pump ya brakes, baby. You got through now. So what's good…you suckin' the snot outta ya man or what?"

"Ooh, niggah-coon, boom! You tryna be messy. And I don't do messy. No, I ain't suckin' no coon-niggah's snot. Well, not unless I gotta suck a lil' dingaling for me a new handbag or some heels. Otherwise, my mouth don't go on no wee-wee, sugah-boo. No gawd. But that ain't why I'm callin'. So don't do me."

I raise a brow. *This ghetto-ass broad.* "Oh, aiight, then get to the point, baby. Why you callin'?"

She huffs. "I'm callin' 'cause I wanna say somethin' to that lyin' bitch from East New York, Quita or whatever that lyin' whore's name is. Boogah-coon, *boom!* You better pop you a molly 'n' spark you a blunt 'n' get yo' gawtdamn mind right. You ain't the *real* deep throat diva, bitch."

I blink. "Damn, baby. Why you goin' in?"

"'Cause that bitch is a fraud. Yeah, she prolly neck gobblin' the dingaling a mile a minute, but she ain't the official cum whore, sugah-boo. She ain't blowin' no real bubbles outta no man's ass."

"Oh, word? Then who is?"

She grunts. "It ain't *that* bitch."

"Aiight, Then if it isn't her 'n' it isn't you, then who is it, ma? You wastin' my time, baby."

"Ooh, thick daddy, see you tryna be messy, boo, with yo' ole tall, fine chocolatey self. And I don't do messy. I ain't gonna say her name on the radio, but if you been down to her salon, Nappy No More, then you know who she is. Now can I give a shout-out, boo?"

I shake my head. "Yeah, aiight. Make it quick."

"Ooh, yes, Fahvergawd! I wanna give a shout-out to all'a my sponsors. Yes, gawd! Y'all been good to me. And I wanna give a shout-out to my homegirl Dickalina 'n' her retarded daughters, Candylicious 'n' Clitina. And my nine sons—Darius, Jah'Mel, Da'Quan, Marquelle, Joshua, Isaiah, Elijah, 'n' da bad-ass twins, Fuquan 'n' Tyquan, 'n' my nasty-azz daughter, Day'Asia. Day'Asia, you better not have no bloody drawz in that muthafu—"

Yo, this broad's shot the fuck out. Bloody drawz? Really? I disconnect the call. *Ratchet-ass hoes.* "Yo, my peeps, ratchet is what ratchet does. And that babe right there sounds like she's the official walking definition for it. Anyway, my freaky listeners, it's about that time. I don't know what *your* plans are for the rest of the night, but ya boy gotta beautiful wife at home waitin' for him to climb up in them sheets 'n' heat it up. Hopefully, you're about to do the same. 'Til the next time, remember this: what you won't do, someone else gladly will. And that's real. Keep it sexy, keep it wet…always keep it ready. I'm out."

Silk's "Meeting In My Bedroom" blares over the air as I hit the switch and remove my headset. I gather my shit, say my good-byes, and hit the door, anxious to get home to my baby to slide this hard dick all up in her.

THREE

Marcel

"Dance for me," Marika says low 'n' sexy, pulling at her thick, dark nipples, pinching them between her slender, manicured fingers. Her juicy lips, glossed and painted with siren-red lipstick, are parted and wet. The thought of her hot mouth wrapped around my dick, staining it with her painted lips 'n' spit, causes me to lick my lips.

Man, fuck. I love seeing lipstick 'n' spit smeared on my dick.

I'm standing in the middle of our master suite, bare-chested and in a pair of Polo boxers, dick stretching down my thigh, hands on my hips, eyeing my sexy wife as she spreads her thighs and slides her hand down her smooth belly, over her distended clit, then letting her fingers trail the rim of her swollen pussy lips.

I grin, dimples flashing deep in my cheeks. I can't front. My dick's getting harder than a muhfucka right now. I wanna fuck! I wanna nut! I wanna bust all up in my baby's guts! But I know she wants me to seduce her. To give her a slow, sexy striptease while she gets off, giving me a show of her own.

She smacks her clit. Her pussy puckers. Drips sweet honey as she runs her fingers over her clit, then smacks it again.

Yo, I'ma spit you some real shit. I'm the luckiest muhfucka in this world. I bagged a real live dime. Hands down. I have a bangin'-ass wife. Brains, beauty, and a bad muthafuckin' body, that's what the fuck I'm talking about. A freak on deck, my baby stays ready to rock in the sheets. And there's nothing she won't do to keep her man happy. But this shit's a two-way street. And, real shit, whatever my baby wants, she gets. Hold up. Don't get it twisted. I'ma real open-minded muhfucka, but I do have a few restrictions just as my baby has hers. And we respect each other's boundaries. But everything else is a go. No questions asked.

So when she sits here with her fingers toying with her clit and playing in her pretty pink slit and asks me to dance for her, a mufucka's gonna dance.

I knew my baby was a freak the moment I laid eyes on her spring semester at Howard, coming out of an AKA rush. It wasn't anything she said or did or what I heard about her that told me she was a freak. It was the way she licked her lips. It was in her walk, the way her long, sculpted legs stepped one foot in front of the other. The way her pelvis thrust when she strutted, the way her hips swayed, the way her ass shook in that lil' plaid Catholic schoolgirl skirt and her full titties bounced in her white low-cut blouse. She walked with a confidence that screamed, "I'm that sexy bitch! And this pussy's good as fuck! Nigga, what?"

No lie. My dick bricked up just from looking at her. And I wanted her...along with practically every other muhfucka on campus who was tryna get at her. But, I laid low, waited until after she crossed the burning sands, the following fall semester, then swooped in and made my move. But I didn't have to put too much work in 'cause she'd been eyeing me as well. And you see where she's at, right? Right where she's always wanted to be. 'Nough said.

I keep my gaze fixed firmly on Marika as her pussy swallows in her fingers. Her juices drip wetly down her hand. My dick throbs in my boxers. Tingles. Pulses. I'm ready to rip these muhfuckas off and pounce on my woman. Ready to slide between her thighs. Ready to kiss her pussy and slide my tongue to the back of her lips. Ready to catch the sweet waterfall of her goodness on my tongue. Ready to lave at her clit, slowly circling my tongue around it. Ready to press my lips tight into her. Ready to push my tongue deep inside of her. Ready to soak in her wetness. Ready to suck her dry of all her juices. Ready to taste how delicious she is. I'm ready, ready, ready! Oh, I'm sooo muthafuckin' ready.

Heat builds up in my heavy balls. I'm ready to explode. I take a quick step forward.

"Oh, no," she warns playfully, wagging a wet finger at me. "Stay. Enjoy the show."

"Shit," I mutter, shaking my head. I pull in my bottom lip.

She knows I'm a voyeur. She knows I get off watching just as much as I do partaking. But right now, a muhfucka isn't tryna watch. He's tryna indulge. He's tryna get his head grasped by both his baby's hands while she clamps her thighs over his ears and fucks her pussy into his mouth.

She grins. "You like watching me play in this sweet pussy, Marcel?"

I slide my tongue over my lips again, anticipating a taste of her hot juices. "C'mon, baby. Stop fuckin' with me. You already know the answer. Let me get a lick of that."

She opens and closes her thighs, mocha stretched over long, sculpted legs. Open. Close. Open. Close. The head of my swollen dick hangs out of the leg of my drawz as she plays peekaboo with her pretty pussy.

Legs open. Marika smiles at me, then drops her gaze down to this long, thick dick as she cups her pussy, then massages her clit.

Precum trickles out of my piss slit.

She licks her lips. A hint of mischief sparkles in her eyes.

I know the game she wants to play oh so fucking well. "Look. But Don't Touch. Don't Taste." She's paying me back for last night's ep. As much as she loves this tongue in her, she loves this dick more. But all I did when I got in from the station last night is fuck her slit with the head. She begged for more. Clamped her legs around my waist and tried to fuck more dick into her wet-wet. But I fought the urge, knowing that I held her—*and* her pussy— in my power without ever having to slide an inch of this dick inside her. So I tip-fucked her nice 'n' slow, letting the mouth of her pussy suck the head of my dick. Word is bond, I love it when her pussy muscles tighten around my head and milks the nut out of it. It feels like she's suckling on my shit.

But now, I am suffering. Waiting. Begging.

I glance at the time. It's already quarter to seven in the morning. All I want is some easy pussy before I head into the office. But, nah, Marika's in the mood to play games. She's gonna make me work for it.

"It's getting late," she says teasingly. "You might wanna hurry up and give me what I want, so you can get"—she takes her hands and pulls open her pussy lips—"this. This *is* what you want, isn't it?"

"C'mon, baby," I practically whine, taking another step toward her. "Let me get some of that pussy."

Her hand goes up to stop me. "Not until you dance for me."

Legs closed. She slides her fingers into her mouth, teasing me with her tongue swirling through each finger.

I squeeze the head of my swollen dick. "You see all this hard dick, baby? You got my shit leakin'."

A wicked smile plays across her painted lips. "And you see all this wet pussy, don't you? You're not getting any until…"

"I know, I know. I dance for you." I smirk, shaking my head. It's all a part of the game. Me pretending not to wanna dance, her pretending not to want me to have the pussy.

In the end, she knows, I know, we're both going to get what we want.

I tug at my dick.

Marika bites into her bottom lip. Lets out a soft moan. Then darts her tongue out over her top lip. "C'mon, Marcel, baby," she coos. Her right hand cupping her left breast, then pinching her nipple. Her left hand moving methodically over the bare mound of her pussy. "Dance for me." Her fingers get lost into her slit. The sweet sound of her wet pussy being fucked by her fingers starts to drive me over the edge.

I finally give my baby what she wants. I switch on one of the CD players—the one with a hundred-disc carousel, loaded with every kinda R&B slow jam to sexy and freaky joints from Trina to New Birth, Floetry, Jill Scott, Janet Jackson, Marvin Gaye, Force MD's. SADE, Kem, Keith Sweat, Pleasure P, Prince, Lakeside, Jodeci, Usher, The Dramatics, Janet Jackson, Marsha Ambrosius, Silk, Tank, Atlantic Starr, Plies, J. Holiday, Beyoncé, Teddy Pender-grass, R. Kelly, Ginuwine, Trey Songz, Maxwell, SWV, Dwele, Raheem DeVaughn, Pretty Ricky, and many others, then set it for RANDOM play.

There's something real intoxicating about fucking and making love to music, yet not knowing what will play next heightens the experience. You can go from slow, deep lovemaking to hardcore pussy pounding. But, uh, dancing for Marika to shit that only a chick should be dancing to for her man, is not my thing. But it's what turns her on. And, like I said, what my baby wants, my baby gets. But I'm not gonna front. I'm silently praying that the track gods only play shit by the bruhs.

Marika grins as Plies' "Get You Wet" floats through the system. I reach for the fly of my boxers, then in one swift motion, tear open my drawz, exposing a trimmed bush of thick, curly pubic hair. I reach down and pull my dick out, let it hang over the torn cotton.

By the time Usher's "Seduction" starts playing, I'm stroking my dick into a thick, long erection. Marika moans, groans, grunts, when I lean forward, extend my tongue out and lick around the head of my own dick, lapping at my sticky precum. I cup my balls.

"Ooooh, yesss…" Marika says in almost a whisper. "Lick that big dick, daddy. Suck it for me."

I look up and wink at her, then flick my tongue over it several more times before standing upright and thrusting my hips at her. She moans, winding her ass into the mattress.

"Mmmm…you're so fucking sexy…you got my pussy *coming*, baby…"

"Yeah, finger-fuck that wet cunt…"

The music throbs around us.

A smile toys at the corners of my mouth as I slowly stalk toward my baby while Trey Songz sings about getting on top. I swing my hips. Dip at the knees. Marika licks her lips as she takes in my body. Dark-chocolate skin sliding over thick muscles. Her fingers match my own strokes as the head of my dick slides in and out of the palm of my hand.

She can't keep the smile from creeping across her face when Beyoncé starts singing about how much she wants to show her man how much she appreciates him. I silently groan. She laughs.

"Oh, aiight, aiight. You think this shit's funny, huh?" I dip at the knees and thrust my hips, lifting my arms up over my head as "Dance for You" plays. The only thing on my mind is easing this dick into her pussy and getting deep inside her. I bunch every muscle in my sleek torso, gliding my hand down the length of my dick.

I move in, closer. Closer, closer, my long fingers caressing my balls with one hand, while my other hand moves faster and faster in short strokes from the top to the bottom of my swollen head, then rhythmically slides into long, deep strokes from the base of my dick, then up, over, and around my head. Long and deep and slow, then fast and short. Stroke for stroke, my knees dipping every so often.

"Yeah, baby," I groan as R. Kelly's "Cookie" pulses through the speakers. I have my dick practically in her face now. Her tongue slides out of her mouth. Her head leans in. Yeah, she wanna taste this dick now.

"Nah, you can't have none," I tease, yanking it away from her open mouth while leaning into her, reaching for her wet pussy. I smack it. Pinch her clit. "Yeah, look at that pussy. All wet 'n' juicy." I slip a finger in. Skim her inner walls with a swirl. She lets out a soft moan, reaching for my dick. I push her hand away. Press my lips into hers. Slide my tongue into her mouth as Trey Songz sings about being a panty wetter.

I twist a hand into her hair. Yank her head back. Bite into her neck. Nip at her ear.

She moans. "Aaah."

"I'ma fuck the shit outta you for makin' me late for work. You know that, right?"

I pull my finger out of her cunt, smack her clit, then plunge two fingers back into her slit. Marika gasps, hisses, then whimpers low in her throat, clawing at the sheets. Her eyes snap open wide. She has that hungry glow in them. My baby wants this dick. Her muscles squeeze my fingers as they curl forward inside of her, finding those crinkly ridges at the front of her pussy.

"Yeah, what was all that slick shit you were talkin'?" I press into spongy flesh, massaging her spot. "Talkin' about I wasn't getting none of this pussy…?"

Her mouth stretches open. Her eyes grow wide as I move my fingers into a slow, steady rhythm, increasing the pressure on her G-spot.

She rocks her hips. Her breath hitches. A scream explodes from her mouth as Jason Derulo croons out "Vertigo."

"That's right. Come for me, baby."

Withdrawing my fingers, I bring them to her lips, smearing gloss and cunt musk together, then pushing them deep into her mouth. "I told you 'bout teasing me when you know I have to be at the office early. Didn't I?"

My fingers slip from her mouth, drawing a wet trail to her pebbled nipples. I pinch, the right one, then the left one.

"Yes," she moans. Then in one swift motion, I lift her off the bed, flip her over, and tell her to get on all fours. I slap her phat ass, then drop to a crouch behind her, taking my thumbs and spreading her cunt open. I sweep my tongue over swollen, glistening lips, then bury it inside of her sticky heat. Marika drops her head forward and claps her ass cheeks around my face, moaning as I tongue-fuck her and stroke my dick through two songs before finally standing and rubbing the thick head of my dick up and down between her damp pussy lips, then sinking it in.

"Aaaaah, shiiiit," I choke out, head thrown back. Her taut, hot pussy causes every muscle in her body to tighten. "Aaah, mutha-fuck, yeah…" I withdraw halfway, then plunge in, deep—until my balls press tight against her cunt lips.

Marika's cries echo around the room, bouncing off the walls. I grind my hips into her nice and slow. "Yeah, baby," I moan, watching my dick slide in and out of her. "Coat my dick with that sweet nut. I love watchin' you take all this dick…aaaah, fuck, baby…nice, wet pussy…"

I pull out again. Fuck her with the head. Then surge my hips forward again, pushing my iron-hard pipe back into her. A soft, feminine rumble of approval seeps from her lips as I change my rhythm, using long powerful thrusts. In, out. In, out. Swish, swish. In, out. In, out. Swish, swish. Each stroke cutting, slicing, sawing into wet heat, gliding out of her wetness from head to base. My balls slap up against the back of her.

I wrap both of my arms around her and pound into her. By the time Xscape starts singing, I'm right where I wanna be. Roaring, buried deep in Marika's shuddering body, fucking my nut into the warmest place on earth.

My baby's wet pussy.

FOUR

Marika

"Your eleven o'clock is here," my receptionist, Shayla, says the moment I step—okay, okay…half-walk, half-limp, thanks to the delicious fucking Marcel put on me this morning—through the sliding glass doors of M&M Publishing, a large publishing company with magazine and book publishing holdings nestled inside a luxury high-rise building on the fortieth floor. The building also houses a record label and a multimillion-dollar public relations and global management agency that manages numerous Fortune 500 companies across the country.

As president and chief executive officer of M&M, I oversee the publishing and operations of our numerous divisions. And I am damn proud of my accomplishments as a thirty-six-year-old, African-American woman.

Straight out of Howard with a degree in communications, I landed a job with a major publishing house where I quickly worked my way up the ladder to executive editor of one of their imprints. Then, after almost two years, I'd had enough and decided to launch, along with Marcel, my own publishing house. Eight years later, M&M Publishing has rapidly become a force to be reckoned with in the publishing industry, becoming the home of many major bestselling authors. And as a result, in 2013, I was presented with the prestigious Matrix Award, a Tiffany medallion, from the New York Women in Communications for excellence in publishing.

I run a manicured hand through my hair, lifting my shades up and resting them on top of my head. The wall behind Shayla's desk is a waterfall with sparkling sheets of chlorinated water splashing endlessly down into a basin filled with shimmering rocks. I glance at my timepiece, then look over toward the waiting area. "*Already?* It's only ten."

She shrugs, pushing a curtain of blonde-colored hair from her high cheekbones. "He said he didn't want to be late." She picks up a stack of phone messages and hands them to me. "Oh. And a Miss Lollipop Lipz called and asked for you to call her on her cell."

I frown. "What kind of mess? *Lollipop Lips?* I don't know anyone by that name."

She snickers. "She said you might say that. She also mentioned something about a manuscript she sent over by Express mail for you to look at. She called it *Cum Stains.*"

"Oh, hell no. I'm not interested in anything titled *Cum Stains* written by some woman who goes by a slutty name like Lollipop Lips. No thank you."

Shayla gives me a knowing look. "If you ask me, she sounded like a real nut. No pun intended. And it's *Lipz* with a *Zee*, not an *Ess*."

I raise a brow. "Well, the next time Miss *Lipz* with a *Zee* calls, you can tell her we're not interested in anything with cum stains on it. And we're no longer taking submissions."

I gather my things to head toward my office overlooking Times Square.

"Oh, and one more thing," she says.

I turn to look at her. "Yes?"

"She said she hopes you have"—she lowers her voice—"two bottles of Sweet Bitch on ice for her."

I blink.

It takes a second for it to register before I burst into laughter. Sweet Bitch is the favorite wine of my friend and line sister Jasmine. We've been best friends since kindergarten, more like sisters. And there's not one secret we haven't shared with the other. Well, okay. Maybe there's one or two that I haven't shared.

"That fool." I wave Shayla on. "I can't with her."

She looks at me inquisitively. "I take it you know her?"

I nod, wondering why she hadn't called me on my cell. "Unfortunately, yes. And, you're right. She *is* a nut."

She shakes her head, then says as I walk away, "Good luck with that."

I chuckle, quickly making my way down the corridor, passing walls lined with framed book covers, autographed author headshots, plaques, and awards. Reaching the end of the corridor, I swipe my laminated ID through the silver card slot, wait for another set of glass doors to slide open, then walk through.

The doors hiss shut behind me.

I turn down another corridor, passing a nest of sleek glass cubicles, then step into my spacious, 1,250 square-foot office with a huge window, Calacatta marble flooring, built-in bookshelves, and a marble-and-steel wet bar over in the far-right corner. On the other side of my office near the window overlooking the New York skyline, there's a plush white leather sofa and two matching chairs and a French vintage gold leaf coffee table.

I smile taking in my sophisticated, yet chic, office. Many years ago, I was a girl with a dream and a plan armed with a degree. Now here I stand. A woman with the kind of life and career most can only dare dream about. And I have a husband, a partner, who loves and supports me in everything I do. Sometimes I feel like I'm living in a fairytale. It feels so surreal.

I have to pinch myself to make sure I'm still breathing, and that everything around me is real.

It is.

My smile widens as I walk around my large, centered desk and stow my Hermès handbag in the bottom drawer. Just as I'm preparing to sit, Shayla buzzes me and tells me Lenora Samuels of LS Literary Agency is on the line. Lenora is the head of one of the top literary agencies in the publishing world.

"Good morning, Lenora. How've you been?"

"I'm fabulous, darling."

"That's great. To what do I owe the pleasure of this call?"

"I have a manuscript I'd like *you* to personally take a look at."

"I—"

"Let me stop you, my dear," she cuts in not giving me a chance to protest. "Before you tell me you're too busy and try to send me chasing one of your lovely editors. Know this. This book is sure to cause a bidding war. Trust me on this. It's so hot and juicy. Flooded with drama and lots of steamy sex."

My ears perk up. "Okay. I'm listening."

"Well, it's titled *Prison Snatch*…"

I blink.

She says it's written under a pen name. Heaven. By a woman who spent several years in state prison after she tried killing her lover. She tells me it's fiction. Erotica. But that it's based loosely on her freaky sexapades during her incarceration.

My mouth waters at the thought of some burly stud-boo salaciously dishing out all her dirty prison deeds. I bite into my bottom lip, imagining a tight-bodied stud*boi* with a twelve-inch dick jutting out of a spiked harness, fucking the shit out of me while a soft, feminine, lipstick and stiletto doll squats over my face and lowers her sweet pussy on my mouth. I lick the drool gathering at the corner of my mouth.

"Have I gotten your attention yet, my darling?" Lenora questions. I can practically feel her beaming over the phone.

I swallow. "Oh, yes, yes…you have. Send it over."

She laughs. "See. I knew you'd see it my way. I'll have it in your inbox by the time our call ends."

I smile, powering up my desktop. "Great. Give me a week or so to get to it."

"Darling, because I'm giving you first dibs at the next *New York Times* bestseller. I'll give you three before I start shopping it."

I thank her before hanging up. And sure enough, before the receiver hits the cradle, there's a new message with an attachment from her.

Shayla calls again. Tells me *Miss Lipz* is on the line.

I laugh, then quickly compose myself as I pick up the phone. "This is Marika Kennedy speaking," I say, trying to maintain every ounce of professionalism while feigning ignorance.

"Yaaass, *bitch*," Jasmine says in her horrible attempt at sounding ratchet. She pops what sounds like chewing gum in my ear. "This is Lollipop. But you can call me Miss Lipz 'cause they real big 'n' juicy. And I know you had better be ready to publish my book. I wanna see *Cum Stains* in everyone's hands 'cause you know like I know, cum is good for the soul."

I crack up laughing. "Jasmine, girl, I can't with you. Your ass is every bit of a damn fool."

She joins in my laughter. "Girl, I couldn't help myself. I was on Amazon this morning looking for a few good books to one-click on this Kindle and my mouth dropped at some of the ridiculous titles. I saw some really crazy shit titled *Gorilla Pussy* and one called

Ratchet Bitch Riding It Raw. Oh and some mess called *Miss Shitty.* Like, really? What the hell is the reading world coming to?"

I laugh. "Ohmigod, no. But I'm not surprised. You should see some of the manuscripts titled with ridiculousness that come across some of my editors' desks. All I can say is: welcome to the digital world, where everyone wants to be in print, hoping to be the next Zane or E.L James."

She grunts. "Mmph. Well, good luck with that. It'll never happen. Not with garbage like that. Anyway, I need something good to read for this flight to San Francisco. Please give me some titles of some books that I can actually stomach. Please and thank you."

I chuckle, then give her the names of a few titles from some of my imprints *(Sweet & Juicy, Drop It Like It's Hot, Lick it Slow, Fire & Desire, and Wet Heat).* Then I rattle off a few titles I'm familiar with from off the list of other publishing houses.

She thanks me. Then asks me if I'm familiar with the author Allison Hobbs. "Girl, who isn't," I say in a tone full of admiration of one of the hottest female authors of erotic fiction. "We've been trying to steal her from her current publisher since the release of her book *Pure Paradise.* And that's been some years ago."

"Well, honey, I just finished reading her book *Munch.* And, girrrrl, let me tell you. My kitty throbbed the whole time. Mmph. That's all I'm going to say. Stevie didn't read the book, but baaaaaaby... he sure reaped the benefits. I wore that man out. By the time I finished draining him, cock dust was the only thing shooting out of that man."

I crack up laughing. "Omigod! Not cock dust! I've heard it all now. Jasmine, your behind is crazy, girl."

She chuckles. "Honey, that man loves it when I have a book in my hand. First thing he wants to know is, 'is that one of your freaky books?' A nod of the head and by the end of the night he's sitting up in bed with his erection in his hand, smiling."

"Hahahahahahaha. Girl, I can't with y'all." I open a drawer and retrieve some tissue from a box to dab under my eyes. Laughing at Jasmine has my eyes tearing. "So what's been going on? How are the twins?"

"Ugh!" she grunts. "Hormonal. I swear they're going to drive me to drink syrup and pop mollies."

I laugh. She has fifteen-year-old twin daughters who give her a run for her money. Jasmine's a jewelry designer and her husband, Stevie, is a multimillionaire entertainment attorney for some pretty high-profile celebrities here in New York and L.A. So her daughters, Amina and Amira, are afforded a fabulous life. Yet they're fascinated with the street life and thugs.

"Girrrrl, I'm serious." She sighs heavily into the phone. "Amina was arrested for underage drinking two weekends ago. And last weekend I spent my entire night in the emergency room with Amira's ass."

I gasp. "Oh, no. What happened? Is she okay?"

She sucks her teeth. "Well, she will be after her jaw heals and the stitches come out of her face." My eyes almost pop out of my head as she tells me Amira and some boy she met on Facebook was caught having sex in his bed by his girlfriend.

"Whaaat? Omigod, no!"

"Girl, yes. Some crazy little ghetto-trash named Clitina—or some damn project mess like that—and some other hood-rat girl she was with, hit her in the face with a wrench, then sliced her face open." I'm speechless. "We live way up here in Mendham Township, okay? But this little Grown Ass finds some way to trek her fast-ass into the slums of Irvington. I'm too through." I ask what happened to the girls who assaulted her. "Oh, honey, we pressed charges on those two little trifling bitches."

I shake my head.

"Anyway, girl. I didn't call you with my family drama."

"Oh, it's no bother. That's what girls are for. If there's anything I can do, let me know."

"Yeah, direct me to the nearest drug dealer."

I laugh.

"Anyway, I'm going to be in the city one day next week. Hopefully we can meet for lunch or an early dinner."

I smile. Tell her I'd love that. I glance at the time. It's already a quarter to eleven. I tell Jasmine I have to get ready for a meeting. We exchange a few more words before hanging up.

I get up from my desk as my private line rings.

"Hello, this is Marika."

"Yo, what's up sexy?"

I smile, sitting back in my chair. "You." I lick my lips. "You miss me already?"

"Always, baby. You already know." His voice vibrates through me. I press my legs together, feeling a sweet throb slowly pulsing in my pussy.

"Mmm. I love the sound of that. And as bad as I'd love to have dirty phone sex with you, I spent the last twenty minutes on the phone with Jasmine. And I have a meeting in"—I glance at the time in the upper-right corner of my desktop—"less than ten minutes."

He chuckles. "Nah, we good, baby. It's a lil' hectic here for all that right now, anyway. I just wanna make sure you don't have anything planned for us this weekend."

I swivel in my chair, glancing out the huge window, taking in the spectacular view of Times Square. "No. Nothing's planned. Why, what's up?"

"I just got off the phone with our pilot. We're going to L.A.," he says coolly. But there's a hint of wicked amusement in his tone.

"Oh, is that so," I say coyly, running a hand through my curls. "And what kind of devilish fun is happening in the City of Angels this weekend?"

"An invite-only party in Beverly Hills. It just came via courier. I'll give you all the details later."

I grin, sliding my warm tongue over my glossed lips as a slow heat rolls up into the center of my pussy. An invitation-only party only meant one thing: a weekend of scandalous seduction. One full of hot, dirty fucking. And *whatever* happens in L.A. stays in L.A.

I ask what time we leave. He tells me our flight is tonight.

8:30 p.m.

"Mmm. I can't wait."

"Me, either, baby."

FIVE

Marcel

"Yo, what's good, pussy," my boy Carlos says, knocking on the door as I'm hanging up the phone with Marika. I could almost smell my baby's pussy juices percolating when I told her we'd be leaving tonight for this mansion freak party out in Beverly Hills.

Carlos steps into my office wearing a black leather biker jacket over a black mesh pullover with a pair of ripped, faded jeans and black riding boots. Swag on ten, his whole getup is from the Ralph Lauren Black Label collection. That's all this muhfucka rocks, that or the Purple Label.

He's a straight-up pretty boy. A mix of Native American, Italian, and African, his exotic looks have always had chicks falling at his big-ass feet. And I'm not gonna front on his dick game 'cause dude stays baggin' mad pussy with his green eyes and all that coal-black, wavy hair, which he wears in his signature ponytail.

We've been boys since junior high. But all through high school we were thick as thieves, hugging the block, turning up at all the hot parties, and fucking all the baddest chicks. Then we graduated. He went off to Morehouse on a track and academic scholarship. And I went to Howard to play for the Bison on a basketball scholarship.

Aside from pledging the same frat and having the same taste in women, we are polar opposites. His family's caked up. Mine lived check to check. He graduated summa cum laude with a degree in biology and a minor in neuroscience. I graduated magna cum laude with a degree in communications and radio broadcasting.

Yet, I'm the one actually doing something with my degree. This niggah decided in his second year at Harvard to drop out of medical school to pursue a career singing and modeling. Garnered by the gossip rags around the globe as an international playboy, he's been linked to several Hollywood starlets, a few R&B songstresses, and several supermodels in Paris and New York. Still, I keep telling his ass chicks ain't checkin' for his kind like that anymore. But the muhfucka still thinks red-skinned niggahs are on top.

Still, I gotta say, he's jet-setting and doing big things. And, although his pops was pissed at him for not becoming a surgeon, like himself and his grandfather, he's finally come around. I gotta give it to dude. He stepped out on faith and followed his dreams. Now, two R&B albums in, several appearances in commercials and film, and a six-figure modeling contract with a major fashion designer, he's posted up on large billboards in his drawz and his face stays plastered on the cover of one magazine or another.

"Oh, shit, ugly muhfucka." I laugh, getting up from my desk, smiling. He's been over in Europe touring and doing some modeling gig for the last six months so it's been a minute since we've linked up. We give each other dap, then embrace in a brotherly hug. The scent of his expensive cologne floats around the space between us. "What up? When'd ya stinkin'-ass get back in the States?"

He joins in my laughter. "Yeah, aiight, muhfucka. I got ya ugly all right with ya chocolate Morris Chestnut-lookin'ass. Big bubble-head muhfucka." I laugh as he pulls back one of the leather chairs situated in front of my desk and takes a seat. He removes his black Aviator shades. "I got in last week, bruh."

I raise a brow, pulling out the other chair and taking a seat. "And you just checkin' me now? Funny-style ass. You coulda at least shot me a text to let me know you touched down. Damn, muhfucka."

He rubs his manicured goatee, framed around full lips. "Nah, man. You know how it is, fam. You right, though. My bad. I got back, chilled with the family for a minute, then had to break my sidepieces off with some of this good wood." He frowns, shaking his head. "Wait. Hold up. Why the fuck am I explaining myself to you? I got back when I got back. I'm here now. What, you want my autograph?"

"Yeah, muhfucka. You can sign over one of them damn checks you collecting."

He laughs. "Yeah, yeah. You're the one making all the paper. So what's good? How's that sexy-ass wife of yours? You ever mess that up, I'ma be snatchin' that up. I'll do sloppy seconds for a life with that fine woman."

I grin. "Yeah, aiight. Never that. Marika is good, man. You should stop down 'n' check for her on your way out. She'd love that."

"I just might. I see life's still treating you right. How's the radio show going?"

"Yeah, man. Radio show is still poppin'. You know the freaks love them some *Creepin' 'n' Freakin' After Dark*."

He shakes his head. "You the only cat I know on the radio melting panties off asses without dropping one damn album or singing one bar. Ya ugly ass can't even hold a note."

I laugh. "Man, what can I say? It's the voice, my dude. The freaks love me. But, yeah, life's definitely good."

He nods his head, smiling and taking in the ice in my lobes and dripping around my neck and wrist. "I see, I see." He inhales a deep breath. "Smells like fresh money all up in this piece."

"Nah, nah. I'm broke, niggah. You the one doin' it big, playa."

"Yeah, okay. The lies you tell, muhfucka."

I laugh.

But truth is, I'm that cat getting it. But bragging isn't what I do. Nah. I learned a long time ago that humility gets you a whole lot further in life than bravado ever will.

Watching my moms wake up every morning—not ever missing a day of work, rain, sleet 'n' snow—with a smile on her face as she left outta the brownstone we shared with my grandmother, aunt and three cousins in Brooklyn, to scrub toilets for rich white folks out in the Riverdale section of the Bronx, then go clean office buildings at night so she could afford to send me to the best private schools the city had to offer taught me a lot about having an impeccable work ethic. About doing whatever it is you need to do to make it.

On everything, Moms was hard on me because my pops wasn't around, thanks to a bullet taking his life when I was five. But she had a mission. She was determined to make sure I had a shot at something much greater than what the hood could ever offer me. And she was dead-ass when she'd threaten to beat the hoodlum, the ruffian, the thug, and anything else that represented the streets out of me anytime I let my pants drop off my waist, or she heard me using slang. Other times she'd threaten to ship me off to Martinique to live with one of my pops' six brothers, or over to Grenada with her family. Becoming a statistic wasn't an option. Prison. Gangs. The streets. All not an option, if I valued my life.

"I'll kill you dead, first, before I ever let the streets have you."

Real shit, everything that I am, everything that I've become, is because of my moms. I owe her everything. She was the poster girl for how to make nothing outta something without looking for a handout. And that's exactly what I did to get to where I'm at today.

On top. And I didn't have to lie, scheme, fuck, bribe, or murder my way up to get here.

But if it weren't for the fact that my face has been plastered in *Vibe*, *XXL*, and *The Source*—to name a few, you would never know that I'm President of MK Records, and one of the most powerful cats in the music industry. Let *Maxim* and *Black Enterprise* magazines and BET tell it. I'm one of the Top Ten Hottest hip-hop and R&B moguls in the game. But, uh, without saying much more. Let's just say—with looks, swag, money stacked, numerous rental properties, a roster of some of the hottest artists in the game on my label, and a bangin'-ass wife—I stay winning.

"Yeah, aiight, muhfucka," he says, laughing. "You're an entertainment mogul. Your name rings bells in the industry, niggah. So save that broke shit for them lames who don't know you."

Carlos cracks me the fuck up, for real, for real. As articulate and polished as he is, you'd never know he wasn't bred in the hood by the way he talks behind closed doors. He has more hood swag than some of the muhfuckas who are actually from the streets.

"Aiight, aiight…" I run a hand up over the top of my head, caressing the deep spin of my waves. "We ain't gotta broadcast the shit. I'm sayin' though. What's good with you? How long you in the States, this time? And when you getting ya ass back up in the lab to drop some heat?"

He nods his head. "Man, funny you should ask 'cause I was just thinking on my way over here that it's time to get back in the studio and make this money. I'm ready. I'ma be here for at least the next six months."

"Oh, aiight, aiight. That's what's up. I got this producer I think you should link up with. This young cat out in Queens; he's got some sick tracks."

He gives me a quizzical look. "So what you saying, bruh? You tryna sign me?"

"Are you ready to grind hard?"

Now I'm not gonna front like I wasn't feeling some kinda way when Carlos signed a two-album deal with another label, but I understood his desire to sign with a major label. At the time, MK Records—the M is for Marcel and the K is for my last name, of course—was just starting out back then and didn't have the kind of star power on its roster that it has now. So I respected his hustle. Still, I kinda wanted to hate on him on the low until his debut song, "Lick Her Slow," dropped and spent weeks on the charts. I knew then he had mad talent. Then when his second single, "Love Box," peaked at number 6 on the Billboard Hot 100 and number 2 on the R&B charts, I knew dude was about to shut shit down. That joint blew up all the R&B and hip-hop stations and his album *Dirty lil Secrets* was not only nominated for both American Music Awards and Grammy Awards, but it also sold over 2.5 million copies.

So on some realness, I couldn't hate. But after his sophomore album, *Ballz on Fire*—which took two years for him to finish because of his modeling obligations—went flat, the label dropped him like a bad habit.

He shakes his head. "Whoa, hold up. Are you shittin' me? Or are you *saying* what I *think* you're saying?"

I laugh. "Yeah, muhfucka. What you think? I'm dead-ass. You been outta the game for a minute, but it's time for you to hop back in 'n' resuscitate R and B."

I can't even front. Right now, the only thing I'm hearing is cash registers ringing in my ears. And all I'm seeing are dollar signs swimming behind my pupils. Carlos is the complete package. He's not only a talented songwriter and singer. Dude is a gifted pianist. And he has mad sex appeal. All of his songs are raw, sexual and sensual about many of his sexapades around the globe and the things he's said and done to get a chick to drop them drawz. And today, like never before, sex sells…lots of it. Straight like that. And this freaky muhfucka has enough heat to turn up the streets.

Carlos reaches his hand out for some dap, grinning. "Then let's make music, baby."

"Yo, that's what I'm talking 'bout," I say, giving him dap. "'Bout damn time you got your mind right 'n' brought ya yellow ass on over to the MK family. Let's go get this paper, bruh."

He laughs, glancing at his watch. "You already know. Let's drop some hot shit 'n' get these streets talking."

"And them drawz droppin'," I add, laughing along with him. I rise from my seat. Tell him to have his manager get at me.

He stands, too. "Aiight, cool, cool. I'ma 'bout to head out." We give each other dap, then our frat handshake, followed by a big-ass hug, which kinda takes me by surprise; especially since his body is pressed into mine a lil' closer than usual. "You've always been my boy," he says, beaming. "And I got nothing but love for you, man."

"That's real shit. Likewise, playboy." I step back from him, abruptly moving around to the other side of my desk and pulling my executive chair out, taking a seat.

I shuffle some papers around on my desk. "Make sure you have your manager holla at me."

"True indeed," he says, heading toward the door. "Let's hit the courts one day next week so I can mop the floor with you."

I laugh. "Yeah, aiight. Never that. You know you can't see me, fam. I'll bust yo' ass, pretty boy."

"Aaaah, shit. Is that a threat?"

I smirk. "Take it however you want, playa."

"Oh, aiight. I got you. I'ma take it to the hoop, bruh. Believe that." He hits me with deuces and I eye him as he makes his way to the door, shaking my head.

When the door finally closes behind him, I take in a deep breath, then slowly blow it out, before getting up and locking my door, then walking back over to my desk and unloosening my Ferragamo belt buckle. *I'm horny as fuck.* I unzip my pants, then slide my hand into the slit of my designer drawz, snaking out my semi-hard dick.

I squeeze the head of my dick a few times, then push back in my seat and grab the base of my shaft. My mouth waters as I lean forward and stretch myself down into my lap, sucking the head of my dick into the warmth of my mouth.

Yeah, I'm a self-sucker. And, nah, I don't see anything gay about that shit. It's my dick. I'm not sucking another niggah's dick. I'm sucking my own. It's no different than jerking it, or playing with it. It's my shit. And it's me pleasuring myself. Only difference is, a muhfucka's using his mouth to add to the sensation. So fuck what ya heard. If I feel like I wanna wet my own dick, that's what I do.

On some real, I learned I was able to suck my own shit by mishap and curiosity when I was like thirteen, during one of my many horny nights of beating my dick in the bathroom. I leaned in to spit down on the head of my dick and realized that I was flexible enough—and my dick was long enough—for me to lick it. So I did. And liked it. But I kept that shit on the low because for some reason, as good as that shit felt, it didn't seem right. And I'd never heard of muhfuckas sucking or licking their own shit. And if they did, they damn sure weren't hanging around the hood or on the courts talking about it.

So licking my dick became my own lil' dirty secret.

And even though I was getting pussy, I still masturbated and locked myself in the bathroom and licked my dick. Then the more raw pussy I started getting, the stronger my urges to taste their juices on my dick got. So I'd finish smashing, then hop up from the bed with my wet, sticky dick swinging and lock myself in the bathroom to suck the cream off my cock. I'd be fucking some chick and the whole time I'd be thinking how I couldn't wait to taste her on my dick. So licking my shit quickly evolved into me sucking it.

Flashes of Marika's fat, wet pussy with my nut flooding out of it click in my head. I lick my lips as if I'm licking her cum-soaked cunt, groaning low. I spit on the head of my dick, stroking my thick shaft and sensually massaging my full, round balls before squeezing them. A mix of spit and precum coat my dick, becoming slippery lube to my shaft. The fire roaring inside of me is trapped, confined behind thick layers of muscle and skin.

"Aah, shiiit, baby…mmm …"

I lean forward and suck the head of my dick, bobbing my head up and down my shit. Horny. I need release. Need to empty this heavy sac. I suck myself to the edge.

Bowing at the crown of my dick, worshipping it, pumping it into my mouth, all the way to my tonsils. *"Aaaah…"*

Here it comes. Here it comes…

I toss my head back, shut my eyes tight, bite into my bottom lip and buck as bolts of hot nut shoot, spurt, then splatter outta my dick.

SIX

Marcel

"Ooh, baby. Guess who came to see me today looking every bit of delicious today?" Marika says, walking outta her walk-in closet. I stare and lick my lips. She's wearing only a pair of red silk panties and high-heel red bottoms.

My dick stirs in my drawz.

"Who?" I ask as if I don't already know.

"Carlos."

I grin. "Oh, word? And he was looking *delicious*, huh?"

She laughs. "Yes, every bit of…with a capital-D. That man is too fine for his own good." She holds up a cobalt-blue strapless dress in front of her. Then tosses it onto our bed. I eye the growing pile of dresses and purses, shaking my head.

She looks at me feigning innocence. "What?"

"Seriously, babe? *More* clothes? Why are you packing all this shit, when you have a ton of things at the crib in L.A.? I thought I said to pack light. Translation: only pack ya purse."

She rolls her eyes. "I *am* packing *light*. These are a few things I want to leave out there; that's it. Besides, a woman can never have enough options."

"Well, how about leaving all that shit here as option one?"

She ignores me and walks back into her dressing room, then comes out with a lil' skirt set. She looks over at me, and smiles, tossing the ensemble onto the bed.

I sigh, glancing at the time. It's a quarter to six. "We're only gonna be out there for the weekend. Damn. And you're still gonna wanna buy shit while we're there."

She walks over and plants a kiss on my lips. "You know me so well." I grab a chunk of ass, then bounce her ass cheek in the palm of my hand. "With this *phat*, juicy ass." I slap it.

She playfully swats my hand away and struts back across the room. She reaches for the chilled bottle of Pinot Grigio sitting in a stainless steel bucket of ice. Then pours some into her half-empty glass and lowers the bottle back into the bucket.

She takes a sip. "You should have seen the tramps in the office today fawning over Carlos and trying to get his attention. That man knows he can stop traffic."

I watch as her ass shakes back into her closet.

I smirk. "Yo, why you sounding like you wanna fuck him?"

She turns to look at me. A smile plastered on her lips, she tilts her head and places a hand up on her hip. "Don't *you*?"

If muhfuckas knew how I got down, they'd be popping a buncha shit and the paparazzi would have a muthafuckin' field day. Though I don't give a fuck what another muhfucka thinks, I'm not beat for the judgment, or the prying eyes. Openly admitting, being a bisexual cat isn't a good look for a muhfucka like me doing what I do in the entertainment industry. Yet, muhfuckas would clap and drool and wave a flag of approval for Marika, wanting to fuck her six ways to Sunday, knowing she's into chicks. But, society still ain't ready for a muhfucka like me getting off on rocking with another niggah. And I ain't ready to make it public knowledge. My sexuality, Marika's sexuality, and how we get down in the bedroom isn't any-muthafuckin'-body's business.

And it isn't up for discussion.

I'm a man, first. A husband, second.

A sexual muhfucka, third.

And sex isn't a guilty pleasure. Not for me, and definitely not for Marika. Nah. Sexual satisfaction is our right. We require it. We expect it. And we ensure it.

And beneath the sheets, behind closed doors, we get it in with one mission in mind: to please each other. To indulge each other, be it with chicks or other dudes. Together. Period. There are no secrets between us. We both like what we like. And we both love making sure the other gets it.

And, nah, I'm not about to go into some long, drawn-out history-sharing story on the hows and whys. All I'ma say is this: My first experience with another cat was back in high school, the summer of my sophomore year. I was fifteen. And stayed horny as fuck. My dick stayed hard. And back then I woulda fucked a cross-eyed, one-armed, legless ho with no teeth on the low if her pussy was clean and I could get away with it.

But this particular summer, it was another muhfucka's mouth I splashed my nut in.

G-Money. A cat I used to smoke weed and chill with from around the way. He was going into his junior year. Six-three. Star point guard for Boys and Girls High.

Dude had a hot-ass girl on the cheerleading squad and a buncha other bad-ass bitches from around the way who stayed giving him pussy. But the muhfucka stayed eyeing me all crazy on the sly. At first I thought it was because he knew I was fucking his girl on the low. But since he never came at me about it, I just let it go. As far as I was concerned we were still cool.

Then one night, I'm at his crib, chilling. We're both kicked back smoking weed and watching some white bitch sucking two muhfuckas off at the same time. The more bud I smoked, the hornier I got. My dick started bricking up watching Becky hold both of their dicks in her hand, rubbing them together, then sliding her mouth back and forth over both heads. The shit had me on rock. And ready to crawl up inside some pussy. But I was high as fuck. And all the hoes were stuntin' on the pussy that night. So I just chilled and smoked and watched the porn flick. Without much thought I slid my hand down inside my basketball shorts and started playing with my shit on the low.

Then out of nowhere this muhfucka gets up and locks his bedroom door, then pulls out his dick and sits down next to me on his bed and starts jacking his shit right in front of me. Real shit, I'm not gonna front. That shit turned me on. I licked my lips and eyed him while stroking my own shit in my shorts.

"Damn, son," he said real low. "Pull that dick out 'n' let me see you jerk that shit."

"Man, get the fuck outta here with that gay shit, niggah."

"Niggah, ain't shit gay 'bout two niggahs jacking dicks together watchin' a bitch suck dick. Pull that shit out so I can get this nut, niggah." Hesitantly, I raised my hips up and pulled my shorts and boxers down. "Damn, niggah, you gotta big-ass dick."

I smirked, stroked my shit and within seconds I bust. But what fucked me up is when he leaned over in my lap and slurped up my nut, licked all around my balls, then took the head of my dick into his mouth. And swallowed me. That shit had my head spinning. And I nutted again. Then when he was done cleaning my dick, he sparked another L, took two deep pulls, then passed it to me.

"Yo, this shit stays between us, feel me?" he said, blowing a thick cloud of smoke up into the air. "I don't need this shit gettin' out."

"True," is all I said, closing my eyes and letting the chronic fill my lungs. From that moment on, every chance G-Money and I got, we got lifted, watched porn, and jacked off, then I'd let him finish me off, sucking my nut out. We even fucked a few broads together that summer, then did our thing after they left. We kicked it real heavy every chance we got. Then the school year came around. I went back to my world and he went back to his.

But that summer stayed stamped in my brain. From his hot mouth on my dick to his wet tongue on my balls to him swallowing my hot loads. Yeah, I already knew what it was like having my own mouth on my shit. And I dug that shit. But G-Money sucking my dick caused electrical sparks to surge through my whole body. Real shit, I never forgot that feeling. And no matter how many chicks sucked my shit, none of 'em ever compared to the sensations that shot through my body and made my toes curl every time he wrapped his mouth around the head of my dick.

And for the next two years, he kept sucking my dick. And I kept fucking his girl.

I swallow, bringing my attention to Marika. "Nah, I'm good on that." I tell her about his visit to my office and how I ended up busting my nut right after he dipped.

"Ooh, you nasty-ass! So you *do* want to fuck him."

I laugh, shaking my head. "Nah, nah. Man, that's my boy; feel me. I don't look at him like that. It's just that after that pretty muhfucka left I got horny as fuck."

A slow, sexy grin slides over her lips. "And you're sure it didn't have anything to do with *him*?"

"Nah, word is bond. The whole time I was handling my dick I had you on the brain. All I kept seeing was that pretty wet pussy."

"Mmmm." She lifts her wineglass to her lips and takes a slow sip. "I like that. But what if I told you I've fantasized about fucking *him*? Tried to imagine what his dick looks like? What would you say to that?"

I smirk. "I'd tell you all you had to do is ask. His shit's long, thick and reddish brown. Then I'd wanna know why you ain't never share them dirty thoughts with ya man? We coulda did some role-play-type shit." I walk up on her. "What, you keeping secrets from me? Is that how we doing it? Let me find out you stay flirting with my boy on the low."

Marika looks up at me and blinks innocently. "You know I'd never do anything like that. Keep secrets. But, yes, I've been guilty of flirting with Carlos a few times over the years, but nothing worthy of concern. And, truthfully, I'd only entertain fucking him, if *you* wanted him in our bed, too." She bats her lashes.

Goddamn, my baby has amazing fucking tits! I lick my lips, reaching for her nipples.

Though Marika and I are bisexual, and non-monogamous—for a lack of a better way of explaining how we define our relationship, our open marriage—don't get shit twisted, we are very much committed to each other emotionally, mentally, and physically. No matter who else we get it in with.

Marika's my fuckin' heart.

My whole muthafuckin' world.

Fact.

"Nah. Besides, I'm about to sign him to MK so you know even if he did get down like that, it definitely isn't gonna pop off now."

"Ohmygod!" she squeals. "That's great news! I wonder why he didn't mention anything to me about it when I saw him."

I shrug. "He probably wanted to keep it on the low until the ink is signed on the contract and we make an official announcement."

"I'm so excited. And I know if you have your way, he'll be groomed to become the hottest, new megastar in the industry."

I grin, rubbing my chin. "True indeed, baby. Carlos is the total package. Talented."

"And sexy as hell," Marika adds, fanning herself.

I laugh. "Silly-ass. Facts, though. He definitely has star power. And all the ladies love him. And wanna fuck him."

She smiles. "Ooh, yes they do. And you're sure you don't—"

I cut her off before she can get the rest of her words out. "Nah, yo…" I shake my head. "Definitely not interested in going there with him. Fucking chicks together is one thing. Having him sucking my dick, *if* he did swing that way, is a whole other level."

"Mmmm," Marika coos. "Even if he doesn't, I'd still love to see him down on his knees with them sexy-ass lips of his stretched around your dick while I lay back and play with myself."

I grin, shaking my head. "Yo, you funny as hell. You know that, right? But, uh, you can cancel that daydream, baby. Not gonna ever happen."

She laughs. "I know, I know. Can't fault a girl for her fantasies, though."

"Nah, definitely can't. I love ya fantasies, baby. And when we get to L.A., we gonna make a few of 'em our reality."

She moans. "I can't wait."

I lean in and give her a deep, tongue-probing kiss. By the time I pull back, my dick is stretching down my inner thigh. "Now, see what you've done?" I show her my dick print. Not that it's hard to miss. "You better get ya lil' ass dressed before I end up tossing you over a chair 'n' fuckin' this dick into you."

"Oooh, I love the sound of that, daddy."

I slap her on the ass. "Yeah, I bet. Hurry up. We have a plane to catch."

SEVEN

Marika

The thing I love most about Marcel is that there is never a dull moment with him. He's meticulous, attentive, adventurous, and intensely erotic. Those are some of the qualities, along with his intelligence, charm, borderline arrogance and hood swag—and not to mention his magnetic smile, and open-mindedness about life, love, and sex—that attracted me to him in the first place. Even after all these years we've been together, this man still never ceases to amaze me.

I love how he seduces me in a way that has always made it easy for me to toss caution to the wind and freely give myself to him. No matter where we are. Like right here, right now, where I'm sitting next to him on our private jet to L.A., reclined back in my chair, my legs splayed open, with my wet pussy pressed against the cool leather seat as Marcel's hand snakes its way up my skirt. His arm is covered beneath the fluffy white blanket I have draped over me.

He finds me wet and ready. His finger lightly trails the rim of my honey-slick lips. I close my eyes. Let myself inhale. I slide down in my seat, inviting him in.

"Nah, baby," he says low in my ear. The deep, richness of his voice scorches over me like melted Belgian chocolate. "I want you to keep them pretty eyes open."

My lids flutter open. I bite into my bottom lip. Fight back a moan as his finger dips into my slit, stirs into my juices, then quickly pulls out. He's going to tease me, taunt me, edge me, until I scream out and can no longer hold on.

My body grows warm.

"Look at me, baby."

I don't right away. I need a moment. But Marcel makes it excruciatingly difficult to think straight, lightly pinching my pussy lips together with his finger and thumb. "You want my fingers fucking this hot cunt, baby? This sweet, slutty pussy?"

He's already sliding two fingers in, deep.

"Oh G-god, yes." I bite into my bottom lip to keep from screaming out.

"Open your eyes and look at me then." My pussy clenches and unclenches ready to burst open as his hand pumps hard, fast. He knows I am on the verge. He slows his pace. Tells me he won't let me come until I do as he's asked. Open my eyes.

I blink. Breathlessly, I turn my head toward him. Eyes delving into mine, he pulls his hand out from beneath the blanket and eases his cum-coated finger into his mouth, tasting me. He licks his lips before leaning in and softly pressing them over mine, the tip of his tongue flicks, and my lips part to greet it, welcoming him—and the *taste* of me—in to deepen his kiss. I suck on his bottom lip, then his top lip, pulling them into my wet, wanting mouth. Oooh, I love this man.

A moan rolls its way up through the pit of my stomach, burns through my chest, then lodges itself in the back of my throat. I gasp. My eyes roll up in the back of my head, spin around in their sockets, then spring open.

"Ooh, please, baby…"

Marcel grins. "Please, baby, what? What, you don't like me fingering you?"

"No, yes...ooh, please...mmm..."

"I love playin' in this pussy," he whispers into my ear. The pad of his finger sweeps over my clit. His breath warms my neck as he continues to whisper dirty talk in my ear. "You got my dick so fuckin' hard. I'ma fuck the shit out you, baby. Mmm. This wet pussy. So fuckin'...hot..." His finger strokes my clit in small circles, pressing ever so lightly, before dipping back into my slit.

A soft moan escapes me.

"Shhh, baby," he says soothingly, even as he slips a second, then third finger into my snug pussy. "You want the other passengers to hear you?"

Although the only ones on our flight besides Marcel and me are the flight attendant and the two pilots, his question is a part of the game. Pretending we're flying with a bunch of other passengers. The threat, the fear, of being watched by others is like an aphrodisiac. The thought of being secretly watched, or overheard, is intoxicating.

"N-no," I push out, shaking my head. I am relieved that we are traveling at night and the interior of the cabin is dimly lit. But in my mind's eye it is the glow of complimentary notebook screens and personal laptops of other passengers lighting the cabin. "But, but...ooh..." Three fingers are now two. "Ooh...ooh...I'm so hot... my pus...sssssy..." Two fingers are now one, again.

I hum deep in my throat.

"Shhh. Milk my finger like you do my dick." He eases his finger all the way out to the tip, teasing my slit, then pushes in his middle and index fingers. My walls clamp around his probing digits, the mouth of my pussy slurping his fingers in. "Yeah, baby. That's it. Just like that."

"Aah...mmm..."

He finger-fucks me slowly, purposefully, as my pussy floods with steaming juices. He pulls out. Slides his wet, sticky finger over the contours of my lips, quickly pulling it back when I open my mouth and attempt to swipe at it with my tongue. He sucks his fingers into his mouth, then leans in and kisses me, again, flicking his tongue over my lips, before easing it into my wet mouth, letting my tongue dance a sultry dance with his.

With a low moan, I wrench my mouth away from his. "I can't take much more of this, baby. It's killing me."

He grins, inching his hand back up between my legs. "You can't take much more of what?" He's back at it again. Toying with my clit, my pussy lips, then the opening of my slit. "This?"

"I'm sooo horny," I whimper. "I want you to fuck me. I need your dick inside of me. Pleeeease."

"Shhh. I know, baby. I know you want this hard dick. Daddy loves this pussy. Hot"—he plunges his fingers in, then pulls out—"wet"—he plunges them back in—"juicy"—he pulls out again. "Pussy."

I gasp, rolling into the swelling wave of pleasure. I am certain that the rest of the cabin can smell my arousal hanging heaving in the air. Its delicious scent filled with sweet musky need.

Marcel teases my clit again. My body shivers. He knows I'm riding on the cusps of an orgasm. I'm panting now. My breasts heave up and down. My nipples tighten. My tongue slides out of my mouth. I am slowing unraveling. My whole body is on fire. I lust to have him fucking me, deep and hard, slapping my ass, and yanking my head back while he guts the back of my pussy, stretching it with his big hard dick.

My hand slinks over into his lap, eagerly grabbing at the bulge in his sweats. Oh, how I love it when he travels in sweat pants. His long dick stretches along the inside of his left thigh. It's as hard as granite.

He presses his legs shut. My hand travels down the length of his wide shaft to the head of his dick, lightly squeezing. "You like that shit. See how fuckin' hard you got that dick, baby?"

"Y-y-yes…oooh, your dick is so hard for me."

"Yeah, that big dick's all for you, baby. I can't wait to get lost in all this wetness." He thrusts his middle finger in deep, then out, then in, then out, exciting my slick opening and causing my legs to quiver. Marcel's thumb flicks my clit. "I'ma fuck this pussy until you can't stand. You want daddy to beat this shit up for you…?"

Marcel's long, talented fingers stroke me into a fever pitch, causing me to almost howl low in the back of my throat. I have to clamp my lips closed, bite down on them, to contain the gurgling sounds.

"Yeah, baby, give me that nut. Cum for daddy."

His fingers slip deep inside of me, stroking my walls, pressing down into my G-spot. My pussy matches the tug and pull of each thrust. I squirm. Wiggle my hips. Fuck into Marcel's hand, deep and greedily.

I snap my head back against the cushioned headrest. Close my eyes and imagine him deep inside of me. "Mmm. Aaah…"

In a lust-induced fog, I let out another moan.

"Shhh," Marcel whispers, swirling his two wet fingers over my clit. I bat my lids open, then sweep my eyes around the darkened cabin, hoping no one has heard me. "Give me that nut, baby…"

He nibbles on my earlobe. His tongue darts in, causing me to squirm. "I bet they can smell your wet pussy." His fingers *click-click* in and out of my wetness. He fucks into my heated center and now I have to wonder if what he says is true. That the flight crew can in fact smell how hot and wet and horny my cunt is.

Marcel's fingers run up and down the lips of my pussy before entering me again. It doesn't take him long to find my spot, that fleshy sponge of swollen desire. He presses into it, strokes it. I whimper. I am thrusting my hips without thought. Too far gone to care as the first warm spasm uncurls in me. My G-spot gushes, making the sticky puddle already beneath me even bigger. My ass is soaked.

I grip the sides of my seat as another wave of heat washes over me. Buck against Marcel, moaning and gasping for air, as Marcel's hand pumps into my weeping cunt, fast and hard, but sweet and steady. A guttural moan escapes my open lips. "Oh, God, oh, God… I'm com…oh, God, ohhhhhh, G-g-g-g-goddddd!"

Disheveled and disoriented, I am thrashing uncontrollably. Pussy pulsing. Clit throbbing. Heart racing. Marcel has done this to me. Damn him!

"Excuse me, Mr. Kennedy?" The flight attendant's gaze bounces back and forth between Marcel and me. "Ma'am…sir? Is everything okay over there?" Her voice and tone, both filled with concern as she assesses the nature of my outburst.

My head lolls over in her direction. I open my mouth to tell her everything is just splendid, but my words come out in a slur.

Marcel keeps stroking into my wetness. My breathing comes in shallow gasps. "Seizure," he says coolly. "My wife gets them every so often."

Panic washes over the attendant's face. She takes in my sweaty face. "Oh, no. Is there anything I can do? What can I bring her? Does she need medical attention?"

Marcel finally withdraws his fingers from my dripping pussy, then eases his hand from in between my thighs. "Nah, we're good." He smiles wickedly. "I'm all the medicine she needs." He licks his fingers, then slides them into my mouth. His lascivious antics cause the attendant's face to flush. "Ain't that right, baby?"

I nod, sucking in his fingers. The flight attendant blinks. Looks down at me, then over at Marcel, realization filling her eyes. Her face flushes. Her mouth drops open as he leans in and slides his tongue into my mouth.

He eyes her as she scurries off, then pulls his lips away from mine, grinning. He reclines his seat back. Drapes his blanket over his lap. Then slides his sweats and his boxers down over his hips, whispering, "Wrap them pretty lips around this hard dick, then come sit on it."

EIGHT

Marcel

"Good morning," Marika says, opening the French doors and stepping out onto the terrace of our Hollywood Hills home. It's a little after nine in the morning. She leans in and kisses me lightly on the lips.

I frown. "Is that all I get?"

Hand on hip; head tilted, she says, "What more would his Highness like?"

"You."

She just looks and smiles at me. It doesn't take much more than that for my dick to stir. I close the entertainment section of the *Los Angeles Times*, setting it on the table beside my half-eaten bowl of fruit salad. "Uh, for starters," I say, licking my lips. "Some tongue would be nice. So let's try this again."

She shakes her head. Then smiles slow and sexy as she leans in so that she is only a breath away from my face. I stare into her long-lashed, brown eyes. My desires swim behind my pupils. I want her.

I always want her.

All of her.

Her kissing. Her licking. Her sucking. Her fucking. Mouth and lips over this long dick. I want her lips glazed by my precum.

Want her wet mouth full of this hard chocolate. Want her neck stretched. Want the back of her throat flooded with this thick, creamy nut. Want her swallowing and gulping and sucking. Want her licking around the inside of her mouth, gliding her tongue over her teeth, tasting, savoring every drop of me.

Fuck what ya heard. My muhfuckin' dick stays hard for Marika. I need her. Lust her. I'm always horny for her. She knows she's the only woman I'm pussy whipped over.

I love this fuckin' woman. Love her hot, wet cunt. Love her wet mouth. Love her wanting tongue—the way it flicks and licks and laps and swirls around my dick. The way it swabs my heavy, cum-loaded balls.

Word is bond. I'm ready to bust this nut.

"Just so we're clear," Marika says. "You already have me." Her lips press mine, and she kisses me like she means it. Her tongue slips inside my mouth, causing my dick to stretch. She pulls back. And as soon as it ends, I want more.

I grin. "Now that's what I'm talking about. It was already a good morning. But it's definitely a better one now." I slide my hand over her ass.

"Oh, no," she says, playfully slapping my hand away. She sits in the chair across from me. "Let me at least have breakfast, first."

I suck my teeth, giving her a "yeah-right" look. "Take them drawz off. I ain't tryna hear all that. I got all the breakfast you need right here in this dick." I drain the last of my cranberry juice, then unfasten the belt on my robe, leaning back in my seat and spreading my legs. I grab my dick. "Come on 'n' get this breakfast nut, baby."

Marika licks her lips. "Well, since you put it like that. How can I resist such a delicious invitation?"

She stands and comes over toward me. I grab her by the waist. Tell her to straddle me. She does. I grin as she eases down onto my lap, opening her robe. She's wearing a tiny lace thong underneath her red teddy.

"*Embrasse-moi,*" I whisper in French, telling her to kiss me. She cups my face and kisses me, moaning into my mouth as my hands roam freely over her body, along her lower back, cupping her ass, kneading her tits, tweaking her nipples. I smack her ass. Not hard. But hard enough for it to echo and give her a sweet sting.

She kisses me harder, her tongue melting into mine.

I smack her ass again.

And again.

She cries out a little. Whimpers. Moans. She bites into my bottom lip. Then groans into my mouth. "Mar*Sell*, baby…"

"Hmmm." I slide my right hand up under her ass, grazing her lips. I slip a finger in. Then another. Then another. Three fingers deep, her pussy clamps tight as I fuck into her. Deep. Fast. My fingertip flicks over her clit, once, twice, thrice.

Marika rocks her hips. Throws her head back. And moans as my fingers fuck and stretch her. My fingertips graze that spot that turns up the heat inside her pussy. My dick leaks sticky heat. My huge balls bubble, filling up with thick cream. I'm ready to bust this fuckin' nut down into my baby's throat.

"*Je veux tes lèvres sur ma bite, bébé.*" Marika's pussy drips onto my lap, wetting the shaft of my dick as I repeat in English, "I want your lips on my dick, baby…"

I pull my fingers out of her, slipping each one into my mouth as Marika slides down onto her knees. Her face inches from my dick. She breathes me in. A mixture of hard horny cock and wet cunt stains.

Marika's mouth engulfs the head of my big black cock. Her head bobbing up and down as I grind my hips forward. She sucks me, one hand squeezing the thick base, then sliding up and down on it. She slobbers and drools and spits all over it.

"Yeah, that's it, baby…mmm…fuck…you love sucking daddy's big chocolate dick, don't you, baby?"

She responds with a grunt and a mouth full of spit-and-drool-covered dick, taking it to the back of her throat.

My cell rings. It's Arianna, one of my many assistants calling from New York, tryna Skype me. I frown. *What the fuck is she callin' me for on a Saturday?* I glance at the time. *At one thirty in the afternoon?*

I accept the call. Arianna's smooth, brown face comes up on the screen. I can't front. She's a beauty. Even without all the makeup. Her hair sits wild and curly all over her head. She licks her lips, then says, "I'm sorry for calling. But it couldn't be helped. I'd thought you'd want to know before you heard it over social media."

"Before I heard what?" I ask, tryna keep my rising annoyance in check.

"J-Smooth was arrested…"

"What the fuck?!" I snap, feeling the vein in my neck pulse. "Again? When? Where? And what the fuck for this time?"

"For assault, possession of weapons, and terroristic threats."

I stand, pacing the floor. "Yo, word is bond. You've got to be… fuckin' kidding me."

She gives me a pitiful look, shaking her head. "I wish…"

Jaquan Samuels, better known as J-Smooth, is one of my label's R&B artists. I'd signed him to MK three years ago and watched his career soar. His last two albums, *Portrait of A Man's Soul* and

Tears & Trepidation, soared to the top of the *Billboard* charts and sold over 250,000 copies in its first week. And his album *Tears & Trepidation* won a 2013 Billboard Music Award.

On some real shit, the cat has incredible vocals and lyrics to match. But lately this muhfucka's been more of a liability than an asset. This is the third time his dumb-ass has been snatched up. The last incident six months ago was due to some corny-ass bar brawl with some rapper over some wet pussy. That of twenty-five-year-old R&B songstress Lydia Miles who they'd both been fucking at one time or another. Allegedly words were exchanged at some Miami nightspot, then the argument erupted into J-Smooth clocking dude upside the head with a bottle, knocking him unconscious and causing gunshots to be fired into the crowd.

He's on three years' probation.

And they're both being sued.

Now this shit.

In the blink of an eye, this musical heartthrob, *Billboard* topper is becoming a pain in my muthafuckin' ass.

"What'd he do this time?"

"Oh, it's ugly," she says grimly. "He slashed Elena Mitchell's tires and then swung a hammer at her, threatening to bash her face and knock her eye sockets in."

My nose flares. Elena Mitchell is his on-again, off-again girl and another R&B singer who'd won season three of *The Voice*.

"There's a restraining order on him and his bail is set at a two hundred-and-fifty thousand dollars. What do you want to do?"

I frown. "What the fuck you mean, what I wanna do? Not a muthafuckin' thing. Let his muthafuckin' ass stay there. If the muhfuckas in his posse can't bail his ass out, fuck him. I'll deal with him when I get back to the East Coast. Until then, I don't wanna hear shit else about that dumb muhfucka. Got it? Get it? Good."

I end the call.

"Who was that?" Marika questions as she's walking into the sitting area of our master suite. She's fully dressed in a sexy lil' skirt and matching jacket. Her hair is pulled back into a ponytail.

"Just some work shit," I say, tossing my cell over on the leather chaise.

She slides her four-carat studs into her ears, screwing on the backs while staring at me through the mirror. "Okay. Not another word. But judging by the bulging vein in the center of your forehead and the one stretching along your neck, it must be serious. And if it has anything to do with that idiot J-Smooth getting arrested early this morning in Atlanta, you need to think about cutting your losses with that one. He's a walking time bomb."

I give her a surprised look, and ask her how she found out before I did.

"Where else? Social media. It's all over Facebook and Twitter. And I just got the heads-up from one of my assistants who is also a borderline stalker of his."

I sigh, shaking my head. "Figures. Yeah, I'm thinkin' I'ma have'ta snatch that muhfucka's contract. I'ma have legal take a look at it when we get back to see if there's a morality clause or some shit we can execute to cut him the fuck off. This shit with him is getting fuckin' ridiculous. He's starting to feel like dead weight right about now. This dumb niggah rather turn up in the clubs 'n' knock women upside the fuckin' head than make good albums 'n' get this paper."

"He's too much of a risk," she says casually, gliding a coat of lipgloss over her cherry-red-painted lips. "Unless he can get his act together, it'll be for the best in the long run." She walks over and leans in, kissing me on the lips. "Besides, you don't need the head-ache."

My gaze flickers up and down the back of her smooth, shiny legs as her ass bounces away from me. "Yo, Hold up. Where you going showin' off them pretty-ass legs 'n' with all that ass bouncin'?"

"To get my hair and nails done for tonight," she says matter-of-factly over her shoulder. "There's a posh new salon over in Beverly Hills that everyone here and back home is raving about. The owner has a salon here and in Jersey. But the one here is supposed to be real upscale."

"Yeah, aiight. How much is this upscale outing gonna cost me?"

She laughs. "You're off the hook this time. It's my own treat."

"Oh, aiight, then. Go do you, sexy."

"I plan to."

"Yeah, aiight. And you better have on drawz, yo."

She laughs, giving me a dismissive wave as she heads out the door.

NINE

Marika

Hair done. Nails done. Feet done. Facial done. My experience at the exclusive salon, Nappy No More II, was more than an experience. It was a pleasurable adventure. Now I'm in my fourth boutique on Rodeo Drive trying on dresses for tonight's *fuck*tivities.

The problem is, Marcel is here with me.

And as much as I love spending time with my husband, this man is impossible to shop with. Time is ticking. And I still haven't found the perfect dress. Yet, here I am—seven dresses hanging on hooks, three others tossed over on the bench—braless, inside a dressing room with Marcel standing in back of me, his tongue trailing down my spine. His strong hands cup my breasts, his fingers tweaking my nipples. He stares at me through the mirror. "Damn, you so fuckin' sexy, baby. *Je une chatte*." I want some pussy.

I gasp and writhe and whimper. I know enough by looking in his eyes that he wants to fuck me. That he wants me right here, right now.

"Mar*Sell*, you're gonna get us…caught…in here."

"So. What they gonna do? Arrest me for fuckin' my wife?"

I shake my head. Try to wriggle out of his embrace. "Not here, baby. We have—"

He presses in close. Licks the back of my neck. Nips it. Causing me to forget my train of thought, to lose my senses.

"Uhh, ooh…you have to stop…mmm…"

I hear voices on the other side of the door, coming closer. I blink. Find my voice of reason. "Baby, someone's coming."

"Yeah, you'll be *coming* in a minute."

"No, I'm serious."

He grins. "So am I."

"But—"

"Shhhh." He turns me to face him and quiets me with his mouth. His warm lips parting my own as his tongue slowly melts away my hesitation. He breaks our kiss, only to step back.

A warm rush of wet passion pulses between my legs as he unbuttons the top button of his jeans, unzips his fly, revealing a vee of smooth, taut skin covered in wisps of dark hair. He doesn't have on any underwear. I swallow, drinking in the sight of him as he pushes his jeans down, over his hips.

Right here. In the dressing room, his dick stretching and thick.

Within seconds, I am in front of the mirror, bent over, the flimsy gown bunched up at my waist, the head of Marcel's dick easing into me.

The heat grows, blossoms, then explodes as he strokes his dick into me. I feel him swelling, pulsing, inside me. Stretching the seams of my pussy.

I hear myself scream.

Hear the wetness of my cunt.

Hear the thrusting of Marcel's dick.

Hear the low grunts and groans lodged in the back of Marcel's throat.

Hear the saleswoman talking to someone on the other side of the door.

"Oooh, yes, yes, yes…"

Oh God, yessss!

Yes, yes, yessss!

I swallow another scream just as there's a soft knock on the door. Marcel rolls his hips into me, his dick sliding in and out, pressing in balls deep, then out to the tip.

"Oooh…"

There's another knock. "Mrs. Kennedy? Is everything all right in there?"

"Uhh…"

"Mrs. Kennedy?"

The doorknob jiggles.

I look up into the mirror. My face is distorted. A film of sweat coats my skin. My freshly done hairdo is slowly becoming undone. "Yes," I manage to squeak out. "I'm good. Give me a sec, oh, uh, ohhhkaaaay? I'll be done in a minute."

Marcel grins, eyeing me through the mirror. "You love this dick, baby?" His voice is a hushed whisper. "*Dis-moi que tue aimes il.*"

He tells me to tell him how much I love it. His dick.

"Are you sure?" the saleswoman inquires.

My eyes roll up in my head. "Yes. Yes. Yes. I'm sure."

"Okay," she says, "if you need any help. Let me know. I'll be up front."

Marcel reaches around me and plays with my clit. His dick strokes are slow and methodical. He fucks into my flesh; fucks into my soul.

"T-thanks," I mewl, sounding like a screeching cat in heat.

Marcel's dick plunges into my cunt, in and out, each stroke stretching my walls and sending waves of pleasure through my body. My pussy clenches.

Oh God.

Oooh he's fucking me so good. A tidal wave of carnal need washes over me, causing me to throw my hips back at him. I fuck him back. My ass bounces and shakes around him.

"Yeah, that's my baby. Fuck this dick, baby…Give me that wet pussy…"

In.

Out.

In.

Out.

In.

Then he is out of me again, his dick long and wet; my pussy wet and aching and greedy. My body shakes with want and need. God-damn him!

He swiftly turns me, backs me into the mirror, lifts me up by the hips, and sits me on the head of his dick. The mouth of my cunt opens wide as he eases me down on him.

I hook my arms around his neck. Gasp. Marcel cups my ass. And makes love to me.

"Vous aimez cette bite, pas vous?"

Love and *dick* is all I can decipher.

Marcel repeats himself in English. "You love this dick, don't you?"

"Yes, yes, yes, yes…," I whimper.

He growls in my ear. *"Je vais venir dans ta chatte humide, bébé."*

A groan slips from between my lips as I wrap my legs around him. "Please tell me what you just said, baby."

He digs his nails into my ass cheeks. "I said I'm gonna *come* in your wet pussy, baby. You want me to nut, huh, baby? Mmm… uh…fuuuck…you want this nut…?"

His words are like kerosene, igniting flames inside of me. Dec-adent heat and pleasure quakes through me as my own orgasm swells.

My cunt clenches. Unclenches. Clenches again. It spasms around Marcel's cock, and gets wetter and hotter with each stroke. His strokes get deeper and faster.

He is on the verge of coming.

I am on the border of an orgasm as well. Marcel is fucking me closer to the edge. I dig my fingernails into his shoulders and bounce up and down on his dick, taking in every bit of his length as he hits the bottom of my well.

I can hear the saleswoman as she returns to the fitting room area, checking in on someone else. I hear the other woman call out and say she is fine.

I moan.

Marcel moans.

The saleswoman knocks on the door again. "Mrs. Kennedy, are you sure you don't need any help in there?"

Marcel's long fingers delve inside my crack. He presses into my asshole. Everything inside of me erupts. "Oh, yes. Oh, yes. Oh, yes. Oh, yes. I'm sure. I'm *com*...ing...mmm...right out."

"All right."

"That's right, baby. Let me get that nut," Marcel murmurs into my neck. "Pussy so fuckin' good." He growls low. Then bites into my shoulder. And unloads a thick river of heated pleasure inside of me.

I cling onto him. Kissing him. Milking him.

Five minutes later, his dick plops out of me. He lowers me to the floor. Then plants one last kiss on my lips, before lifting his pants up from around his ankles and stuffing himself back inside.

"Let's get home so we can finish this up." He grins, opening the dressing room door and slipping out, leaving me wet, disheveled, and deliciously fucked.

TEN

Marika

The black-suited driver rolls the stretch Bentley with its tinted windows through the ornate iron gates of the Beverly Hills mansion where tonight's extravaganza will take place. He slowly pulls in front of its circular driveway, then stops the car and slides out of the driver's seat, walking around to open the door for Marcel and me.

Marcel leans over and kisses me lightly on the cheek. He takes in my white draped, sleeveless Azzaro Capricieuse jewel dress with its plunging V-neckline and long slit in the middle, revealing my inner thigh. I'm wearing the six thousand-dollar dress—that is sure to catch the eye of many of tonight's elite guests, shakers and movers in the movie and music industry as well as some well-known sports figures—with a pair of white Valentino Garavani six-inch, rock-stud sandals.

His gaze drops down to my perky nipples peeking from underneath the thin fabric of my dress, then onto my smooth, shimmering thighs.

He licks his lips. "Damn. You look sexy as fuck, baby."

I smile, breathing in the scrumptious scent of his cologne, Creed Royal Oud. Every time he wear this, it drives me wild. "Thank you. You don't look too bad yourself." The glint in the diamond studs in his earlobes is blinding. He's donned in an elegant, black-fitted Valentino suit with a matching pair of loafers. "And you smell delicious, I might add." My hand slides between his legs, finding his meaty dick. I gently massage it until it starts to thicken.

"Yo, c'mon, baby," he says, grinning while trying to pull away. "You better stop before shit gets serious back here 'n' I end up ripping that dress off you 'n' beatin' that fat pussy up in this backseat."

"Ooh, yes, daddy," I coo into his ear. "Beat this pussy up. Fuck it until it stretches and burns. I want to feel you still inside of me throbbing and pulsing long after you've pulled out."

Marcel leans in, and whispers, "Hold tight, baby. By the end of the night, I promise. I'ma be doin' just that. *Putain la gueule d'ya cul sexy.*" Fucking the shit out of ya sexy ass. "But, for now, let's save the foreplay for the onlookers inside."

I press my thighs together, reluctantly retrieving my hand from his hard dick.

The back passenger door swings open.

Marcel winks at me, grinning. "You ready?"

I lick my lips as sordid scenarios of lewd sexapades flash through my freaky mind, causing heat to creep inbetween my thighs. My clit tingles, causing my pussy to instantly moisten.

"I'm always ready."

"So, what...or should I say *who*...are you in the mood for tonight, baby?" Marcel asks as we maneuver our way through the maze of designer-clad and diamond-studded guests, giving customary smiles and head nods, along with generous hugs and handshakes.

"I'll know when...."

There are several VPs and A&R executives from various record labels and numerous A-list celebrities and athletes milling around the room, drinking flutes of some of the finest champagnes while mingling, flirting, groping, and sidling up to their objects of desire as bare-chested waiters wearing black bowties and tuxedo pants circle with champagne on silver trays.

"Ooh, the two of you are simply delicious together," says a sultry voice in back of Marcel and me. We both look over our shoulder and our eyes flicker into the face of Nairobia Jansen—the half-Dutch, half-Nigerian author, model, and sex goddess who has graced the covers of both *Penthouse* and *Playboy* and has built a multimillion-dollar empire with her adult toy line.

"Mmm," she purrs, running a finger lightly down my spine, causing a burst of sensations to erupt inside of me. She's dressed in a scandalous white sheer dress sans bra and panties, brazenly revealing the assets she's most famous for—her voluptuous breasts, curvaceous hips, and beautiful round ass. "I'd love to have the two of you in my chambers tonight doing all sorts of naughty things."

"Nairobia, my darling," I say saucily, casting my gaze to the swell of her breasts, "you're looking irresistibly scrumptious as always." I lick my lips zooming in on the outline of her dark areolas and thick chocolate-tipped nipples.

She air-kisses both my cheeks, then hungrily eyes Marcel as he leans in and kisses her lightly on the lips, cupping her delightful ass.

He licks his lips, then says, "Good to see you, baby."

Gray eyes lit with mischief, Nairobia stands on her tiptoes and whispers, "And it would be even better to *feel* you deep inside me again." Before giving Marcel a chance to respond, she presses the mounds of her breasts against him and nibbles on his earlobe, taking his hand and sliding it between the long slit in her dress, placing it between her legs. "I've missed the feel of you inside my pussy."

Marcel gives her a lopsided grin. "Oh, word? You miss this long, hard dick, baby?"

She moans in response, pulling me into her, cupping her hand at the base of my neck for a tender kiss. My pussy moistens. She parts my lips with her tongue, while her other hand finds its way to my breasts. She brushes her mouth against the column of my neck, her warm breath heating my skin.

My hand slinks between her legs to join Marcel's. Index and middle fingers brush lightly against her slippery nub while Marcel's fingers get lost deep inside her heat. The scent of her pussy, wet and hungry, flows freely over Marcel's hand.

My mouth waters for a taste of her sweet nectar.

In between gasps and moans, Nairobia says, "I want…mmm… both of…you…*fucking*…me…in my *mouth*…my *pussy*…my sweet, tight *ass*…"

Marcel's thick fingers open her, wide and wanting, making room for my two slender fingers to slide in alongside his. Together we finger-fuck her. I can feel the silken swell of her cunt as she nears orgasm. She's getting wetter with each stroke.

Marcel leans in, kisses me, tongues me, then does the same to Nairobia. She hums deep in her throat, her cunt contracting around our probing digits, causing my own pussy to pulse. And thicken with desire.

"Spread your legs wider," I urge. She is close to coming. I can smell it, feel it, around our fingers as she thrusts her hips; four fingers fucking into her juicy cunt. The sound of wet pussy swallowing our fingers causes a deep throb to take root inside of me.

"Yeah, baby, nut on these fingers," Marcel murmurs, his voice deep and husky. "Bust that pussy for me, baby…"

And she does.

Like a tidal wave, warm juices erupt, washing over our fingers, soaking our hands. Nairobia squirts and shudders and gasps. Her skin flushes hot. And then she comes again.

A few seconds later, when her body is no longer trembling, when her cunt is vacant from our prodding fingers, Nairobia kisses us both, whispering promises of sweet, nasty things to come, then floats away.

"Damn, I love how wet her pussy gets," Marcel says, kissing me, then pressing his cum-slick fingers to my lips, offering me Nairobia's cunt juice. I suck his fingers into my mouth, sweeping my tongue around his fingers.

He smiles, and I moan as he pulls his wet fingers from my mouth. "Mmm, and she tastes so good."

Across the room, there's a set of eyes watching us. I'm not sure who spots him across the room first—me or Marcel, but when my eyes land on him I know he's the one I want eating my pussy alongside my husband.

He's gorgeous. And tall, at least six feet five, with a shock of dark, wavy hair and dark, piercing eyes. From where I'm standing, he looks as if he's been sculpted from a delicious batch of caramel, then drizzled with hot fudge.

"Him," I say, sliding my sticky fingers into my mouth, then licking them as I would a hard dick. "He's who I want for us tonight."

"Yeah, that muhfucka's real sexy, baby. Good choice."

He doesn't shift his gaze when he sees us looking back at him. He smiles. I smile back. Marcel acknowledges him with a head nod. "Yo, I think he likes what he sees."

"And so he should," I say, feeling my skin heat at the thought of sucking his dick and licking his balls while Marcel fucks me. I pick up a crystal flute off one of the trays. I hand it to Marcel, then grab a flute for myself.

Marcel smirks. "Let's hope the muhfucka doesn't have a lil'-ass, infant-size dick. I'm not tryna see them pretty lips wrapped around no tiny-ass dick, baby."

I clink my glass with his. We both take slow sips. The fact that Marcel enjoys seeing my mouth wrapped around another man's dick, the fact that he revels in the sight of seeing my lips painted with another man's semen, is what makes me desire him even more. Not many men could or would handle having their women—let alone giving her permission—to suck another man's dick. And he damn sure wouldn't be willing to kiss her with another man's cum on her tongue. But Marcel…he's uninhibited. Freaky. And secure enough in his manhood to enjoy it. Encourage it. And indulge in it.

"Oh, no," I say, eyeing Mr. Sexy across the room. "The way he's standing, all wide-legged and confident, tells me that whatever is hanging between those long legs of his is quite substantial."

"Yeah, well. It'd better be."

I grab his dick. Squeeze the head a few times. Then tell him I'll be right back. He kisses me on the cheek, his hand gliding over the globes of my ass. "Go get 'im, baby."

"I plan to," I say, gulping down the rest of my drink, then pulling Marcel into me. "For the both of us." I reach up and press my lips against his, parting them easily, my warm tongue prodding around his mouth before breaking free and prowling in the direction of the mystery man.

The smell of wet pussy and freshly fucked ass wafting around the room is intoxicating.

The thing I love most about sex clubs and private parties, there are no pretenses. No judgments. No limits. No shame. No room for games. No space for confusion. Everyone is always here for the same reasons, to fuck and be fucked shamelessly. To explore rapturous fantasies with whomever they choose. To be sexually fulfilled.

"You are one fine man," I say, walking up to him. I am already wet, but now I've become wetter with eager anticipation. I set my empty glass on a nearby table.

He flashes a megawatt smile, revealing straight, white teeth. "And so are you, beautiful. I enjoyed the show."

I smile, reaching for another flute of champagne as a bare-chested waiter in black tuxedo pants saunters by with a full tray. "Oh, there's a whole lot more to see," I assure him, my tone full of seduction and promise.

"Hmm. I love the sound of that." He places his empty glass on the tray, taking another one full of bubbly. "So who's the man I've watched you work the party with?" I tell him it's my husband. He grins and nods his head in approval. "Aah. And he doesn't want to join us?"

"Not at the moment." My gaze, full of fire and hot desire, skims his body, pausing over what looks like a growing bulge, thick and heavy. "But he will, trust."

He grins. "I look forward to it. The more the merrier." He pulls in his bottom lip, slow and seductively.

I give him a knowing smile. "So, what shall we drink to?" I ask, reaching up and pulling the diamond hairclip from my hair, letting my hair cascade over my shoulders.

"Why not to a night full of endless possibilities," he says with a wink.

I toss my hair, shamelessly flirting with this fine hunk of man. "Well, my husband and I"—I nod my head over in Marcel's direction—"would love to end the night with *you* in our bed."

He waits a beat, then glances over in Marcel's direction, lifting his flute. Marcel returns the gesture, along with a head nod. He smiles, returning his attention to me.

"Oh, and what an endless night of possibilities it shall be." His eyes scan my entire body, from head to toe. "I have a thing for pretty feet," he says, licking his lips. "And beautiful, open-minded women."

I grin, holding his gaze. "And I have a thing for fine men who aren't afraid to indulge their desires. That's a real turn-on. What are your desires, uh…I didn't get your name."

He grins back. "I didn't give it. Names aren't necessary. Just know I'm a freak, here looking for a good time. And I have a whole lot of energy for more than one round."

"Okay, Mister No Name Freak Looking For A Good Time, what do you desire tonight?"

He glances back over at Marcel, who is being entertained by two buxom vixens wearing nothing but glitter and gold body paint over their gym-Pilate-toned bodies.

A sly smile eases over my moist lips as I eye Marcel slide both his hands in between each of their legs. The two sex kittens lean in and kiss. And I swallow, imagining the feel of their warm flesh against his fingers, imagining the taste of their wetness on my own fingers, on my tongue.

A vision of sharing the two vixens with Marcel causes my pussy to spasm and my nipples to peak hard.

"For starters," Caramel says, bringing my attention back to him, "to answer your question. I desire a night with *you*." He tears his stare from mine, glancing over at Marcel. "And *him*. But for now…" He eyes my feet again. "I'd like to taste them pretty toes." He slides his lusty gaze back up to meet mine. "Then lick you to climax."

My breath catches.

Then, without another word, he's whisking me off outside toward a row of cushion-padded benches. The backyard is dimly lit with gaslight sconces and tiki torches.

The walls of my pussy literally tremble as I watch this tall, sculpted hunk of a caramel-coated man gulp down the rest of his drink, then drop on one knee, unfasten the straps of my heels, remove them, then gently fold his large hands around my ankles, lift a foot to his face. He kisses my feet with warm lips. Then runs his tongue along my arch, kissing the tips of my toes, then putting them into his mouth. I can't help but moan as his tongue slides around, and in between, each toe as his hands slip up the back of my calves, my thighs, then back down. He sinks all five of my toes inside his mouth. And I feel myself melting into the sensation. Erotic and sensual, my clit tingles.

I arch forward, aching for him, devouring him with my eyes. He sucks and licks my toes as if he's sucking and licking on my clit, sucking and licking on my cunt, sucking and licking on my swollen lips, sucking and licking as if each toe were a tiny, hard dick. Heat dances over my body. Spreads out over my skin. And stirs my simmering lust.

"Do you want to taste my pussy, too?"

His head nods. "Mmm…yes."

"Say it then. Say you want your tongue in my sweet pussy." I brazenly part my legs, allowing my already open split to spill open further, showing the damp patch of triangle fabric covering my moist cunt.

A dark smile crosses his lips as Marcel finally walks over to join us; the imprint of his dick showing his approval, stretching down the left part of his thigh like a third leg.

Marcel greets my toe licker with a grin, then leans in and kisses me. His heated tongue lustfully probes the inside of my mouth while his hand travels inside the neckline of my dress and caresses my breast.

I let out a soft moan as Mr. Caramel slides his finger back and forth over my swollen clit. I feel a climax coming from somewhere deep inside me. A spark of fire ignites low in my gut as he finger-fucks me, tormenting my clit with his tongue. He pulls out, then slides his long, slick fingers up and down on either side of my thick pussy lips. His tongue lolls out and traces its way up my smooth lips, ignoring my distended clit. And I feel myself on the verge of a scream.

I reach for Marcel. Grab his dick. Squeeze it. Stroke it. Beg for it. Groan with pleasure. Moan with want. Whimper with need.

With his tongue flat and firm—sticking out like a hot slab, Caramel licks my clit, repeatedly, while Marcel pinches my nip-ples so hard that I shriek in delight. Caramel licks again and again, then licks long and hard against my wet, juicy hole, eventually darting his tongue in and out.

My pussy muscles clench. "Yes, right there," I say breathlessly.

And then comes the sucking again, and the slurping and more sucking as my hot nectar spills out of me. Caramel growls into me, and the vibrations send shivering waves of pleasure through my cunt. Then he opens wide, taking my whole pussy into his mouth, sucking my labia, letting his tongue dip down into my asshole.

My cunt coils, then weeps.

I unashamedly moan and groan and tell him how to eat my pussy, when to suck my clit, when to fuck his fingers into me. I grind my pussy into his mouth. Aftershocks reverberate up and down and around the walls of my pussy, along my spine. And I come. And come again.

I pull him into me and kiss him, vicariously tasting my sweet-ness on his lips and his cum-coated tongue. "Are you ready for the real show?"

"What you think?" He rises to his feet—his chin glistening and his mouth gleaming with juices—and grabs the thick bulge in his own pants. "Let's take this party somewhere more private."

I lick my lips, glancing up at Marcel as the two men's eyes lock, sizing the other up. "Then let's go get freaky," I finally say, standing up with my sticky juices glazing the insides of my quivering thighs as I lead the way.

ELEVEN

Marcel

Marika raises her voluptuous hips to my every thrust. Her eyes widen with heated pleasure as I pound into her pussy. Her slick walls tighten around me as I groan with each plunge, until I am balls deep, until I am hitting the core of everything she is.

My baby's pussy is so muthafuckin' deep.

And wet.

And muthafuckin' hot.

My tongue slides into her ear. My teeth nip at her lobe. My breath is hot on her neck. She whimpers as my thick dick slams into her wetness, relentlessly parting her swollen pussy lips with each stroke. I growl low in her ear. Tell her how much I love her. How much I need her. How much I appreciate her. How much she means to me. How good she feels. How good she makes me feel. Oh, how fucking good she is. How I live for the sight of her, the taste of her, the touch of her. Her smell. Her skin. Her lips.

I increase my pace. Pound in and out until I can hear the smack of flesh on flesh, mine against hers, our bodies becoming one.

"Mmm…fuuuck…oh, shit…"

Marika screams. Clasps her long legs around my muscular hips, her pussy slurping in my dick and capturing it deep inside her.

"Oh fuck…deep, wet pussy…mmm…I love being in this pussy, baby."

"Marcel…" Her voice comes out muffled, sounding more like a cry than my name. "Ooh, yessss, baby…mmmm…fuck meee…" Her fingernails rake the muscles of my broad back and shoulders.

In response, I lower my head and cover her mouth with mine, biting into her plump bottom lip as I fuck harder, deeper, swirling my tongue around hers.

My baby's hot, wet pussy melts all over and around my dick as she slides her tongue into a sensual dance against mine, her parted thighs spreading wider, inviting me into her bottomless well, her juicy cunt clutching my dick.

"Ooh, Marcel…oooh…your dick…mmm…uhhh…is…mmm…oooh…so…good…"

I groan.

The deeper I stroke, the wetter Marika gets.

The hotter she gets, the harder my dick gets. Her pussy becomes a swell of tingles. Her walls are a silken wrap of tight heat and pleasure. I lose myself in her wet passion, growling.

"Fuck! Aah shit! Aah! Motherfuck…mmm…!"

I palm Marika's right tit, toying with her nipple, rolling it with my finger and thumb—a squeeze, a pinch, a tug, a gentle brush, I keep my fingers fastened on her swollen chocolate nub, causing her juices to splash out of her pussy.

"Yes! Fuck me, baby! Oooh, yes! Yes! Yessss…!"

She gasps as I lower my head and nip at her nipple. Take it into my mouth. Sweep it with my tongue, curling, laving, suckling, then switching over to her left tit.

"Oh, yes; oh, yes; oh, yes; oh, yessss…"

Marika's eyes flare open. Her head snaps to the left, then the right. Her hot gaze filled with pleasure and lust and need. She arches her back, thrusts her pelvis up into me, fucks me back as she eyes the onlooker.

Yeah, we have company.

An invited guest.

Sitting naked.

Watching us.

Getting off on us.

His long, lean legs spread wide.

His hard, fat, hairy dick in his hand.

His smooth-shaven balls lightly bouncing as he slowly glides his hand up and down his shit.

Marika moans.

"Yeah, baby," I whisper in her ear, stroking into her. "You want that dick in ya mouth? You wanna suck that muhfucka's cock?"

She moans again, taking in his body with hungry eyes.

"You want that muhfucka to stretch ya neck out...huh, baby? Tell daddy what you want..."

She whimpers low in her throat. I can tell she's nearly out of her mind with desire and need and greed as much as I am.

We both want him to join us.

We both want him to fuck his dick into her mouth.

We both want him to bury his face between her legs.

Then curl his tongue inside her gushy pussy, tasting her; tasting me.

Eating her pussy clean.

Then dropping down on his knees, sucking in my dick, licking it clean.

Marika moans.

I grin.

Our naked onlooker stands up. Dips his knees and fucks into his hand, the head of his dick popping in and out of the opening of his palm.

I grunt my approval, thrusting harder in Marika, rocking into her, lifting up on my arms and long stroking into her, tip to base. In. Out. In. Out.

Then plunging back into her.

I grunt.

She grunts.

"Beg for that niggah's dick, baby," I urge.

He grins slyly, his dick gliding in and out of his hand. The head of his dick glistens with droplets of precum.

I growl. "Yeah, muhfucka…jerk that shit, niggah…"

He lets out a moan.

Marika moans.

His strokes match my rhythm. The faster I thrust, the faster he strokes. The deeper I pump, the deeper he strokes.

He meets my gaze.

"Yeah, muhfucka…you wanna suck my baby's pussy juice off this long dick, don't you?'"

He grunts.

I grin.

Holding myself up on my forearms, I thrust steadily in and out of Marika, keeping my stare on the sexy muhfucka standing in the middle of the floor. I glance down at Marika and smile. Then wink. Her face is a collage of expressions. She moans and groans. Her tongue hangs out of her mouth. Her legs are wrapped high around my hips, sucking me deeper into her pussy. "Yeah, baby…nut for me," I say in a low, husky voice. "Let me feed that muhfucka over there this nut, baby…"

Her fingernails dig into my shoulders in anticipation. She bucks and thrashes and screams and cums around my dick, soaking it in her warmth. My dick is thick and hard and aching. I grunt, feeling my own nut gathering at the base of my spine.

"Yeah, muhfucka…come over here and get this nut…"

Marika moans.

Then groans, my thrusts fucking the noise out of her. The head of my dick strokes her G-spot. I can feel it. She's about to cum again. Hard. Wet. Long. Dripping.

And she does. Then she is fucking me back. Her hips thrust. Her pussy glides up and down the shaft of my cock. Her juices dribble out, drenching the sheets beneath her.

The aroma of her pussy is all around me.

I'm about to bust.

"Come get this nut, niggah…"

Marika moans again as I grunt, and a gusher of hot nut bursts outta my slit into her pussy. I quickly pull out as our guest drops to his knees in front of me. He takes my cunt-and-cum-soaked dick into his hands and sucks my giant head into his mouth like he's sucking the juice out of a tangerine, stroking my shaft.

He moans as I nut again. Three more ropes of thick cum shoot out of me, hitting the back of his throat and flooding his mouth. He sucks out every drop, then pulls his head back and caresses my dickhead between his lips.

I pull out of his mouth, groaning, as one last spurt of nut splashes his face.

TWELVE

Marika

The rules are simple.

Our tête-à-têtes are always agreed on.

We choose each other's sexual pleasures for the night.

We must both be physically attracted to them.

We never, ever, engage in any extramarital trysts without the other's permission and presence. Never.

Discretion is a must. Each conquest must have as much to lose as we do if our secret rendezvous were to ever become public knowledge.

And they're all always...beautiful.

Every shade of black, every hue of brown, every tint of red, wrapped around taut, sculpted bodies; firm breasts, round hips, tight asses to sensual lips, chiseled chests, rippled abs, and long dicks.

We participate or not in the other's salacious night.

And, together, Marcel and I embrace our bisexualities, testing sexual boundaries while indulging our *sinful* fantasies, and turning them into sensually heated realities; like right now.

With this delicious hunk of caramel perfection, sliding his spit-and-cum-soaked dick from out of my mouth as Marcel's cum-soaked cock flops out of my sticky cunt. Caramel's thick cream coats my lips. Marcel's warm nut coats my walls.

Both of them spread their dicks over my respective lips, then lean in and kiss them, licking their semen up, tasting themselves on me. Dark hunger flashes over Caramel's face as he slides his tongue over my lips, then slips it into my mouth. His lips are soft and moist. I can still taste Marcel's nut on him. Can taste and smell my pussy on him on his lips from having sucked Marcel's cock less than five minutes ago.

Mmmm...

Deliciously decadent.

My insides throb as Marcel's tongue skims the mouth of my pussy, then flaps up and down inside my wetness. My cunt clenches. My hips shift in response. Wind. Thrust. Pump. Marcel's long tongue slides further up inside of me. My ass churns. My pussy juice flows like a never-ending river. I have become a plush rain-forest.

A moan hitches in the back of my throat as I soak Marcel's face with my juices. A rushing well of pleasure flooding his mouth, soaking his tongue.

Marcel groans into my pussy as I reach out and grab Caramel's curved dick. Caramel groans into my mouth, gliding his tongue around mine as my soft hand strokes his dick back into an erection while Marcel lavs and nips and suckles my clit.

"Mmmm...you're so wet, baby," Marcel says in between tongue licks, fingering the wetness between my legs. My pussy burns. He scissors a second finger into me, stretching into my heated cunt.

I cry out.

Gasp for air.

I eye a droplet of precum caressing the tip of Caramel's bulbous, copper-colored head. Then reach out and pull him by the base of his shaft toward my waiting, open mouth. And suck him in. I keep my gaze on him as his head snaps back and he groans. Slowly, I shift my body. Crane my neck so that my head is now between his opened muscular legs. I get lost in the intoxicating scent of his skin, his manliness. Licking around his musky balls, I open wide and wait for him to lower them down into my mouth. I suck them in one at a time.

"Yeah. Wet them motherfucking balls up…"

He groans again.

Marcel's finger…a thumb, I think—or maybe it's his tongue— flicks over my clit. I hear him say over the pounding of my heart in my ears, "Suck that muhfucka's dick, baby…"

And then Marcel is up, leaving my pussy and the space between my thighs vacant, standing next to Caramel, his big beautiful dick sliding in and out of his wet hand. The head of his dick hovering over my face, his mouthwatering balls clack in sync to his hand strokes.

Marcel wants me to change positions. Wants me to sit up. I do. My feet sink into the plush carpet. Through blurred passion, I lovingly eye Marcel as he palms the back of Caramel's neck and draws him into a kiss, sliding his tongue into Caramel's mouth— offering him a taste of me, and himself.

Instantly, my walls spasm and a flash of searing pleasure shoots through me as my cunt creams, causing me to suck Caramel with feverish enthusiasm. Tears gather in my eyes as his dick hits the back of my throat; his thick curve snaking and stretching its way down into my neck, then sliding back out.

I am no porn star, but I have perfected the art of sucking a big dick, thanks to my years of sucking Marcel's. And I have mastered a no-gag reflex. So there isn't a dick that I can't handle. Caramel's isn't as long as Marcel's, but it's equally as thick so I handle him like a pro. Suck him until his legs tremble and he is on the brink of another orgasm.

I pull him out of my mouth. And reach for Marcel's dick, flicking my tongue over its swollen head, lapping at the shimmering pre-cum as it trickles out of his slit. I press their dicks together, then alternately suck them both; my hot mouth gliding over each one.

My eyelids flutter up, taking in the sight of these two masculine men kissing fiercely, groaning as their tongues dance around in each other's mouths. They both have a hand on my breasts, caressing each one, pinching and tugging at my nipples.

My clit throbs.

My pussy burns hotter.

My outer lips get slicker.

I need, want, Marcel's dick back inside of me, feeding me his width and length. Slamming in and out of me, over and over. Oh, how I need to be fucked, again.

Deep and delicious.

I tell Marcel so. Beg him. Urge him. "Fuck me…Please. Put your dick back inside of me…"

But my demand goes unanswered. Instead, I am being pushed back onto the bed, my legs spread apart. My cunt splayed open by eager hands as Marcel and Caramel drop to their knees, bow their heads, and worship my pussy.

I bite into my bottom lip.

Count the number of times their tongues move over my clit—Marcel's and our secret lover's, along the folds of my pussy, then up and down my throbbing pussy lips, then again back over my clit. I lean up on my forearms, panting and moaning. Force my eyes to focus on the decadent performance of their swirling tongues, flicking against the others as they paint wet circles over my engorged clit. Perfect eights.

I count each lick in my head. Count each stroke. Up and down. Up and down. Up and down. Around and around and around, the heat from their greedy tongues teasing me into an orgasm.

"Ooooh, yes…lick my pussy…mmmm…yes, yes, yes, yesss… ooh, ooh, ooooh…right there, right there…"

Marcel cups my clit with his tongue. Our lover slides two long fingers inside of me, curling his fingers inward, beckoning an orgasm out of me; taunting a moan to escape my lips.

Lapping and nibbling, probing and flicking, wet tongues, wet fingers, stroking between my legs; spreading my wetness, moving over my clit, sliding around my ass, pinching my erect, aching nipples until I am moaning and moving my hips, shuddering.

I blink. The room spins. My eyes are hazy with want.

I scream out in need as they both stroke their dicks with one hand while tongue-fucking my wet and wanting cunt, their tongues echoing the smack-slap and thrust and withdrawal of their cocks sliding through their palms.

Desire and heat creeps up in me. Sweeps through my pussy and snatches my breath. I want them both inside of me. Marcel's thick, dark chocolate slicing into my cunt. Caramel's curved dick sawing into my ass.

Fucking me.

Stroking me.

Gutting me.

Before the sun rises…I'll have them both.

And then I will savor watching Marcel mercilessly fuck himself into Caramel's gaping wet mouth again, coating his throat with another round of his sweet semen before sending our secret lover on his merry way.

THIRTEEN

Marcel

After a taking an early morning run on the beach, then sitting out on the terrace looking out over the Pacific Ocean, Sunday afternoon finds Marika and I are already getting in round two with our second guest for the weekend before we have to board our private jet and head back to New York in another three hours. Bret Morrison. Six-four star point guard and one of the NBA's hottest draft picks. And another cat who loves pussy, but digs getting it in with another muhfucka on the low whenever the opportunity presents itself.

Like right now.

Marika and I have gotten it in with Bret several times over the last two years when we're out on the West Coast and feel the urge to indulge with a repeat. Kicking some real shit, I think Marika's crushin' on him on the low.

But it's all good.

I'm diggin' the long-tongued, thick-dicked muhfuckah's swag on the low, too. With his sexy dark eyes, lean, muscular frame and tattooed flesh, he's the only cat I can actually close my eyes and visualize his sensual mouth wrapped around my dick—sucking my shit like it's the last thing he'll ever slide into his wet mouth, sucking this dick with a whole lot of spit—and my dick will brick up without stroking it.

There's something 'bout this sexy muhfuckah that does it for me. But still I keep that shit in check. Keep it in perspective. It's strictly physical.

Aiight, aiight…and part mental.

But that's it. I'm not tryna wave some rainbow flag and wife the muhfucka. But keepin' shit a hunnid, I've definitely considered fucking him in his ass a few times. Word is bond. This niggah has a juicy muhfuckin' ass.

And it's the only muhfucka's ass I've ever stuck my tongue in. Tongue-fucked the shit outta it while he sucked my shit.

Sixty-nine.

His ass hovering over my face.

My tongue flicking around in his asshole.

My legs bent at the knees and spread wide.

His mouth on my dick.

Marika sucking and licking on my balls, then inching up and sucking his hard dick into her mouth.

It was the first time I bust off mad fast.

In less than fifteen minutes.

"Ooh, yes, baby," Marika says in between soft moans and low groans. "Uh, uh, uh, uh…" She fucks back on my dick, her pussy gulping in all but two thick inches of it. "Oooh, yesss…uh, my pussy…mmmm…feels so good…oooh…"

With my hands on my hips, I keep still. Allow Marika to clap her ass up and down and around my dick, her wet cunt sliding back and forth on it.

Slap!

"Yeah, baby, get that dick," I coax, watching her ass bounce and shake as I slap it.

Slap!

I reach over Marika and slap Bret's ass. He's on his knees in front of her, his hanging balls dangling in her face.

Doggy-style.

The both of them.

"Lick that muhfucka's ass, baby," I grunt, pulling open Marika's ass cheeks. I spit into her asshole, smear it in with my finger, then stick my thumb inside of her. Her back arches. While I'm fucking Marika from the back, I lick my lips as she licks Bret's muscular ass cheeks, then pulls them open and starts licking on the inside of his ass.

Dude moans and wriggles. His hard, swollen cock swings and bounces. I lean forward and stretch my long arm around and reach for it, stroking it in my hand. I kiss Marika on her shoulder, then nip at her ear as I move my own dick in and outta her soppy-wet hole, fucking her with slow precision in sync with my hand strokes up and down Bret's cock. His precum drips over my hand as I grab his balls; cup and squeeze them muhfuckas.

He groans.

Marika moans. Her tongue dipping in, then flicking out, then swirling over his puckered hole.

I moan. "Yeah, baby...fuck that hot tongue all up in his juicy asshole."

"Oh yes, oh yes, oh yes...mmm...uh...oooh..."

"Aaah, shit," Bret grunts as Marika's finger goes knuckle deep into his ass. She pulls his dick to the back with her free hand and sucks the head. His body trembles. "Fuck. Uh. Oooh, fuck..."

"Yeah, that's it, baby...make that muhfucka bust..." I reach for a set of black vibrating anal beads with a *T*-shaped handle on the end beside me. Pull open Marika's ass. Then drip more spit into her asshole, before pushing the first bead in. *Pop.*

Marika gasps. Burrows her tongue inside Bret. He groans. Buries his head into the pillow. Backs his ass up on her tongue.

Slap!

I slap Marika's soft ass.

Slap!

I reach over Marika, and slap Bret's muscled ass. Then thrust my hips and fuck another inch of my dick into Marika's warm, creamy cunt. She moans into Bret's ass, reaching between his thighs again and pulling his dick and balls back, licking around his balls, then the head of his dick, before sliding it into her mouth.

Slowly I push the second bead in her ass. This one's a little bigger than the first. *Pop.* I grunt. "Yeah, baby…look at that pretty asshole…" I push the third—*pop*, and then the fourth—*pop*, and finally the fifth bead in—*pop*, each one bigger than the other.

I can feel the beads vibrating against the thin skin between her ass and juicy pussy, pulsing along the shaft of my wet, sticky dick. Heat sizzles up around my balls causing me to tremble.

"Uh, fuck, baby…you got that good, juicy pussy…"

"Yeah, fuck your pussy, baby…" she murmurs, greedily licking up and down Bret's shaft.

I reach under her and slide my fingers over her clit. Marika digs her nails into each side of Bret's ass cheeks, her nose pressed into his hole as she sucks his dick deep into her mouth.

He grunts. "Aah, fuuuuuck! Shit! Goddamn…!"

"Yeah, baby, suck that shit," I say, slapping his ass again.

Slap!

I slowly twist the vibrating beads slowly in and out of Marika's ass, gliding my dick in and out of her slit. In. Out. Mmm, her pussy walls feel like silk. In. Out. In. Out. Damn. The way her wet heat caresses my shit is making my toes curl. I shut my eyes. Throw my head back. Try to hold the nut working its way out of me.

"Oooh, fuck, baby…mmmm…uhhh…aaah, shiiit…motherfuck… this wet pussy…mmmph…"

Marika shakes. Cries out. Bucks her hips. She's on the edge. Burning hot. "Yes, yes, yes…I'm cumming, baby…oooh, yesssssss!"

I quickly pull the beads from her ass. *Pop, pop, pop, pop, pop…*

Then reach over and push them deep into Bret's ass.

He trembles. Groans. Begs. Arches his back. He's on the verge of busting his nut. "Aaaaah, shiiiiit…yeah, fuck…suck that shit. Fuuuuuck!"

I shudder. Moan. Give in to ecstasy. "Aaaah fuuuuuuck…I'm cuuuummin'…"

The three of us nut in unison.

Bret in Marika's mouth.

Marika all over my cock.

And me…deep inside my baby's hot cunt.

FOURTEEN

Marika

Late Monday morning finds me standing in the middle of the kitchen with Marcel pulling me into him, his hands gripping my ass. I can feel his dick pressing into my abdomen. And the juices soaking through my black La Perla Brazilian briefs and glazing my heated cunt lips is evidence of how aroused I am.

"I had a great weekend with you, baby," he says before kissing my forehead. "I don't know how I ever got to be so lucky to have such a fine-ass, freaky wife."

I look up into his eyes and smile. Great is an understatement to describing this past weekend in Beverly Hills with him. We are both still floating from our weekend getaway. It was everything I'd hoped for, and more. Delicious. Raunchy. Seductive. Sinful. Taboo.

We didn't bed any women this trip. Only men.

Two of them.

And it left me satiated. My pussy well-fucked. Throbbing. Aching. Quivering. And lustfully awaiting our next rendezvous point.

The beautiful island of Saint Lucia.

Four months from now.

And there, we will feast on pussy and ass and bouncing breasts.

"I'm the lucky one," I say, placing my hands up on his muscled shoulders. "I needed that. And there's no one else I could ever imagine experiencing any of it with."

Marcel grins. "Likewise. We both needed that, baby." He kisses me on the lips. "There's nothing more intoxicating than being surrounded by a bunch of obnoxiously beautiful muhfuckas."

"Mmm…" I lick my lips, remembering all the beautiful scantily clad vixens and handsomely, sculpted men, all in search of a salacious night of scandalous fucking.

Marcel leans in. His tongue traces the seam of my lips before I part them and he slips his tongue inside. I shut my eyes, imagining being locked in a candlelit suite filled with the musical sounds of grunts and moans and *oohs* and *aahs*.

Marcel is blindfolded.

Anticipation and desire building into a slow fire as I wait for the naked man wrapped in bronze-colored skin and rippling muscles to slap his hard dick up against Marcel's lips. He tells Marcel to stick his tongue out, then slides his dick over it. Tells Marcel to kiss his cockhead. Marcel kisses the tip and kisses around it, then licks it.

He moans.

I moan.

I play in my pussy watching. Delighting in the debauchery unfolding in front of me. I reach for a dildo, slide it up and down and over my clit, then push it into my wetness as Marcel's mouth opens around the nameless man's dick and he massages the tip with his lips.

I moan as Marcel sucks Mr. Nameless' cock deep into his mouth, every inch filling his mouth. I fuck myself silly as Marcel fucks the nameless man with his tongue.

His dick is thick, very thick. But not as long as Marcel's, then again…not many of our male lovers are ever as long as he is. Some have come very close to it—eleven, eleven-and-a-half, even twelve. But still none to match or surpass what Mother Nature has blessed Marcel with. Thirteen inches is a lot of dick to come by. And it's all mine. And whomever else *we* allow to share it with.

I come over and over, bucking my hips as Mr. Nameless bucks his dick hard into Marcel's mouth, moaning and grunting as hot semen splashes the back of his throat and floods into his mouth.

I swallow. A half-smile plays on my lips.

"What are you thinkin'?"

I shake my head. "Oh, nothing."

"Nah, nah, baby. Don't do me like that. Go 'head 'n' say it." He chuckles. "I know it's something nasty."

I feign insult. "Now what makes you say that?"

He grins. "Yo, c'mon. Who you think you talkin' to? 'Cause I know you, baby. That look means you have something dirty on ya mind. So spill it. You know I love the way ya dirty mind thinks."

"Wellll, since you put it that way," I say coyly. "I was hoping you would've sucked either Cameron's or Brets dick for me, or at the very least with me."

He laughs, shaking his head. "Nah, baby. You know I'm not sucking no dick."

I tilt my head. "Why not?"

"'Cause you know that's not me, baby."

I reach between us, rub on his dick, feigning a pout. His abs clench. I try not to stare, but it's difficult. I lick my lips. "But it's what I want. I want to see you suck a dick. Do I ever deny you?"

The corners of his mouth curl up. "Nah. Never. Anything I want, my baby gives me. No question."

Heated lust shoots through the pit of my pussy, causing a burning pleasure to build up inside of me. "And *any*thing I want, you give me, no?"

"*Tu veux que je suce une bite*?" Marcel says in French. He knows how hot he makes my pussy whenever he speaks in his native tongue. He kisses my right cheek, then along the column of my neck as his right hand snakes its way up my silk blouse, then under my bra. He fondles my breasts.

"Mmmm…"

"Is that what you really want, baby?" his voice is low and husky. There's a hint of mischief and horniness dancing around in his eyes. "To see ya man on his knees sucking another muhfucka's dick?"

I nod. "Y-y-yes. Mmm…a big, long, juicy one. Then I want to get on my knees and suck it with you. Our tongues flicking against each other's as we lick his dickhead."

Marcel's dick instantly stretches and thickens.

"N'est pas sucer ma bite assez pour vous?"

Suck and *dick* are the only two words I make out in his sentence. He loves teasing me. He grins. Translates in English: "Isn't sucking my own dick enough for you?"

"Yes. It is. You know seeing you suck your dick turns me on. But I've been fantasizing about us sucking dick together."

He takes what I've said to him with a bemused smile. "Oh, word? Is that so?"

"Yes. That's what I want. From you, baby.

He starts laughing. "So let me get this straight. You want us to become the Bonnie & Clyde of cock sucking?"

I punch him softly in his hard chest, trying to stifle a laugh. "No, silly. But the next time we bring a man to our bed, I want you to suck him with me." I bat my lashes for effect. "Pretty please."

Marcel cups my ass cheek in one hand. *"J'adore ce gros cul juteux."*

I moan. Marcel knows how to make me feel slutty and sultry at the same time. *Fat* and *juicy* are the only two words I can decipher. "Say it again. This time in English."

"I said"—he squeezes my ass—"I love this fat, juicy ass."

"Mmm." My pussy is soaked in juices. "I thought that's what you said. Now back to my question. Will you suck a dick with me?"

He smiles that lopsided smile of his, flashing his dimples. The smile that lets me know nothing else needs to be said. My wish will be fulfilled.

A soft moan slips out of me as he gently squeezes my left nipple, then my right. "You're going to make me late to the office," I whisper, allowing him to undo my blouse with his free hand. Of course I have no intentions of ever putting up much of a fight where Marcel and sex is concerned. My Scorpion blood runs hot for him. Always hot. Always ready. Marcel's other hand is now up my skirt, his fingers skimming along my pussy lips.

And I am wet. So very wet. My panties are a sodden mess.

Marcel pushes two fingers into me until they can't go any deeper. "Damn, baby, you so fuckin' hot. *Putain tellement humide pour moi.*" Pleasure ignites all through me as he tells me how fucking wet I am for him. The feral look in his eyes tells me he is going to fuck me deep and good.

The sharp scent of my overheating pussy slowly seeps out from beneath my skirt, revealing my hungry need.

"You might wanna call the office 'n' tell 'em ya man's got you runnin' late." Marcel pulls his dick up and over the waistband of his boxers. "I don't need much time." He leans in. His tongue dips into my mouth again. The thought of him sucking another man's dick with me causes a deep, throbbing ache to pound inside my flaming cunt.

I am a wildfire.

My skirt hiked up over my hips. My panties and pussy soggy with lust, Marcel lifts me up and carries me over to the island counter where dozens of stainless steel pots are strung high over it, setting me up on it.

He nips at my ear, then whispers, "*Je veux te baiser profound dans ta chatte, bébé.*"

Something *fuck*. Something *pussy*. Something *you*. Whatever it is, it causes shivers to dart through me. "W-w-what did you say?" I ask, panting. "You know it drives me wild when you speak in French, Marcel. Stop teasing me."

"I'm not teasing you, baby." He kisses the left side of my neck, then the right side. "I said…I want…to fuck…you…"—more kisses—"deep…in…your pussy, baby…"

"Then fuck me," I murmur, wrapping my arms around his neck, pulling him in closer.

My mouth finds his and my tongue delves deep into the warm, wet space between his lips as he pinches my clit just enough to bring me to the edge of an orgasm, and keep me there. I know he can see the rapacious hunger in my eyes staring into his.

Marcel does this to me. Always.

"Mmm." Marcel moans, pulling his fingers out of me and sliding them into my mouth as he inches the head of his dick into my slit. I suck his fingers as if I'm sucking his dick as he pushes it in. I gasp as he pulls his fingers from my mouth. "I'm about to stretch this pussy open."

I stuff my fist into my mouth to keep from screaming as my orgasm slams into me as Marcel pushes his dick further into me. Slowly. Purposefully. His hips move steady. His dick pulls out. Then slides back in. Pulls out. Slides back in. Pulls out. Slides back in. Four inches, six inches, seven inches, eight inches…

"Ooh, oooh, oooooh…yes, baby…fuck me like that. Mmm…"

He pulls all the way out to the tip. Fucks the mouth of my pussy with the thick mushroom head of his dick. Then slides back in. Nine inches, ten inches…

I am peaking. Urging Marcel on through hissed breath as he stuffs more of his dick inside of me. I arch into the burning heat, throwing my head back.

"Whose dick you fuckin', huh, baby?"

"It's mine," I push out. My breath catches in the back of my throat. "Alllll...mmm...your dick is mine...uhh..."

"Yeah, that's right, baby. This's your dick. C'mon nut on your dick, baby..."

Nails digging into his flesh, I moan. Fight to keep my eyes from rolling up in the back of my head. "Fuck. Oooh, fuuuuck!"

"That's right. Let that nut go. Give Daddy that pussy, baby..."

Hot nectar sprays out of my slit each time Marcel pushes in, then pulls out. Pushes in, then pulls out. He is fucking into my cunt. Fucking into my G-spot. Fucking an orgasm out of me. Fucking me over and over and over.

"Ohgodohgodohgodohgod...yesyesyesyesyesyessss..."

Marcel now has about eleven inches of his dick inside of me now, slowly rolling his hips, gliding his dick in and out of me. *"Mmmm...j'adore cette humide. Il fait tellement chaud. Serré..."* He translates as I moan. "Uh, fuck...I love this wet pussy. It's so hot. Tight."

I gasp.

"Yeah, that's right, baby...nut all over your dick...*donne-moi cette crème douce, bébé.*"

I try to decipher what it is he's said. Something *sweet*. Something *cream*.

I come.

And cry out.

And come again.

FIFTEEN

Marcel

Arianna walks into my office carrying her iPad while holding her iPhone in her hand and says, "J-Smooth is in the conference room with his manager."

I look up from my computer screen, glancing up at the crystal clock up on the wall. It's eleven a.m. And this muhfucka just shows up here without an appointment. I knew he was bailed out by his manager earlier this morning, but I didn't know he was gonna show his ass here. Then again, I'm not surprised. But I'm not beat to deal with his ass until I hear back from our attorney.

"He knows he doesn't have an appointment, but his manager says they've been trying to reach you all morning."

"Yeah, fuck 'im," I say, getting up from my desk and walking over to the huge floor-to-ceiling window overlooking Times Square. "I've been iggin' their asses. Let 'em sit. And wait." I take in the ridiculously amazing view, which includes several large billboards of advertisements—one of them being Carlos's ass posing in his damn drawz. It's like the muhfucka's gazing back at me smirking 'n' shit.

I shake my head and then turn to look at Arianna. "I need for you to get Lance Green on the line."

Lance is another one of my frat brothers and also my attorney.

I'd already put a call into him while I was out in L.A.; now it was time to follow-up with my plan of axing J-Smooth's ass.

Arianna walks out of my office. A few minutes later, she buzzes and tells me Lance is on line two.

"Yo, Lance, my dude…tell me something good. Can I drop this muhfucka J-Smooth or what? This muhfucka's bad-boy-rebellious image is becoming a PR nightmare. Turning up in clubs 'n' shit is one thing, but this shit with him slashing tires 'n' tryna knock his girl's eye sockets out is shit I ain't cosigning. And that's some real shit, feel me?"

"I hear you, man. But perhaps we should hang tight to see how it all pans out in court before we drop him. He hasn't been convicted of any wrongdoing as far as the domestic violence case goes."

All morning long, J-Smooth's name has been rolling off the tongues of radio personalities and the damn social media bloggers have been dragging his dumb ass. And it hasn't helped matters that Elena's camp released a statement pretty much saying the shit she's alleging is true. Somehow photos of her Benz slumped to one side where J-Smooth allegedly flattened two of her tires was leaked over the Internet.

"Nah, fuck that. Wait hell. You know like I do, whether he's found guilty or not, that doesn't mean the muhfucka didn't do the shit. I'm done with his ass. Let him take that ratchet shit on over to some other label. I want him the fuck off mine."

"All right then. Although the language around the morality clause is vague, it's definitely a bail-out provision, so if you wish to terminate his contract, then so be it."

"That's all I wanna hear. I'll let his manager know effective today, he's been dropped." I end the call, then buzz Arianna. "You can tell them muhfuckas they can come back this afternoon. At four."

A few seconds later, she buzzes me back.

"Yeah?"

"Umm, you have a call on line one. The caller refused to give me her name."

I frown. "Did she say what she wanted?"

"No. When I told her you were busy, she simply stated she'd stay on the line and wait until you were available. And she didn't care how long it'd take."

Probably some thirsty wannabe songstress tryna bum rush her way into a studio audition. "Aiight. No worries. I got it." I disconnect from her and pick up line one. "Mar*Sell* Kennedy speaking," I say, leaning back in my executive chair.

"Ooh, I couldn't wait until Thursday," a sultry voice coos into the phone. "I needed to hear your panty-soaking voice today. I wanna suck the nut out your dick."

"Oh, word?" I say, tryna figure out the voice on the other end of the line. There's a hint of a Spanish accent. "Who am I speaking to?"

"Te preocupes, papi. I'm not a stalker or anything."

"Yo, so do I know you? Have we met?"

"No. But I *feel* like I *know* you. For almost four years you've been my fantasy boo. *El hombre me jodido yo escuchando. Quiero follar mi coño. Quiero que me folles.*"

I swallow, feeling a slight stir in my drawz. I don't know what the fuck she just said. But whatever it is got my balls starting to heat.

"Yo, hold up, *mami,* my Spanish is mad rusty, so you gonna have to translate that sexy shit you spittin'."

"Ooh, no worries, *papi.* I said you're the man I've fucked myself listening to on the radio for the last four years. I want you"—she lowers her voice to almost a whisper—"to *fuck*…me."

I lean up in my seat. Press my legs together. She's not the first chick to come at me like this. Hell, there's always some chick offering up midday and late night propositions and wet panties, or sending me videos of them playing in their pussies, so I'm used to it. Still, there's something different about this chick. I don't know if it's that sexy lil' accent, or what. All I know is, my muthafuckin' dick is starting to stretch.

And, on some real shit, she's lucky I'm a faithful muhfucka or I'd be calling her bluff. Word is bond. I'd be telling her to come through so I can rock her fuckin' drawz off. I'd have her leaving up outta here on her knees, feeling around on the floor tryna find her way outta here.

"Yo, dig, baby. I 'preciate you hitting me up, but I'ma need to bang on you, feel me? You can't call here comin' at me talkin' that sexy shit."

She giggles. "I can't help myself. *Te quiero, papi. Tu voz hace que mi coño tan mojado.*" *Motherfuck! Shit!* Hearing that shit causes sparks to shoot up through my balls. "And in case you're wondering what I just said," she says, turning up her accent. "I want you, *papi.* Your voice makes my pussy so wet."

And then she hangs up, leaving me sitting here at my desk with my balls bubblin' and dick harder than muhfuckin' granite.

Later that evening, I'm stepping outta the master bath with a towel wrapped around my waist and beads of water still sliding down my bare chest. I walk into the bedroom and find Marika sitting up propped up in bed looking sexy as fuck in a red teddy with a glass of wine in one hand, her iPad in the other. She looks up from her screen and smiles, brushing a strand of fallen hair from outta her face.

I wink at her, grinning. "Yo, I forgot to tell you that some lil' hot-in-the-ass broad called up at the office today, talking some real sexy shit in Spanish to me. Talkin' about she wanted me to fuck her. And how she's been fucking herself listening to me on the radio for the last four years or some shit like that."

She shakes her head. "What else is new? The thirst is real. It's the price I pay for marrying one of the most sexiest men alive."

I grin, flexing my chest muscles. "Yeah, no doubt. But the crazy shit is, when she hung up, my dick was hard a fuck."

She gives me an amused look, taking a slow sip of her drink. "Isn't that something? Do you at least know what she looks like?"

"Nah. But her voice was mad sexy." I furrow my brow as realization dawns on me as to where I'd mighta heard her voice before. "Damn. I knew her voice sounded familiar. I think she's the same chick that called up to the radio show last week."

"Who? Not that loudmouth chick with the twenty kids who kept calling you some sugar boo, or whatever that mess was?"

I frown. "Oh you got jokes, huh? Hell nah. Not that ratchet-ass broad. The chick who said she wanted to borrow me for the night, and you could come along as my chaperone."

She rolls her eyes. "Oh, that one. Miss Anonymous."

I nod. "I can't be for certain, but it def sounded almost like her."

"Well I'm not going to pretend that she didn't have a nice voice, because she did. I'd love to see what she looks like."

I chuckle, walking back into the bathroom. "She's probably got a face like an orangutan."

"Mmph. Or has hair on her back." We both start laughing. "If she calls in again, tell her to send you one of her selfies. And a snapshot of her snatch."

I laugh. "You so nasty, baby. But, yo, I just might."

She gives me a sly grin. "And if she has a big clit and fat pussy, I might show you just how nasty your baby can be."

I chuckle, heading back into the bathroom. "Oh, I know how my baby gets down. But watching you turns me the fuck on."

I turn the faucet water on and brush my teeth, staring at my reflection in the mirror. All I see is a fine, sexy, black muhfucka staring back at me. I wink at myself. Then rinse my mouth out.

When I step back out into the bedroom, Marika is leaning back on her pillows—comforter off her, with her legs bent at the knees and spread wide. My eyes zero in on the puffy print of her pussy. But she's so wrapped up into reading something on her iPad that she doesn't even notice me standing here staring at her. I watch as a hand slides down between her thighs. She opens and closes them.

"Damn, you ready for this dick already, huh, baby?" I drop my towel. Dick swinging, balls full.

She looks up from the screen and laughs, reaching for one of the king-sized pillows on my side of the bed and throwing it at me. "I can't stand you."

I smirk, dodging the pillow. I bend down and scoop it up, walking toward the bed. "Yeah, aiight. What I tell you about lying? You know you stay ready for daddy."

"This is true. But daddy's going to have to wait until I finish what I'm doing."

I climb in my side of the bed, pulling the comforter back and leaning over and kissing her on the lips. "Damn," I say, frowning. "What, I can't get no tongue? What's good with that?"

She grins, reaching over for her wineglass on the nightstand and taking a sip. She looks over at me, smirking. "Tongue leads to wandering hands that will eventually lead to my legs getting spread."

I give her a perplexed look, raising a brow. "*And?*"

"And right now, that's going to have to wait."

"Oh, so what you gotta do that's more important than taking care of ya man's hard dick?"

She tells me nothing is ever more important than me, but my hard dick will still have to wait because she's reading a manuscript. I roll my eyes upward.

"Yo, since when you start reading manuscripts again? I thought you gave that up."

"I have, for the most part. I got a call from an agent looking to shop her client's manuscript. It's a special request. And when Lenora Samuels calls you and offers you first dibs on one of her clients' manuscripts, you take it. And so far this book is one hot, juicy read."

"Oh, aiight." I glance over at the time. It's almost ten p.m. "I guess I'll just sit over here and play with this dick until you ready to make time for me." I fold my arms over my chest, looking over at her. "I still want some tongue, though."

"No," she says, smiling.

I frown. Then quickly recover, sliding my hungry gaze down to her nipples. Chocolate nipples. Peaked. Hard, swollen nipples. Pressing against the fabric of her nightie, beckoning for release. Drool pools around the corners of my mouth. And the second I move in to seize one into my mouth over, Marika covers her chest with her arm.

"Oh, no you don't," she says, wagging a finger at me. "There'll be none of that until after I finish my reading. I will not be distracted."

"Yeah, aiight." I smirk, gliding a hand over her right leg, along the inside of her inner thigh. Her silky skin feels good against the palm of my hand. "Well, how about I eat your pussy while you read?"

She hesitates, bites her lip. I can tell she's thinking about this tongue sinking into her slit, licking up and down her lips; flicking up and down on her clit. Yo, real shit. I can almost taste the arousal creaming in her pussy.

She moans softly. "Mmm. It sounds so tempting." She removes my hand from between her thighs, clasping her long legs shut tight. "But not now." She leans over and kisses me on the lips. "I promise to make it up to you."

I grab my hard dick. "Tonight?"

She leans over and kisses me again. This time I nip at her lower lip until she lets me in and I deepen the kiss. Marika moans as my tongue swirls with hers. And then her fingers curl around my throbbing cock, stroking the heat of my shaft and causing me to groan.

"Fuck, yo. You better stop now, before I end up taking that pussy. I'm telling you now." I feel my nut swelling in my balls. She cups them. And word is bond my shit starts leaking nut juice.

"You want my mouth on this big, hard dick?" she whispers, squeezing my balls. Her gaze measures the length of my dick. "You want me sucking you into my wet mouth?"

The crown of my dick gets wetter. Precum slides down my shaft. I wrap a hand around her neck and draw her head closer. "Yeah, let me get some mouth, baby."

Marika grins, shaking her head. "Well…so much for reading," she mutters, then leans forward and sucks my shaft deep into her mouth until it hits the back of her throat.

I groan as she starts to suck me hard. "Aaaah, fuck. Yeah, suck that dick. Mmm." My hand clamps around the back of her head, my hips move to the pulsing rhythm of her mouth. "Motherfuck, motherfuck…shit, baby. I love this fuckin' mouth…mmm…"

My head snaps back. I close my eyes. And get lost in the wet-suck-smack sounds her mouth makes as it sucks in seven, eight, nine, ten inches of dick, drawing each inch in and out of her mouth until my head starts spinning and I can barely stand it any longer.

She goes in for the kill. Suck, suck, slurp. Suck, suck, swirl. Suck, suck, slurp. Her mouth, lips, tongue and hands work in sync. Marika had perfected deep throating eleven inches of this dick after two years of marriage and now my baby's a dick-sucking beast. She swallows and gulps and lets her throat muscles massage my dickhead.

"Oh. Oh. Shit. Shit. Shit. Oh, fuck, fuck, fuck. That shit feels so fuuuuckin' *gooood*!!!"

She slowly pulls off my dick, sucking all the way up. When she gets to my head, she tongues my slit, catching the flood of precum oozing out. She looks up at me, her lips slick with spit and precum, and smiles.

Then she catches me by surprise and says, "I want you to talk dirty to me in French. Make believe I'm that Spanish bitch who called your office today sucking your dick." And, then, she is sucking me back into her mouth, down into her throat.

I blink. Close my eyes. *"Oui, vous chienne méchante. Sucer la bite, bébé. Merde! Sucer cette mere baise bite, salope. Donne-moi cette bouche de latine chaude. Vous allez me faire encule dans cette chatte humide espagnole avec cette grosse bite noire, hein, bébé?"*

She grunts. Her mouth rapidly sucks me as I repeat what I've said in English: "You nasty bitch. Suck that dick, baby. Suck that motherfucking dick, slut. Give me that hot Latin mouth. You gonna let me fuck you in that tight, Spanish pussy with this big black dick, huh, baby?"

She groans. Her hand glides up and down my shaft. Her head bobs. Her mouth gets wetter, hotter, as it stretches over me. She wets my dick, soaks my balls. I can feel spit sliding down into my crack. My dick moves inside her mouth, fucking into a wet river of hungry need.

Marika is sucking the shit out of my dick. She strokes it with her hand as she sucks my balls into her mouth. Twirls her tongue around them. Licks them. Every so often, her tongue sweeps around the crack of my ass.

I slide a hand between her legs. Reach for her pussy. But she grabs my hand and brushes it away, shaking her head *no* as she sucks me.

"Hold up, baby…wait, wait…wait…aah, shit…"

I feel tingles brewing at the base of my spine. The head of my dick brushes against the roof of her mouth as she slides it in and out of her throat.

God, how I love the way my dick feels in her mouth. So fucking hot. So fucking wet. "Aaaaah, shiiiiiiiit, baby. Oh, baby, baby… oooh, fuck. Aaah, shit. Baby, wait…hold up…"

Marika ignores me. She's caught up in a dick-sucking zone. Determined to make me crack this nut. And as hard as I'm tryna fight it. As hard as I am tryna hold back this surge of sensations. She's taking me there. She has me right at the edge. Ready to explode. I can feel it. Rolling up and crashing like a tidal wave. My dick is pulsing. My balls are swelling tight. I feel my tongue starting to thicken. Feel it sliding out of the side of my mouth.

I groan low in my throat. "Oh, fuuuuuuck…" I hear the words tumble out of my mouth, but they sound almost slurred as I pump into Marika's mouth, as she sucks and siphons out every last bit of my thick nut, leaving me dizzy and spent.

SIXTEEN

Marcel

"Yo, what's good, my beauties, cuties, hookers, hoes, pimps, and playboys…this is ya boy, Mar*Sell*, coming at you live with another steamy Thursday night of *Creepin' 'n' Freakin' After Dark*. You already know how it goes down here at 93.3 The Heat: hot, raw 'n' ohhhh so nassssy. I hope everyone had a hot cum-filled week with lots of toe-curlin' sex. I know I did.

"But ya boy's back 'n' now we're about to get it in. So drop them drawz, sit back…relax…light a candle…pour yourself a glass of your favorite wine…pull out your favorite lube…your favorite toy… or hit up that special someone…and prepare to be stimulated beyond your own imagination. Let me mentally lick you into climax as we get into part two of last week's hot topic: Cunnilingus.

"That's right, my freaky peeps. Oral sex. Eatin' The Peach. The Cooter. The Twat. The Penis Fly Trap. Whatever lil' name you call it. Puttin' ya face up in it is the name of the game. And like I said last week, I don't care if you're a man or woman. It's not an option. It's a requirement. And tonight we're gonna pick up where we left off last week. On our last segment of *Creepin' 'n' Freakin' After Dark*, we had the beauties call in, letting us know how they get down poppin' the top. Giving that Becky. Tonight, I'ma need the fellas to get at me.

"If you're puttin' in that tongue work, if you know how'ta make her toes curl 'n' her uterus shake, if you've got her clutching 'n' clawing at them sheets, if you have her speaking in twenty-seven different languages 'n' her body vibrating, if you have tears springing from her eyes 'n' have her squirtin' 'n' shoutin', holla at ya boy. 1-212-FreakMe."

Within seconds all the phone lines light up. Now, on some real-ness, I know that most of the mofos who call into the show are more than likely lying about their stroke games. Most of 'em aren't even knocking down half as much pussy as they get on the air and claim they're getting. Most of 'em just wanna hear them-selves talking on the radio. But what I care? At the end of the night all I care about are the ratings. And as long as these numbers stay up, this show stays up.

"Yo, what's good…you're on the air with ya boy, Mar*Sell*. Whom am I speaking to 'n' where you calling from?"

"Yo, what's goodie, fam…this ya boy, D-Dot, from Newark. I tried to get at you last week, but, yo, you had them lines on fire, bruh. But dig, I'm sayin'…I need one'a them dic—*bleep*—suckin' hoes to hit me up, for real, for real. I need me a nasty, sloppy, dome-lickin', ball-suckin' broad whose head game is real live 'n' messy, feel me, bruh? I'm talkin' spit bubbles, strings of drool 'n' watery eyes from gaggin' 'n' getttin' that skull-fuc—*bleep*—ed. I just need a slutty whore to suck the meat juice outta this thick six-inch."

I frown. "*Six* inches? Damn, fam. You hanging like a horse, knocking teeth loose."

He laughs. "No doubt, no doubt. I beat the neck up."

I roll my eyes, glancing over at Nina, who is in the booth cracking up. Instead of moving on to the next caller, I decide to fuck with this delusional short-dick muhfucka. "That's what it is, bruh—six inches of tonsil strokin' 'n' throat-guttin'. I bet you gotta long tongue, too, to match that long dong."

"No doubt, no doubt."

"Oh, aiight, aiight. So you love doing them tongue laps up 'n' down 'n' around them sweet, puffy kitty lips, then dippin' it deep into that wet slit, huh?"

"No doubt, no doubt. I gotta tornado tongue that'll have a ho climbin' the walls. Not scared of the pus—*bleep*—sy. Love the taste 'n' will pretty much suck the skin off that thang, feel me."

"No doubt, no doubt. And there you have it, my freaky peeps. You heard it right here, Long Dong with the tornado tongue is ready to wreck shop. Yo, thanks for callin' in, my dude. Next caller, you're on the air."

"Yo, word is bond, son. Hahahahaha. Yo, you dead wrong for gassin' B's head up like that. You got that niggah thinkin' he a daddy long stroke now. Hahahahaha."

"Hey, I do what I can to keep hope alive. Who am I speakin' to?"

"Hahaha. I heard that. Yo, this is ya boy, King, from East Orange."

"What's good, King. So you lickin' the gumdrop?"

"All day; every day, fam. I love eatin' the snatch, bruh; word to mother. All baby girl gotta do is lay back 'n' hit the blunt while I get all up in that. And, nah, we don't have to get it in, but if chick gets horny enough from the head, then no doubt I'll beat dat back out for her if she wants this thick nine; ya heard?"

"Loud 'n' clear, my dude. Next caller."

"Yo, fam, this Whalik from Elizabeth. What it do, yo?"

Muhfucka, you called me. Fuck you mean what it do? You eatin' pussy or not, niggah? "You tell me, bruh. You puttin' in that tongue work or what?"

"Hell naw, man. I ain't eatin' no broad out. That shit nasty, yo."

Then what the fuck you callin' in for? "And what makes it nasty, playboy?"

"Yo, pus—*bleep*—sy's made for fuc—*bleep*—ing, not lickin'. That shit's dirty, feel me?"

This whack-ass mofo. "Yo, my dude, you ever try it?"

"Ugh! Yeah. Once. And it was disgustin', yo. I couldn't get past the smell or the taste. It was fishy."

"Fishy? Bruh, I don't know what kinda foul punanni you had ya mouth up on, but sounds like maybe you had a bad batch of tuna. Unless her diet is real crazy or her insides are rotted, that thing-thing should be real tasty. And it damn sure shouldn't *smell* or *taste* fishy. Real spit, bruh, if a chick spreads open her legs 'n' she's leakin' shit that looks like clam chowder, you need to hop up 'n' run for the door. Mmph. Sounds like the chick you had ya tongue in needed to invest in some antibiotics 'n' a douche. My advice, next time do the two-finger test. Slide them fingers up in 'er. Play with that thing-thing. And, if them fingers come back missing, covered in slime, or smellin' like the back of a garbage truck, then you already know what it is. Baby girl got some hazardous waste in them drawz."

"Nah, fuc—*bleep*—that. There ain't gonna be no next time. My mouth ain't goin' no where near a ho's hole."

I glance over at Nina, giving her my "what-the-fuck" look.

She shrugs, shaking her head.

"Bruh, sorry ya first experience was a bad one. But, yo, you need to get ya mind right 'n' face the clit tongue-on. Try again, play-boy. Thanks for callin' in. Yo, my freaky peeps. Before I take my next caller, we're about to go into a quick break, but let me say this to all the beauties out there listenin' right now. Check this out. If you're with a mofo who is pressin' you to drop down on his top, but dude isn't 'bout that tongue life, then baby, you need to shut that slurp shop down. If he ain't suckin', then neither should you. Unless you're not beat 'bout gettin' head 'n' only enjoy giving it, then do you. But if you want some face-time, too, then it should be an equal opportunity suck-a-thon. And if dude tells you he only eats his girl or wifey out, then you need to tell him to take his ass on back home to her 'cause the head doctor is on leave." I laugh. "Yo, let me shut these clit lickers before I get some'a you dudes tossed up outta ya cribs. Don't let me disrupt y'alls' bed-flow, I'm just sayin'…You gotta know a place where you can kiss to bring ya baby to bliss. You want the key to her heart, you gotta go down low, nice 'n' slow…"

I pull back from my mic as Mariah Carey's "Bliss" bellows over the air, which means I have about three minutes or so to hit my baby up with a few nasty texts before I'm back on the air. I reach for my phone and hit her up, letting her know I'm thinking about her and can't wait to crawl up in bed and caress her clit with my tongue, then slow-lick her pussy lips, before sliding my tongue into her slit.

I set my phone back on my desk, then look over toward the glass booth and grin at Nina as Mariah sing-whistles about taking it slow and letting the feeling grow. Nina smiles back at me, knowingly. She always knows what to play next. Real shit. We're a perfect fit. She feeds off my energy and knows exactly what songs to play to tie into the heat. And it's been like this ever since I stepped foot through these studio doors and took my seat at this desk. We just clicked.

She signals me that we're on in five…four…three…two…one…

I press my legs shut, pressing the swelling in my balls. "Aiight,

aiight, aiight…what it do, my people. I hope all of my beauties out there in radio-land are somewhere ridin' down on a face as I speak, glazin' some wet tongue 'n' horny mouth with them sweet juices. Next caller…you're on the air with ya boy."

"Yo, what's good, Mar*Sell*. This Q from East New York, yo. Why mafuckaz be stylin', yo? How you not eatin' the twat? Man, that mafucka who called in earlier is mutha—*bleep*—ing whack, yo. Tell that niggah I said it's snack time, niggah! I love givin' head, yo. Give me a hairy wet hole 'n' I'm feastin' on it 'til she passes out. I love them bald beavers, too. But a lil' fur is mad sexy, yo. Work between them sexy thighs 'n' spread open them juicy wet lips 'n' go to work suckin' that puffy clit; word to mother, yo. Tell that whack-azz mafucka he can send his girl on over to me. I'll eat her out, suck her insides out. Flip her over on all-fours 'n' eat that shit from the back, tongue all up in that slit 'n' bootyhole, then run this big-azz di—*bleep*—up in 'er. Then after I bust up in her guts, I'll lick my nut out 'n' send 'er home to his corny-azz."

I lick my lips. "Damn, son, sounds like you stay gettin' it in."

"Word to mother, yo. I gets it in, fam. I'm real 'bout mine. Them niggahs out there frontin' on that good-good better wake up. They can sleep on it if they want, but it'll be a horny mafucka like me givin' his broad the business, then climbin' outta his window at night. That's real shit, yo."

"I heard that. Keep on lickin', playboy. Yo, y'all heard it here. If ya man ain't lickin' it, there's someone else out there—willing 'n' ready—who will. Next caller."

"Oh, yassss, *daddy*," the raspy-voiced caller says, sounding like the character Sheneneh from the old sitcom *Martin*. "This is Princess from Bushwick. No tea, no shade. But you give me life. I live for Thursday nights."

"Oh, word? That's wasssup. So you puttin' in that tongue work?"

The caller coughs. "No *hunty*. I'm allergic to *fish*."

I blink. *What the fuck?!* "Yo, then why you callin' in, my dude? Wait. Yo, you are a dude, right?"

"No. I'm transsexual. And I gets my kitty tongued *down*. I keeps me a piece of trade on speed dial to handle this cat. And I love sucking dic—*bleep*. Oral sex is my ish. And for all them lazy non dic—*bleep* sucking fish who ain't giving head, they best believe I'm more than willing to give their men what they need. A tight, wet throat. Trust. Mmmph. I've probably already had most of 'em anyway. But they know their secret is safe with me 'cause I don't kiss 'n' tell."

"Oh, aiight, aiight. Well, Princess from Bushwick. Thanks for callin' in."

"Wait, daddy. I'm not done. I wanna know would you ever get head from a dude?"

I blink. Shift in my seat. What the fuck this muhfucka think I'ma say, "Hell yeah. I dig seeing a masculine muhfucka on his knees sucking the nut out this long-ass dick"? This niggah buggin' if he thinks I'ma admit some shit like that on live radio.

"Nah, my dude," I tell him. "I'm good on that."

Dude pops gum in my ear. "Well, I feel like each gender should get head from the same sex at least once."

I glance over at Nina behind the glass. She's looking at me, smirking and shaking her head. "Oh, word? And why is that?"

"Why else? Because same sex give head way better."

Yo, you ain't lying about that shit. I lick my lips. Although I've gotten some premium head from multiple females, and Marika knows how to suck the hell out of a dick. But damn...there's something about the way another muhfucka locks his jaws and sucks on this dick. For a quick second G-Money's mouth wrapped around my dick flashes through my head. The way he'd flick his long, wet tongue out and lick my big-ass, meaty balls before sucking them into his mouth. The way he'd use his tongue like a paintbrush and make long, wet strokes up and down the length of my veiny shaft, leaving wet, hot streaks while he massaged my nut sac. The way I'd pump deep into his mouth and he'd suck 'n' swallow this creamy nut, then have my muthafuckin' head spinning.

I shake the memories.

"Nah, partner…I'm good on that. But, yo, thanks for hittin' me up." I end the call. The next three cats who call-in all profess to be pussy-eating specialists going into full details of how they put in that tongue work and slay the pussy. My dick doesn't stretch, pulse, jump, or get hard as they share their skills, so of course I'm only half-listening as they gas themselves up.

We go into a quick commercial break, then kick shit up with an old R. Kelly joint, "Seems Like You're Ready." I shoot a look over at Nina, smiling and shaking my head.

This shit is one of the joints I love eating pussy to. And on some real shit, I've been snacking on pussy since I was thirteen. My oral instructor was a twenty-five-year old, hot-in-the ass, neighborhood oral-freak named Alyssa. She was the first older chick I'd rocked with. Alyssa had a thing for young, hard dick. She felt it was her duty to break all the young cats from around the way in. To get 'em ready "for the next bitch." And she was serious about getting her nut off. She wouldn't let you fuck her, but she had no problem sucking a young cat's dick and glazing his mouth with her cream.

Alyssa rode my face and sucked my dick every day for two weeks straight until I got that shit right. She showed me how to turn this tongue into a weapon of clit and slit destruction. Showed me how to whisper my hot breath against her pussy, and hum while I sucked in her clit. She coached me how to lap at her pussy lips and lure her whole cunt into my mouth and coax orgasm after orgasm outta her with deep strokes of my tongue. Then once she felt I had mastered the art of eating her pussy, she shut shop down and moved on to the next. And I've been eating pussy ever since.

Nina taps on the window from behind the booth, breaking up my trip down memory lane. I adjust my headset. We're back on in five…four…three…two…one…

"Aiight, my freaky peeps as we make our way to the top of the hour, let ya boy stretch out ya mind 'n' take ya imagination to a place way beyond what you've ever imagined. Spread them thighs 'n' let me lick ya spot, get it real hot as we rap up another segment of *Creepin' 'n' Freakin' After Dark*. Next caller, ya on the air with ya boy, Mar*Sell*…"

"Yo, whadddup,….this Shawn from Marshall Street in Irvington."

"What's good, playboy. You eatin' the cookie?"

"Word to mother, yo. I got them deadly tongue skills. I'm like R. Kelly, yo. I turn up 'n' lick the middle like an Oreo. Gobble that thang up. Make a broad forget her name, feel me?"

"Oh, aiight, aiight, Cookie Monster. That's what's up. Gobble that thang up, playboy. Thanks for callin' in. Yo, we have time for one last call. Next caller. What's good? You're on the air…"

"Mmmm…I'm so wet for you, *papi*," purrs a female voice on the other end. "I would love to give you a taste of this sweet, juicy fruit."

I grin, shaking my head. "Oh, word? Who's calling?"

"Oooh, I can't believe you've already forgotten my voice and it's only been a few days since my last call to you."

I lean up in my chair. "Oh, aiight, aiight. What's good, Anonymous?"

"*Haciendo dulce el amor para mi es lo que es bueno* with that big, long, black...uh, it is big...and *loooong*, right?"

I chuckle. "Yo, ma-ma, you talkin' mad filthy right now. I don't know what you just said, but it sounded mad sexy."

"I saaaaid, *papi*, you making sweet love to me is what's good."

"Oh, word? Yo, hold on for a minute." I place the call on hold, then close out tonight's segment with some shit about doing what you need to do to spend a lifetime pleasing and being pleased. Then sign off. Maxwell's "Lifetime" comes on the air as I remove my headset and pick up the phone to get at this lil' Spanish *mami* who has my dick bricked.

I hit her with my gmail addy and tell her to hit me up with some hot flicks so I can see what she's looking like. She says some more slick shit in Spanish, then tells me she'll send a few pics so I can see how wet I get her.

"Yeah, aiight. Cool, cool...do that." I end the call just as Nina makes her way over to me, grinning.

"Great night." She takes a seat beside my desk, crossing her slender legs. I glance at her toned calves, then into her brown eyes. "Sounds like you have another admirer on your hands. But this one sounds like she's *really* trying to *have* you."

I shake my head, laughing. "Nah, nah. She's tryna *borrow* me. Remember?"

She playfully rolls her eyes. "Yeah, that's right. For the night."

"Well, if her body's on point and her face doesn't look like it needs a wrecking ball to it, I just might let her. *Borrow* me...for the night."

She gives me a *yeah-right* look. "Umm, last time I checked, you were still a married man? And that still looks like a wedding band on your finger."

"Correction," I say, stretching my long legs out. "I'm *still* a happily married man." She glances at the bulge in my pants, then shifts in her seat. I grin. "What, would you rather I jump ya bones instead?"

She rises from her seat. "No. What I'd rather *you* do is go home."

I laugh. "Yeah, aiight. That's what ya mouth says. Why ya drawz wet?"

"*My* drawers are *not* wet," she says. Although her tone is indignant, her eyes flicker something different.

"Yeah, aiight, with ya lyin'-ass. Then why I smell them hot juices, huh?"

She playfully swats at me. "Ohmygod! You're so nasty."

I grin, flashing her my dimples. "You have no idea, babe." She shakes her head, walking out. Maybe her panties aren't wet, but I bet her pussy is sucking them shits in, wishing it were a dick between her legs.

SEVENTEEN

Marika

One-thirty a.m.

I am sitting propped up in bed, the sixty-inch, wall-mounted plasma playing low, with my iPad in my lap reading through this *Prison Snatch* manuscript when Marcel walks into the bedroom.

I can't lie. So far this manuscript is a good, entertaining, and a very hot, nasty read. A few times I've had to squeeze my legs to shut off the pulsing in my clit. Or found myself absentmindedly rubbing my erect nipples, slowly winding my hips and grinding my bare ass down into the sheets and mattress as I read about Heaven's sexapades while she's incarcerated. From fucking CO's—male and female—to fucking other female inmates, all I can say is, this is one freaky bitch.

And I love it.

"Hey, babe," Marcel says, sauntering toward me.

I smile, taking him in as he makes his way over to me. My gaze locks on the long, thick bulge dangling in his sweats. "Hey, beautiful man."

"How you?" He leans forward and kisses me on the lips. His hand caresses the side of my face. Little does he know, listening to him on the radio tonight and reading this manuscript for the last hour has my pussy on fire, and I'm ready for these flames to be stoked, hard and deep.

"Horny," I say, reaching for his dick. My pussy clenches.

He grins. "Aaah, that's what I'm talkin' about, baby." He plants another kiss on my lips. "I got something for that."

"Ooh, I hope so."

He reaches for one of my nipples. Plays with it over the fabric of my silk teddy until it pebbles, then lightly pinches it, causing a low moan to escape from me. He leans in and kisses me again.

"I can't wait to slide my tongue in some pussy," I tell him in almost a whisper. "Some sweet, tangy, wet pussy."

"Mmm. I want some pussy, too, baby. So let's make it happen."

He removes his shirt. I eye his chiseled chest and arms, allowing my gaze to drift along the ripples of his stomach to the light trail of hair that dips down into the waistband of his sweatpants. Marcel unties the drawstring, then drops his sweats to the floor and steps out of them. His dick hangs low. The head is peeking out from under his boxers.

I swallow as he drops his underwear. His long dick causes my mouth to water. "I enjoyed the show tonight," I say, licking my lips. "Some of your callers crack me up."

He chuckles. "Yeah, they're a piece of work. You see Miss Anonymous called again?"

"Mmhmm. I heard her talking all dirty in Spanish."

He grins. "That shit sounded sexy, right?"

A smile flits across my face. "It did." I reach over for my wineglass, then take a sip before setting it back onto the coaster on the nightstand. "It's been a long time since we've had a sexy Latina in our bed."

"No doubt," Marcel says. I stare at his muscled ass as he walks into our bathroom. "We definitely need to make that happen, soon." He leans up on the doorframe, holding his toothbrush in his hand.

"Anyway, I spoke to that Miss Anonymous chick after the show and told her to send me some flicks. I almost told her, 'So my wife can see what that pussy looks like.'"

I laugh. "Well, there's nothing wrong with looking. It's not like we're going to be inviting her into our bed."

"True, true." He goes back into the bathroom and runs the water in the sink. I hear him brushing his teeth so I decide to go back to my place in the manuscript and start reading some more before he climbs in bed, or should I say before he climbs on *me*.

My skin heats as the character describes being down on her knees under a desk in the control center of her unit alternately sucking the dicks of two correction officers—one Hispanic, the other black—who sit back in their chairs sharing in the pleasure of her warm, wet mouth while the rest of the inmates in her unit remain locked in their cells.

"Ooh, Marcel, baby," I call out to him. He pokes his head out of the door. "Listen to this: 'My cunt was so hot and horny and needy as I sucked on COs Martinez's and Corbert's hard cocks. Both were thick and long. And heavy. And ribbed with veins. Lots and lots of winding veins along the top of their shafts that I trailed with my wet tongue before swirling my tongue over their piss slits, collecting the sticky treats that drizzled out. Their dicks were so tasty. Martinez's cockhead was shaped like a large stuffed mushroom. And leaked lots of precum that tasted sweet and salty. I loved that his foreskin slid all the way back. Corbert's dickhead, on the other hand, was a giant plum-shaped head...'"

A hot sexual urge ripples through my cunt as I fantasize that I am the one on my knees, my throat being fucked deliciously and dangerously deep. I reach for my wineglass and take another sip, then set it back on the nightstand.

I swallow hard.

"Yo, don't stop now," Marcel says, popping his head back out. His voice is smooth and deep. "Keep reading that shit. You got my attention, baby."

I smile. "I knew it would. Okay, where was….?" I locate my spot and continue. "'I hated these two bastards. But I wanted them both taking turns fucking me deep in my pussy until it burned and screamed and begged. I wanted them fucking me in my ass, pumping into the loose heat, stretching it out like the Lincoln Tunnel, my asshole wide enough for a small fist or double-dick fucking. But none of that would happen tonight. These grimy fuckers only wanted head, with lots of spit. And I gave it to them. My right fist slid up and down Corbert's shaft while I sucked on Martinez's thick, throbbing cock. I sucked and sucked until a gusher of cum burst out his slit, splattering the back of my throat and soaking my tongue. I swallowed. Then swallowed again. Gulping down the hot frothy juice.'"

"*Daaaaayummn*," Marcel says, reaching down and rubbing his dick. "That broad sounds like a real live freak."

"Yes, she does. She writes like one, too."

"So are you snatchin' her up?" He walks back out into the bedroom. Naked. Still not showered. Dick swinging. Balls hanging.

"More than likely. It definitely reads like a bestseller, that's for sure. I'll forward her manuscript to one of my senior editors and let them make the offer."

He smiles. "Although looks shouldn't matter, hopefully she won't look like some wildebeest. The last thing an erotica reader needs is to have their wet dreams fucked up by some mad ugly broad."

I chuckle. "Or possibly looking like a garden gnome, like your radio stalker, Miss Anonymous."

He laughs. "Right, right. All that nasty shit she was talking, she probably has a body like Shaq 'n' a face like a bulldog"

I join him in laughter. "Honey, you're a mess. That is sooo not nice."

He shrugs. "I'm dead-ass. But I ain't tryna talk about that right now. I wanna hear more of what that chick's writing about." He grabs the base of his dick and shakes it. "Yo, that shit got my dick twitchin'."

My pussy starts to spasm as he stalks over toward the bed and tells me to pull the covers back and spread my legs. I grin, slinging the covers back. "Oooh, you nasty man."

"Aaah, yeah, you like it when ya man's nasty." He lies on his stomach and stretches out between my legs. He blows on my clit. His fingertip grazes my labia. And I shudder in anticipation. "Damn, baby, your pussy's wet as hell."

"I know. Reading this book."

His smirk teases. "Yo, don't have me tearing nothin' up. Let me find out that book's turning you on more than ya man."

"Ooh, don't be jealous, lil' daddy," I tease back. "Nothing or no one ever wets this pussy like you."

"Yeah, aiight. I got ya *lil'* all right." He taunts my pussy with his finger, then plunges it inside. Instantly, desire swells in my belly.

Oooh, yes!

Marcel lifts his gaze up at me, pulling his finger out of my cunt. His eyes are dark and hungry. "Keep reading."

"I-I don't think I'll be able to concentrate."

He licks his finger, then grins, pushing it back inside of me. "You'll manage." I squirm as he slips his wet finger in and out of my slick opening, teasing gently. I try not to close my eyes. Try to focus on the words on my screen. But they slowly start to fade in and out, the way his finger slides in and out of me. "Read to ya man, baby…"

I blink. Blink again. Then pick up where I left off. "'I sucked Martinez until I drained the last drop of his man juice and his dick went limp…'"

Marcel buries his tongue thick between my pussy lips.

I moan. "Ooooh, yes. Yes. Yes. Mmmm."

"Keep reading," he murmurs. He fucks me with his tongue, then laps at my slit, then my lips, then wriggles the tip of his tongue across my clit.

I draw in a breath, bite my lip, and choke back a groan. "N-no. I-I can't. Think. Can't. Focus. Oooh…" I try to steady my breathing. I fight to keep reading. To keep from stuttering out words, but it's for naught. Marcel kisses my pussy. His tongue circles it slow and steady, tracing my swollen folds. Then curls deep inside.

My eyes snap shut, then flutter open as he urges me toward an orgasm.

"Read," he says into my juicy cunt.

"'I l-let out a s-soft moan. With there being no windows or circulating air, the control room held the pungent scent of my wet pussy. The smell heightened my arousal, intensifying my need for a long, hard pounding. I swallowed the thick remnants of Martinez's cum that clung onto my tonsils as I reached for Corbett's cock. I wanted, needed, my pussy ate, ass tongued, and to be fucked from the back on all fours with both of my arms pulled back, like reins. I wanted it rough. I wanted my hair pulled and my ass spanked, hard, until it reddened and bruised. I wanted these two no-good, dirty motherfuckers to treat me like the kinky little cumslut I was…'"

Marcel's tongue dances and skips across my sensitive folds.

I gasp, then keep reading.

"'A thread of precum dripped from his dick. My mouth watered, and I licked away his sticky nectar. Then sucked the head of his dick into my mouth…'"

Marcel groans into my cunt. "Mmmm. This sweet muthafuckin' pussy." He lifts his gaze to me. "Don't stop now."

He curls his tongue inside me and strokes my clit, causing my eyes and mouth to gape. He presses his middle finger inside, then a second finger, curling them forward into wet heat, finding the crinkly ridges at the front as he cups my clit with his tongue, then flicks it before sucking it into his mouth.

My eyelids pop open wide.

My inner walls spasm.

My iPad hits the carpeted floor.

Fuck a manuscript. Fuck trying to stay focused. Marcel strums a sweet, slow symphony with his fingers, pressing into my G-spot. My cunt and clit throbs, tingles, pulses as he taunts my insides.

My orgasm rises, tightens in my belly, and spreads through my body. My wet pussy swallows Marcel's fingers. A deep throb sweeps through me. And I groan. And growl. And grunt.

Fuck.

Shit.

Goddamn.

"Oooh, yes, baby…mmmm…eat my pussy, daddy…yes, yes, yes…fuckfuckfuckfuckfuck…ooooooh, baaaaabbbbbyyy…"

My body flutters. I pinch my nipples. And cry out. Four thick fingers fuck into my cunt, sending waves of pleasure splashing out of me.

Marcel's wicked tongue licks my clit in slow cunning strokes. His fingers go in deep. Plunging in and out, fast and purposeful. My back arches. My body shudders. And trembles. His tongue slides over my clit, down my cunt lips, teasing into my hole, savoring the wet, delicious heat, licking into my ass, into my pussy.

I shut my eyes tight as they water.

A burst of vibrant colors swirl behind my lids.

As my body relaxes and my pussy unclenches, I open my eyes.

Marcel slowly pulls his mouth away from my whimpering cunt and looks up at me with a slow grin; his shiny lips wet and sticky with juices. "You wanna finish reading to ya man, or you ready for this hard dick?"

Is he kidding me?

No words are needed. I bend my legs at the knees. My thighs spread and my fingers splay open my pussy, wet, hungry and ready.

EIGHTEEN

Marcel

Seven a.m., barefoot and butt-ass naked, I'm down in the kitchen making breakfast. Scrambled eggs with cheddar cheese, green peppers, chives, and onions; chicken and apple sausages; home-made blueberry waffles; and sliced fruit. And, yeah, we have enough money to hire an entire staff to wait on us hand and foot. But Marika and I prefer to keep shit simple. We do it ourselves. And cooking is one of those things we both enjoy doing for each other whenever our busy schedules allow for it. This morning happens to be one of those occasions where I can toss it up in the kitchen for my baby.

Sipping on my third glass of pomegranate juice, I walk over and pick up my chiming cell sitting on the kitchen table next to my laptop, signaling I have incoming emails.

I type in my passcode, then pull out my S-pen and tap the EMAIL icon on the screen.

In my gmail account there are several emails, but only one catches my eye.

It's from hotmami@hotmail.com.

The subject heading reads: 4 YOUR EYEZ ONLY

I click on the message, opening it. There are three attachments. I quickly read the short message—I WANT YOU. I WANT TO TASTE

YOU. AND FEEL YOU INSIDE MI MOJADO, APRETADO COÑO. THIS IS HOW WET YOU MAKE ME—before clicking onto the first attachment. A video.

Of her, Miss Anonymous, from the neck down. I can't front. Her body's right. Plump tits, tight waist, skin the color of café au lait stretched over curved hips. Her nipples stand out stiff and brown. She parts her smooth thighs slightly, showing a trimmed patch of pubic hair. "Ooh, *papi*," she coos. "I hope you like."

She cups her tits. Tweaks her nipples. Then her hands dip between her thighs. She peels open her swollen lips, showing her slick pussy. Her pink clit pops out from its hood, rigid and ready.

I swallow.

"You're all I think about," she says, playing with her clit. She gasps. "I play in my wet pussy thinking about you." She lets out a soft moan. "I'm so wet for you, *papi*. *Estoy muy muy mojada para ti papi…*"

Her fingers disappear. Then I hear the wet clicking sound her fingers make fucking into her cunt. I bite into my bottom lip as images swell through my head: her on all fours, her arms pulled back like reins as I fuck into her wetness. Her down on her knees, blindfolded, as she sucks my dick and my nut melts into her hot, hungry mouth.

"Oooh, I wish you could fuck me with your black dick." She gasps again. "I love black dick, *papi*."

"Yeah. I bet ya freak-ass does," I say aloud.

She pulls her fingers from out her, then puts them to her lips. Her tongue flicks out and she licks her fingertips, before sliding them into her mouth. She moans as she sucks them.

"Mmm, *papi*. I taste so good, rich, creamy Latin pussy for you, *papi*. All wet and ready for your hard dick. Are you hard for me?"

"Fuck nah," I murmur staring at the screen. "You gonna have to give me a lil' more if you tryna get my shit rocked."

She runs her hands over her tits, pulls at her nipples, then slowly turns, giving me a slow-motion view of her entire body. When her voluptuous, round ass comes into view, I lick my lips. She has a heart-shaped tattoo on her right ass cheek. "Goddamn, this freak gotta fatty."

"Who has a *fatty*?" Marika says, walking into the kitchen, wearing nothing but her robe. "Good morning." She plucks a strawberry from off the tray on the isle counter.

I glance from the laptop over to Marika as she saunters over to me. The belt of her robe is tied loosely around her waist, allowing her robe to slip open. Before leaning in and kissing her on the lips, I cup a hand over my mouth and huff into my palm, then breathe in.

Although brushing my teeth was one of the first things I'd done when I rolled out of bed at five this morning, I still like my breath fresh when I'm tryna get some tongue. A kiss on the lips is one thing. Tonguing my wife down is another. And my breath has to be right.

It is.

I lick my lips, then pull Marika into me, covering her mouth with mine, slipping my tongue in. The sugary-sweet taste of the strawberry she'd bitten into lingers in her mouth.

"Good morning," I finally respond, pulling back from her. I cup her ass, then smack it playfully.

She moans. "Mmm. What a way to start the day. A wet kiss from a sexy, naked man served with breakfast. It smells delicious." She grabs my dick. "I'm starved."

I grin. "Yeah, I bet you are. Keep grabbing my dick like that and you're gonna end up with it in ya mouth."

She laughs. "I'll keep that in mind." I eye her as she takes a seat. "So, what—or should I say, whose *fatty*—had you so engrossed on the computer before I walked in?"

I point to the laptop screen. Tell her about the email.

She grins, reaching for the pitcher of cranberry juice on the table, pouring some in a crystal tumbler. "So Miss Anonymous did email you. Nice. Let's see what she looks like?"

"Well, we still don't know what her face looks like, but here's what she sent."

Marika stares at the screen. A slow smile creeps over her lips. "Ooh, she has the nerve to have a nice body."

"True indeed," I say, scooping eggs out onto her plate. "You want one or two sausage?" She doesn't respond. "Babe?"

"Huh?" I repeat myself. "One, please. Thanks."

I laugh. "Yo, let me find out she got you all caught up."

"I will say this, she's definitely tempting."

"True," I say, walking her plate over to her.

"Thanks. Everything looks good." She bows her head and says grace, then slides a forkful of eggs into her mouth. "Mmm, these eggs are delicious."

I join her at the table, sitting in a chair next to her. She chews and swallows, pointing at the laptop.

"So, what do you plan on doing with her?"

I smirk. "Uh. What would *you* like me to do with her?"

She tilts her head. "Would you fuck her?"

I grin. "Would you?"

She shrugs. "Under different circumstances, maybe. Depends on what her face looked like. And whether or not we clicked. You know it's always about the mental and physical connection."

I nod knowingly. The "different circumstances" being if Miss

Anonymous was someone we met at a private event instead of her being some horny radio listener tryna get a good fuck.

"Oh, by the way," I say, reaching for my napkin and wiping my mouth, "before I forget. I got an email from Arianna. There's an album release party for Laila Evans next Tuesday."

"Ooh, I love her music," Marika says, taking a sip of her juice. With the highly anticipated release of her sophomore album, Laila Evans is R&B's hottest chick next to Beyoncé right now. A cross between Amel Larrieux and Rihanna, the five-foot-eight bombshell beauty has the whole industry turned upside down with her fiery talent and exquisite beauty. "Where's the party being hosted?"

I tell her at Club Amnesia over on 29th Street. That the doors open at ten and close at four a.m. "We can slide through real quick, make an appearance, then bounce before the party goes into full swing."

Her brow furrows. "Please don't tell me this is open to the public. If so, I'll pass."

Although Marika loves to mix and mingle, she's not really big on industry parties. And she typically doesn't attend them unless it's an artist she really digs or if I press her enough to go, which I usually don't.

"Nah, nah. Invitation only, baby. You know better than that. It's real exclusive. I'll have you home and tucked in bed by midnight."

Her eyes sparkle, as if she's already planning the night out in her head. "Oh, I'll be ready to get *tucked* in bed all right, but it won't be to sleep," she says teasingly.

"So that's a yes? You're going?"

She nods. "I'd like nothing more than to be there. Laila can sing to me anytime."

I grin. "Real talk, baby. She could get the dick if she wasn't on our label."

Marika smirks, running a hand along her neck. "I'd have to taste her juices, first."

My mouth waters. "Oh, no doubt, baby. She'd definitely have to sit on that sexy tongue of yours." She slides her tongue over her lips, then flicks it up and down. My dick twitches. "Let me get some of that."

I lean over and kiss her, parting my lips as she slides her tongue in. Chills slide down my spine as her slick tongue slides around mine. Her robe comes open at the belted waist, exposing her bare thighs, her naked pussy. Shit. I groan into her mouth, feeling my dick stretch. Marika's the only woman who knows how to fuck my head up with just a kiss.

I reach for her. Squeeze her right breast as my free hand eases between her legs.

Marika's eyes slide closed as my fingers skim her pussy, pushing her lips apart and making her gasp. She's already wet. Real wet. And hot.

A deep sigh escapes her. "Oooh, baby. Mmm…you're going to make me late."

I groan. "Fuck 'em. They'll survive."

"But…."

"Just a taste, baby," I murmur into her neck. I nip at her ear. "*Juste un avant-goût.*" I repeat in French.

She moans. "You know it drives me crazy when you speak French in my ear."

"I know, baby. *J'aime vous faire fou.*" I tell her I love making her crazy.

She moans again as I slip a thumb into her mouth. Let her suck it into her mouth like a thick clit. And right then, the shit makes me go weak with want.

Fuck.

She holds my hand in hers. Pulls my thumb out of her hot mouth and closes it around my index and middle fingers. She sucks them forcefully, causing my dick to throb as I finger-fuck her with my free hand. Her wet heat smothers my fingers, coats my hand.

I can't take much more of this teasing shit. I'm ready to put in some work.

Tongue, first. Dick, second.

My dick bows upward, bouncing and pulsing. I stand up and scoop Marika up in my arms, sweeping the dishes off the table with an arm, making room to lay her on her back. Glasses and plates, eggs and sausages hit the floor.

"Wait, baby," she says breathlessly. "What are you doing?"

"I want you in…my mouth…on my tongue. All of you."

I push her legs back. My fingers spread her open. Then my face disappears. I lick and lave and kiss her folds. Smear my lips into her juices. Then bury my tongue deep inside of her.

"Ooh, yes…yes, baby! Eat my pussy! Oh, God, yesss…"

Marika has me going crazy with need.

The crazy need to taste her sweet cunt, to tongue her, to lick her, to suck her in.

And then…

I'm gonna slide this dick in her and coat her pussy walls with my nut.

NINETEEN

Marika

Six-thirty p.m., I'm whisking through the glass doors of Tamarind Tribeca—a trendy Indian restaurant on Hudson Street, to have dinner with Jasmine. She'd called earlier today to say she was in the city. And wanted to meet for dinner and drinks.

The moment I walk in, I spot her sitting at the bar talking to a tall, delicious, dark-skinned man, with a smooth shaven face and bald head, donned in a black suit. Jasmine sees me and waves a hand in the air, sliding off the barstool. The gentleman smiles and welcomes me as she wraps her arms around me, kissing me lightly on the cheek. "Hey, girl."

"Hey," I say, hugging her back. "I see you found your way to the bar."

She laughs. "And if I were single"—she nods her head in the direction of the maître d'—"I'd find my way into the arms of that fine specimen of a man."

I glance over my shoulder, eyeing him on the sly. "Girl, he *is* fine." He looks over at us, and smiles.

Her mouth curves in a familiar smile. Then she looks back over at him. "Yes he is. And Nigerian." She wriggles her eyebrows up and down.

I grin, knowing all too well her deep attraction to African men.

All through high school and college all she dated were men from Africa. Her three serious boyfriends were Nigerian, Kenyan, and Sudanese, respectively. Yet, she married Stevie, who is handsome nonetheless, but far from African.

"Ooh, straight from the Motherland," I tease.

"Yes, Lord." She shakes her head and waves a hand, causing her jet-black, shiny bob to swing. "I'd love to see him in a loincloth."

"Ladies, your table is ready," the attractive hostess interrupts, walking up to us holding a set of menus. She escorts us to a table upstairs.

We take our seats, and within seconds, a server appears and asks us for our cocktail selection. We both order mango cosmopolitans, then eye him as he walks off to place our drink orders.

"So, how are the twins making out since we last spoke?"

She rolls her eyes, giving me a dismissive wave, sending her diamond and gold bangles jingling. "Girl, please. Don't even get me started. Amina is two seconds from being shipped off to a boarding school in the Swiss Alps somewhere. And unless I find a chastity belt to lock her in, Amira is mostly like going to end up being shipped to a convent once she's healed and her stitches are removed."

I chuckle, but I'm silently relieved that Marcel and I don't have any children. Not that we haven't talked about it. But we're both so career-driven and so into each other that having children hasn't made the top of our "to-do" list, especially not since the two miscarriages four years ago. And after watching Jasmine get dragged through the wringer by her daughters, living vicariously through her woes of motherhood has definitely made the idea of having kids less and less appealing.

"Hopefully they'll see the light. And things will get better."

She lets out an exasperated sigh. "When? Before or after they run me ragged?"

I reach over and grab her hand, giving her a gentle squeeze and a sympathetic look. "I feel your pain."

"Thanks. Okay, enough about my drama," she says as the waiter returns. He sets down our water, and drinks, then gives his spiel on tonight's specials. We listen to him rattle off a list of delectable dishes, before I tell him we'll need a few moments to decide.

Grabbing one of the menus, Jasmine looks it over. "Mmm. Everything looks delicious. I can't decide between the Tamarind scallops or the Lobster Masala."

"Girl, they're both delicious," I say, flipping through a menu as well. "You can't go wrong with either dish."

Tamarind's is one of my favorite Indian restaurants in the city. I'd been looking forward to tonight's meal all day while enjoying the company of my soror and best friend.

"Are you ready to order"—Jasmine nods at the approaching waiter—"I'm starving." She licks her lips, lifting her glass and taking a sip from her drink.

He leans in and attentively takes our orders. Jasmine orders the scallop dish with a side of lemon rice. And I order the spinach and garlic rice along with the spinach patties with intentions of sharing some with Marcel when I get home.

The waiter takes our menus, then saunters off. I toss my linen napkin over my lap, then lean forward, resting my forearms on the crowded table. "So how's Stevie?"

She drolly rolls her big doe-like eyes and sips from her cosmo. "Compulsively obsessed with work, always looking to make his next million."

I smile knowingly. For as long as I've known Stevie he's always been a go-getter. Driven. Even though he was born into a well-to-do family, he's always prided himself on making his own way, which is why he opted to not work in his family's billion-dollar hair care business.

"But no matter how much he works, he always makes time for the three most important women in his life," she adds. There's a hint of admiration and lots of love in the way she says this. And I can't help but think of Marcel and his love for me. "I wouldn't trade him in for nothing in the world."

"We both married great men," I agree, taking a sip of my drink.

The waiter returns with our dishes, setting our plates down in front of us, then checking to see if we need anything else. My stomach rumbles. And I think I hear Jasmine's rumbling as well. Neither of us wait for the waiter to walk off before we're quickly saying grace, then digging in.

"So let me ask you something," Jasmine says, between chews of scallops. "If Marcel ever cheated on you, what would you do?"

I blink, caught off guard by the random question. I chew the portion of food in my mouth, then swallow. "Well, I'm not sure how to answer that," I say, setting my fork down on my plate and raising my brows. "I mean. There's no reason for him to ever have to cheat on me. I'm open enough to allow him a free pass to screw whomever he wants with some rules, of course."

Her eyes widen in surprise as if they're ready to pop out of their sockets. "You'd do what? *Give* him the okay to cheat on you?"

Although Jasmine and I are very close, and she knows Marcel and I have had threesomes, I've never disclosed to her just how open my marriage to Marcel is. She doesn't know about the men whom we also share our bed with. That tidbit is none of her business, or anyone else's.

As freaky and open-minded as Jasmine might profess to be—and, yes, she's been known to fuck her husband Stevie in public places and allows him to fuck her in all three holes, her freak flag does not—and probably will never—fly as high as mine. And I don't feel like having to explain or defend my acceptance of Marcel's bisexuality, or the fact that I, too, am bisexual and enjoy watching him share himself with other men. And vice versa.

Yes, she's aware I've slept with other females. But as far as she knows it was a phase during college, a period of experimentation and self-exploration.

Nothing more.

What she doesn't know is how much I love the taste, feel, and smell of another woman. How I love sucking Marcel's dick after it's been coated in another woman's juices; although that—Marcel fucking his dick into another woman raw—has only happened twice and with the same woman. Nairobia. All others have been sexed using condoms.

But with Nairobia, it felt right. And it's what the three of us wanted.

To fuck and be fucked…raw.

Jasmine gives me an astonished look. "Ohmygod! Girl, you have got to be kidding me. You mean to tell me, you'd be okay with Marcel sleeping with another woman?"

I nod. "A one-night stand is simply about sex. So yes. If Marcel wanted to share his dick with another woman, I'd let him. The physical act is of no threat to me. At the end of the day, I know Marcel loves me. And I know, without question, that he's *in love* with me. I have him emotionally."

She shakes her head. "Girrrl, you're more woman than I'd ever be to be okay with some shit like that. Emotional connections or not, love should keep his dick in his goddamn pants. Trust. If Stevie ever cheats on me, I'm taking his ass to the cleaners. And he knows it."

"Well…" I pause when the waiter returns to see if we're enjoying our meals. We nod in unison. He smiles. Tells us if we need anything else to let him know. Then whisks off to a nearby table. "For me it isn't cheating, if I've given him permission to indulge if that's what *he* feels he wants to do. But he understands that that works both ways."

She grunts, twisting her lips. "Mmph. The one thing I am not ever signing up for is having some side bitch disrupt my home."

"Well…" I pause again when then maître d' stops by the table in all of his deliciousness to see how we are enjoying our dining experience. "Everything is fabulous," I say, grinning; almost certain I have spinach stuck in between my teeth. I glide my tongue over my teeth. Then reach for my glass of water, and take several sips. "I always enjoy eating here."

He smiles. "I'm glad to hear that. We appreciate your patronage." He looks over at Jasmine. "And you? Did you find everything to your liking?"

"Oh, yes. Everything is delicious."

He nods, smiling. Tells us to let him know if he can be of further assistance, then makes his rounds to the next few tables. Jasmine and I both eye him.

Ooh, I bet he has a long, thick dick with lots of veins and a big meaty head. Mmm. I bet Marcel would enjoy him in our bed.

"Girl, if I were single and slutty, I'd suck his dick raw and swallow my way back to *Roots*."

I laugh, almost choking on my drink. "Okay, Miss Lollipop Lipz. With a *Zee*."

She smacks her lips together. "That's right. Get it right."

I shake my head. "Girl, you're a damn mess."

"So," Jasmine says, taking a quick sip of her drink. "You were getting ready to say something before Mister Tall Dark and Delicious came over."

I take a sip of my drink as well, then set it down on the table. "Oh, right. I was going to say the *side bitch*—as you called her, isn't the problem. She's never the problem. She's not the one who disrupts anything. It's the one who invites her into his life. But I thought we were talking about simply going out and fucking someone else. Not having an affair with them. Those are two different things. Fucking someone once doesn't constitute as an affair, in my eyes. But if there's a side chick in the picture, then it's an affair. Now if Marcel were to have an affair with someone, then that is something I might struggle with."

She gives me a confused look. "Well, what's the difference? He's still fucking someone else." She finishes her drink in three long gulps while waiting for my response. It's still cheating," she says as she motions for the waiter.

"Hon, it's not cheating if it's mutually agreed on." I pause when the waiter returns to our table, and Jasmine orders another drink. "You asked me what I'd do if Marcel cheated on me," I continue when the waiter is no longer in earshot. "And I'm simply saying he has no reason to ever cheat on me."

"Well, what if he did? Would you want to know about it?"

I take another sip of my drink. "Of course I would. I have a right to know. And I have a right to decide how I want to deal with it."

"But what if he didn't tell you? Would you leave him?"

I shift in my seat. Run a hand through my hair. "No, I wouldn't leave him. I married Marcel with the intention of growing old with him, till death do us part, so leaving him isn't something I entertain. Would I be disappointed? Yes. Would I be hurt? I'm sure I would. Why? Because like I said, there's no reason for him to ever do anything behind my back. And vice versa. Marcel extends to me the same opportunity to sleep with other people if I choose to. Marcel is everything to me. So anything I experience sexually, I intend on experiencing it with him included. Period."

She blinks. "And have you?"

I feign ignorance. "Have I what?"

She leans in, lowering her voice to a conspiratorial whisper. "Slept with other men?" I tell her I have. "Ohmygod! You tramp. I hate you. Stevie would blow a lid if I even thought to part my lips and tell him I wanted to fuck someone else. And I know as greedy and selfish as I am, I'd be ready to slice off his dick and toss it in a meat grinder if he came to me with that. I'm not one for sharing, especially when it comes to my man. And neither is he."

"Trust me. I definitely understand."

The waiter returns with Jasmine's drink, and sets it down in front of her.

"So let me ask you this," she continues when he walks off. "I know you've said many times how well Mar*Sell* satisfies you sexually. Then if that were so, why would you need, or even want, to sleep with another man?"

I smile, sliding my bang over forehead, tucking the curled end behind my ear. "It's not that I *need* to sleep with other men. But I enjoy it because it adds excitement. There's not much Mar*Sell* and I wouldn't do to please the other. We both do a wonderful job at satisfying each other. But we're also always looking at ways to fulfill each other's fantasies. So if having someone else share our bed is a part of said fantasy, then we do what we can to make it happen. In the end, we are both pleasured and well-satisfied."

I swallow back the rest of my drink, slowly starting to feel the effects of the Absolut and Cointreau. "Wait. Why are we having this discussion, anyway? Is there something going on with you and Stevie that you wish to talk about?"

She shifts in her seat. Takes two gulps of her drink. Then tells me she thought she was going to have to cut up his clothes and claw out his eyes a few months ago when he started acting distant, not wanting to sex her down as much.

"Girl, I'm embarrassed to say this, but I literally worked myself up thinking Stevie was fucking his secretary, or one of his paralegals. You should have seen me doing drop-ins two and three times a week at random times trying to catch the bitch with her panties wrapped around her ankles. I even cornered her ass and told her I had my eyes on her."

I gasp. "Girl, no."

She hangs her head. "Girl, yes. I went there. Every ounce of class and charm school etiquette went out the window once my imagination went to the left. You know a horny, wet pussy will have you doing and thinking some crazy shit when it's not being taken care of at home."

All I can do is laugh at her nutty ass.

At nine o'clock, after three more rounds of cosmos, we're finally ready to go and the check arrives. I pull out my AMEX to pay the tab, but Jasmine insists on paying the two hundred-dollar bill. I agree only if she allows me to pay for the tip. I reach in my wallet and pull out a hundred-dollar bill, handing it to her.

Once the bill is paid, we gather our things. "Girl, I needed this," she says, pushing open the glass doors and stepping out into the cool night air.

I smile. "Likewise." I wait with her outside of the restaurant while she hails a taxi, then give her a hug and kiss when one pulls up and stops for her. "Girl, it was good seeing you. Thanks for dinner."

She hugs me back. "No, thank you for always being here for me. I don't know what I'd do without you."

I smile. "That's what sisters are for. I love you."

"Ooh, and I love you more," she says as she opens the cab door and slides in. I shut the door behind her, then wave as the driver pulls off.

Just as I'm making my way to my car, my cell rings. I maneuver the takeout bag in my hand, fishing out my phone down in my handbag. "Hello."

"You good?"

I smile. "Always."

"Cool. I got two hard dicks here waiting for you."

I lick my lips. "I'm on my way."

TWENTY

Marcel

Dick slaps my lips, hard and thick. And I try to keep from scowling. Real shit, yo. I have to catch myself from snapping on this muhfucka. I know it's all a sex game. A role. But still. I'm not used to a muhfucka slapping my mouth up with his muthafuckin' dick.

I look up at Bret, then quickly glance over at Marika, who's on her knees alongside me—one hand diddling her clit, the other playing with her breasts. Her glossy lips curl upward. Anticipation and lust sparkle in her eyes. She's finally getting her wish.

To have me sucking another muhfucka's dick with her.

"C'mon, man, suck this dick," Bret says, pressing the head of his dick to my closed mouth.

I breathe deeply and exhale slowly, trying to get my mind right. Sucking my own shit is one thing, but having my lips wrapped around another muhfucka's dick is taking shit to a whole other level.

And, yeah, it was my idea for Bret to come through when he hit me up earlier and said he was in the city for a few days. Hell, after tossing back a few shots of Rémy white, my hormones were wide open and I wanted to get my freak on. And I already knew Marika was down for the get down since she'd already mentioned earlier this morning that she'd love to rock with him again. So when I hit her up and told her I had two hard dicks here for her, she knew what time it was.

So here he is.

Standing in front of Marika and me, with his balls dangling and the eye of his dick, wet and sticky, staring me dead in the face.

"Suck it," he murmurs. "Slow and deep." His tone is all husky and gruff with horny desire. The muhfucka licks his lips. He's been tryna get me to wet his dick for a minute. And now the moment has come.

Real shit, when I fuck with a muhfucka, kissing is a go. Jacking cocks is a go. Grinding dick to dick, no doubt...is a go. Ass eating, or rimming as it's called, is a go. But, uh, um...dick sucking, except for my own, hasn't been on the menu.

Until now.

Mouth open, tongue thick and wet, I bring my lips to his dick and kiss; swallow; lap it with my tongue, then run it along my lips.

"Aaah, shit." He grabs the back of my head. "Damn, man. Them fucking sexy-ass lips feel so good on my dick." He thrusts his hips, fucks my mouth open wider.

Marika moans. "That's right, Marcel. Suck his dick, baby."

Bret grunts. "Uhh, fuck. Shit. Suck it deeper, man. Let me feel that throat." He grinds into my face, the head of his dick, splashing into a mouthful of spit. "Damn, I wanna fuck your mouth, baby. Aaah, fuck..."

I look up at this muhfucka likes he's a three-headed clown. How the fuck is he gonna tryna to gut my neck out when I told his muhfuckin' ass to go easy? Yeah, he's seen me suck my own shit, so he knows sucking a dick isn't some new shit for me. Sucking *his* is, though. And I need this muhfucka to relax. Let me get my mind right.

I grip his shit at the base, then bob my head, controlling how much dick hits the back of my throat. But, yo, sucking this muhfucka's dick on my knees isn't the move for a muhfucka like me. Nah, fuck that. I'm six-eight, feel me? What I look like in this submissive permission? On my knees, no less, like I'm about to worship this muhfucka's cock with him towering over me. Nah. I'm a dominant muhfucka. And, yeah, I gave Marika my word that I'd put in some throat work with her. And I'ma real muhfucka. I stay true to my word. So I'ma suck the shit outta his muhfuckin' dick. But not like this.

I roll my tongue around his dick twice, then come up for air, pulling back from his dickhead.

Bret's eyes snap open. "Yo, why you stop? That shit was feeling good as hell."

I stand. "I got you, playboy. But I ain't about to be on my knees worshipping your dick, or submitting to you, yo."

I grab him by the dick and pull him into me, kissing him on the mouth. I jerk his dick, smearing his precum over the head. He groans into my mouth, sucking my tongue into his mouth.

Marika moans.

I kiss along his muscular neck, bite into his clavicle, then kiss back up his neck, stroking his dick in my hand, until my lips are at his ear.

"You liked my hot mouth on this big-ass dick, muhfucka," I say hoarse and low.

He grabs my dick. Strokes it. "Hell, yeah, man. That shit felt good."

I cup his balls. Squeeze them. "You wanna bust ya nut down in my throat, muhfucka? You wanna give me that hot, creamy load?"

He dips at the knees. "Hell yeah. Aah, uh…fuck, man."

Marika moans again. Her fingers click in and out of her wetness. Between her thick scent hovering in the air, and Bret's manliness, my dick is throbbing. Aching.

I tell him to get on the bed. He steps backward until he comes into contact with the edge of the bed. He sits. Leans back. And spreads open his legs, holding his dick in his hand. "C'mon and let me feel that wet mouth back on this hard dick."

"Nah, muhfucka, turn around," I say, shaking my head. "Let me get that shit from the back."

He opens his eyes wide. Gives me a confused look, then looks at my hard, throbbing dick, shaking his head and putting his hand up. "Nah, man, hold up. You're not about to run that big-ass horse dick up in me. I told you I'm not into nothing going in my ass, except a tongue. Fuck that."

I deliberately lick my lips, then smirk, grabbing my dick. "Relax, man. I ain't tryna take that ass." I glance down at Marika, who's fingering her pussy and licking her left nipple. "Although that shit is nice and *phat*, though." I laugh. "You know I ain't with that extra shit. I'm tryna eat that shit from the back, then suck that dick."

He breaks into a relieved grin, flashing a sexy smile. The two of us stare into each other's eyes. Forbidden lust between us, surrounding us. The attraction between us is strong. The need, the urge, to indulge our sexuality is even greater. *This fine-ass muhfucka. He's lucky I'm not into fuckin' muhfuckas, I'd bust his shit wide open.*

"Oh, aiight," he says, moving up on the bed. "That's all you had to say."

"Get ya sexy-ass on ya knees, yo," I say gruffly, walking up on him, feeling back in control.

I push him forward on his elbows, grabbing him by the hips, pulling him toward the edge of the bed. I slap him across his ass, drop down on my knee, then pull open his cheeks and dive in, rimming his hole with abandon until he groans and squirms. I get his shit all slick and wet with my spit and tongue, causing him to moan loudly.

The hairs in his crack tickle my nose as I press my tongue in, deeper, deeper, until it can go no further.

The hot, erotic scent of his ass is intoxicating.

With my tongue snaking into his ass, I grab his dick and stroke it. He groans.

"Yes, yes, yes," Marika chants in a singsong voice. "Tongue his sexy ass. Make him beg for it, baby." She smacks herself. Her clit, I'm sure. "Yes, yes, yes…mmm…oooh…Does that ass taste good, baby…?"

I grunt my response as Bret rocks his hips. Grinds his ass into my mouth. "Yeah, that's it. Lick that shit, man. Aaah, shit…yeah, like that, muhfucka."

I lap at his hot, tight hole stuffed between his muscular ass cheeks. Bret's body judders as I dig my fingers into his ass, pulling his cheeks farther apart, my big dark hands splayed over the copper-brown skin of his ass. I can't front. The shit is sexy.

He reaches in back of him and grabs my head, shoving it deeper into his crack, suffocating me. Intoxicating me. My nose fills with the scent of his ass.

And I groan.

"Mmm…oooh, yesss," Marika moans. "Eat his ass, baby." I hear the slick-click-click of her fingers fingering in and out of her slit. "Lick his sweet manhole. Oooh, oooh, oooh…mmmm…"

I slurp and lick and gulp in the heat from his ass. My shit bobs up and down, the enlarged head of my dick, leaking.

Bret grunts. Pushes his dick backward. Tells me to put it in my mouth. "Suck that shit," he murmurs. Finally feeling ready to take the cock dive again, I kiss the tip, then tickle the head with my tongue, licking at the precum that dribbles out of his slit. Then lick the underside, sticking a finger into his asshole. I suck his dickhead. Lick it. Kiss it. Lick it again. Then suck it again.

He bucks his hips and moans.

Marika lets out another moan. "Yeah, that's right, baby." She crawls over to us, her mouth at my ear. "You look so fucking sexy with his dick in your mouth, baby." She reaches up and slaps Bret's ass.

He grunts.

She plays with her clit as I suck Bret. Then wriggles closer to me, reaching between my legs and grabbing my dick. Her wet fingers grip my shaft. My shit's leaking like crazy. "Ooh, your dick is so hard. And it's so wet." She runs a finger over my piss slit, swiping at the string of juice, then slides her finger into my mouth, then hers.

She moans in my ear. "Mmm. You taste so good, daddy. My pussy's so wet."

"Yeah, I know it is, baby," I say real low and deep.

"Lick his dick, baby," she urges. "Let me see you run your long tongue up and down it. Make my pussy cream, baby."

I suck the head of his dick, then lick the pinched skin on the underside of it.

Marika's excitement, the fact that she's so turned on by the idea of my taking another cat's dick in my mouth, makes my dick throb even harder. The more turned on she gets, the more turned on I get. The more I want to please her.

Marika gives me a one-hand dick stroke while she buries her fingers, knuckles deep inside her wet pussy. "Let's suck his fat dick together, baby," she says breathlessly.

I slide my tongue back up into Bret's ass. Sink my tongue into his moist hole. Then tongue-fuck him while Marika's hand grips the base of my dick tight, then uses both her hands to stroke up and down my shaft.

My shit is pulsing.

"Aaah, fuck," I groan into Bret's ass.

Marika takes one hand off my dick and reaches over and slaps Bret's ass cheeks. Left, right, left, right. *Pop, pop, pop!*

He lets out a deep groan.

Marika pulls my face away from his ass, her sticky fingers pressing into my cheeks as she covers her mouth over mine. She slides her tongue in. Greedily sucks it. Then sucks on my lips, tasting Bret's ass on my mouth and tongue.

"Mmmm." She moans. "Let me taste."

I grin. Lean back. Give her space. She pulls open his ass, then buries her face inside. I sink two fingers into the back of her hot cunt. She's so wet and slippery.

"Goddamn, baby. Ya shit's so juicy."

I shift my body. Inch up behind her. Spread her ass open. Then press the head of my dick at her slick opening. I can see the mouth of her pussy opening and closing. Hungry, wet, and ready.

My balls are so fucking heavy. I'm ready to bust. Fast. Hard. Now.

But I have too much dick to drive in deep, thrusting inside of her in one forceful lunge. I'm not tryna hurt her. But I wanna hurt her. Make her pussy sting and burn. I press into her, the head of my dick sinking into her heat. She's on fire.

She moans, pulling Bret's dick back and sucking it into her mouth. I slowly push in, feeling her entire pussy quiver and tingle around my dick.

"Aaah, shit, baby." I spit down into her asshole, then press my thumb inside. Instantly, her pussy opens up, wider, taking me all the way in. "Mmm, fuuuuuck…aaah…shit!"

I bite into my lip and close my eyes. I'm ready to nut. Ready to flood her cunt. Then tongue my nut out of her. I move my hips, slowly. Slow-fuck her.

"Oh God, yes," she moans, pulling her mouth off Bret's dick.

Marika knows my body. She knows when I'm about to spit. "No, no, baby, don't come yet."

I can't hold it. Not this time. Sucking Bret's dick got my whole body overheated. Knowing I liked the way that shit felt hitting the back of my throat got me going through it.

I press my lips at the back of her neck. Bite into her skin. She groans. Winds her hips. Her pussy slurps and sucks my dick in, deep.

I growl. Thrust my hips.

I eye Bret as he strokes his dick, his balls dangling low and heavy, looking like two big chocolate eggs. "Yeah, muhfucka stroke that fat dick, niggah. Aah shit, yeah. Big-dick muhfucka. Look at them big-ass balls."

I lean in, moan in Marika's ear. "Suck them big balls, baby."

She groans. Grabs them and slurps them into her juicy mouth. Then groans again. The vibrations cause him to stretch open his toes. He's on the verge of nutting.

"Not yet, muhfucka. Don't bust that nut, yet."

I grunt, flooding the inside of Marika's walls, then slowly pull out. My dick wet and heavy and still hard, I pull open her ass and bury my tongue inside her creamy slit, slurping and tonguing out my nut, sucking on her pussy lips, then sucking her sticky clit into my mouth.

"Uh, uh, uh, uh, uh, uh, uh, uh, uh…ooh, ooh, ooh, ooh…yes, yes, yes…" Her body shakes. "Oh, baby, your tongue feels so good…"

I suck her pussy clean, then rise up and crane Bret's head to me and slide my tongue into his mouth, giving him my nut and Marika's.

He eagerly sucks on my tongue and my lips, moaning. When he finishes, I tell him to get on his back. He rolls over, his legs over the edge of the bed, his size fourteens planted to the floor. He spreads his legs. Places his hands on the back of his head. Gives Marika and me an open invitation to feast on his rock-hard dick and swollen balls.

Together, we suck and lick him. And then I reach for his left foot, and suck his toes into my mouth, causing the muhfucka to grip the sheets and thrash his head.

"Aaah, shiiiit. Goddamn, man. Aaah…Damn. I've never had my toes and dick sucked at the same…uhhh, shiiit…time. Aaah…"

I stroke my dick, fast and hard, feeling another nut building up in me.

"Ah, baby," I groan over his toes. "Catch his nut in your mouth for me."

Marika slinks a hand between her legs and plays in her soaked pussy while taking Bret deep into her mouth. His eyes roll back in his head as I lick the balls of his feet, then suck his heel, then lick the back of his toes before sucking them back into my mouth.

"Aaaaah, that's so fucking good," He moans. "I'm coming. Aah, fuck. I'm coming…uhh, uhh…"

I reach over and lightly pinch one of his nipples, pushing him completely over the edge. He grunts. Growls. Then bucks his hips, grabbing ahold of Marika's head.

She moans, gasps, as thick ropes of nut shoot into her mouth. I jack my dick faster, sucking Bret's toes harder, biting into them, as surges of heat rip through my body. I grunt. The base of my dick thickens as my own cum shoots out in thick, hot bursts, gushing up into the air, then splashing down and hitting Bret's chest and stomach.

I grin as Bret takes his finger and scoops up a glob of my nut, shoveling it into his mouth as Marika takes his sticky dick and smears the remaining bit of nut seeping out from his piss slit over her lips, glossing them.

My dick is still hard, and horny.

I wanna nut again.

Wicked smiles ease over Marika and my lips.

It's about to be a long muthafuckin' night.

TWENTY-ONE

Marcel

Just before eleven, Tuesday night, Marika and I step out of our chauffeured Bentley and hit the red carpet outside Club Amnesia for Laila's album release party. The entire block is blocked off by security. Onlookers, groupies, and tons of paparazzi hoping to snatch tomorrow's front-page headlines are outside behind barricades. Marika hides her face as a gaggle of cameras start snapping our pictures, bulbs flashing everywhere.

The bouncers quickly pull back the red rope so we can enter the club. And there's no surprise here. The music is thumpin'. The party's packed. The energy's on full-blast. There are wall-to-wall muhfuckas in all of their bling everywhere, profiling. And scantily clad vixens and video hoes and broads looking for a come-up scour the club, trying to snag their next meal ticket.

I reach for Marika's hand and snake our way through the massive three-level club. On the main level, I greet a few kats from A & R, then say what's up to Keshia from BET's *106 & Park*. A lot of shit's definitely changed in the industry. I'm not gonna front.

I pull Marika onto the dance floor and dance up on her when DJ Chunky Monkey—this cool-ass cat who also deejays real heavy down at some spot over in Jersey. Newark, I think—slides on Laila's new joint "Booty Clap."

"Make that booty clap, baby," I tease, grabbing a chunk of Marika's ass on the sly. She laughs, spinning out of my grasp. On the right of us, I spot the singer-songwriter Jason Derulo and some sexy Dominican-looking beauty, doing their thing on the floor. I give him a head nod.

Then focus my attention on some wild-ass chick with a big, juicy ass stuffed in a sexy-ass white mini dress with the back cut out dangerously low. I eye her as she spins around in the middle of the floor. She has muhfuckas swarming around her like flies to shit, all dancing and tryna keep up with her energy. "Yes! Yes! Make it clap, gawtdammit!" She drops down low, then pops back up and starts making all her ass clap. She fucks my head up when she bends over and pops each ass cheek. Real shit, I almost nut in my drawz.

That ass is real juicy.

I blink. "Goddamn she gotta fat ass!"

Marika grins. "Oh, you like that, huh?"

"She a bit ratchet for my taste," I say over the beats, "but that ass, though…"

Juicy Ass spins, then dips, then hops up and down. "Goddamn you, Chunky! Goddamn you! Owwww! Make it clap! Make it clap! Can't a bitch clap it like me! Take a look and weep, bitches! Booty clap! Booty clap! Owww! Owww! Yes, goddammit! They call me Big Booty, bitches! Oww! Yes, gawd! Laila tore her muthafuckin' drawz with this shit…!"

Pretty in the face, small in the waist, Juicy Ass bends over again and pulls out a string of anal beads, then swings them shits over her head, dropping it like it's no thing.

That's it for me. Marika and I stop dancing, staring in disbelief. I shake my head. "Yo, this chick's shot the fuck out," I say, grabbing Marika by the hand. "Let's get the fuck up outta here."

"Um, did she just do what I think she did?" Marika asks, furrowing her brows.

"Straight-up freak shit, baby. Where they doin' that at? Pulling beads outta their ass. Then swinging them shits in the air."

Marika shakes her head. "Nasty-ass."

"No doubt." I take Marika's hand and put it on my thigh. "But you feel that, right? I ain't gonna front, baby. She got my dick hard as hell when she did that shit."

She laughs, squeezing it. "Nasty."

"It's all for you, baby," I shout over the music as another Laila joint plays.

She playfully rolls her eyes, giving me a yeah-right look.

We finally make our way through the second level and like the main level, it's packed here as well. But more heads are dancing than standing around holding drinks in their hands.

Marika and I bump into Nina, who's looking sexy as fuck in a black, low-cut wrap dress. She has her hair pinned up.

She waves at us, shifting her drink from one hand to the other, then stepping in to give me and Marika a hug. "Girl, you're working that dress," she says, giving Marika an approving look. "Good to see you."

Marika waves her on. "Girl, please. Not like you're wearing yours. Good seeing you as well."

"Damn," I yell over the music, spreading my arms out. "Don't you see me standing here? Can a brotha get some love around here, too?"

She rolls her eyes, pressing her body into mine. "Happy?" she says, stepping back. "Girl, I don't know how you deal with his spoiled behind."

Marika links her arms through mine. "Girl, it's a challenge, but somebody's got to do it."

Nina laughs. "And it might as well be you."

"Yeah, aiight. Keep talkin' slick." I kiss her on the cheek. "See you Thursday night, yo."

"Yup. Let me go get my dance on." She smiles. "Marika, as always. It's good seeing you."

"You, too, hon." They give each other hugs. Then Marika and I eye her as she zigzags her way through the crowd. "She's sexy," Marika says, grabbing my hand.

"No doubt. I bet you'd tear that sweet ass up, too."

Marika laughs. "Oooh, you know it. All night long."

I grin. *Damn, I'd love to see that shit.* Yo, real shit. Nina's lucky I'm not into breaking cardinal rules. Otherwise I'd have her hanging upside down on this dick.

When we finally hit the third level, I immediately spot my boy Carlos flanked by two exotic beauties, posing for the cameras. Tonight, he has his wavy hair combed out, and he's rockin' all white. See-through linen.

And the muhfucka's dick is swinging like he isn't rockin' a pair of drawz.

I shake my head, nudging Marika. "Look at that pretty muhfucka over there."

"Oh, I see his sexy behind."

"Muhfucka looks like he ain't wearing drawz, either."

Her lips curl. "Oh, I see that, too. And I see whom he's with. Ooh, that man knows he's a magnet for beautiful women."

I nod knowingly. "No doubt."

Carlos grins when he spots us, breaking free from the two lovelies clutching either side of him. "Oh, shit. What's good, playboy?"

We give each other dap. "I see ya ugly ass cheesing for the camera."

"Yo, don't hate me 'cause I'm everything you can't be. I can't help if I'm a pretty muhfucka." He brings his attention to Marika, scooping her up in his arms and kissing her on the cheek. "Hey, beautiful. Why are you with his ugly ass?"

She laughs. "Let's see. He's my beautiful beast. And I love him."

"Good answer." He drapes his arm around her.

"Hey, hey," I say, knocking his arm away, "fall back from tryna run off with my wife."

He laughs. "Man, you lucky I got love for you, or I'd been snatched her away from you."

"Now, now, boys," Marika teases. "Play nice." I see the look in her eyes and know what she's really thinking: *I have enough pussy for the both of you, boo.*

I spot Kandi Burrus and her husband, Todd, along with a few cats from the Brooklyn Nets. I also peep the heavy-hitter himself, DJ Camilo in the building with his peeps. And Solange. I blink. Then quickly scan the area to see if I spot Jay-Z or Beyoncé in the vicinity. I don't.

"How long you been here?" I ask Carlos, bringing my attention back to him. He says about thirty minutes or so. He waves over the two chicks he'd been hugged up snapping flicks with, and introduces them. Sienna and Summer. Two twin models from the U.K.

Real shit, they're fine as fuck.

Carlos leans into me, the heat from his breath tickling my ear and says, "You know I'm fuckin' them down tonight. Too bad ya ass married. You could be pounding their shit out with me."

I laugh, reaching for Marika's hand. I give it a squeeze. "Do you, playboy."

We talk it up a few minutes more, then decide to link up before either of us gets ready to roll out. He gives Marika a kiss on the cheek, then daps me up. Marika and I both eye him as he snatches up the twin beauties, then cups a handful of their ass cheeks.

I can't help but laugh at his nasty ass.

Laila's face lights up when she spots me. She hurries over and gives me a hug. Thanking me for coming out to support her. I introduce her to Marika. And she wishes Laila much success on the new album. More hugs, then she's off to greet the rest of her guests.

I take Marika by the hand and lead her to a booth not too far from the bar reserved for M&K executives, which also overlooks the dance floor. There's already two bottles of Bollinger on ice in a bucket on the table along with flutes.

Marika and I are on our second glass of champagne when we both lock eyes on the bangin' beauty with the melon-sized titties and plump ass—rocking a red skimpy, low-cut blouse and red short skirt, perched up at the VIP bar, sipping from a martini glass. I'm not sure where she's come from, but she definitely wasn't sitting in that spot ten minutes ago. Or maybe she was.

All I know is, she's there now. And I'm diggin' what I see. And so is Marika.

"Now she's sexy," Marika says, leaning into me.

I grin. "You think she got good pussy?"

"There's only one way to find out," she says, placing her flute to her lips, then slowly taking a sip. She licks her lips, setting her glass back on the table.

I glance back over toward the bar. Whoever chick is, she's someone I've never seen before. And judging by the way the vultures are swooping in on her, no one else knows who she is either.

I like that. She wasn't one of the regular groupie chicks who stalked industry parties.

I rub my chin. *Fresh meat to pound this dick in.*

"How much you want to bet, her panties are red, too?" Marika says, bringing my attention back to her.

I eye her as she takes her tongue and glides it around the rim of her drink as if she were licking the head of a fat dick. She dips her tongue down into her drink, then takes another slow sip. She sets her empty glass on the bar, licking her juicy, glossy lips.

I feel my dick slowly stirring in my drawz.

"You see that?" Marika says low, leaning into my ear.

"No doubt." I bite my bottom lip, imagining her long, pierced tongue lapping at my balls, then sliding over my…

Marika playfully pinches me. "I know that look."

I hit her with a sexy grin, feigning ignorance. "What look, baby?"

"Don't play coy with me. That 'I'd love to feel that silver ball rolling over my hole' look."

I laugh. "Yo, you know me so well. Guilty as charged." I narrow my gaze. "Don't front like you weren't thinking the same thing."

Now it's her turn to laugh. "Busted."

"So, what you think? Latina or Italian?"

She glances over at the bar. "Mmm. It's kind of hard to tell with the lighting. She could be Italian."

I lick my lips. "Nah, she's definitely Latina, baby. Look at that ass on her. And them juicy made-for-dick-sucking lips."

"And clit sucking," Marika adds teasingly.

I lean in and kiss her on the lips, catching the eye of our prospective lay for the night if things kick off the way I hope. Although Marika and I rarely indulge our sexual appetites at these types of industry parties, every now and then someone worthwhile becomes an exception to the rule.

Tonight, it might be the beauty at the bar.

Marika brings her flute to her lips, taking another sip. "She's still looking over here. I think you should go over and invite her to join us."

I lean in and give Marika a long sensual kiss, then slide out of the booth and make my way over toward the bar. Baby girl is checkin' me hard as I head her way. Her eyes seem to light up as she arches her back, poking her titties out more.

"What's your name, beautiful?" I yell over the music into her ear, placing my hand on the small of her back.

She smiles, flashing a set of straight white teeth. "I'm everything you need me to be."

I grin. "Mar—"

"Oh. I know who you are, *papi*," she says, licking her luscious lips. "Mister Creepin' and Freakin' After Dark. Who doesn't know whom the sexiest man alive on radio is. You never emailed me back to let me know how you liked the pictures I sent you."

I blink. "Oh, shit. It's *you. Miss Anonymous?*"

She slides off the barstool. "Yep. It's all me. In the butter pecan flesh, *papi*." She slides her hands over her hips, then slowly turns, giving me a full view of her entire body. Ass for days, damn! "You like?"

Hell the fuck yeah. I nod. "True, true." My gaze drops to her cleavage and lingers there, before licking my lips and looking back into her face.

"Good. We're all aduts here. I'm grown. So forgive me for being straightforward, but it's no secret that I wanna fuck you, *papi*. I wanna feel my pussy wrapped all around your cock."

Ah shit! Freak-ass. Baby, I'll fuck ya ass inside out, then watch Marika blow ya guts out. The two of us will rock ya muthafuckin' lights out!

"So how'd you get an invite to this?"

She tells me her *friend* won two VIP tickets to the release party over the radio last week after trying for three weeks to win them.

She glances over at Marika. Then reaches for her drink and lifts it up at her. Marika does the same, smiling. "Your wife's very beautiful." I give her a look, surprised that she knows Marika is my wife and not some date. "Oh, don't be so shocked," she says, grinning. "I know who she is. Who doesn't? As many times as you've talked about her on the radio and I've seen the two of you in photos, how could I not know? Still, I'd rather have *you* all to myself."

She bats her thick lashes, tucking her hair behind her ear.

"Nah, baby…no dice. It's a two-for-one special. We're a package deal."

A sly smile eases over her lips. "That's sexy, *papi*. Real sexy."

"Yeah, like you." I decide to test the waters, to see just how open this beauty is. I put a finger to her jawline and gently trace it. "What color panties you have on?"

She bats her lashes. "Red. I'm hot like fire, *papi*," she says over the music. "And you are making them wetter by the second."

"Damn, baby. I love wet panties." I glance over my shoulder at Marika. She smiles at me. And I wink at her.

I glance at my watch. We've been here almost two hours. It's time to roll out. "Where ya peoples at?"

She takes a slow sip from her drink, easing back up on her stool. "Oh, her." She tsks. "Please, man problems."

My eyes soak in her voluptuous lips, imagining them wrapped around the head of my dick. *Damn. I bet she can suck a mean dick.*

"Oh, word? Then how about you come join my wife and me"— I nod my head over toward our table—"and get to know *us* a lil' better. I promise. We won't bite."

Her wet tongue swipes over her lips again, then spreads into a mischievous grin. "Who said I didn't want to be bitten?"

"Oh, my bad, baby. Then you good."

"Oh, I know I am." She tosses her long hair over her shoulder, causing her titties to jiggle. Damn. All I can think about is having my hard dick sandwiched in between them big bouncy mounds, then busting my nut all over them. "I *love* being bit...in *all* the right places."

Laila's new track "Paradise" starts playing and the club goes wild.

Miss Anonymous pops her fingers, then two-steps. "Oooh, this is my shit. Come dance with me, *papi*."

"Nah, I'm good on that," I say, taking in the scene around us, then bringing my attention back to her. "What I'd rather do is go somewhere 'n' fuck."

She slides back off the barstool. "Ooh, *papi*. If you only knew how long I've fantasized about being with you."

I smirk. "Then let's go turn that fantasy into a reality."

She guzzles her drink back, reaches for her beaded clutch, then says, "Let me go freshen up. I'll meet you back at your table."

TWENTY-TWO

Marika

My breath quickens. Buzzed from countless flutes of champagne, arousal sparks the air around us. Marcel lowers his mouth to mine, kissing me with a heated passion, as he slides the hotel's key card along the slot. His tongue is hot and wet as it sweeps around mine. He pats my ass, then cups and squeezes it. And I moan low in my throat as our tongues tangle and clash.

"Let's turn her world upside down, baby," he whispers against my mouth.

I crane my neck over my shoulder, taking our prey in. She's inebriated, but still very sexy.

Her gaze locks with mine. My lips curl. "Yes. Let's."

The door clicks open. And the three of us stumble inside, letting the door shut behind us.

Marcel doesn't waste any time with chitchat. As soon as we hit the bedroom suite, he pounces on her, swift and with a purpose. I eye him as he hikes up her skirt, then in one-swoop lifts her up on the dresser and wedges himself between her thighs. "You sure you want this? You think you can handle the heat?"

"Yes, *papi*. I know I can," she responds breathlessly. "Give it to me. All of it."

Her scent, wet and needy, fills my nostrils.

"Yeah, you want all of it? All thirteen inches?"

Her eyes widen. "Yes. Oooh, yes."

I watch as he unzips his pants and digs the heavy length of his cock out. He isn't wearing any underwear, which makes its release easier. The crown of his dick is damp with arousal.

I lick my lips.

She licks her lips.

My mouth waters for a taste.

Of him, of her…

Her cunt is thick and juicy, the imprint of her bulging sex beckoning for release as Marcel grinds up into her, against the silky fabric sheathing her core.

She moans.

My breath catches. I snake my right hand down into my panties, while my left teases my right nipple.

"You like that," he rasps, reaching under her panties with his thumbs and pulling at her cunt lips out of the sides of the crotch.

"Yes, yes," she whimpers.

Marcel presses his shaft up against the center of her panties, right between her swollen lips, up against her engorged clit.

"Imagine I'm fucking your wet pussy," he tells her. "Squeeze your tits. Play with your nipples."

She does, cupping them.

My fingers slip into my pussy, slinking into my own wetness.

Anonymous moans.

Marcel rolls his hips into her again. His ass, thick muscled humps, looks so delicious clenching and unclenching with each stroke.

I moan, coating my fingers with heat and excitement.

"I'm gonna make you nut in ya panties," Marcel taunts, thrusting into her. "You wanna come on my dick?"

"Yes, *papi*. Yes," she pants. "You have my pussy so hot. So wet. So ready."'

My fingers sink deeper into my cunt as Anonymous wriggles and begs. I can tell the friction and the heat is pushing her over the edge.

I can see Marcel's hard dick straining toward her panty-soaked pussy.

She reaches for it.

Marcel grabs her wrist. "Nah, *mami*. You don't get to touch this dick." He grips both of her small wrists in his one hand, holding them up over her head.

Between gnashed teeth, she hisses, "Fuck me, *papi*. Give me that big black cock. Let me feel it deep inside my pussy." She thrusts her hips upward. "Oooh, *papi*…feed *mi coño* with your big, hard dick. Give it to me."

Marcel pulls her panties to the side, exposing her puffy cunt, swollen and wet with lust and heat and want. Then assaults her clit and the center of her slit with swift pumps, sawing back and forth over her cunt.

Marcel steps back, gazes at her pussy, slides two fingers in and fucks into her. She moans low, her head falling back.

It doesn't take me long to step out of my cum-soaked panties and fasten my harness on, readying myself.

She reaches for Marcel again—his thick and hard and aching dick, wanting him, begging for him, but he pushes her hands away. "What I say, yo? You don't get this dick yet. Not until my baby fucks you; until she opens you wide for me. She's gonna fuck you deep until your pussy drips."

Her gaze flickers over at me, then glides down to the silicone jutting out from its harness.

I lick my lips. Stroke my ribbed cock, purple and thick. I cup one of my breasts in one hand, lift it up to my parted mouth and suck my nipple in.

Marcel takes me in. His eyes alight with fire as his gaze glides down to my long cock. He licks his lips.

Anonymous spreads her legs wider, winds her hips upward. Moans. Talks dirty in Spanish. Tells Marcel how he's driving her insane. Making her dizzy with lust.

Marcel bends forward and bites into her cunt, causing her to howl out in ecstasy. "Yes, *papi!* Oooh, yes!"

I stroke my cock, pressing the base of my harness into my clit, watching Marcel trace the sides of her labia with quick, wet strikes of his tongue until his bottom lip stretches under her slit. His tongue licks and nibbles and flicks at her clit, then he sucks her deep into his mouth.

Marcel stands, plunges two fingers inside her, then treats her to her own juices. He tells her to suck. And she does. Her head falls back and she sucks in his fingers in delight, in hungry want.

He works her panties back in place, then steps back.

I let out a moan, fisting my cock faster. My pussy juices splatter along the edges of its base. I'm ready.

Ready to sink my cock into her clenching cunt. Ready to feel her spasm along the ridged width. Ready to fuck into her guts.

Warm and wet, Marcel palms the front of her sodden panties, then smacks her cunt over the thin lace material.

"Ooh, yes, yes, yes…more. *Yo quiero más.*" She says she wants more.

Whap!

Marcel smacks her crotch again.

My own pussy tingles. And drools. And is eager for attention. A finger, a tongue, a long hard dick…anything other than my own fingers fucking into my pulsing heat.

Marcel's gaze flickers over at me as if he's reading my mind, as if he can smell my aching pussy's need.

"I got you, baby." He winks at me. "Sexy ass."

My lips curl as he tells her to get down from the dresser, get down on her knees and crawl over to me. She does. Submits without a blink of an eye. "Suck my baby's dick," he orders. "I wanna see that pretty mouth working all over her cock."

"Anything for you, *papi*," she says over her shoulder.

He stalks behind her, slapping her on her ass as she prowls toward me. When her lips meet the tip of my cock, Marcel feathers a hand over her jaw and tells her to open her mouth.

"That's right. Open wide. Say 'aah.'"

Her lips part and I fit the crown into her mouth, easing in while Marcel holds her head.

I moan. "That's it. Suck it."

She closes her eyes and sucks me deeper into her mouth, past her tonsils; down into her throat, her nose pressing into the base of my harness. Marcel lies flat on his stomach in back of her, his face flush with her ass. He eats her pussy from the back. I can hear the wet licks of his tongue; the wet slurps of his lips as he gobbles her sex into his mouth.

She groans into my cock. He uses his fingers to spread her open and tongues her, fingers her, curls into her heat and presses into her G-spot.

Anonymous bucks and gasps, sucking feverishly on my cock. I reach up and pinch my nipples, tweaking them, rolling them.

"Baby, fuck her mouth," Marcel muffles out in between licks. She frantically pushes back against Marcel's mouth, his tongue, while I stroke her tonsils. Her mouth tightens against me, pressing into my throbbing clit. My orgasm rises. Ignites. Crackles and blazes. Spreads like a wildfire.

My body shakes.

Her body shakes.

Faster, wetter, the slick sounds of my cock sliding in and out of her juicy mouth, diving in and out of her throat, brushing her tonsils.

I close my eyes and cry out, imagining a jet of hot semen hitting the back of her throat. Imagining her swallowing my hot nut spurting from my cock and spilling over her lips.

A pulse pounds, thick and heavy, in my pussy. I come, over and over and over, still wanting, needing, more. Oh God, yes. Hips still moving, I shudder. And Anonymous shivers, too. Drool and lots of spit, pooling out of her mouth and cascading down her chin.

Round one is finished. But the party's just begun…

And now I am fucking Marcel, riding his dick, bucking my hips as Anonymous straddles his face, facing me. She fondles my breasts, then leans in and suckles them into her mouth. She lavishes them with sweet affection, then bites into each nipple, causing heat to ripple through my entire body. The rush begins low in my body, then fans out into flames as Marcel thrusts hard. Rapidly stroking deep.

Anonymous leans in and kisses me, her fingers caressing my swollen tips, cupping my breasts. She sucks my tongue into her mouth. And before long, we are both melting; me over Marcel's dick, her over his mouth and tongue.

I keep coming, watching Anonymous watch me.

Then reluctantly, I slowly lift up from him. His dick is still rock-hard and ready for more. Anonymous joins me in sucking his dick clean. Our tongues laving up his shaft, then meeting at the crown, twirling our tongues over it before wrapping our lips over each side of his mushroom-shaped head and sucking. We French kiss his tip, then slide back down his shaft, before each sucking one of his balls into our mouths.

"Aaaah, shiit, fuck…that's what I'm talking about. Suck them shits. Yeah. Mmmmhmm. Just like that."

She moans, rubbing her pussy. She begs for her turn to feel Marcel's hard dick. She eases up over him, readying to mount when I grab hold of her ass and stop her.

"Wait a minute, sweetie. There'll be no raw dick tonight."

Her mouth turns into a crooked, drunk grin. "I'm clean, *mami*."

"That's nice," I say, reaching over and grabbing the gold-foiled wrapper. "And so is this condom." I tear it open, rolling the Magnum down over his shaft. "Now you can have at it."

She glances over her shoulder at me, and smirks as I reach underneath her and guide Marcel's dick to her entrance, then slap the mouth of her pussy a few times with it before letting her sit down on it. She gasps. I push her forward as Marcel wraps his arm around her back and glides his dick through her wetness.

"*Dios mío! Ooh, mmm…su pinga es tan grande!*" She steadies her breathing, then rocks back and forth, slowly easing down on his dick. She gallops up and down on Marcel's dick. Rides him like a skilled jockey riding a thoroughbred. She speaks more Spanish. Tells him how wet he makes her pussy. "*Mmm, papi. Tu pinga es bien garde y chocolate como mi gusta!!!!* Oooh, yes…your dick is big and chocolate how I like it!"

There's a growing heat in Marcel's gaze, and hers…

She's trying to out-fuck my man. Trying to outshine me.

I am surprised at the tinge of jealousy that washes over me. I know she is no threat to me. But…it's as if Marcel is making love to her, not fucking her. He's touching her, and filling her, spreading heat and good dick all through her. And the look in her eyes tells me she may not be able to separate feelings from sex.

"Oooh, *papi*…" she mutters, rocking and rolling her pelvis. "It feels so good in me. Oh, I love the feel of this big dick. Mmmm…"

She has every inch of Marcel's dick stuffed inside her. Deep. Balls deep.

And, yes. I am impressed.

Her eyes glaze with passion.

Or maybe it's craziness. Yes, that's it. Call it women's intuition. But I know crazy when I see it. And this bitch has a crazy look in her eyes that I hadn't noticed before now.

But I shake the thoughts, the nagging feelings, and stay in the moment. Her pussy is hot and wet and very juicy.

She lifts up and squats and lets Marcel thrust up in her. "Turn around on this dick, yo," he says huskily. And, slowly…she does. She rotates her hips, and her juices slide down Marcel's shaft. She turns until she is facing him and her back is toward me.

I reach out and smooth my fingers over her skin. Caress her ass. Reach around and fondle her heavy breasts. Her nipples are swollen thick.

She moans, "Aaaah…," then leans in and kisses Marcel. I pull her face from his, breaking her kiss, covering her mouth with mine as Marcel's dick slides in and out of her body.

I tear my lips from the kiss, then position myself behind her and kiss the small of her back, then let my tongue slide up her spine, then down it until my tongue dips into the crack of her ass.

I lick further down until I am flicking at Marcel's condom-sheathed shaft, until I am lapping her cunt juices from his balls.

Marcel moans, "Aaah…shit, yeah…do that shit, baby…"

I know he's talking to me. But Anonymous feels the need to respond for me. "You like that, boo? You love how this good pussy wraps around that big dick, hmm?"

I lick back up to her crack, then along her spine, feathering wet kisses over her damp, heated skin.

I inhale her musky scent of arousal, feeling my pussy coming alive again. Aching with desire. Pulsing with a burning need. And knowing.

"You like that big dick in your pussy?" I nip at her earlobe. She grunts her response. "Then you'll love one stuffed in your tight little ass." My thumb lightly brushes over her nipple. "You want it in your ass, too?"

"Mmmmm...yes. Give it to me in *mi culo*..."

I smack her ass again. Then walk over to my handbag and return with a Trojan Fire and Ice condom and lubricant before crawling up behind her.

I tear open the wrapper, then roll the condom down onto my cock.

Marcel reaches around and slaps her ass, both cheeks alternately. "Arch ya back, babe. Get that sweet ass in the air for my baby."

Marcel's gaze meets mine. He licks his lips and winks at me as I squeeze out some gel onto my fingers. I smear some over her hole, then finger her, working the lube inside and out, finally stretching her with my fingers.

She whimpers.

"You ready to have me inside your ass? To have the both of us fucking you?"

She yells out something in Spanish, then bucks her hips.

"Fuck her good, baby," Marcel says gruffly, watching as I position myself, guiding my purple cock between her ass cheeks.

Anonymous gasps.

Marcel cups her face in his hands and soothes her with tenderness. "Ssh, relax. Lean into it, baby…look at me. Give in to it, *mami*."

She inhales deeply.

I palm her ass, pushing every inch into her tight space. Determined to fuck her guts in, then out.

Marcel groans, feeling her pussy clamp around his dick like a tight fist as I fuck into her ass until we are both bathed in fire. My breasts sweep across her smooth back.

I lean in and meet Marcel's gaze again.

Whatever niggling of jealousy I'd felt earlier is now gone. I feel in control. I *am* in control.

"Can you feel my cock fucking into her sweet ass, baby?"

Marcel grunts. "Fuck yeah. Aaah, shit…"

She moans loudly and leans farther into Marcel as I push forward and gently rock my hips into her ass, sawing her hole with heat from the ribbed dildo and the tingling sensations caused by the warming effects of the condom and lube.

Marcel curls his fingers underneath Anonymous' ass and lifts her slightly. We both take turns thrusting and retreating, fucking her holes.

Squishy, squish-squish…

Her wetness splashes out of her.

She cries out in Spanish. "*Dios mío!* Ooh, I never thought this would feel sooooo good. Ooh, ooh, ooooooh…yes!"

Our bodies slam together. Our rhythm in sync, Marcel and I are in our own zone. I silently know, he silently knows, we are both ready to explode.

Sensation starts to tumble inside of me, roiling up from my clit, bubbling up inside my cunt. My head lolls back. My eyes roll upward. The room starts to spin.

Then the entire bed shakes as I pound into her ass, striking my clit with each delivered stroke, watching the eye of her hole stretch and pucker around my cock.

Anonymous cries out.

Marcel growls.

And my own cry mixes with theirs.

Slowly, the three of us lay, sweetly heated, panting and wet and quivering, still shaking from the multiple aftershocks of pleasure.

Deliciously fucked…

TWENTY-THREE

Marcel

"Man, get the fuck outta here!" I snap, smacking the palm of my hand down on the long conference table. I've been in a meeting with J-Smooth and his punk-ass manager for the last thirty minutes listening to these two morons try to convince me why I shouldn't release this muhfucka from his contract with MK Records. "Don't get it twisted. I'm not the one who fucked you over, man. You did. I'm not the one ruining ya career. You are."

I stare at him. He's five-eleven, slender, mocha brown, with sleepy dark eyes and a neatly trimmed goatee perfectly framed around full lips. And real talk. He could definitely get this dick in his neck if he got down like that. I know a lot of muhfuckas in the industry who do, but J-Smooth's name isn't one of them on the list.

"You know I'm talented, Mar*Sell*, man," he says, running a hand over the waves of his freshly cut hair. "And you *know* I can get in the studio and drop a hot album. Don't let some BS get in the way of us making this money, man."

Muhfucka, you can drop down on those knees and wet up this dick; that's it. I take a deep breath. "Yeah, you're a talented artist. No one can deny that. But I'm not the one gettin' in the way with us gettin' this paper. You are. At the end of the day, talent doesn't mean shit if no one is checkin' for you. And right now. You're going down faster than a plane. Your fans aren't feeling you. Money or not, you're becoming reckless and too risky. And *you* and your antics are becoming a liability."

"C'mon, man. If you'd just ride it out with me, this'll all blow over. I know I can win my fans' trust and respect back. I've already made a public apology."

I give him a blank stare. "And you think some half-assed public apology means shit when you keep doing the same bullshit?" Then to add to his already fucked up image, this morning someone leaked some photos of this dumb muhfucka with a bong pressed to his fucking lips smoking weed. The muhfucka looked lit the fuck up. When I saw that shit this morning, all I could do was shake my damn head. Then when I called him on it during the first half of this meeting, this muhfucka said he took a few hits because he's stressed. I knew then I'd made the right decision dropping his ass.

I shake my head. "Nah. MK Records isn't that pressed for drama. I'm not checkin' for gangster R&B artists. You seem better suited for Thug Records or some other label that supports slashin' tires 'n' crackin' bottles upside muhfuckas' heads. But you can't be here."

J-Smooth gets up from his seat and walks over to the huge picture window that overlooks the city that never sleeps. He stares out as his manager tries to persuade me to reconsider. He tries to convince me that his current situation is simply a minor misunderstanding between a passionate couple who loves hard, and fights harder.

"Mar*Sell*, J's been loyal to you. And…"

"And MK Records has been more than loyal to him. But given these recent events, and with him now being dropped from his endorsement deals, it's best we part ways."

J-Smooth turns from the window and sighs. "Man, this is fucked up. I don't know why that bitch had to call the cops. None of this would be happening right now if Elena's dumb ass woulda fell back. She knows how I am. She knows I wasn't going to cut her throat or stab her. She blew shit way outta proportionate. We had an argument. Things got heated and got a little outta hand. That's it."

I frown. "A *little?* You think? Man, do you hear ya'self right now? You pulled a blade on her! Threatened to slice her throat if she tried to leave you! Then went out a slashed all *four* of her damn tires!" I slap the back of my hand into my opposite palm as I speak. "You get arrested and charged with a domestic violence! Not once! Twice!"

"I only slashed *two* tires," he says, correcting me as if two slashed tires is better than four.

I frown, rocking back and forth in my executive chair. *This dumb muhfucka.* "Okay, two. Big deal. The point is, you slashed her damn tires! And now you have a restraining order slapped on you! By yet another woman! There's something wrong with this picture, man. And the one common thread in all this shit is *you.* I don't know what sort of issues you have with women or how you deal with them, but that you can't see that you have a problem is fuckin' disturbing. You need help to get your shit together."

As J-Smooth makes his way back to the table, I have to fight the urge to stare at his lips and check myself for looking at him all crazy, wondering if he likes being spanked and fucked in the ass on the low.

Word in the industry is his tongue game is fire. But his dick stroke falls short, real short. Not that that shit matters to a muhfucka like me since I wouldn't be doing shit with his dick, any-fuckin'-way; except, maybe, grabbing it or jacking it off a few times.

But, if the rumors are true, there isn't shit these big-ass hands can do with a lil-ass short dick.

Still, short-dick or not, J-Smooth's a sexy-ass muhfucka to look at.

Man, what the fuck is you doing? This isn't the time to be tryna imagine what this muhfucka looks like stretched out butt-ass naked! Get ya mind outta this niggah's drawz!

I shift back into the soft leather of my chair. Then blink away the image of stretching open J-Smooth's mouth with my dick.

"Man, it's all a big misunderstanding," he says, pulling out the high-back chair next to me and taking a seat. "I can fix this, man. All I'm asking is for you to not give up on me."

I shake my head. Then lean back in my seat and casually cross my leg. Real talk, I dig J-Smooth. And I say this. I let him know this shit isn't personal. It's strictly business. And until he gets his mind right and starts moving right, he's not welcomed here.

There's nothing else to be said. I've already wasted enough time on this bullshit.

I stand, straightening my silk tie. "Well, gentleman. Unless either of you have something to say worthy of more of my time, I'm done. I have an important lunch meeting, and I—"

J-Smooth scowls. "So that's it? You just gonna dismiss me like I'm some random cat on the streets?" He pushes back in his chair, hard, standing; almost knocking the chair backward. "This is bullshit! Some real foul shit, man! And you know it! How you gonna just turn your back on me after all the records I've sold?"

I sigh, smoothing a hand over my tie. "Look. I'm gonna ask you nicely to bounce before I call security and have you escorted outta here. Don't let this get ugly, fam. Roll out 'n' go get ya shit together."

His manager tries to talk some sense into him. "C'mon, Jaquan, man. You're already in enough mess. Let's not add more insult to injury."

I pull my buzzing phone from out of my pocket. It's a text from my assistant, Arianna, letting me know the front of the building is swarming with the paparazzi.

I shake my head, sliding my phone back into my pocket. "You might wanna take the stairs and exit outta the back of the building. There are cameras out front. I'm sure waiting for *you*."

"I'm not running from them. I have nothing to hide."

His manager tries to dissuade him from flapping his gums to the press. To just fall back before he digs himself into another hole. But this muhfucka is a Know It All.

I cock an eyebrow, shaking my head. "Suit ya'self." I walk over to the door, then pull it open.

J-Smooth stares me down, then reluctantly stalks toward the door. "Man, fuck this shit. I'm out." He brushes by me as he walks out. I grit my teeth and fight to keep from punching him in the back of his muthafuckin' head.

"Hey, baby, I say, leaning down and kissing Marika on the lips. She's already seated at the sushi bar at Masa's—a twenty-six-seat Japanese restaurant in the Time Warner Center with a $450 menu price per person, not including the two bottles of sake and tip. As pricey as this shit is, I dig this spot and how they change the omakase for every season. And watching Chef Masa do his thing is worth every penny.

Marika smiles at me, then glances at her watch. "I didn't think you were going to make it. How'd the meeting go?"

I give her the condensed version then quickly change the subject, draping my arm on the back of her chair. "But enough about that. I don't wanna talk about that dumb muhfucka. How was your morning?"

"Busy. Spent my first half of the morning in an editors' meeting, then the last half of it with publicity."

I smile, then lean in and kiss her on the neck. "You're so fucking sexy."

"So are you."

I nuzzle my nose in her neck. "Damn, you smell good." She's wearing my favorite scent, Lolita Lempicka. Real talk, every time she wears this shit I wanna lick her up. I whisper in her ear, "You getting my dick hard, baby."

She playfully sucks her teeth. "Your dick stays hard."

"Ah. What can I say? You have that affect on me. I'm weak for you, baby. And so fuckin' turned on by you."

I eye the chef as he grinds fresh wasabi root in front of us, then goes about the business of preparing our first fish dish. Each dish afterward becoming progressively more elaborate than the one before.

Just as we're finishing up our lunch, my cell rings. I pull it out, then glance at the screen and smirk. I show Marika who's calling. She smiles, taking a sip of her sake.

"Yo, what's good, beautiful?"

"Aaah, Marcel, *mijn liefde. Uw stem maakt mijn kut nat.*"

I grin. *"Je ne sais pas ce que la baise que vous venez de dire mais il ma bite dur."* I tell her I don't know what the fuck she just said to me but it's got my dick hard.

Marika shakes her head, grinning.

Nairobia gives a low, sexy chuckle. "I said, 'my love. Your voice makes my pussy wet.'"

"Just how we like it," I say, glancing over at Marika. She meets my gaze and I wink at her. "Nice and wet."

"And I hope to have all of my wetness smeared all over your

wife's beautiful lips. Oh how I long to feel my aching clit throbbing against her greedy tongue and her fingers fucking into the folds of *mijn natte, sappige kut*."

I fan my legs open, then shut as she talks about being fucked in her wet, juicy cunt with Marika's fingers. "Oh, word? Is that all you wanna feel?"

She moans, softly. "And your big black cock. Mmm. You know I love big dick, Mar*Sell*."

Nairobia's freak-ass knows she can get this dick raw…whenever. In her neck, that is. Although, on some real shit. One time I did fuck around and run this dick up in her without a condom. In the heat of passion, Marika and I were so caught up in the moment that we were on some crazy impulsive-type shit that night. But, I ain't gonna front. That raw pussy was good as hell.

But after the nut was popped, and all the freak-dust settled, Marika and I raced down to our doctor's office to get tested. Even though we get tested every three months, and we only fuck with muhfuckas who get tested regularly too, that was some real scary shit. I was stressed out for almost a whole damn week waiting to hear back from the doctor with my results.

"Yeah, I know you do, baby. So what's good? You in the city?"

"The day after next," she says real low 'n' sultry. "And I will see you and Marika, no?" I tell her we'll have to check our schedules, first. But more than likely we'll be there. Marika eyes me, gesturing for me to hurry up off the phone.

"But dig, baby," I say, gliding a finger along the side of Marika's cheek. "I'm out having lunch with my beautiful wife now. Why don't I have Marika hit you up a lil' later, aiight?"

I tell Nairobia to hold on as Marika gestures for the phone. The two of them chat it up for several minutes with Marika pulling out her own phone, then scrolling through her calendar. I take a sip of my sake as Marika tells her so far she has nothing planned for Friday evening.

Marika's gaze settles over mine as she slips her hand down into my lap. Her hand slides along the inside of my thigh, along the length of my semi-hard dick. She squeezes the head. Then one corner of her sexy lips curls in a half smile. I settle back in my seat and wait for the call to end, grinning.

TWENTY-FOUR

Marika

Late in the afternoon one of my assistants cheerfully whisks into my office. "These just came for you," Natalie says, her heels clicking against the wood floor.

I look up from the manuscript I'm reading and smile. She's carrying an exquisite large floral arrangement.

"Oh, my. They're beautiful."

"Yes, they are." She breathes in the bouquet. "And they smell delightful. Looks like you have made someone very happy. Where would you like these?"

"Sit them over there," I say, pointing toward the Florence Knoll credenza centered in front of the window. "I wonder who they're from."

"Oooh, let's hope it's a secret admirer," she says plucking a small white envelope from the arrangement. She waves the card, grinning. "Ooh, lalalala. Look'a here."

Out of all my assistants, Natalie is my favorite. She's intelligent, quick-witted, has lots of sass, style, and a splash of sophistication that most girls her age seem to lack. And aside from the fact that she's a sexy piece of eye candy, she's proven herself trustworthy over the three years she's been with me.

I take her in, admiring her flair for fashion. Today she's wearing a vintage arc-hemmed, shoulder-baring flower power tunic dress that clings to her hips and C-cup breasts.

"Save the secret," I say, dismissively. "The *only* admirer I'm interested in is my husband. Hand over the card."

She sucks her teeth, dramatically rolling her eyes. "Oh, what a dream killer. Where's the scandal in that? Here." She pokes her lips out, sliding the card on my desk. "I'll be at my desk," she says, heading for the door.

"Bye, Natalie," I say cheerfully. She gives me a stiff beauty pageant wave. I shake my head, chuckling to myself. "Oh, you can leave the door open."

I eye her as she walks out, then pick up the card from my desk. A light feminine scent wafts out as I pull out the stationary note card. My brows draw close as I read the cursive that flows across the card in black ink.

I still taste you on my lips. Still feel you deep in my ass. Thank you for making love to me like no other woman ever has. I'll never forget it or you.

—Anonymous

I blink, blink again, then reread the note for a second time. *I can't believe this! How did she even know where to send this? Easy, fool. Look who you're married to.*

I shake my head. I don't want to make a big deal about the gesture. After all, the flowers are gorgeous. But this note card...what if Natalie or someone else from here had read it? Then what? Couldn't this bitch simply written a simple "thank you" for the other night, instead of being so goddamn descriptive?

I mean. Where the hell is the discretion in this?

Better yet, how about not sending anything at all?

Relax, Marika, girl. Don't blow this out of proportion. It's just a card and some flowers. Accept it for what it is and move on.

Just as I'm pulling out my cell to call Marcel, Shayla buzzes me. "Lenora Samuels is on line two for you."

"Thanks," I answer absently. Thoughts of this Anonymous chick start to take space in my mind. *What if she's a lunatic? What if this ho starts harassing us? What if she tries blackmailing us?*

The last thing Marcel and I need is drama.

And that's why you never, ever, fuck anyone who doesn't have anything to lose.

I shake the unnerving thoughts from my head for the moment, clearing my throat as I pick up the phone. "Hello. This is Marika."

"Marika, darling, Lenora Samuels here."

"Yes, how are you, Lenora? Forgive me for not getting back to you. Life has been ridiculously crazy."

"I'm fabulous darling. No worries. Now let's cut through the cheese and get right down to the meat, darling. You know I have no time for idle chitchat. The manuscript. You've read it. And you loved it, no?"

I can't help but chuckle at her brashness. "Yes, of course I did. And I loved it. I actually forwarded it to Andrea." Andrea is the senior editor for our erotica imprint. "She should be calling you in a few days to discuss an offer."

"Oh, fabulous. I'll be going to the prison later this afternoon to share the news."

"Wait. I thought you said your client was released."

"Oh, yes. She was. But she's had a minor slip-up."

I blink. "*Minor* as in what? A traffic violation?"

"No, not exactly. She sort of violated her restraining order."

I frown. "Define *sort of*, please. The last thing I want is to sign someone to…who hasn't been fully rehabilitated, or is mentally unstable." I glance over at the floral arrangement, then down at the card on my desk. *I still taste you on my lips.* I flip the card over, cringing. "We don't need that sort of publicity here."

"Oh, Marika, darling. Don't go getting all *Judge Judy* on me. It's simply a case of a broken heart. Heaven loves hard, that's all. And she has a hard time letting go. And, yes, she's a little extreme and, maybe, even a bit touched."

Translation: she's fucking crazy!

"Then again, passionate is more like it. But she means well. And she has, as you've read, one helluva juicy imagination."

"Well did she try to kill anyone, again?"

"My goodness, no," she says, sounding appalled. "Since her last incarceration, she's against gun violence."

I dramatically roll my eyes. "Well, that's a relief."

"Yes. She stabbed her victim this time."

My mouth drops open. She says this Heaven chick violated her restraining order by trespassing onto her imaginary—because he was never hers—ex boyfriend's property, then attacked his girlfriend, stabbing her in the chest and neck.

I gasp, clutching my chest. "Ohmygod!"

"So needless to say, she won't be available for any book signings for a long while, unless she can sign from her cell."

Oh, she has got to be kidding me! I lean back in my chair and shake my head in distress. There is absolutely no way I can consider offering her a book deal in light of this new information. Then again…

It had makings of a bestseller, girl.

She probably won't see a dime of it.

That's not your concern.

I clear my throat. "You know, I'm thinking maybe we should hold off on offering your client a contract until she's—"

"Now, now, darling. Let's not be hasty."

I feel like saying, "Sweetie, being hasty is the bitch sitting behind bars." I pick up my pen and repeatedly drum it against my desk, trying to wrap my mind around what I've been told. I can't. It's simply too much to digest.

"I'll tell you what. Let's not lose focus here. How about I give you a call the middle part of next week?" she offers as if she's trying to accommodate me.

"Sounds great," I say as Natalie pokes her head through the door and says in a low whisper so not to disturb my telephone conversation, "There's a Marisol Rodriguez on line three for you. She says it's personal."

I hold up an index finger and mouth, "Whoever she is, have her hold for a second."

She nods, backing out of my office.

"Lenora, I hate to end our conversation, but I have another call. We'll talk next week. Okay?"

"Perfect darling," she says, and hangs up.

I click over to the third line. "Good afternoon, Marika Kennedy speaking."

"Hey, *mami*."

My pulse quickens. "Excuse me? Who's this?"

"Ooh, is that how you and that fine hunk of a man of yours do it? Bring someone back to your suite. Fuck them real good and filthy, then forget who they are?"

I blink. "*Anonymous?*"

"Yes, *mami*. Who else would it be? And before you get all spooked out. I promise you, *mami*, I'm not some nut case. I just want to make sure you got the flowers I sent. And to say, I'd love a repeat of last week's mind-blowing performance."

Yes." I frown, totally caught off guard while trying to keep my tone even, and my attitude from flaring up. "They're lovely. But it really wasn't necessary. Thank you."

"Oh, I know it wasn't. I just wanted you to know how much I enjoyed—"

"Listen, Marisol, or if that's even your real name I—"

She cuts me off. "No, *you* listen. Before you start getting all messy. Let's meet for drinks tonight. I can be in the city around seven."

I blink. *She can't possibly be serious.* "That's not a good idea," I say, calmly. "But thank you for the invitation."

She huffs. "Soooo, you're saying after the romantic night we spent practically fucking until the sun came up that you're too good to meet me for a drink now? Is that it?"

I blink. "Of course not. Not wanting to go out for drinks with you has nothing to do with thinking I'm better than you. It simply means we're not friends, nor will we ever be."

"Oh, okay. If that's how you want it."

"It's for the best." I get up and walk around my desk, then shut my door. "Listen, Anonymous, I mean Marisol…" I pause, shaking my head. "That night…in all honesty, Mar*Sell* and I had a great time with you." I sit back at my desk. "But it's no more than that."

"Uh-huh. No worries, *mami*. Fuck the drunken girl, then act like it never happened." She tsks. "Real classic."

"Listen. We were all pretty lit up that night, but not to the point where we weren't aware of what we were doing. We were all consenting adults that night. So I don't want to sound harsh or anything, but I need to be honest with you. We're never going to be friends. Nor are we going to become acquaintances. So, there'll be no after-work dinner dates, or future late-night rendezvous."

"Well, I don't want to be friends with *you* either. But I was hoping to get your blessing to keep *fucking* that fine husband of yours."

My eyes widen. I am totally taken aback that this woman has boldly come out and tells me that *she* wants *me* to allow *her* to keep sleeping with *my* goddamn husband. All I want to know is, where the hell they teaching this shit at?

She laughs. "Ooh, *mami*. He has some delicious dick. And it's so huge. I thought my last *papi*'s cock was *mucho grande* but he—"

"Excuse *you*?" I say, cutting her off. "Are you serious? You want *me* to give *you* permission to keep screwing *my* husband?"

"Well, of course. I don't see the big deal. Out of respect, I'm coming to you as a woman. Yes. I want *your* man, *mami*. I think we have something special. And I'm willing to share him for now. But eventually I'm going to want him all to myself. So get ready."

Oh this bitch has got to be fucking kidding me?

I hop up, walk around my desk, stalking over to the credenza. "Oh, no, sweetie. Let's get something clear right here, right now." I snatch the flowers from out of the vase. "You will *not* be fucking, sucking, or doing anything else"—I toss them into the garbage— "with *my* husband under any circumstances. Now I appreciate the flowers, but I'm going to have to insist that you not contact either of us again. Please. Respect our privacy *and* our space."

"Oh, okay, then. I can take a hint. You're not interested in being friends. And you're not willing to share your man. *Your* man." She laughs. "What a joke. But fine. I'll play nice. Keep him…I'll just borrow him."

Keep him?

As if I planned on doing anything less.

"Oh, and no worries, *mami*, your secret is safe with me."

I frown, placing a hand up on my hip. "And what secret is that?"

"That you and Mister Creepin' and Freakin' After Dark are a bunch of certified freaks. I'm sure you wouldn't want that getting out."

I blink. "Well, of course I wouldn't. Discretion is of the utmost importance to us. And I assumed for you as well."

"Well, of course it is. Lucky for you I don't kiss and tell." There's a pregnant pause, before she says, "But don't cross me."

The line goes dead.

I slump back in my seat as if the air is being sucked from my lungs.

Dear God...

TWENTY-FIVE

Marcel

"Can you believe that *bitch*?" Marika hisses, kicking off her heels and removing her blouse. She steps out of her skirt, then stomps over toward the liquor cabinet. I absently lick my lips eyeing her ass bounce in her panties with each step. I imagine it's my tongue that's wedged in between the crack of her ass instead of them muhfuckin' laced drawz. I lick my lips again, shifting my eyes from her juicy ass to her silky legs, then back up. All I have on my mind is having them long, sexy legs wrapped around my hips, or one up over my shoulder and the other around my waist.

I slide a hand over the length of my dick, then squeeze the head a few times. *Fuckin' balls heavy as hell. I'm ready to bust this nut up in that sweet pussy. Sexy ass.*

"Marcel, are you listening to me?"

I'ma tear that shit up tonight.

"Marcel?"

"Huh?"

She blinks. "Ohmygod. Are you kidding me?" Hand on hip, head tilted, she narrows her gaze. "I'm telling you what the hell that little Spanish hussy said to me today and you haven't heard not one thing I've said." She throws her hands up. "Why do I even bother?"

"Yo, c'mon, baby. Don't do that. You know I heard everything you said.

"Yeah, right," she huffs loudly, while grabbing a bottle of Merlot. She cracks open the wine bottle, then fills a glass, and tosses it back in a matter of seconds. "You're not listening to one word I'm saying."

Guilty as charged. "Nah, seriously. I heard every word. That shit's crazy."

"Mmmhmm. Sending me some goddamn flowers like that shit was supposed to mean something. Bitch, please."

"Maybe she didn't really mean anything by it," I say coolly.

She scowls. "Are you kidding me? That ho meant a whole lot by it. Trust me. She's a sneaky, conniving bitch who got a taste of some good dick and is now whipped."

Yeah, I did put this dick on her ass...

She pours herself another glass of wine, tossing it back. "Asking me some shit like that. Can she keep fucking *you*! I *knew* there was something a little off with her ass the minute she started riding your dick. That bitch was scheming then. Trying to show me up."

Damn. She def rode the shit outta this dick. "C'mon, now. Can't anyone *show* you up, baby. She can scheme on the dick all she wants, it ain't gonna happen. You got this shit on lock. She was just enjoying herself."

She shoots me an incredulous look. "No. What she was enjoying is pretending she was me. That bitch carried on like she was your wife, and *I* was the side dish."

I laugh. "Yo, c'mon, baby. Now you're being ridiculous."

She slams her glass down. "Don't call me ridiculous. And I don't see anything funny. I *know* what I saw. I was there; remember? Or were *you* blocking me out, too?"

What the fuck?

I frown. "Hell nah, I wasn't doing no dumb shit like that. Where's that coming from?"

She sucks her teeth. "Forget it."

"Nah, nah. You don't get to say some shit like that, then tell me to *forget it*. That's not how we get down. Talk to me."

"Whatever you say, Mar*Sell*," she mutters nonchalantly. "I talk, you ignore. Where's the communication in that?"

I sigh, running my hand over my mouth. "Damn. Really? This is how you doing it? We're supposed to be able to talk about *anything*."

"Yeah, well. I'm aggravated. I was talking, telling you how that bitch called my office and rattled my damn nerves with her shit, and you're sitting over there playing with your damn dick, probably thinking about fucking."

I grin all sheepish 'n' shit, flashing her my deep dimples. "Hey, what can I say? You turn me on, baby."

She scoffs, raising her voice a decibel. "*Really?* You're turned on? *Now?* I'm rattling on about that Spanish ho trying to disrupt our lives, and—"

"What we have is untouchable," I say calmly. "She, or anyone else, can't disrupt shit, baby. Not over here, unless one of us lets her. And I know I'm not letting the animal outta the cage to devour shit we've built. So don't you let it, or her, either."

She fills her glass again. "Oh, good answer, Mar*Sell*. I wonder how calm you'd be if the shoe were on the other foot and some big-dicked Mandingo came at you telling you he wanted to keep fucking *me*. I bet you'd have those big thick cow balls of yours all up in a bunch."

"Is that what *you* want?"

"Maybe."

I go silent for a few seconds, try to collect my thoughts and ignore the sarcastic dig.

I take a breath. "I'm not letting another muhfucka keep fuckin' you unless *you* wanna keep getting fucked, so we're not going there. And the only woman I'ma keep fuckin' is *you*, for the rest of my life. All that other shit is irrelevant. Neither one of us can help what another muhfucka wants, or desires. It's what *we* want that matters. *We* built this shit, baby. Me and you. What we have is solid. So relax, and stop letting that broad get all up in your head."

She lifts her wineglass to me. "I'll keep that in mind."

My gaze drifts down to her breasts and her already hard nipples. I lick my lips as I imagine sucking them into my mouth. "See you got jokes, right?"

She holds my gaze. "No. I have a headache."

"C'mere 'n' let me take care of it for you."

She walks off, shaking her ass.

I frown. "Yo, you kidding me, right? Where you going?"

"To go relax," she says over her shoulder.

"I got something to relax you."

"No thank you. You stay there. And keep *playing* with your dick."

I blink as she disappears.

Oh hell nah. *I'm tryna get some pussy tonight.* That's all I've been thinking about all day. Fucking. And I'll be goddamned if I'm about to let this shit with some dizzy-ass, nonfactor broad spiral into some bullshit-ass tiff between Marika and me. Not tonight.

Damn. I fucked up. Muthafuckin' dick hard! I shoulda just fuckin' let her vent.

I get up and sulk over toward the bar, pouring myself a shot of 1800 Coleccion, then toss it back. *I'ma give her ass a few minutes to chill.* I lift the pewter decanter and pour another shot. *No way in hell I'm going to bed tonight without some pussy. Fuck that.*

"Fuckin' broads, man," I mutter, shaking my head. I uncork a bottle of 2008 Domaine de la Romanée-Conti, then grab two wineglasses and fill the glasses. I glance at my watch and drop my drawz, letting them fall around my ankles.

I step out of them, leaving them in the middle of the floor.

Her two minutes of shittiness is up.

I make my way toward the back of our loft.

And there she is…

Looking sexy as fuck, submerged in our huge, sunken whirlpool tub.

Candles lit, the sounds of George Tandy Jr. playing through the speakers, Marika's head is back on the neck rest.

Steam billows around her as she sways to the rhythm and her legs fall open. Her eyes slide shut.

I swallow hard, but keep my mouth shut as I watch her juicy titties bobbing in the water, and her thick chocolate-colored nipples puckering just above the suds. Marika's breathing hitches when the water laps at them. I lick my lips. And stand in awe, leaning up against the doorframe, eyes smoldering, holding our wineglasses.

I imagine how slick her pussy must already be as her hand reaches between her legs and she strokes herself.

Fuck.

Chest heaving, dick now pointing straight out, rock-solid, copper-hard, my heavy gaze drifts up and down the bathtub as I watch Marika edge herself to an orgasm.

Yeah, that's right, baby. Get that pussy ready for me.

With her free hand, she thumbs her nipples and arches her back.

I hiss in a breath and grip the wineglasses, feeling a heavy nut swelling in my balls. Sighing with my own need, I push off the doorframe, sauntering across the bathroom until I am standing next to the tub staring down at her.

"You thinkin' about this dick, baby?"

She gasps, cracking open her eyes and looking up at me. She blinks. "How long have you been standing there?"

I grin. "Long enough to know how much I love you. And need you. You're sexy as fuck, baby. Even when you're mad at me."

"I'm not mad at you," she says softly. "I was somewhat irked by your nonchalance, though. But I'm over it now." I hand her a glass of wine. "Thank you."

I lean down and kiss her on the head. "I apologize, baby. You know everything you share with me is important to me. And if someone fucks with you, then they're fuckin' with me."

"I know." She takes a sip of her drink. "Mmm. This is delicious."

"Yeah, it is," I say, staring at her rigid nipples.

She catches my gaze and shakes her head. "The wine, silly."

"Yeah, that too." I sit on the edge of the tub. "I love you. You know that, right?"

"Of course I do," she says softly. "I love you, too."

I reach out to touch her wet cheek, stroking the curve, then down her jaw with the back of my fingers. "Don't let that broad get to you, aiight. She's a nonfactor in our lives."

She nods. "I know." She takes another sip of her wine, then sets it up on the ledge of the tub. "The nerve of her."

"Yeah," I say, dropping my hand down, delving into the water. "The nerve." I gulp back my wine and set my empty glass on the floor, caressing her nipple until she lets out a moan. "Silly-ass broads. Can't stick to the fuckin' script."

"I…I was so…so damn taken by surprise at her audaciousness that….I let it get to me." I thumb her nipple. "Oooh."

"Fuck her, baby."

I slide my hand down over her belly, then dip down between her thighs.

Marika sucks in her breath. "Yessss. F-f-fuck. Her."

Daley's—this cat from UK—joint with Marsha Ambrosius, "Alone Together," is playing now. I can't even front. The muhfucka's voice is mad sexy.

I tweak Marika's clit between two of my fingers, causing her to gasp.

"You like that?"

"Yes," she says softly, licking her lips. "You drive me crazy, Mar*Sell*."

"I'm all yours." I stroke my thumb over her nipple again.

"Uhh. I know, baby." I pinch her clit again. She gasps again. "Oooh, yess…"

My fingers skim between her lips. "Whose pussy is this?"

"Y-yours," she says huskily. Her lashes flutter.

I can feel the heat pulsing over her erect clit as I circle my fingers back over it, kneading and stroking. I lean over into the tub and flick my tongue over her nipple, wetness and warmth and steam coating my tongue.

"Uh. Oh, Mar*Sell*. Yes, baby…"

My fingers dive into her cunt, causing water to swirl and ripple around her.

"You want me to get in?"

It's a loaded question.

She licks her lips again. "Yes. Get in." She grinds her hips down into the tub. Fucks herself onto my hand. "Get in. Get in. Get in. Aaah, yes…Get. All. Up. In…meeee."

I remove my hand from between her legs, causing her to gasp. "Ohmygod, why you stop?"

Jamie Foxx's "Freak'in Me" eases through the speakers.

I grin, lust gleaming in my eyes as I rise from the edge of the tub and lift a leg over the side and into the water. My dick bounces in her face. A smile eases over her lips.

"You still need to ask?" I tease as I turn to face her and slide into the suds and steamy water. I reach down for her feet, lifting her right one up to my mouth and sucking all five of her wet toes deep into my mouth. She moans as I lick the ball of her foot, then suck her heel into my mouth. Then go back to making love to her toes with my tongue and mouth all over again. I move onto her left foot. Do the same thing. My dick sticks straight up into the air, clearing the surface of the bubbles.

I moan, laving her toes. She lodges her right foot into my crotch, pressing my dick up against my stomach as she slides her foot up and down my shaft, stroking it. I try to suck her foot into my mouth.

"Oh, God, yessss. Mar*Sell*, baby…"

I ease her toes out of my mouth, then reach for her, pulling her toward me.

"Straddle me."

With a sassy grin, she gets up on her knees, water cascading down her body as she straddles me, situating one knee on each side of me.

"Sexy-ass," I rasp, wrapping my arms around her waist. Our wet bodies collide as she cradles my dick against her pussy. I lower my head in, run my lips over the swell of her breast, then suck her nipple into my mouth, gently tugging it between my teeth.

"Oooh, yes…"

I suck harder, finding a rhythm that causes her heart to beat wildly against me.

August Alsina starts singing about a chick riding him like a porn star as I slink one of my hands between Marika's thighs, brushing my fingers over her swollen pussy lips, then flicking over her clit. Never taking my mouth from her nipple, I toy with the front of her slit. My fingers circle it. Tease it. Then dip inside. Deep.

"Uhhh, yes…"

"You like that, baby," I whisper, gazing into her eyes. My fingers go deeper. Caress her slick pussy walls, then press into that magic spot.

"Ooh, yes. Ooh, yes. Ooh, yessss…"

Her G-spot swells as she closes her eyes and throws her head back.

"Damn, you…uh. Mmmm…oooh…aaah…"

"You ready for me to drown this pussy?"

"Yes, daddy. Drown it." She rides my fingers. "Uhhh…flood this pussy, Mar*Sell*…"

I suck and nip at her nipple.

She palms my shoulders and curls her fingers into my back. And when I lift her hips up and lower her onto the head of my dick, her nails sink into my muscles. She rocks and rolls her hips. Moans and groans. Rolls and rocks, splashing water up over the edge of the tub.

She buries her face into my neck, sucking in deep breaths as her pussy muscles suck me in. "There you go, baby. Get that dick. Daddy gotta big nut for you."

I squeeze her ass. She bites into my neck.

"Oh, God, oh, God…" Marika grinds her breasts against me, sliding further down onto my dick, water and bubbles slosh up over her ass, like waves as she rides me.

"Yeah, there you go, baby…Let that hot pussy suck the nut outta daddy's big dick. Yeah, get that shit, baby…"

I reach around, slide my fingers along the crack, then push my middle finger into her ass.

"Aaaaah…aaaaah…uhhhh…ooooh…"

She's panting, hovering over the edge when I say—in a voice

hoarse with lust and emotion, "I don't want *any*one but you, Marika. Don't *ever* doubt me. Or us."

And then I come.

Deep inside.

Filling her with everything I am.

TWENTY-SIX

Marcel

Keyshia Cole's "Woman to Woman" slowly fades out as I adjust my headset and lean up in my seat. "What's good, my freak-nasty peeps…if you're just tuning in to the Tri-state area's hottest radio station, 93.3 *The Heat*, sit back…relax…light a candle…pour yourself a glass of your favorite wine…pull out your favorite lube… your favorite toy…or hit up that special someone…and prepare to be stimulated beyond your own imagination as we finish up tonight's topic: Man sharing. That's right, peeps. Tonight's segment goes out to the other woman. The Sideline Ho. The Side Chick. The Mistress. The Jump-off. The Home Wrecker. The One-Time Trick. Eff what ya heard, cheating is real. It's at an all-time high. And tonight we're gettin' down 'n' dirty. Is monogamy extinct? Is it nonexistent? Holla at ya boy. Let's turn up the heat 'n' get it in. 212-FreakMe…"

My phone lines are lit up. "Yo, what's good…you're on the air…"

"Yo, what's goodie, Mar*Sell*? This L-Rock from East Orange, yo."

"Aiight, aiight. What's on ya mind, playboy?"

"Yo, fam. Real shit. Niggahs stay trippin' wit' all that love shit. Fuc—*bleep* a bitch 'n' keep fuc—*bleep*—in'. I don't have sex to please a bitch. I have sex to get a nut. Feel me? All that extra shit is for the birds, man. I gotta girl 'n' three hoes 'n' they all know what it is."

What the fuck this gotta do with the topic? Dumb fuck! "Oh, word?

Well, how 'bout you let the listeners know what it is," I say, shaking my head and rolling my eyes up in my head. These ignorant-ass muhfuckas kill me.

"Man, they all know not to come at me wit' no bullshit. Feel me? Don't come to my crib. Don't step to my girl. Respect my space. And we good. Come outta pocket 'n' feel my wrath."

I glance over at Nina, who has a lollipop stuck between her plump lips. She shakes her head.

"So basically what you're saying is, ya girl is cool with sharing *you* with other broads?"

"Hell naw she ain't cool wit' it!" he snaps. "But she knows there's nothin' she can do about it. I holds it down at home. And I do what I do. I put this good D on 'em 'n' turn 'em out. But my girl knows I love her. She knows she's got my heart. But all these basic broads out here who stupid enough to let muhfuckas like me dig in that ass whenever we want, knowin' we got a girl at home, can fall back wit' all that lookin' for love ish."

"Oh, aiight. And you don't think ya girl sitting at home is just as stupid, knowing her man is out doing him?"

"Hell naw! Like I said, she knows what time it is. And my girl ain't goin' nowhere, anyway. So what's ya point, dawg?"

I chuckle, shaking my head. "Yo, the point is, stupid is what stupid does." I end the call. "Next caller."

"Hi, Mar*Sell*. This is LaToya from New Haven. I'm currently going through this situation right now. I mean, I don't know if I'm the main chick or the side chick."

Another silly, rabbit-ass broad. "Yo, why you say that, ma-ma? What's good?"

She sighs. "Well, I live with my baby father and we have sex like two to three times a week, but on those nights we don't, it's because he doesn't come home. He says he's out making money, but I go through his phone and find all kinds of naked pictures and dirty text messages from other females. And a few times I got in my car and rode around until I found his car."

I blink. "Damn, ma-ma. Sounds like you doin' too much. It's obvious you aren't the only one. But you're still with him. So riddle me this, ma-ma: Are you good with sharing ya man?"

There's a silent pause.

"Caller, you still there?"

"Y-yes." *Sniffles.* "H-he's even brought females into the house and sexed them while I was in the other room sleep." She blows her nose. "Sometimes I feel so stupid. But I'm so scared I'll lose him."

Sometimes? Really? "Well, babe...like I told the last caller. Stupid is what stupid does. If *you* choose to allow ya baby father to disrespect you, then you get what you get."

"So you judging me now? You think I deserve what he's doing to me?"

"Nah, ma-ma. No judgment. I think you *deserve* to get ya mind right 'n' do better. You already lost him. The day you let him dog you out, the moment you accepted his disrespect, he checked out on you. And if you want the truth, you've been reduced to being his in-house cum dump. So if that's all you aspire to be, then my advice, baby...strap up 'n' hope he doesn't bring you home something you can't get rid of. Next caller. You're on the air..."

"Hey, boo. This Marquita. I'm a Sideline Ho. And PROUD of it! What? My man pays my bills and gives me the dic—*bleep*, then goes home to his wife and kids. And trust. I got my shit together. I'm not some broke, uneducated chick. And I'm not the problem, or his wife's problem. He is. His stupid-ass wife knows he's a filthy-ass pig, yet she chooses to stay with him knowing he's out here breaking his wedding vows to her. Stupid ass."

"Wow. And you're good with being the sidepiece?"

"Yup. Why wouldn't I be? I get the benefits of having the man without having the drama and headaches of his lying, cheating-ass ways. At the end of the day, I might be on the sideline, but I can drop him at any time and move onto the next. These silly-ass chicks always wanna blame the other woman, like we're the enemy. No, hun. You're *sleeping* with him. You're sucking him. You're having his babies. If anything, you're the one doing too much. If you ask me, most of them dumb-ass hoes should be celebrating the sidepieces. We're the ones giving her man stress-free sex 'n' most times keeping him from coming home and beating her ass."

I blink. "Well, damn, baby. Tell us how you really feel."

"Ha. Truth hurts, boo. Them hoes married cheaters. Don't blame me for him cheating. Most of these tricks know what kind of man she has *before* she marries him or lets him knock her up. So why they stay acting surprised that he's out getting his creep on is beyond me!" She laughs. "All I'ma say to them stupid hoes is, see you in divorce court or the STD clinic!"

Click.

"Well, daaaaayum. She had some real fire in her veins, huh? I guess she told us." I laugh. "Yo, but on the real, like it or not, some of what she says is truth." I let 'em know we're going into a quick break. "But before we do, riddle me this: how many of you beauties who're being cheated on have played the other woman? Keep it gangsta, baby. What goes around comes around."

I remove my headset as Monica's "Sideline Ho" eases over the airwaves and check in with Marika real quick. Then hit up Carlos to see if he's down at the studio.

I glance over at Nina and smile as Soul Children's "I'll Be the Other Woman" eases over the air. She's taking them way back with this classic old-school joint. The shit cracks me up. The jump-off singing about being cool with dude cheating on his wife with her, but ain't checking for him if he's cheating on her too. Un*fuckin*-believable. But there are plenty of broads who think like this.

I ease my headphones back on and take the next caller...

"Hi, Mar*Sell*. This is Teirra from Paterson."

"Yo, what's good, Teirra. What's your situation, ma-ma?"

She sighs into the phone. "Well, sad to say, but right now I'm going through something similar to all the other callers. I've given my man six years of my life. Fast-forward three children and a home later, I find out he's been cheating on me, and now I'm not sure if she's the sideline piece, or if I am. And the crazy thing is, he's been fu—*bleep*—ing her for five years. Not once has he ever given me any signs that he was cheating on me. He's home every night, in our bed, answers my calls whenever I call him through-out the day, and makes sure I'm taken care of in and out of the bedroom."

"Damn. How'd you find out?"

"The *bitch* called me at my job! She said she couldn't take the lies and fakeness anymore and thought it was time we had a talk woman to woman. And you won't believe what she had the audacity to say to me." She doesn't give me a chance to ask. "That whore *told* me I needed to let him go because he was no good for me. That he doesn't want me. That bitch wants me to leave my man 'cause he's no-good for me, but he's good enough for her. Bitch, please."

"So whatchu gonna do?"

"I don't know. I still love him, though."

I cock an eyebrow and shake my head. "Yo, check it. You need to love *you* more, ma-ma. Unless you think you deserve to be reduced to ya man's sidepiece, my advice: cut ya losses. Let ya Facebook gal-pal have him. Let me know how you make it. Next caller."

"This is Raqaunnaleesha from Union."

What the fuck?! I'm not even about to try'n pronounce that shit. "Yo, what's good with you, ma-ma?"

She grunts. "What's good is *that* dirty bitch, Marquita, calling in. I'm the wife. Always have been, always will be. Ten years. And what? That stupid ho calling-in with a buncha damn lies. Yeah, that bitch been fuc—*bleep*—ing my husband. But that trifling ho forgot to tell you how many times she's tried to get pregnant by him. Yeah, Marquita, trick-ass bitch! Why you ain't tell him how many times *you* fished through the trash for my husband's used condoms, you filthy bitch! And how many times *you've* poked holes in 'em just so you can have what I got?"

"Oh, word? Daaaaamn. It's like that?"

"Yeah, it's like that. The thirst is real, boo. That skank-bitch knows I got a good man. And a damn good father to my two kids. And she's jealous. Yeah, she might get the dic—*bleep* and she might even get a few dollars out of him, but there's two things that bitch will *never* get. And that's his baby. Or for him to put a ring on it."

"Yo, hold up, ma-ma. Let me get this straight. So you're good with sharing ya man, is that what you're saying?"

"Uh, nooo. Follow the yellow brick road, boo. What I said is, that bitch will never have what I got. No matter how many times my man crawls up in her bed. Honey, get your shit together. You got on national radio and made a fool of yourself. It doesn't matter if my man spends the night with you, his home and his heart is somewhere else. Aren't you tired of playing the sidepiece? You disrespectful bitches need to grow up and find you your own man."

"Um, dig, ma-ma. No disrespect. But, uh, sounds to me like *you* need to get *your* shit together as well. You've just made a fool out of ya'self, too. Aren't you tired of playing the role of disrespected wife? Aren't you tired of playing victim? You know what ya man is doing 'n' you sounding like one big hot mess, ma-ma. Be well, baby. Next caller…"

"Yo, fam, this ya boy, Two-Tone. Bedstuy, niggah, what? Do or Die! Stand up! I wanna give a shout-out to all my niggahs who still payin' for pus—*bleep*—y after the club let out."

I frown. *Yo, this muhfucka…*

I let the retarded muhfucka live and disconnect on his ass. We go into another quick break. I stand and stretch my arms up over my head. Then crack my neck from side to side, reaching for my cell. The chiming sound lets me know it's a text from Marika. I type in my password, then retrieve my text. Marika sends me a picture of herself posing in front of the mirror in black heels and her panties on. My mouth waters.

ME: DAMN! Y U FUCKIN W/ME?

MARIKA: U MAKE ME FEEL SEXY

Nina waves her hands to get my attention. We're about to go back on the air. I hit Marika back real quick. Let her know I gotta run. Then tell her to hit me with some more of them sexy-ass flicks.

I sit back in my seat and adjust my headset as Mary J's "No Happy Holidays" fades out. I glance at the time. It's eleven thirty. *Thirty more minutes!* I'm ready to get home and crawl up in bed with my wife. Real shit.

"Yo, what's good, my freaks…we're back with more *Creepin' 'n' Freakin' After Dark*. And man, listen. Y'all got the phone lines going nuts tonight. And judging by the number of listeners who've already called in, infidelity appears to be an epidemic. Let me get back to the phone lines." I pick up line three. "Yo, what's good; it's ya boy, Mar*Sell*. Who's this?"

"This is LaRhonda from Uptown."

"Oh, aiight, LaRhonda from Uptown. What's good, ma-ma?"

"Mmph. I'ma tell you what's good, boo. This good-good; that's what. Them bitches out here calling in and hating on us side chicks. Ha! Call me what you want, like I'm supposed to give a fu—*bleep* about what your invisible asses think. I'm still that chick. And, bitch, *trust*. I'm coming fo' yo' man. Get used to it. Because bitches like me ain't going nowhere. We don't mind sharing. At least, I know I don't. All I want is the dic—*bleep*. He leaves me with a smile on his face. Yeah, he's running home to you. But I'm the one he's thinking of when he's lying in bed next to you. I'm the one he's missing. I'm the one he can't wait to see again.

"I'm the one he's sneaking text messages and phone calls to. I'm the one he can't get enough of. Not you, hon. So for all those miserable-ass broads sitting at home, or riding around tryna find where their man's getting his creep on at, get yo' life, dumb-ass. I'm happy with playing the sideline while you play wifey or the mainline chick. Ha! The real fools in the room are you, clown-ass hoes. I get to fuc—*bleep* your man, run his wallet, then send him home to ya stressed-out ass. I don't wanna keep *him*, boo-boo. You do. Truth be told, I feel sorry for you."

Click.

"Damn, yo. She just hit us, straight like that. Raw 'n' hard."

The next four callers go off on the women who get down with playing the sidepiece, calling them all types of snake-bitches, whores, home wreckers, etc.

"Daaaamn," I say, feeling a headache creeping up in the center of my forehead. "Y'all goin' in on the side chicks like they're really ya problem. Like one caller already stated, she's *not* your problem. Ya man is. And, real shit. I gotta agree. But know this, if you rockin' with a mofo who creeps, you are not the cause. He or she makes a conscious choice to step outta the relationship to get it in with someone else, whether it's a one-time stick 'n' move, a weekend fling, or some ongoing affair, it's purposeful, my peeps. And that's real shit.

"But, yo, hold up. Don't get it twisted. Broads are real grimy, too. They cheat just as much as the fellas do. The only difference is, chicks real sweet with how they get it in. Ya heard. Bottom line… the only home wrecker in the room is the one who steps outta their drawz to get it in with someone else without consent from their mate. And for you dumbo broads putting in applications for all those vacant sidepiece spots, don't feel the least bit guilty for gettin' ya swerve on. Do you. But don't be messy with ya shit. Don't disrespect a mofo's situation just because he is. Stay in ya lane. Play ya position. Respect the game. You have ya reasons for doing what you do just like the chick who stays taking her man back or frontin' like she doesn't know what time it is, does.

"My advice to everyone else who ain't beat for all the extras that come with creepin' is this: Keep them freak flags flying. High. Keep shit spicy in them sheets. Keep them lines of communication open. Keep ya sexy on. And, yeah, fellas, you need to keep ya situations tight, too. Give ya women something to look forward to. Give 'em a reason to want to jump up 'n' down on ya bone without you having to ask for it. Stimulate her mind. Seduce her. That is all I'ma say on that. Get at me on Twitter or Instagram. Thanks for tuning into another bangin' segment of 93.3's *Creepin' 'n' Freakin' After Dark*. It's been real. Until the next time…keep it sexy, keep it wet…always keep it ready. I'm out."

TWENTY-SEVEN

Marika

Hot breath.

Slick tongue.

I spread my quivering thighs wider, opening my sweet pussy to Nairobia's gaze. She traces a finger along my delicate folds, opening me wider, taking in my cum-and-spit slick cunt. Heat spreads like wildfire through my veins as she groans into my wet, tingling flesh. "Aah, mmmm…so delicious. So pretty."

She licks, softly at first, swiping the entire pad of her wicked tongue over my slit and up my clit, swirling around the velvety pink nub. It swells and throbs as she delicately pulls it between her teeth with a light sucking motion.

I fight to catch my breath as Nairobia lovingly caresses my clit, then sucks and licks my pussy lips. Nibbling. Kissing. Licking. Laving. Nairobia's tongue scorches over my sex as she circles my clit, then plunges inside of me.

I gasp. "Oh yes, oh yes, oh yes…Mmmm, yessss…tongue my pussy. Yes."

She stops licking and starts sucking, alternating quick up-and-down strokes with darting and dipping, fucking into me.

I am beside myself.

Crazy with want.

Crazy with need.

Crazy with desire.

Nairobia takes my pussy with an open-mouthed kiss, purring, "Give me your sweet juices."

I welcome her tongue with a deep moan, knowing she's pulling another orgasm from me. I am almost there. She spears me with her tongue in anticipation.

Yes, God!

My body purrs.

Nairobia raises her face, licks her lips and smiles softly. "My mouth waters to suck more of your sweet juices. My own cunt drips for you."

I gaze down at her through lusty slits. And then she disappears, both her hands on my thighs, parting them wide as her warm tongue feathers across my clit, sending chills along my spine. She whispers something I am unable to decipher in her native tongue that sends me teetering on the brink of climax.

"Mm-hmm…oooh," I whimper, losing myself in the sensations flowing through me. "Yes, yes, yessssss…"

Nairobia whispers, her hot breath against my cunt, "Precious pussy."

My ass lifts slightly up off the bed and Nairobia cups and squeezes it, hungrily feasting on my flowing honey. Sweet and thick and heated.

Marsha Ambrosius' "Tears" plays. Nairobia hums the tune into my cunt, her curling tongue-tricks causing me to claw at the sheets.

Oh, how I love coming in a woman's loving mouth, on her sensual tongue, over her sumptuous lips. If I could, if I were to, ever fall in love with a woman, Nairobia would be the type of woman to capture my heart. Sensual and raw and rough. Feminine, bold, and deliciously aggressive.

I close my eyes and get lost in the wet, smacking sounds of her mouth. Get lost in the wetness of my dripping cunt.

"Oooh, yes," I whisper.

My nipples tighten as she licks over my sweet pussy again. I grow wetter over her tongue, bathing her in sensual heat.

My breaths come quickly as I glance over at Marcel. Behold his bare chest, packed with rigid slabs of muscle. His flat stomach muscles ripple as he takes in the view. His veined length bobs and pulses as a bead of nectar clings to the head of his dick, glistening in the glow of candlelight.

Marcel leans forward and extends his tongue and licks his precum.

My mouth opens, drools, for a little taste of him.

He watches.

He touches himself.

His nipples.

His balls.

His cock.

My nipples pucker tighter. Ache to be sucked. Long to be pinched.

"Spread your thighs wider," Nairobia commands, rising above me, then positioning herself between them. Her eyes flash with excitement.

I blink up at her. Cupping my breasts from the bottom, she nearly circles them with her soft hands. Avoiding my nipples, she lightly kneads them, then tightens her grip on my breasts and my skin heats as they begin to swell.

"Mmm…oooh…lick 'em," I beg.

Nairobia lowers her head; her mouth barely touching my skin, her breath laps over the sensitive tips, causing me to arch to her, begging and panting, as she slides her hot creamy sex over my mine; silky smooth, sensual skin pooling in juices.

Sweet heaven.

She nips her way up my neck to my ear, then kisses a line down my jaw, then back to my ear. She nibbles softly at my lobe and then sucks it into her lush mouth. Her body against mine, she has my pussy and ass on fire; every inch of my flesh inflamed.

God how I love the touch of a woman.

Pleasure rips through me and I fight back a scream.

Clit to clit, I arch into the flames as Liv Warfield sings about her soul lifting to a higher place. Nairobia grinds into me, her wet cunt dissolving into mine, melting like liquid silk. Smooth and warm.

It's a sweet torture.

Excruciating arousal.

Rapture.

The sheets beneath me are soaked. Soaked by need. Soaked by want. Soaked by unbridled hunger and passion.

I let out a moan. Glide my hands down Nairobia's back as she kisses me, stroking her tongue deeply over mine, allowing me to taste my sticky juices, to savor the sweet musk clinging on her tongue, drenched on her lips.

Mouthwatering cunt.

Hot and juicy.

And on fire.

Grinding and bucking.

"Yeah, that's right," Marcel says huskily. "Grind them pussies together. *J'aime l'odeur de vos chattes humides.*"

I moan as he tells us how he loves the smell of our wet cunts. How he wants to fuck himself deep into our wetness.

Nairobia lowers her mouth, letting her breaths torment my already throbbing peaks. She darts her tongue to flick kisses along the sides, swirling it all around my areola, purposefully, methodically, neglecting my nipples.

My back bows to get closer to her mouth. "Suck them," I rasp out. "Please."

"Like this?" she murmurs, wrapping her lips around the tip, wetting it, licking it, then blowing on it before languidly moving on to the other.

For the love of God...

"Nairobia..." Pupils dilated, voice flooded with lust, I beg. Whimper. "Fuck me. Please."

"Is your sweet pussy horny for me?"

"Y-yes," I push out breathlessly. "It's so horny for your mouth, your tongue, your fingers."

She grinds harder. Her hips move rhythmically to India.Arie's "Beautiful." I thrust up into her, moan into her, latching onto one of her swaying breasts, sucking her nipple into my wet, juicy mouth.

Nairobia groans, her hand slinking between us, her long finger finding its way to my clit. I dig my nails into her ass.

"Mmm. *Zo nat. Zo heet. Zo lief,*" she murmurs. "So wet. So hot. So sweet."

Yes, yes, yes...

"Yeah, baby," Marcel urges, his voice thick with heat. "Grab that fat, juicy ass. I wanna run my dick all up in that."

Nairobia moans and kisses her way back down to my breasts, tonguing my left nipple into a rigid peak before suckling my right nipple into her hot mouth. She licks, then sucks, then nips, pushing me closer to nirvana. One finger, two fingers, then three, then four, then five.

In and out.

In and out.

"Yes, fuck my pussy," I whisper before sucking in my breath and reveling in the sensation. Burning. Stretching.

"Oooh, yessss…Aaaah, yesss…fuck me. Mmm, yes, yes, yes…"

Amel Larrieux's "For Real" plays and the room goes blurry around me as my orgasm builds and builds, tightening and coiling in my belly. I squeeze my eyes shut. Curl my fingers into tight fists. Grind my teeth. Oh God, I can't take much more of this. I am stretched tight over her fingers. My ass bucks. My pussy clenches. Unclenches.

It aches.

It throbs.

I need dick.

Marcel's dick.

I need to be fucked.

Want to be fucked.

Marcel fucking me; and fucking her, alternately, filling me, and filling her, with his cream.

Everything I am heats and burns, starting at the balls of my feet, then roaring upward. My ass. My pussy. My clit. My belly. My breasts. My skin.

Embroiled in desire.

I am floating. Dangling over the edge of delirium.

Marcel groans. The rapid *slap-slap* of his dick sliding in and out of the palm of his hand, up and down his shaft, he grunts and stands; dips at the knees.

"I'm about to bust this nut. Aaah, shit, motherfuck…I'm ready to get up in that pussy, yo…"

Then in one swift move, I am on my back and Nairobia is turned around to straddle my head. She murmurs in Dutch, *"Maken graag mijn kut. Voeden mijn poesje je tong.* Make love to my cunt. Feed my pussy your tongue."

She lowers her heat against my lips. My fingers spread her wet lips, and I open my mouth and feast, greedily tonguing her.

She spasms around my tongue and fingers, causing me to gasp.

Marcel is hovering over us. His balls swinging back and forth as he brings himself to the edge. "Yeah, baby...eat that pussy..."

He reaches over and slaps Nairobia's ass.

She moans loudly, then fucks into my mouth and sucks on my clit, her fingers fucking into my dewy slit.

My eyes glaze.

I am coming.

She is coming.

Marcel is coming.

Delirious with pleasure, I drink in Nairobia's steamy juices; sucking and sucking and sucking, feeding my need; swallowing her in.

Every last drop...

TWENTY-EIGHT

Marcel

I'm sitting behind the keyboards at the studio—eyeing one of the engineers as he maneuvers a few levers up and down the expensive equipment with his headphones over his ears, rhythmically nodding his head to a beat—when my cell rings.

I glance at Carlos through the glass as he plays the piano in the booth. It's a little after midnight. We've been here for the past four hours working on the tracks to his new album, *Seduction*. And so far the shit is sounding sexy as fuck.

"What's good, baby…?" I get up from the system and walk over into the lounge area.

"Thinking about you," Marika says all low 'n' sexy.

I grin. "Oh, word? I've been thinking about you, too. How was the Empowerment luncheon?"

"It was great. The whole day has been very inspiring and encouraging. It's nice to see so many women from all ages and walks of life coming together."

I smile, nodding my head. "Word. That's wassup, baby. I wish I could be there with you."

"I wish you were here, too. I do understand, though. Duty calls. But you're here in mind and spirit."

"No doubt. And I'ma be deep in that body soon as you bring ya sexy ass home."

"Oooh, I love the sound of that. Promise?"

"Oh, it's most def a promise," I say low and deep. "You already know. So whatchu gettin' into the rest of the night?"

"They're having a private reception party here in one of the ballrooms. Then I might head to the lounge for a nightcap before turning in."

"Oh, aiight. No slot machines?"

"Already played."

I chuckle knowingly. Marika digs playing the penny machines. That's all she'll fuck with. She'll take a grand and sit all night playing three machines in a row until one of them hits. Then she'll cash out and spin off. But me? I'ma run them tables. I'll drop ten grand—my max, and play them shits to win.

"I won sixteen hundred," she says coolly.

"That's what's up, baby." I laugh. "Now you can take ya man out to lunch."

"It'll be my pleasure." She wants to know where I am. I tell her at the studio with Carlos. "Oh, tell that fine man I said hello. I can't wait to hear the new album."

"Yeah, it's gonna be a real panty soaker, for sure."

"Ooh, I bet. I'm really glad you signed him."

"No doubt. Me too. But enough about that. You miss me, baby?"

"Always," she says softly.

"Yeah, that's what I'm talkin' about."

"You miss me?"

I smirk. "Yeah, what you think? You didn't give me any pussy this morning. Left up outta the crib mad early leaving my dick all dry 'n' shit."

She laughs. "I gave you some last night?"

"Yeah, aiight. What that got to do with this morning, huh? See.

You stay on that BS. You know this dick needs its morning dose of that wet-wet."

She laughs. "Horny man, you. Is that all you ever think about?"

I grin. "Nah, I think about that wet throat, and that *phat*, juicy ass. But you already know how much I love that wet, tight pussy."

She moans. "Yeah, I do. But let me hear it again, anyway."

"I miss that sweet, wet pussy, baby."

"Mmmm. And what are you going to do with it?"

"C'mon, baby. Don't start that shit. You know I'm in the studio."

"And? When has that ever stopped you?"

I smirk, shaking my head. "Yo, you terrible. You know that, right?"

She's not fazed by the comment. "What are you going to do with this wet pussy, Marcel?" Her voice is low and sexy.

"Yo, c'mon, stop playing. You already know."

"I want to hear it, Marcel. Make my pussy purr, daddy. Tell me what you want to do to it."

I lick my lips. "Shit. I can't wait for you to get home so I can get you up in them sheets so I can slide my tongue all up between them sweet lips and suck on that clit, then slow-fuck this hard dick into you. Damn, baby. I wanna lick, tongue, and fuck it down, period, point blank." I grab my dick. "Fuck. Just talking about it, got my shit on rock. I need my dick sucked."

She laughs. "You're so bad."

"I stay fuckin' horny for you, yo."

"I know you do, baby," she coos. "Ooh, I have to go." She sucks her teeth. "Now I have to go back up and change my panties. You have me soaked. I hate when you do this to me."

"Nah, you love it."

She sighs. "Yeah, when I know it's going to be followed by a hard dick and a delicious fuck."

I reach down and squeeze the head of my dick. "Shit. How you think I feel, baby? Now I gotta go back up around a buncha muh-fuckas with my shit stretchin' down my leg."

She teases. "Baby, stop. You love it when the boys glance down and see all that dick. Admit it. You're a cock tease. You love seeing the look on their faces."

"Hahahahahaha. Yo, you shot out, baby. But, uh, no comment."

She joins in my laughter. "Uh-huh. None needed."

"Yeah, well, your wet tongue is *needed* on this hard dick."

She moans. "I'll make it up to you when I get home tomorrow. Promise. In the meantime send me a video of you sucking and playing with that big, beautiful dick. I need something to get me through the night."

I pull in my bottom lip. "Word? That's what you want, baby?"

"No. I want the real thing," she says, causing the head of my dick to swell. "But for now I'll take what I can get."

I grin. "I got you, sexy." I glance over at the booth again. Carlos is still in there doing his thing. "But, dig. What's it looking like down there? Any eye candy?"

She chuckles. "You know I'm *strictly dickly.*"

I smirk, glancing over my shoulder. "Yeah, aiight. Maybe ninety percent of the time." I laugh. "But the other ten percent you on pussy patrol. Clit stalking. Who you fooling? You know I know."

"Oh, hush," she chides playfully. "I can't stand you."

"Yeah, aiight. Keep lying to ya'self. You can't live without me."

"I wouldn't want to," she says softly.

I smile inside. "Aaah, that's what I'm talkin' about. So tell me. What them beauties looking like? Anyone catch your eye on the low?"

She chuckles. "There were a few who I'd say could get it."

I pull in my bottom lip. "Damn. All that sweet pussy in one spot."

"But none as sweet as mine."

It isn't a question. Marika already knows what it is. Still, I know enough to make it clear. "Oh, you already know, baby."

"Mmhmm. I thought so." She laughs. "Ohmygod! Wait! You are not going to believe this. Guess who's here?"

I take a seat on the sofa and prop a foot up on the wood table. "Who?"

"Ramona. And I almost didn't recognize her. She's dyed her hair a fuchsia color."

I furrow my brow. "Who is that?" She tells me the Spanish chick we fucked the night of Laila's album release party. I frown, a mixture of surprise and befuddlement on my face, followed by flashes of that night. It's been over a month since we rocked in the sheets with her. I swallow back a rush of filthy thoughts flooding my brain. I grab at my dick. "Yo, get the fuck outta here. Word? What the fuck is she doing there? And why you calling her Ramona? I thought her name was Maribel or some shit like that."

"Marisol," Marika corrects. "She first said her name was Marisol. But today her nametag said Ramona. And she claims she was invited."

"Interesting. Did she come at you crazy?"

"Surprisingly, not. She was as sweet as pie."

"Yo, let me find out she's stalking you, now."

"Ohmygod. Don't say that. It's an isolated incident, Mar*Sell*. Let's not blow it out of proportion. I haven't heard from her since the flower and phone call incident. You know I told you I thought she was a little off that night we had her, but…"

"But now you think she isn't?"

"I'm not saying that. Maybe I was a bit presumptive. After all, it isn't like either of us has heard from her since I kindly asked her to leave us alone."

I raise a brow. "True." Come to think of it, she hasn't called into the radio station either on Thursday nights.

"Besides, she seemed really surprised to see me here when she walked over and gave me a big hug."

"Mmm. I don't know, baby. Something doesn't sound right."

"Although I could have done without the hug, I don't want to turn this into more than what it is. Whatever that is. I kept it cordial. But then right after the luncheon, she turns around and sends me a friend request on Facebook."

I shoot up in my seat. "She did what? Yo, now she's tryna be on some ole other shit."

"I went onto Facebook and saw it with my own eyes. I didn't accept her, though. But I think she's following me instead."

"Yeah, I can see that." I shake my head. "Yo, she's fucking buggin'."

"I don't mean it like that, silly. I meant on Twitter."

"Yeah, well, I did."

"Well, she hasn't said or done anything to cause alarm. Maybe it's coincidence that she's here."

Yeah, right. Coincidence my ass, maybe that ho's cat-shit crazy. "And she just happens to hit you up with a friend request, too, right? Yeah, okay."

"Maybe. I mean, after all, my contact info was in the packets everyone received."

"Nah, I don't know. That shit doesn't sit right, babe."

"Don't go getting all *CSI* on me. She seemed harmless," Marika offers calmly. "Worst-case scenario, she asks for another round in the sheets with us, and I have to kindly shut her down, again."

"Or her ass's really a fuckin' nutcase." I let out a heavy breath. "You're awfully calm about this, though."

"That's because I'm trying to give her the benefit of the doubt. I'm taking your advice and not letting her get in my head. I'm not saying I trust her. But she did apologize for how she came at me."

"Yo, the last thing we need in our lives is some crazy-ass broad tryna turn up. But I'm thinkin' this chick might become a mutha-fuckin' problem."

Why the fuck it seem like most of the broads with the killer pussy are fuckin' psycho-ass whack-jobs?!

Marika sighs. "Let's hope not."

TWENTY-NINE

Marika

"Your pussy tasted so sweet on my tongue…"

That's what that crazy-bitch had said to me as I drained my wineglass.

Okay, so maybe I should've listened to my gut and gone straight up to my suite, instead of going to the Ultra Lounge here at the hotel. But I didn't. Instead I found myself sitting in a leather chair with my third drink in my hand and a spectacular view of the Atlantic Ocean, talking to Ramona, or Marisol, or whoever she is—who, admittedly, is a beautiful woman.

But I noticed something about her. Something odd. The more she drank, the more vacant her eyes looked. Glazed. Empty.

The compliment had caught me totally by surprise when she leaned forward and said it. Although she'd been discreet in her revelation, it still made me feel uncomfortable just the same.

"The three of us were so good together…"

"We were simply enjoying each other's company."

"Oh, stop. Don't play coy, mami. We did more than just *enjoy* each other's company. We enraptured each other. Now that I enjoyed. Being ravished. Being fucked savagely. And would you like to know what I enjoyed *most*? I enjoyed riding your pretty face, feeling your tongue wedged between my pussy lips…"

"Please. Let's not have this discussion here."

"*That night is all I've been thinking about. And that husband of yours, I can't get his naked body out of my head. All of that long dick. All of that masculine beauty on display for the both of us to savor...*"

That remark was my cue to get up and leave. I glanced at the time. Then graciously stood and excused myself to head up to my suite, but not before she'd gotten the chance to growl out her last words: "*That night in that hotel room, my pussy was his. But this tight ass was all yours...*"

I blink, staring at my reflection in the mirror as I remove my diamond choker and earrings, then placing them inside the safe.

I don't believe this mess.

I swallow, hard. Step out of my clothes. Remove my bra and panties. Then saunter into the bathroom and step into the bath, easing down into the steaming water.

I think to go back out into the bedroom and retrieve my phone from my purse. To call Marcel and share with him what transpired up in the lounge, but I decide against it. The scented bath is relaxing. The hot water surrounding me is soothing. I can feel it slowly melting my tension away.

I lay my head back against the headrest, and close my eyes, inhaling deeply. Marcel's naked body comes into view. His strong hands cupping my ass, kneading my flesh, parting and spreading my ass, pausing as the head of his dick touches my open slit, then stretches me around his width, his thickness, as he pushes inward.

My arms pinned over my head, my legs stretched wide, I imagine Marcel digging his thick fingers into my waist, then slipping down to my hips, pulling me into him, onto the length of him and him fucking me gently, pulling out to the head only to ease his way back in. The wetter I grow, the easier he glides in, the welcoming warmth of my pussy engulfing him.

I sink further down into the tub, reveling in the sensation. Submerged in bubbles, my breasts bobbing in the water, I can feel how slick my pussy is. And I haven't even touched myself…yet.

All I can feel is Marcel; him inside of me, him fucking into me, taunting my cunt, flinging me perilously closer to an orgasm. Slowly, I trail my palms over my breasts, lightly pulling at my nipples, twisting them. They immediately pucker, sending a delicious shiver through me.

"Oooh," I moan, grinding my ass into the bottom of the tub, feeling the heat of the water as it sloshes up against my pussy, licking into my clit. "Aah, yes…"

My hands travel over my belly, over my waist, then along my inner thighs. I imagine Marcel's lips against my flesh, against my weeping pussy, as I glide my forefinger over my lips, pulling them open. My free hand traces over my clit, finding it swollen and sensitive. It pulses and aches.

I suck in warm air. Gasp. Exquisite tension simmers between my legs. I pinch my clit, setting my whole body on fire. When I sink my fingers into my cunt, my entire body spasms. My toes open and close, grasping bubbles between them.

I moan softly, easing my fingers from my pussy.

And then…

There's a knock at the door. I barely hear it. It's a light rapping, at first, and I have to strain to be sure. The knocking continues. Becomes more incessant.

What the hell?

I squint through my haze. Listen. There it is again. The knocking. *Who could possibly be at my door at this hour?*

I scramble from the tub, reaching for a plush white towel, wrapping it around my body before tossing it for the robe hanging behind the door. I use the towel to wrap my head instead, then head for the door.

"Yes? Can I help you?" I say, standing at the door. I peer through the peephole.

"It's me," says a soft feminine voice. "Can we talk?"

I frown. *Oh you have got to be fucking kidding me!*

I swing open the door. "*Ramona?* W-what are you doing here?"

She bats her lashes, tossing her hair. She sweeps her gaze over my half-wrapped body, beads of water still clinging to my skin.

"I hoped we could talk."

This chick can't be serious. Is she? I scowl, pulling my robe tighter. "I believe you said more than enough up in the lounge. So I'm going to need you to leave." I go to shut the door in her face, but she blocks it with her foot. And hand.

"Wait. *Please.* All I need is a few moments of your time. I promise. I won't take up much more than that."

Reluctantly, I step back, opening the door and inviting her in. "You have two minutes." I cross into the sitting room, then turn to face her, folding my arms across my chest. "Okay, what is so important that you felt it necessary to hunt me down and come up to my suite?"

I hold my breath, waiting.

She frowns. "Don't be nasty. And let's not be foolish. I didn't *hunt* you down. That sounds so…*stalker-ish.*"

"Well…it's starting to look pretty *stalker-ish* to me."

"Oh, look who's sounding paranoid. I simply found out which room you were staying in." She opens her arms dramatically. "And here I am."

"Oh, is that so?" I say in disbelief. "I suppose just like you *found* out I would be at this exact hotel speaking?"

She shrugs. "That was simply fate. But to answer your question: I'm here because you raced out of the lounge so quickly that I didn't get a chance to finish what I was saying. And besides, I wanted to check on you."

I give her a look of disbelief. "Oh, I think you said enough for the both of us. Actually, you said more than you should have. And as you can see, I'm fine. So why are you *following* me?"

She puts a hand up. "Wait a minute. Don't flatter yourself. I'm *not* following *you*. I mean you're a sweet piece of ass and all, but don't go there, boo."

I huff. "Then why are you here?"

"Aww, *mami* don't be like that. I planned on staying away, I mean, I wanted to. But I can't stop thinking about our magnificent night together. Then seeing you at that luncheon earlier brought all those sweet memories flooding back. And I found myself listening to you today give your precious speech, getting all wet and horny. Seeing you and hearing you had my pussy so juicy sitting in my seat. All I kept thinking about is your tongue. And that long purple dildo you fucked into my ass."

The air around me suddenly goes thick. "That night was a lot of fun. But please don't make me regret it. It was a one-night stand. So please. Let it go."

"Are you serious?" she says incredulously. "*Let it go?* Just forget that it ever happened? Oh, no. Sorry, *mami*. I can't do that. I know what went down with the three of us was supposed to be strictly No-Strings-Attached sex. And maybe for you it was. But not for me. Oh, no. It was so much more. I felt a connection."

Memory floods me. The way she rode Marcel's dick. The gentle way he coaxed her, touched her, and...made love to her. The way she looked at him. And now this bitch stands here confirming what

I'd already suspected that night, what I'd already felt deep in my gut. That she wouldn't be able to keep things in perspective. That she'd potentially try to turn it into something more than what it was.

Sex. Uninhibited fucking. A meaningless ménage à trois.

"You need to leave," I say, cinching the belt around my robe tighter. "Clearly you're intoxicated."

"I'm not drunk," she says, defiantly placing a hand up on her hip, nostrils flaring. Her Spanish accent sounds thicker than I remember hearing it.

I narrow my eyes. "Then you're in need of some serious medications for those delusions."

Hands fisted at her side, she snaps, "I'm not crazy, *puta*. Don't ever call me *that* again. And I'm *not* leaving. Not until I'm done talking."

I blink. Okay, so she *is* a little off, like I initially thought. So provoking her might not be the wisest thing to do at this very moment. And the last thing I need is a scene or hotel security swarming in, like members of a SWAT team.

Stay calm. And keep this bitch calmer. I sigh. "Sweetie, I didn't call you *crazy*." *Although you obviously are.* "I said you were *delusional*."

"Same difference," she snaps. Her eyes grow cold. "And I'm neither. I know what I felt. And I know what I saw. You were uncomfortable seeing the chemistry between that fine, chocolate man of yours and me. You couldn't stand seeing me handle his dick better than you. You saw how he loved being up in this sweet *coño*."

I shift from one foot to the other. "That is utterly ridiculous. What happened that night between the three of us was strictly sex; nothing more. It was to fulfill a need, a want, for three consenting adults. That's it."

"So the two of you *used* me. Is that it? You preyed on me!"

"You weren't used. And we didn't *prey* on you. If anything, you *preyed* on us. That *is* why you're standing here now, isn't it?"

"I already told you why I'm here! Don't play games with me."

Oh this bitch's elevator is definitely stuck in between floors. I shake my head, grappling with growing frustration and annoyance. "Listen, Ramona…that is your name, right?"

She gives me a dirty look. "No, *puta*. It's your momma's."

I blink. "Let's not turn this ugly, okay? I'm not calling you out of your name so I'd ask that you refrain from doing the same. Please."

Neck rolling, finger jabbing the air. "Well, *you* called me *crazy*. So I'll call you whatever I want."

I cast my eyes around the room for a weapon in case things get messy and I have to fight this bitch and beat her to death. My gaze lands on the lamps on the end tables.

"Listen," I say calmly. The last thing I want is a brawl ensuing. And I definitely don't want the hotel's security getting involved. Still, I refuse to allow her to bully or disrespect me. "I'm not going to get into this with you. Clearly, you've had a full night at the bar and there's no talking rational to you."

She waves me on dismissively. "Oh, obviously you're the *delusional* one, hon, so you go right ahead and keep telling yourself whatever you need to in order to sleep at night. But if you *think* pretending you didn't see it, the connection, for yourself is going to change anything, you're wrong." She swipes a strand of hair from her face. "You were jealous that night. And rightfully so…"

My brow furrows.

Her lashes flutter.

"Mar*Sell* is a wonderful lover in bed…"

I cringe.

"And the way you fucked into my ass…" She licks her lips.

My face flushes as I stare wordlessly at her.

"I never knew taking it in the ass could feel so damn good. I'd never come so hard in my life than I did that night with the two of you. You and Mar*Sell*..." She pauses, licking her lips again, relishing in the memory. "Fucked me so good."

I blink.

I am not even aware that I am holding my breath until I start to feel lightheaded and my lungs start to burn.

"Ramona, what is it that you *really* want? From me...from us?"

She tilts her head. "I want love...I want *you* to disappear."

I suck in my breath.

"And I *want* your husband."

I blink.

"But for now"—she undoes the sash to her coat—"I want *you* to tongue my pussy, then..." Her coat drops to the floor and gathers around her ankles. "Fuck me *en mi culo*, again."

THIRTY

Marcel

I'm sitting in my office staring at the pile of contracts in front of me. It's been two weeks since that shit with Marika and Marisol—or Ramona, aka Anonymous or whatever other alias that nutty broad goes by—popped off down in Atlantic City, and so far neither of us have heard from her since then.

I still can't believe she told Marika she *wanted* me. That she wanted her to disappear. Then turned around and told her she wanted her to eat her pussy and fuck her in her ass again.

I asked Marika had she. Eaten her out. Fucked her. And the crazy thing is, a part of me lusted at the idea. Hoped that she'd fucked her raw, fucked her out of our lives. But when she averted her eyes, fidgeted with her diamond choker, then met my stare with silence, my fuckin' heart leapt in my throat.

"Is that what *you* think of me?" she finally asked incredulously. "How dare you ask me some damn mess like that? Fucking her was the furthest thing from my mind."

And, yes, I was relieved. Real shit.

But, then the following day, that fuckin' broad hit me up, talkin' reckless. "Did your wife tell you how she fucked her purple cock into me, stretching my asshole over every inch of her?"

"Yo, fuck outta here, man. I'm not tryna hear that dumb shit. Your ass is delusional."

She huffed. "Oh, what, you don't believe me, *papi*. Check your email; you can see it for yourself. My asshole fucked open by your wife."

"Yo, real shit, I'm asking you nicely. Make this the last time you call me. Keep fuckin' around and I'ma have ya ass arrested for harassment."

Then she flipped her lid. "Motherfucker! You pussy! You ain't shit, Mister Big Shot Mar*Sell* Kennedy! You turn my life upside down, then want to act like what we shared doesn't mean anything to you."

My nose flared. "Yo, will you listen to ya'self? You sound fuckin' ridiculous right now. It was meaningless sex. You stupid fuck! That shit wasn't 'bout nothing, but catching a nut."

She snorted. "Oh, really, Mar*Sell*? Well, I don't believe you. It *did* mean something. It still does. And I know it meant something to you as well, *papi*. Fight it if you want, *papi*. One day you'll see how we're meant to be together."

I rubbed my throbbing head. "I see there is no reasoning with you. I don't know why I thought that was possible. You're insane. Real shit, baby. You're crazy as fuck, yo."

"Motherfucker! *Voy a hacer de su vida un infierno viviente!* Do you hear me, Marcel? Cross me if you want, I promise you. I will make your life a living hell! You will pay for using me, mother-fucker! You and that stuck-up bitch of yours! You're mine! And if I can't have you, neither can she!"

I stared at the phone baffled at how she'd easily flip her lid from one extreme to the other, cussing and threatening me in one breath, then begging me to feed her this dick again in the next.

I finally had enough and banged on her dizzy ass.

I blocked her from emailing me, but she's made up bullshit-ass email addies and went from sending naked shots of herself to sending me faceless videos of herself going off on Marika and me, talking real slick at the mouth. Every day for a whole fucking week she sent them shits, spazzing out, calling us users. Saying I wasn't shit for leading her on. That she was going to make me pay for hurting her. Then she threatened to expose us, if I didn't speak to her.

I was like, "what the fuck?"

But luckily, we haven't heard from her since then. She still hasn't even called into the radio station. Hopefully, she's found another couple to be the object of her obsession. Real shit, I've never been more relieved. I know I'd told Marika to not let her get all up in her head, but that broad's been relentless. Word up.

I'm still kicking myself for stepping to her in the first place, then inviting her into bed with Marika and me. I shoulda left that shit alone. Good pussy or not, that shit wasn't worth the headache.

I'm just glad it's finally over. Fingers crossed, we're done with the likes of her crazy ass. Still, that stunt she pulled in Marika's hotel suite was fucking out of control. On some realness, my mouth dropped open when Marika called me two o'clock in the morning and told me what went down.

"That crazy bitch came up to my hotel room and opened her coat—butt-naked, telling me to eat her pussy and fuck her in her ass again."

"Yo, she did *whaat?*" I snapped, jolting up in bed, then reaching over and turning on the lamp. "What the fuck you mean she came up to your room and wanted you to fuck her?"

"Just what I said. She refused to leave."

"What do you mean, 'she refused to leave'? How the hell did she get in?"

"How the heck you think she got in? I opened the door and there she was. She said she only wanted a few moments to talk. So I let her in."

I blinked, scratching my head in confusion. "Yo, what the hell? And why would you do that dumb shit?"

"She kept banging on the door. And I didn't want her causing a scene."

"Oh word? And that's all?"

"Ohmygod, Mar*Sell*," Marika screeched. "What the hell are you trying to insinuate here? You're making it sound like I asked for this shit with that crazy-ass woman."

The one thing about Marika and me, we have our disagreements, but yelling and hollering at each other isn't what we do. I can count on one hand the number of nasty fights we've had. One.

Going at each other's neck is not how we get down. But, on some real shit, that shit with this chick had us about to go there.

I took a deep breath, checked myself real quick and said, "Nah, nah, baby. My bad. That's not what I'm saying, or tryna imply."

She grunted. "Well, it sounds like it to me. And I don't appreciate your tone."

"I apologize for coming at you like that. But this, broad, yo, is fuckin' nuts."

"Yeah, well, you're the one who had to fuck her like you loved her. Now you got this bitch thinking *you're* in love with her."

I frowned. "I wasn't *making* love to her. I *fucked* her."

She grunted. "Well, tell that bitch that. It looked that way to me. So I can see why she'd get it in her nutty-ass head that you have a thing for her."

I sighed. "See. Now you're blaming me. You're talking like I invited that broad into our lives to harass us. How was I supposed to know her ass was unstable?"

Silence.

"C'mon, baby. Look. I don't wanna beef with you. This is the shit that broad wants us doing. Going at each other. You know this isn't even us."

"Do you want that bitch, Mar*Sell*?"

Real shit, when she came at me with that, heat washed all through my veins, had every fucking vein in my forehead and neck pulsing. I frowned. "Are you fuckin' serious right now, yo? *Vous parlez baise fou!*"

She huffed. "Oh, now you want to speak in French, knowing I don't know what the hell you've said. So typical."

I sighed. "I said, you're talking fuckin' crazy now."

"Oh, am I? Well, crazy is the bitch that just left here telling me she wants my husband because she knows *he* loves *her.*"

Hands curled into a fist, I got up and punched a hole in the wall, barely missing a beam. "What the fuck, man! No, I don't want that broad. You think I'ma throw away fifteen years with you for some one-night stand that *we* both wanted to fuck?"

Silence.

"What, now you're gonna ig me?"

"I'm tired, Mar*Sell*. I'm drained. And I'm going to sleep. I'll talk to you when I get home."

She'd hung up on me. But fuck what ya heard! Two hours later, my ass was in Atlantic City and I was the one banging on her room door. Believe that.

I snap out of my reverie when my door opens and in walks Carlos. "Hey, what's good, playboy?" he says, shutting the door behind him.

"Nothing, man," I say, getting up and walking around my desk to give him dap. "What's good with you?"

He takes a seat in one of the chairs in front of my desk. I sit back in the chair behind my desk. "Nothing much, man. You know, just tryna put the finishing touches on this album. Laila's interested in being featured on my joint, 'Unforgiveable.'"

I nod my head, digging the idea. "Oh, aiight, aiight. That's definitely a good look. The two of you together spitting that hot, sexy shit will be straight fire."

"Exactly. And since we're label mates, who are both sexy as fuck, it's a win-win."

I chuckle. "Man, listen to ya ugly-ass. You stay suckin' ya own dick."

He laughs. "Yeah, well, it beats letting another muhfucka do it."

Suddenly the room fills with an awkward silence. Then Carlos gives me this strange look, as if there's something else on his mind.

I shift in my seat. "What, what's good, yo? Why you giving me that look?"

"Nah, man. It ain't nothing. Just some bullshit; that's all."

I frown. "Aiight, then holla at me with it. If there's something on your mind, speak your piece, bruh."

He leans up in his seat. "We're boys, right?"

My brows bunch. "Yo, what the fuck you mean, 'we boys, right?' You know we fuckin' boys, niggah. For life. Where's this coming from, man?"

"I need to know."

I eye him suspiciously. "Man, fuck outta here with that. I can't believe you'd ask me some shit like that. You already know what it is."

"True, true. I just need to know I can trust you to always keep it straight with me no matter what."

"Man, fuck. Say what you gotta say."

"Well, you'll probably feel some kinda way for me even coming at you with this, but you know how punk-ass muhfuckas in the industry like to gossip…"

I narrow my eyes. "Yeah, and?"

"Well, there's this bullshit-ass rumor going around that you're on the DL."

I shoot him an incredulous look.

He repeats himself. Tells me some muhfucka said some shit about me being on the down low and that Marika and I have some kind of open understanding.

I frown. Although I was aware that there'd been talk over the years of muhfuckas speculating behind my back how I get down behind closed doors, no one has ever been bold enough to step to me with the shit.

And the one time the shit popped up on some blogger's website and in some blind item celebrity gossip, instead of going on the defense, Marika and I agreed to ignore the shit. Muhfuckas can think what they want.

"Man fuck outta here."

Carlos leans forward in his seat. Looks me dead in the eye, and says, "You know I don't get caught up in bullshit like that, but this is like the third time I've heard this over the last several years, and I always igged that ignorant shit. But last night, man…" He shakes his head. "I had to check this muhfucka for coming out of pocket. The muhfucka was talking real slick, and I wasn't digging it."

I narrow my eyes. "Who was it?"

"Man, it doesn't matter." He opens and closes his fist. "Hatin'-ass muhfucka, that's all. Niggah mad 'cause his shit got dropped. I handled it." I peep his swollen knuckles, and it's clear: He took it to the muhfucka's head. He eyes me. "So is it true?"

I swallow. Now it's my turn to look him dead in the eye, and say, "Hell naw, muhfucka. I ain't on no down low shit. That DL shit is for pussy-ass niggahs. I've never crept on Marika to rock with some muhfucka in the sheets."

Well, it's not a lie. I'm not *DL*. And I've never slid off to chill with a muhfucka behind Marika's back. And I never will. Don't get it twisted. Being DL and bisexual are two separate things. I'm not with that DL shit; period, point blank.

"Oh, aiight. I didn't think so. I've known you for years and have never seen you look at another muhfucka, licking your lips or winking at his ass."

That's because I know how to move, muhfucka.

"Nah, that's not me, playboy. I love pussy. And lots of it."

No lie there.

And having a muhfucka suck on this big, thick-ass dick…

"But I'ma say this, man. Real shit, I wouldn't give a fuck if you got down like that or not. We boys. Always have been; always will be. But I'd be kinda hurt that you couldn't trust me enough to share something like that with me."

"Man, I appreciate you, real shit. But being a DL muhfucka is one rumor you can def ignore. And that's fact."

And, nah, niggah, I'm not about to offer up being bisexual to you or anyone else. But on some real type shit, if he asked me if I was a bisexual muhfucka, I'm not so sure I'd tell him. I mean, what the fuck for? As far as I'm concerned, shit like that only matters if you're tryna rock in the sheets with a muhfucka. And, yeah, it isn't a secret how Marika feels about having him beneath the sheets with us, but we know that's not about to happen so there's no need in him knowing how I get down.

Boys or not.

He glances at his Rolex. "Yo, let me get up outta here. I'm meeting up with Laila real quick."

I stand. "Oh, aiight, that's what's up." I walk around and give him dap, and a brotherly embrace. He presses his body into mine.

"Damn, muhfucka, get ya dick up off me," I say, playfully nudging him back.

He cracks up laughing. "Yo, B, you shot the fuck out, man."

He walks toward the door. "Yo, come get at me later tonight on the court. Me and a few other cats are tryna get in a quick pickup game. Paper on the table. Fifteen hundred a point. You down?"

"No doubt. Whose team am I playing on?"

He grins. "Mine, muhfucka. Who elses?"

"Oh, aiight. Tell them muhfuckas, then, to get their money up."

He laughs. I eye him, shaking my head as he walks out the door. The minute the door shuts, I flop back in my chair, wondering who the fuck is flapping their jaws, running their muthafuckin' mouth about me.

Fuck.

THIRTY-ONE

Marcel

One week later, Marika and I are in Monte Carlo, Monaco for the Twenty-Fifth Annual World Music Awards, an international award show designed to recognize the world's best-selling artists in various categories, hosted at the world-famous Salle des Etoiles. Although I wasn't really beat for coming out here, I knew not coming wouldn't be a good look.

So here we are.

I glide my hand over Marika's hip. She rests her hand over mine. Her sexy ass is wrapped in a beaded, form-fitting couture gown. The sight of her makes blood rush to my dick.

I lean into her ear, and whisper, "I wish I could take you somewhere and slide this dick up in you real quick."

She smiles. "Not yet, but soon. I'll have my lips sliding down over that long, delicious cock of yours, coming all over it."

"Damn…" I groan. "You're killing me, baby."

She chuckles. "Softly, I hope."

"Always."

I scan the room and peep Alicia Keys taking a photo with Rihanna. Someone says something that makes the two of them laugh and share a sisterly embrace.

"And look what the angels have blessed upon us," I tease, nodding my head in the direction across the room.

Marika gasps. "She looks so fucking gorgeous," she whispers, slinking her arm through mine.

Nairobia sashays over wearing a long, flowing, ultra-sheer dress that hangs off her smooth shoulders, showcasing her long legs, tiny waist, mouthwatering tits, and magnificent ass. The only things covered—*barely*—are her nipples and pussy. As usual, her dress leaves nothing for the imagination, and every muhfucka in here is envisioning fucking her, her legs wrapped around them, swimming in her juices. Heart stopping, jaw dropping, real shit... Nairobia Bryant has a body made for all-night fucking.

All eyes are on her. Conversations go on pause as she saunters by, and muhfuckas soak her in. The flimsy garment she's rocking parts down the front, and causes muhfuckas' eyes bulging from sockets. She looks like an Egyptian goddess.

My dick starts to stir as she nears, her expensive perfume swirling around me and making my mouth water.

Marika slyly slides her tongue over her glossed lips.

"Marika, my sweet," Nairobia coos, voice throaty, smile wicked. "You look ravishing."

"So do you. And you're wearing the hell out of that dress, girl."

She waves Marika on. "What, this old rag? Darling, please." They giggle, then lean in and air kiss.

"You smell divine." Nairobia squeezes Marika into her. "My tongue thickens to taste you, my darling. You know how to get my sweet juices flowing."

Marika flushes with heat. "Oh, hush," she whispers. "Seeing you, and I'm already a wet river."

"Damn," I groan low. "Both y'all about to have me nut in my drawz."

Nairobia eyes me, licking her lips. "Aah, Mar*Sell. Ik heb je mijn sexy* *chocolade gemist.*" Translation: I've missed you, my sexy chocolate.

I grin, then lean in and kiss her on the cheek, placing my hand on the small of her back. The back of her dress drops into a sexy V-shape that tapers down to a sharp point, stopping at the crack of her ass.

A photographer with fucked-up skin and shiny hair stops in front of us and snaps our picture.

"Nairobia, baby," I whisper out of the corner of my mouth as our photo is being taken, "you're so good for my ego."

Marika waits for the photographer to move out of earshot and chimes, "And we both know what a *big* ego he has."

"Ooh, yes, darling. We do." They share a knowing smile. Desire darkens her expression as she grabs Marika's hand. "Mar*Sell*, may I borrow your beautiful wife for a spell?"

"No doubt." I glance over her shoulder and spot J-Smooth—eyes hidden behind dark sunglasses—with…I blink, then frown… with Lydia Miles on his arm and a posse behind him. "I'ma go holla at Lydia Miles."

"The singer?" Marika asks, glancing over her shoulder.

She's wearing a pearlized gown that clings to her curves. A gaggle of photographers spot her, and rush over to her, snapping photos. She quickly lets go of J-Smooth's arm and smiles for the cameras as he eases back.

Marika gasps. "Ohmygod. Please tell me that isn't J-Smooth she's here with." She lets out a grunt of disgust. "I thought she had a restraining order out against him."

I shrug, shaking my head. "Nah. His other chick does."

Marika shakes her head. "Oh, that's right. For slashing her tires or something."

"Let's not babble over folly tonight," Nairobia says, giving a two-finger wave and half-smile to a young Middle Eastern-looking cat dressed in royal garb. "Ooh, there's my sweet prince with the dick of a spider and the balls of a bush cricket." She blows him a kiss. "But he has the tongue of a giraffe."

I can't help but chuckle. "Yo, you shot out, baby."

"I'm ovulating," she shares, snapping open a bejeweled fan and fanning her crotch area.

Marika laughs. "Nairobia, girl, you're a mess."

Licking her red pouty lips, Nairobia says teasingly, "And I'm wet and juicy." She loops her arm through Marika's. "Come, darling. Let's go quickly...*freshen* up...before the festivities begin. Then I want to introduce you to the princess of Sweden."

I eye them as they strut off—the two finest women up in this muhfucka, then make my way through the crowd.

Lydia smiles when she sees me approaching. "Oh, there he is." She sassily struts over, titties bouncing freely, with her arms out-stretched.

"What's good, beautiful?" I lean forward and wrap my arms around her, enveloping her into a friendly embrace, lifting her up off the floor and kissing her on the cheek.

She giggles. "Mar*Sell*, you're so lucky I'm already taken."

It's a loaded statement. But I know she's referring to record labels. "You aiight?"

She flashes me her pearly whites. "I'm great. Thanks."

I don't acknowledge J-Smooth. I front like I don't see the muh-fucka standing here.

"Oh, aiight. I wanted to congratulate you on another number one single, baby. You're doing your thing."

She smiles. Thanks me. Then nervously shifts her weight from one foot to the other.

J-Smooth clears his throat. "What, you drop me from your label, and now wanna act like you don't know me."

"Oh, damn. J-Smooth? Damn, man. I didn't even know that was you." I laugh. "You standing there looking all incogneegro 'n' what-not. What's good with you?" I lean in, offering a fist to him. One of his cronies in his lil' entourage takes a step forward.

I narrow my eyes. "Yo, there a problem?"

He throws a hand up to stop his lapdog from advancing.

Muhfucka, I wish the fuck you would.

"Nah, we good," J-Smooth says.

"Oh, aiight. Just checkin'."

He reaches out and gives me dap. But for some reason the shit feels fake. But I'm cool with it. The muhfucka's pretty much on the verge of becoming a has-been, anyway, now that he's lost all of his endorsements and no one else in the industry is checking for him.

If he wants to be heard, or seen, he'll have to put out an independent project, or keep leeching off the spotlight of chicks like Lydia, too fucked up to peep he's only using them.

Lydia steps closer to J-Smooth. "Mar*Sell*, I hope to see you opening night at my concert at the Garden."

I glance over at J-Smooth on the sly. *What the fuck?* I notice a tight lump over his left eye. And it looks like there's a bruise under his eye. But I can't be for certain.

Muhfucka was probably somewhere running his mouth.

"Damn, bruh, whose fist you run into?"

He scowls, touching the frame of his shades. "Oh, nah, nah; just some bullshit-ass squabble. Nothing major."

But then something *major* saunters in, causing murmurs through the crowd and everyone to turn their heads, including Lydia and

J-Smooth. It's Laila Reynolds—sexy as shit in a shimmering bronze mini and knee-high gladiator-style heels—on the arm of my boy Carlos in a tux, with his long, wavy hair slicked back. Both looking like they've been airbrushed to perfection.

Photographers swarm them, blinding them with flashing bulbs. I shake my head, grinning. *This muhfucka here.*

"Pussy-ass niggah," one of J-Smooth's cronies, Leon, mumbles under his breath. Cat is about six one, two-thirty, eyeballing Carlos, like he's ready to get it in.

I can almost see the hairs on the back of Lydia's neck raise as she eyes Laila with what looks to be envy. As talented as they both are, she seems threatened by Laila's success. And J-Smooth seems fidgety all of a sudden, stretching and rolling his neck.

I open my mouth to call cat out for that slick shit just as Marika sidles up beside me. "You ready."

I kiss Marika on the cheek; quickly letting dude's comment slide, then introduce her to Lydia. "Lydia, this is my wife, Marika. Marika, Lydia Miles."

Lydia smiles. "Nice meeting you."

"Oh, the pleasures all mine," Marika says warmly. "I love your last album. I think I kept it in rotation for almost a month straight. Isn't that right, sweetheart?"

I nod absently, eyeing J-Smooth as he shoots glances over at Leon, who smirks.

"There's this bullshit-ass rumor going around that you're on the DL."

I cut my eye back over at J-Smooth. I think to pull this muhfucka to the side to see if he's been coming outta his face sideways about me, but then decide the shit's not relevant. I'm good with who and what I am.

"Well, we better get going," Lydia says briskly. "The show is about to start. It was great seeing you, Mar*Sell*."

"Yeah, you too, beautiful." I lean in and give her a kiss on the cheek. "Again, congrats on all of your success."

She smiles, waves goodbye to Marika, as J-Smooth quickly grabs her hand and whisks her toward the auditorium.

My forehead creases as they walk off.

"Wow, that felt awkward," Marika says, arching a brow. "What was that all about?"

"C'mon, let's go to our seats," I say, taking her hand in mine. "It doesn't even matter."

She squeezes my hand as we stroll down the red-carpeted aisle. I lean in her ear and tell her how beautiful she looks, and how much I love her.

She smiles, then whispers out the corner of her mouth. "I can't wait to fuck you."

I groan low, letting my hand slide over her ass as we take our seats in the front row. I get settled in my seat, draping an arm along the back of Marika's chair. When I glance over my shoulder, I catch J-Smooth seated in the third row over in the next section, staring at me behind his shades. He gives me a head nod.

Carlos' voice replays in my head. *"I had to check this muhfucka for coming out of pocket. The muhfucka was talking real slick…"*

"Niggah mad 'cause his shit got dropped…"

THIRTY-TWO

Marika

"Girrrrrl, so how was it?"

I dab the corners of my mouth with my linen napkin. "How was what?"

Jasmine scoffs. "Monaco, girl?" We're in Midtown finishing up an early dinner at Megu, a Japanese restuarant in the city. Unfortunately, I enjoy coming here more so for the décor and ambiance than its menu. The overly priced food is okay. But since Jasmine enjoys chic, trendy restaurants, here we sit.

Jasmine called me earlier stating she'd be in the city and wanted to meet for early drinks and a bite to eat. Besides, we haven't talked in a few weeks so catching up in person instead of over the phone is always nice.

I run a hand through my hair, swiping curls from my face. "We've been back over a week, and I'm already ready to go back. It was fabulous."

"I'm so jealous."

I wave her on. "Girl, please. You and…" My voice trails off. I squint. Take in the beautiful woman who has walked into the restaurant wearing a pair of skin-tight jeans and an off-the-shoulder blouse. I blink. "Oh, for the love of God!" I hiss looking over at the table she's being seated at in disbelief. I blink again as she has the goddamn audacity to sit directly facing in my direction. "You have got to be fucking kidding me."

"What?" Jasmine asks, glancing over her shoulder in the direction of my glare.

I shake my head. "Girl, nothing. Anyway…like I was saying, if you really wanted to go out to Monte Carlo, with all of Steve's connections, he would have made it happen. And you know Mar*Sell* could have gotten you seats."

I take a deep breath. Will my eyes on Jasmine, instead of across the room, where I can feel this bitch's eyes on me.

Why the hell is this bitch here…? She has to be stalking me.

"I'm ready to get out of here."

Jasmine gives me a confused look. "Why? Wait. You know her or something?"

Yeah. Real well. Marcel and I fucked her. "Not really."

Jasmine tilts her head. "Well, whoever she is. She must have really gotten under your skin. You should see your face."

I glance up at one of the giant lamp pillars, willing myself in my seat. But when the bitch winks and gives me a four-finger wave, smirking, I snatch my napkin from off my lap, tossing it up on the table, and quickly standing up. "I'll be right back," I say to Jasmine.

She eyes me as I stalk my way over to her table. "Hello, Marika," she says, smiling. "Surprise seeing you here. You look wonderful."

I cut through the niceties, getting right to the point. "What are you doing here? Following me?"

She laughs. "Oh, don't flatter yourself." She glances around the restaurant, lowering her voice. "Yes, you were definitely good in bed. Not as good as my *papi*, though. But you're definitely in my top five Clit Lickers category. And you know how to work a strap-on like no other."

I cringe.

"Still, last *I* checked, this was a public place, so why would *I* be following *you*?"

She tilts her head.

I place a hand up on my hip. "Well, that's what I'd like to know."

"If I were going to *stalk* anyone, sweetie. I'd be stalking that fine-ass husband of yours. After all, he's the one with the *real* dick. And big at that."

"You have some serious issues, hon."

She glares at me. "I'm not your *hon*. So do us both a favor and run along or *you'll* be the one with the issues."

I shoot her an incredulous look, trying to keep my tone even. "And what exactly is *that* supposed to mean?"

She flashes a smug smile, then tosses me a dismissive wave. "Look. I'm here to have a delicious meal and enjoy the ambiance. We're not friends, remember? Nor will we ever be. You made that perfectly clear. So go back over to your table. Leave me to my own dining experience. And stop letting your imagination get the best of you."

I stare at her, hard. Then arch a brow. "Good day. Enjoy your meal."

"You do the same," she says acidly. Then she says, as I'm turning on my heel to walk away, "Tell my *papi* I said I miss him. Me and *mi coño*."

The bitch starts laughing and it takes everything in me not to snatch her glass of water from off the table and toss it in her face. She smirks. "Relax, *mami*. I'm only teasing. He'll be *all* mine in time."

My face flushes with anger. "In your fucking dreams," I hiss.

"And, oh, what sweet dreams they are."

My nostrils flare, indignation flashing in my glare. I walk off, annoyed; yet relieved she hadn't raised her voice at any point.

"What was that all about?" Jasmine asks, eyeing me the minute I return to our table. "Who is that?"

I huff, taking my seat and signaling for the waiter to bring the check. I clench my teeth. "Some psychopath *bitch*."

She blinks. Shakes her head. "Wait a minute. Name-calling. Dropping the *B*-bomb at another woman. Oh, it must be serious. What's the deal?"

I pull out my compact. "I don't really want to talk about it." I glide a fresh coat of lipstick over my lips, then snap my compact shut, tossing it back in my purse.

The bitch is eyeing me.

I glower over in her direction. Then roll my eyes.

"Where the fuck is our check," I mutter.

"Ooh, now the *f*-bomb. Oh, she's really bad news, then. Do I need to take off my jewels and tie my hair up in a knot?" She starts sliding off her diamonds, slipping them into her purse.

I can't help but laugh. "Girl, no. She's annoyingly harmless."

Jasmine glances back at her. "Well, who is she?"

I sigh. Then hold a finger up at her. "Not a word. But I think she's stalking me."

"What? Why?" I pull out my wallet. Jasmine stops me. "Oh, no. My treat. Now tell me who this heifer in back of me is before I go over there and introduce her to a hometown ass whooping."

"No, that won't be necessary." I lean in and whisper, "She wants Mar*Sell*."

"*Whaat?* Get out of here. And how do you know this?"

"Oh, she told me. The bitch was bold enough to call me at my office and ask me for permission to fuck him."

I decide not to mention about our romp in the sheets with her.

"Ohmygod, that scandalous skank!" Jasmine exclaimed. "And you didn't drag her by the front of her hairline? Oh, hell no."

"Shh!" I sweep my eyes around the restaurant to make sure no one has overheard Jasmine's outburst. "I don't need you broadcasting it to the world."

"Girl, please. I wish a bitch would. These hoes today are downright treacherous."

I shake my head. "Tell me about it. The bitch needs to go find her own man."

"Well," Jasmine says, reaching for the leather check binder when it's brought to our table, "at least there's a bright side to all this."

I cock my head. Arch a brow. "Oh really? And what's that?"

"At least she asked if she could *fuck* him, instead of going behind your back."

I buck my eyes. "Are you kidding me? Where they teaching that at?"

She shrugs. "Hey, I'm saying. You know how these trifling hoes are. They'll smile in your face while trying to screw your man. At least, she wanted permission." She pauses, glancing at the bill, then sliding her Black Card in the sleeve, closing it.

"Well, trust me. She didn't get it. And…" I stop talking when the waiter returns to take the check. "I'm not about to hand over my man to *her* or any other woman."

She wants to know what makes me think she's following me. I tell her about her showing up in Atlantic City at the conference.

"And now she's here."

Jasmine reaches over and grabs my hand. "It could be another coincidence."

I shift in my seat. Give her a "yeah-right" look. I glance back over at her, then bring my gaze back to Jasmine. "I don't know what that bitch is selling, but, trust me, I'm not buying it."

THIRTY-THREE

Marcel

"What's good, my freak-nasty peeps…if you're just tuning in to the Tri-state area's hottest radio station, 93.3 *The Heat*, sit back… relax…light a candle…pour yourself a glass of your favorite wine… pull out your favorite lube…your favorite toy…or hit up that special someone…and prepare to be stimulated beyond your own imagination as we get into this week's segment of *Creepin' 'n' Freakin' After Dark*. Tonight we're gonna switch it up a bit 'n' do a lil' Speak Ya Peace segment. That's right, peeps. Call in 'n' express ya'self. I wanna know what's on ya mind. So let's turn up the heat 'n' get it in. 212-FreakMe…"

As soon as the phone lines light up, I hop right into it, picking up on line two. "Yo, what's good…you're on the air. What's on ya mind?"

"Hi, boo. This is Stacy from Parsippany. I love your show. I listen to it faithfully every week."

"Oh, cool-cool. Thanks for the love, ma-ma. So what's on your mind, beautiful?"

She sighs. "Well, I met this guy on a Christian dating website about a month ago. And everything was going real good with us. I was even thinking about giving him a little taste of goodness after Bible study last night, but do you want to know what this heathenish fool had the audacity to say to me?"

I lean up in my seat. "Nah, ma-ma. Tell us."

"This nasty baboon asked me if he could come over and get him a little taste."

"Oh okay, okay. But you wanted to give him a lil' sampler of the goodies anyway, so what's the problem?"

She huffs. "The problem is, the devil is a boldface lie. I thought I had me a good Christian man with a healthy sexual appetite, but instead I got me some ole nasty freak."

I roll my eyes up in my head, glancing at the time. I don't know why the fuck these hoes call in without getting to the muthafuckin' point.

"Damn, baby. Give me something good. What kinda nasty was he askin' for, ma-ma?"

"Oh, that nasty heathen wanted me to squat over him and pass gas in his mouth, then go to the bathroom on him."

I frown. *Oh that muhfucka mad nasty. He's one of them shit-stained teeth 'n' tongue muhfuckas.*

"Then he wanted me to let him clean me up back there with his...*tongue*. What kinda nasty devilishness is that? The devil is a lie if he thinks I'ma do some nastiness like that."

I blink. "Wait. Hold up, ma-ma. Are you saying ole boy wanted you to squat over him 'n' pull open them big, fluffy booty cheeks and take a dump in his mouth, then let him lick out ya shitty hole?"

"Yes. That's exactly what I'm saying. Ole nasty shit eater. I'm so appalled. Why couldn't he tell me he was into this level of devil work before I let him stick his serpent tongue in my mouth?"

"Damn, ma-ma. Sounds like you're gonna need a deep cleansing, no pun intended."

She groans. "I'm going to pray on it. And just call out on the Lord to send me a man with a good sexual appetite who isn't into filthy sex."

I bite the inside of my lip to keep from laughing. "Yo, beautiful. There's nothin' wrong with a lil' ass-lickin'. It's a real treat. As long as it doesn't taste like shit. Next caller. You're on the air."

"Yo, what's poppin', fam? This ya boy Mike, yo."

"Oh, aiight. What's good, Mike…where you calling from, play-boy?"

"Nyack, son."

"Oh aiight. That's what's up. What's on ya mind, bruh?"

He sighs. "Man, what's good with these light-skin bitches these days, yo?"

I furrow my brows. "I don't know, man, you tell me."

"On some real niggah shit, yo, them hoes becomin' basic as fuc—*bleep* these days. And they all starting to look the same, actin' like every muhfucka out here can't live without 'em. Bitch, boo! Go have ya pancake-batter-face ass a seat somewhere. All I'm tryna do is fuc—*bleep*. That's it."

I chuckle to myself. "Damn, bruh, you sound angry."

"Nah, yo. I'm just tired of the games 'n' the stink-ass attitudes them hoes be bringin'. And most of 'em's mouth game is whack as hell, anyway. If you gonna act all stuck up, at least know how'ta suck a goddamn dic—*bleep!*"

The line goes dead.

I shake my head. "Well all right then. That sounded like one wounded bruh. Next caller, you're on the air."

"Hey, boo. This is Ronzella from Union City."

"What's good, Ronzella. What's on ya mind, ma-ma?"

She sighs heavily into the phone. "I'm so sick of dumb chicks. These thots be thinking 'cause a dude rocks a few Polo shirts and a Gucci belt that he's ballin'. But ask him how much money he has in the bank, or what he's driving, or where he lives and I bet he doesn't even know what the inside of a bank looks like. He's riding shotgun in his boy's whip, or he's on foot. And his mattress is on the floor of his momma's house. It's pathetic."

"I hear you, ma-ma. Sounds like you got your ish together."

"You got that right. And I can't wait for my man to get home from his bid. So we can ball out."

I blink. "Yo, what's he down for?" When chick says something light, as in armed robberies, I almost fall out of my chair. "Yo, you call armed robbery something *light*."

"Well, yeah," she says nastily. "It's not like he raped or killed someone."

"Oh, aiight. Sounds like you definitely snatched ya'self a real baller, baby," I say sarcastically, but it goes over her head.

"You damn right, boo. And as soon as he gets out in twenty-twenty-five, I'ma show these silly bitches what a real baller looks like."

I smirk. "Oh, I'm sure the world can't wait. Thanks for calling in, baby."

George Tandy Jr.'s "March" eases over the airwaves as Nina comes over and tells me Marika's on the station's private line and that it's important. I frown, picking up my cell and removing my headset, wondering why she'd be calling the station instead of hitting me up on my cell.

"Hey, baby, you good?" I say, picking up.

"I am now, *papi*," the caller says. I cringe the minute I hear her voice. "Ooh, you sound so delicious. It's so good to hear your sexy voice, *papi*. I've been missing you so much. You have no idea how badly my body aches for you. I need some more of that *buen pene*."

My nose flares, but I try to keep shit in check. "What the fuck do you want, yo?"

"Don't be mean. I've missed you. I've tried to stay away, but I can't. I want you, *papi*. And I want some more of that good dick."

I huff. "Yo, you can't be hitting me up at the station like this, pretending to be my wife 'n' shit. What the fuck is wrong with you?"

"Well, I wouldn't have to keep calling you if you'd just respond to my emails, and stopped avoiding me. I can't believe you actually blocked me from your Twitter and Instagram."

This crazy-ass chick's back flooding my email with naked flicks and videos of her playing in her pussy, and sending me direct messages on Twitter for the last week. Just when I thought shit was over, here she comes popping back up.

"That was mean and childish," she says softly. "Make love to me, Mar*Sell*, baby."

I scowl. "Yo, real shit. What's really good with you, huh?"

"I told you. I miss you. I wanna see you."

"Not gonna happen. I thought I made that clear."

I glance over my shoulder at the booth, then lower my voice. "Did you get dropped on your head or something? I'm tryna keep this light, but you can't seem to follow the fuckin' script, so let me help you out. If a muhfucka doesn't hit you back after the tenth email and he blocks ya ass from all social media, then, uh, what the fuck you think that shit means?"

She huffs. "Now, baby. Don't be like that. All that means to me is you're playing hard to get."

Is this broad fuckin' serious right now?

I take a deep breath. "No. What it means is, a muhfucka's not interested in ya ass. So why are you still hitting me up?"

"Because I love you, *papi*. And I can't stop thinking about you."

"You *love* me?" I laugh. "Yo, you funny as hell. You don't *love* me. You're confused; that's what you are."

"I'm *not* confused, *hijo de puta!* I know what the hell love is. And I know what I feel for *you*. So don't tell me what I don't feel for you. I *love* you, *papi*."

I pull the phone away from my ear and stare at it in disbelief for a few seconds before placing it back up to my ear. "Listen, yo. That shit you feel isn't love. It's lust. And it's clear it was a big-ass mistake on my part to ever link up with you."

"Don't say that. It wasn't a mistake. It was fate, *papi*. Don't you see that? I was supposed to win those VIP tickets." *I thought this broad told me her girl won them.* I shake my head. "I was supposed to be sitting up at that bar. And I was supposed to be in bed with *you*...and her."

I sigh, frustrated. "Look. That shit we shared was a night of good *fuckin'*. Not love. But you're obviously confusing the two. How much paper is it gonna take for you to leave me and my wife the fuck alone, huh?"

"Motherfucker!" she yells. "I don't want your *money*, asshole! I want *you* to leave your fucking wife!"

I laugh. "Yo, you shot the fuck out if you think I'd ever leave my wife for *you* or any other chick."

"Mar*Sell*, baby. Let's not fight, okay? Why are you doing this to us? We're good together, and you know it. I know you felt it. I felt it when you were looking into my eyes, making love to me."

"I *fucked* you. Get that through your fuckin' empty-ass skull."

"Okay, Mar*Sell*, baby. Whatever you say, boo. I'm not going to argue with you. I know what you did. I was there, *papi*. And if you'd stop fighting it, you'd see it too. Baby, we can be so good together, like magic. That stuck-up bitch doesn't deserve you."

I raise up in my seat. "Yo, hold up. Now you way outta pocket, yo. Don't call my wife out her name. You got that?"

"Oh, so you're going to defend that *puta* when she's the one trying to keep us from being together? She knows what we have. And that's why she doesn't want you to see me again. She's jealous of us."

"Yo, will you stop sayin' that shit. We don't have shit; feel me? And my wife has nothing to be jealous of. You're no threat to her, period, point blank. Believe that."

She laughs. "Oh, I'ma threat all right. And I'm going to have you, *papi*. We're gonna be together real soon, baby. You wait and see."

I laugh.

"Oh, you think this is funny, huh, motherfucker? You think you can toy with my emotions, then dismiss me? Laugh all you want, Mar*Sell*. But I promise you. We're gonna see who's laughing last."

I grit my teeth. "Yo, you're delusional as fuck. And I'ma tell you again. Stop fuckin' callin' me!"

I hang up.

"What the fuck?!" I snap, running my hands over the top of my head. I take a few quick breaths and adjust my headphones, then we're back on in five…four…three…two…one…

"Yo, what's good, my freaky-peeps, we're back. And tonight it's your time to speak ya peace. That's right, peeps, tell ya boy what's on your mind. The phone lines are open now. 212-FreakMe." I answer line one. "You're on the air, what's on ya mind?"

"What's good, fam? This Peanut from Flatbush. Man, I don't know what's up with these chicks out here. It's like they say they want a good man, but then when one is looking them right in the face, he's not good enough. I'm like, what the hell. Real ish, man. Me and my mans, we are all college-educated cats, business owners, Wall Street-type cats between the ages of twenty-eight to forty, and none of us can seem to get a decent *black* woman. What's up with that?"

I shake my head. "Yo, that's crazy, playboy. Maybe you and ya peeps are looking in the wrong spots. I know there are lots of black women who want a good man."

He huffs. "I can't tell. Seems like all they want is a thug. Somebody to beat their asses, disrespect them out in the streets, and knock 'em up, then leave 'em for the next chick. It's real funny the shit chicks do for the bum guy. I own my own home, drive a high-end luxury car, my credit's on point, and I keep my passport stamped up, but that's not good enough."

"Man, that's crazy. Don't give up. That good woman you seek is out there for all of you."

"Man, fuck it. I'm gonna sag my pants and tell these sistas I flip burgers for a living, or push weight, then I bet I'll get some damn respect. If I had a state number instead of a college degree, I bet they'd be tryna worship me. But it's all good. I'ma start dating snow bunnies. They seem to know how to treat a brotha. Get me a white woman; she'll know how to appreciate a man with a Black Card."

"Bruh, keep hope alive. Yo, my black beauties, stand up! Where you at? Represent 'n' let my man Peanut know that there are good black women out there who still exist and who want good men. Next caller, you're on the air."

"Hey, Mar*Sell*. This is Juicy from East Orange."

"Juicy? Damn. Why my mouth get all wet saying that." I chuckle. "But I'ma leave that alone, ma-ma. What's on your mind, baby?"

She giggles. "Mar*Sell*, ooh, you're so bad. I love me some you, boo. But I gotta get this shit off my damn chest before I kill somebody."

"Damn, baby. We don't want you going out there doing something you'd regret. Go head 'n' speak ya piece."

"I found out my man…George Gregory the Third, aka Freedom

Lord God Rush has been fuc—*bleep*—ing some dirty bitch named Temeka Bush he met on Facebook. And I want him to know live and direct that he better let that gremlin-looking bitch pay his child support and his fines from now on because I'm done with his cheating, lying-ass. So, George Gregory, you can come get all your shit I just cut up and bleached up and tossed out in the yard because you ain't stepping foot back up in here. That crusty bitch can ride it out with you from now on."

Ghetto! "Daaaaaayum, ma-ma. That's wild. How'd you find out about ya man gettin' his FB creep on?"

"I hacked into his Facebook account and read all his inbox messages from that ugly, horse-faced bitch. That moose head bitch must suck a good dic—*bleep* and take it in the ass for him to fuc—*bleep* up five years. I tell you. Niggahs ain't shit! I'm done with 'em. I'ma turn gay and find me a damn stud."

Nina comes over and slides me a note stating the chick Temeka is on line four and she wants me to put her through. *Aww, shit. It's about to get real.* "Yo, Juicy, hold on a minute. Your man's Facebook boo is on the other line; let me bring her on." I place Juicy on hold, then pick up line four. "Yo, Temeka you there, ma-ma?"

"Yeah, I'm here," she says with lots of stank.

"Oh, aiight, aiight. Cool. Hold on." I click Juicy back on the line. "Yo, Juicy, you still there?"

"Uh-huh. I sure am."

"Oh, aiight, cool. Aiight, we have Temeka on the line as well. So we're—" Before I can get the rest of my sentence out, they start going at it, calling each other every dirty bitch, ratchet trick, hot-ass, disease-carrying name you can imagine.

"Bitch, am I suppose to give a fuc—*bleep* what your invisible ass thinks about me?" the Temeka chick snaps.

The Juicy chick snorts, "Umm, no bitch, just like I could care less what a dumb bird who sells her EBT card and calls herself Boss Bitch thinks about me."

"And I don't care about what some dry-pus—*bleep*-y-ass bitch who calls herself *Juicy* thinks about me. And so the hell what if I sell stamps off my EBT card, why you all up on my hustle? I'ma businesswoman, bitch."

"Oh cry me a river, you ghetto-ass, man-stealing bitch!"

"Why you mad, boo? It ain't my fault Freedom left ya ass for a real woman who knows how to handle him. And lets him be a man."

Juicy laughs. "Code for: 'I let him beat my ass and run the streets.' Bitch, aren't you late for some niggah's dic—*bleep* sucking? You sound stupid as hell."

They both start talking mad reckless about clawing 'n' stabbing each other up that I finally have to disconnect the Temeka chick from the line.

"Yo, beauties, hold up, hold up…time out," I say, shaking my head at the ridiculousness of these two chickenheads fighting over some bum-ass mofo who clearly is only good for slinging dick 'n' fucking dumb-ass chicks silly. "Temeka is no longer on the line. But I'ma say this. Both of you need to chill. No man is worth disrespecting 'n' beating each other up over. Juicy, baby, obviously this cat Freedom moved on. So let him. Yeah, aiight. Dude hurt you. We get it. And its effed up that he put you through whatever *you* allowed him to put you through. But guess what? He's not beat for you. So go do you. Be grown with your shit; cutting up dude's shit 'n' talking all reckless is not the move. It makes you look crazy."

She huffs. "No, boo. It makes me look like a bitch who is about to fuc—*bleep* his life up for tryna fuc—*bleep* over mine. That's why I called his parole officer on his black ass. And he's probably get-ting locked up right as we speak. Ha! I jailed with his ass, now let that bitch jail with him. And no worries, boo. I *am* doing me. And

I'ma be doin' his boy in a minute. That's right George Gregory the *Third*, you piece of shit-ass trash. While you're locked up takin' a dic—*bleep* up the ass, I'ma be out here fuc—*bleep*—ing your boy, Knowledge. And what?" She cracks up laughing. "Oh, and one more thing, bitch-ass. Don't drop the soap."

My head is pounding. I take a deep breath.

"Desperation is at an all-time high," I say, disconnecting Juicy from the line. "Like I always say, stupid *is* what stupid does. And fighting the next chick or the next dude over someone, who obviously doesn't wanna be with you or doesn't have enough respect for you to simply end the relationship is straight-up stupid. Get ya minds right, peeps. You can't make someone love you if they won't. On that note, thanks for another interesting night on 93.3's *Creepin' 'n' Freakin' After Dark*. I'm ya boy, Mar*Sell*, bringing you the heat, keeping it turnt up in the sheets. Until the next time... keep it hot 'n' oh so nasty, my freaky peeps. I'm out."

I lean back in my seat and remove my headset as Tank croons out over the air his rendition of Bonnie Raitt's "I Can't Make You Love Me."

"Some night, huh?" Nina says walking over to my desk as I'm gathering my shit. My fucking head is still pounding from that nutty-ass broad calling here talking all slick 'n' shit. Real shit, that broad still has me muthafuckin' hot.

I force a smile. "No doubt. These broads are fuckin' crazy." I shake my head. "It never ceases to amaze me the clown-ass shit chicks will do to try to keep a muhfucka who isn't beat to be kept."

"That's why I'm still single," she says, sitting on the edge of my desk. She sighs, locking her gaze on me. "Besides, seems like all the good ones are already taken."

"Nah. Weren't you listening earlier? Peanut's still looking, baby. You want me to get back on the air 'n' have him get at you?"

She laughs, playfully swatting my arm. "No, thank you. I think I'll pass on that. He's not who I was referring to. Besides, I'm saving myself."

"For who? *Me*?"

She averts her gaze and says, "Don't flatter yourself. A man like you is only good for two things starting with the letter *f*. And flirting is the other one."

I smirk. "Oh, and what's the first thing?"

She pushes up off my desk, brushing by me. "You figure it out."

THIRTY-FOUR

Marcel

"Mister Kennedy," Alise says through the intercom, "there's a call on line two. The caller says it's urgent."

I frown. "Who is it?"

"She wouldn't give her name. But she said you'd take the call. And if not, she'd call your wife instead."

Fuck.

Without another word, I know who the caller is. This broad is slowly starting to get on my muthafuckin' nerves. "Aiight, thanks, Alise." I take a few seconds to collect my thoughts, then pick up. "Yo, what the fuck is you doing?" I hiss. "You called the fuckin' radio station 'n' now you calling me here. What the fuck is up with you, huh?"

"Oooh, I love it when you talk dirty, *mi papi chulo*."

My jaws tighten. "Yo, what the fuck, man. I asked you nicely to stop fuckin' calling here."

"You did, *papi*. Don't be mad. I just needed to hear your voice."

"Look, you can't keep calling here."

"I want to see you, *papi*."

I huff. "Stop calling me that shit. I'm not ya *papi*. I'm not shit to you, aiight. I mean, damn."

"Don't be nasty, *papi*. Can't you see how much I want you?"

"Nah, what I see is you actin' like a fuckin' nut, yo. What part of Leave. Me. The fuck. Alone. Don't you get? The leave? The fuck? Or the alone?"

"*Fuck* me, again," she says, low and throaty. "*Chupar tu pinga para sabe como yo puerbo.*" Let me suck your dick so I can see how I taste.

I suck my teeth. "Look, I don't have time for this shit. Stop fuckin' calling here."

"*Ay papi. Quiero montar mi choca en tu cara.*" I wanna ride ya face with my pussy. "*Quiero que me folles tan duro en mi apretado, dulce, cono Latino.*" I want you to fuck me so hard in my tight, sweet Latina pussy. "Do you want some of this sweet pussy?"

I sigh. "Yo, what the fuck is wrong with you, huh? If you think talking all that nasty Spanish shit is gonna get a rouse outta me, you dead-ass wrong. The shit is a turn-off, and you fuckin' starting to piss me off, yo."

She moans. "Then let me stir your big, chocolate dick inside my mouth. I wanna suck your nut, *papi*. Let me taste that sweet *leche*."

I clench my teeth. "Yo, will you fuckin' quit this shit. What the fuck you want from me? More dick, is that it?"

"Yes. But I want you. *All* of you, Mar*Sell*. Not just your big hard dick. But your heart, too. Let me love you, *papi*."

"Not gonna happen. Next."

"Then I'll take that big juicy dick, if that's all you're willing to give."

I stare at the phone, and frown. *Is she fuckin' kidding me?*

"Don't you see, we belong together?"

Fuck outta here. "Nah, ma. The only thing I *see* is that you belong in a padded muthafuckin' room somewhere strapped to a gurney. That's it, period. Now, this is the last time I'ma fuckin' tell you. Stop. Fuckin'. Calling here. Now beat it, yo."

"Motherfucker, don't cross me!" she snaps. "You don't get to fuck me, then dismiss me. And call me goddamn crazy! I love you, but all you want to do is fuck me over. And hurt me. Don't—"

"Listen, what the fuck's it gonna take to get you to disappear, huh? Fifty thou? A hundred? Two hundred? Name ya fuckin' price and I'll cut you a check write now."

"Ohmygod. You really want me out of your life?"

I frown, staring at the phone. *What the fuck you think?! Stupid bitch!* I restrain from snapping on her ass. Pushing her over the edge is probably not the smartest thing to do. But right now. I don't. Give. A. Fuck. All I want is for this broad to bounce. Now.

I take a deep breath. "Listen. I don't wanna hurt your feelings. And I'm not tryna be nasty, but you need to hear me clearly: We're not. *Ever.* Gonna be together."

"Why not?"

I bite into my lip. "You want the truth? Nah, on second thought, I can already tell you can't handle the truth. But I'ma hit you with it, anyway. I don't love you. I don't want you. And I'm not *ever* leaving my wife. Period."

"You don't mean that."

"Yo, for real for real, I mean every word of it. I want you to stop fuckin' calling me. Don't call here. Don't call the station. Stay the fuck out of my life. And leave my wife alone. Now I'ma ask you again. How much is it gonna cost me to get you to leave us the *fuck* alone?"

"I'm pregnant with your baby."

I laugh, ending the call. *Fuck outta here! Stupid-ass broad! This shit is crazy!*

I blow out a deep breath, swiveling in my chair. *Good pussy or not, this shit isn't worth the fuck, or the nut!*

I hop up and walk around my desk over to the window and stare out.

We shoulda never fucked that dizzy-ass broad. Fuck! We really fucked a muthafuckin' screw loose outta her ass.

Two minutes later, Alise is buzzing in again, "Mister Kennedy. I have that same woman on the line. I know it's none of my business, and I'm probably out of line for saying this, but she sounds like she's really cuckoo-crazy. She said get back on the phone or you're going to be sorry you didn't."

I clench my fist, then storm over to my desk. "I got this." I snatch up the phone. "What the fuck is your problem?"

"*Don't* fuck with me, Mar*Sell*. I'm sick of motherfuckers like you thinking you can come into my life and fuck me over."

I scowl. "Do you hear ya'self, right now, yo? I mean. Do you *really* fuckin' believe what the fuck is coming outta ya face at this very moment, huh? How have I fucked *you* over, huh?"

"You're dismissing me like I'm last night's trash."

"I'm dismissing you, yo, because I'm not beat for you. All you were is a one-night stand. One that I'm starting to fuckin' regret ever happened."

"No, no," she quickly says, changing her hostile tone. "Don't say that. I'm sorry. Do you really want me to leave you alone?"

I huff, tension coiling around my neck like a fuckin' rope. "What the fu—" I catch myself from spazzin' the fuck out. I take a deep breath. "Look. Whatever it is you think you feel for me ain't real. And if love is what you're looking for, I can't give it to you."

"But we could be so good together, baby."

"Stop acting desperate, aiight. We fucked. That's it. Now move the fuck along."

"Fine, Mar*Sell*. If that's how you want it to be, then…"

I shake my head. "Yo, name ya price and let's be done with this shit."

"I don't want your money. I want *you*. But since you're forcing me to leave you alone, I want a little something to get back on my feet. Give me fifty grand."

Fifty grand? That's it? This ho got some lil'-ass feet. "Done. Give me ya bank information and I'll have it transferred to you right now, but first ya ass gonna sign a confidentiality agreement. Then I want you outta my fuckin' life. Got it?"

Silence.

"Yo, you hear me?"

"Yes. I fucking heard you. I don't want it transferred. I want you to bring it to me. Personal check is fine."

I glance at the time. It's a quarter to eleven in the morning. Something tells me to have the shit couried to her, but ignore the voice in my head. I just want this broad gone.

"Aiight, meet me at Fifty-Ninth and Columbus. Two o'clock. Sharp."

I hang up.

THIRTY-FIVE

Marika

After a deliciously decadent weekend lounging in the house naked, I am at my desk still basking in the afterglow of scandalous fucking when Shayla buzzes through. "Missus Kennedy, your eleven o'clock is downstairs at the security desk. They won't let her up because her name isn't on the list."

"What eleven o'clock?" I ask, puzzled. "I don't believe I have anything scheduled for today."

I reach for the portable mouse on my desk and wait for my PC to power up. I click into my calendar on my desktop, as well as check the calendar on my iPad. "Are you sure? I don't see any appointments scheduled for today. There must be some mistake."

"I thought so," she says. "I checked my calendar as well and didn't see anything scheduled. She wouldn't speak with me on the phone so I went downstairs and told her that I'd be more than happy to take her name and number and have you call her back. Needless to say, she did *not* seem happy to see me and wasn't trying to hear anything I had to say. She insisted on seeing you, *today*."

I sigh, glancing at the time. It's a quarter to eleven. "Did she give you her name?"

"Yeah. Alexandria Maples."

I purse my lips. "Alexandria Maples? Hmm. Name doesn't ring a bell. Did she say where she's from?"

"No. She didn't. Hold on." A few seconds later, Shayla returns and says, "Ronald says she says it's a personal matter and she will only speak with you."

I ask Shayla what she looks like. The second she describes her as a J.Lo lookalike, my heart drops.

Oh no! Now this bitch has gone too far! Coming here to my place of business!

I reach for my cell and immediately call Marcel, but the call rolls over to his voicemail. I end the call, and send him a text. CALL ME. ASAP.

"Did she look armed and dangerous?"

She chuckles. "Uh, armed? No. Dangerous? No. Hella crazy? Maybe. When I went downstairs to talk with her, she was pacing back and forth in the lobby like some caged animal and talking to herself." She lowers her voice. "Is everything okay? Do you know this woman?"

"No, no," I say quickly. "Not really. Can you call and let the desk know I'll be down in five minutes."

"I think you better make it in three," Shayla quickly says. "Um, I have Roman on the other end. He says she's down there talking reckless. She just told him that she's with The I'ma Turn This Bitch Upside Down Society if *you* don't hurry up and get downstairs. He's ready to call it in."

"No, no. Tell him I'm coming right down."

I quickly hang up and send Marcel another text: SHE'S HERE!!!! IM GOING DWNSTAIRS NOW

When he still doesn't respond back, I pick up the phone and call up to his floor.

"MK Records…this is Alise. How may I direct your call?"

"Hello Alise. Is Mar*Sell* around?"

"Oh, hi, Missus Kennedy," she says instantly, recognizing my voice. "Let me see." She puts me on hold. A second or so later, she returns to the line. "Um, he's actually in a meeting until about one. Would you like me to get a message to him?"

"No. That won't be necessary. I sent him a text. Thanks."

I hang up, and put my head in my hands and sigh, trying to gather my thoughts for a second before I collect my badge. Shut my office door and practically sprint in my six-inch heels through the building, heading for the elevators.

"Ramona," I say frantically, walking over to her. "What are you doing here?"

"It's *Alexandria*," she says tersely. "And I'm here because we have some unfinished business."

I bristle. "Umm, okay, Alexandria. Or whoever the hell you are. No. We don't. So I'm going to ask you nicely to leave now before I have you escorted out of the building. And don't *ever* show your face here again. Or the next time I will have you arrested."

She scowls, snapping a hand up on her hip. "*Vete a la mierda, puta…!*"

I blink.

Then my worst nightmare suddenly starts to unfold before my eyes when she hisses, "You do that. And I'll tell the world all about our lil' lesbian love affair. You pussy eater."

I cringe.

Oh, dear God, no! My eyes widen in shock. I can feel the blood draining from my face. I glance over at the security desk, hoping the two guards haven't heard her. The last thing I need to become is the spectacle. The sideshow.

They don't seem to be listening. Still, I've never felt more humiliated than I am at this very moment.

I clench my teeth. "There was no love affair." I take a deep breath, trying to conceal my real emotions. On the inside, I'm screaming, "*You stupid bitch! Get a life! And leave mine the fuck alone!*"

"Bitch, you eat my pussy and fuck me in my ass, then *think* you can dismiss me like I'm some whore-ass trick. I don't think so. Just like the night up in your hotel room, I thought we could be women about this, but I see you prefer it messy."

I need to get this ho somewhere private and out of everyone's earshot.

"Please, let's not do this here," I say with pleading eyes.

She narrows her gaze at me, placing a hand up on her curvaceous hips. Hesitantly, she agrees to talk privately. And I quickly usher her into one of the empty conference rooms, then shut the door.

I whirl around to face her. I'm livid. "Look, what is it you want from me, huh? Money?"

She laughs. "*Puta*, don't insult me. Do I look like I *need* money? No. I don't *want* your fucking money, bitch. I told you what I want. I want you to leave Mar*Sell*."

I scoff. "*What?* I don't know how many times I have to keep telling you to stay the *fuck* away from my husband and me. He and his dick are *not* available to you. So you need to go find you some other woman's husband to *stalk*, because mine—and his dick—are off limits."

She sneers. "Oh, you think you're real slick, don't you, bitch? But newsflash, sweetie: Your happy home isn't so happy. And that man you're so desperate to hold onto isn't happy with you. He doesn't love you. He loves me. I'm who he wants to be with."

"Bitch," I snarl, slamming a hand up on my hip. "You're fucking delusional. Mar*Sell* doesn't love you. And he damn sure doesn't want some crazy bitch like *you*."

She laughs again. "Then you're the dumb one, hon. How many late nights do you think we've spent on the phone talking, sexting, FaceTiming, while you're asleep, right *after* he's fucked you to sleep, huh? How many early morning email exchanges do you think we've shared behind your pathetic back?"

I blink.

She covers her mouth. "Oops. I guess he didn't mention that, huh? I guess he's keeping secrets from you, after all. Just like I bet he didn't reveal being with me last week."

I frown. "You're fucking lying."

"Oh really? Am I? Ask him where he was last Friday at two o'clock."

My mind quickly searches through my mental Rolodex.

"I have a two o'clock meeting."

My stomach lurches. My heart pounds in my ears.

"Oh, don't bother asking him. You know how men are. They have selective memory and they leave out all the important details. So I'll tell you. He was having a late lunch." She lewdly pats her crotch. "Between my thighs." She smirks, then licks her lips. "Ooh, his tongue is sooo addictive. I can see why you don't want to let him go."

This bitch is trying to bait me. But I'm not falling for it.

Yeah, right. Meeting my ass! What if he was with her ass Friday?

"I know you saw it in his eyes that night I was riding his big, long dick. It killed you, didn't it, *puta*? Seeing me give it to him so good. It tore you up watching the man you love fall for another woman, didn't it? *Él está enamorado de este coño.*" He's in love with this pussy.

Flashes of that night shoot through my head. Yes, Marcel was more passionate with her than he's been with other women we've brought into our beds, then again…those other women were women we'd met in different countries, or private parties. None of them were some obsessed woman who'd sent him nude selfies, or constantly called into his radio show.

She finally pushes me over the edge when she rubs her belly and says, "I'm pregnant with his baby."

"Bitch, you're delusional."

"Oh really? You think? Then riddle me this: Why did he give me"—she digs in her purse, yanking out a folded piece of paper—"this, huh?" She slings the paper at me.

I kneel and pick it up, opening it. My insides drop. It's a personal check for fifty thousand dollars written out to her from Marcel.

What the hell is going on here?

"It's hush money. He wants me to have an abortion, then disappear. But I don't want his money. I want him. And I'm keeping his baby."

"You lying, conniving bitch!" I lunge for her, slapping her face. My nails graze her face.

She touches the side of her face, then looks at the blood on her fingertips. Her eyes darken, making her look possessed. She clenches her teeth. "Oh, you just fucked up, bitch. You are going to regret ever putting your motherfucking hands on me. I'm going to turn your whole. Fucking. World. Upside down."

I lunge for her again, but she slips from my grasp, swings open the conference door and makes an erratic dash out of the conference room. I give chase after her not caring who's around, but she surges past the security desk.

"Bitch, I'm going to start letting everyone know *que me cogió en el culo!*"

My stomach lurches. She's going to let everyone know that I fucked her in her ass. I only know this because she's nice enough to translate it back to me as she yells out, "Marika Kennedy is a lesbian bitch!"

I stop in my tracks, mortified, feeling my gut clench as she shoulders her way out the glass door. My whole body shakes. I attempt to grab ahold of the wall to keep from falling, but one of the security guards catches me before I hit the floor.

"Missus Kennedy, is everything okay?" he asks, eyeing me cautiously. "Should we call the police?"

I shake my head. "No, no. No police," I say, the tremble still evident in my voice. "I don't want them getting involved. We'll deal with this in-house for now." I take a deep breath. Try desperately to steady my nerves.

"Marika Kennedy is a lesbian bitch!"

It's hush money!

He wants me to have an abortion…

I swallow back a scream. I fight to keep my composure as I calmly say, "And I'd like to *know* I can count on the two of you to keep what you witnessed and *heard* today quiet. I don't want this mess getting out."

"We have no idea what you're talking about," he says, sounding genuine. Still…I know how everyone loves spreading rumors and juicy gossip. Although all of our employees sign non-disclosure agreements, you can never be certain. They both lock their gazes on me and assure me that nothing will ever be repeated.

I want, need, to believe them. Desperately. But I can see it in their eyes. Judgment.

"But if she ever shows her face here again, I want the police called, immediately. No questions asked."

"Say no more," Roman, the younger of the two, says. I make a mental note to write them both a hefty check for their loyalty and to ensure their silence as I walk off, feeling their eyes on me as my heels click against the polished marble.

I don't fucking believe this shit! Crazy bitch!

As I'm making my way down the hall, one of the elevator doors slide open, and Marcel is stepping off.

The last person I wish to fucking see right now!

My nostrils flare and my eyes blaze.

"Marika," he says rushing to me. He glances around the lobby. "What happened? I got your texts." His Bvlgari cologne sweeps around me as he steps up to me. I try not to take a deep whiff of him, but he smells delicious. Any other time the smell of his cologne would be an aromatic aphrodisiac that makes my pussy pucker with lust. But the fact that some dick-hungry bitch is after him has me coming unhinged all over again, quelling any possible desires for him.

I turn away from him, and stalk off toward the bank of elevators, unwilling to have this discussion with him. I am still beside myself with rage. I've never been more humiliated in my entire life. *That dirty bitch!*

"Marika." Dead silence. I'm too drunk with anger to speak. "Marika, tell me what's going on. What happened?"

I whirl around to face him. "That *bitch*," I hiss, "is what happened. Now leave me alone so I can think."

His face tightens. "Yo, really, Marika?" He glances over at the security desk. Once again, we have a small audience. Marcel lowers his voice. "You see around you? Are you sure you wanna do this right here?"

Before I can catch myself I blurt out, "I'm sick of this shit. I didn't sign up for some whore-ass, nutty bitch disrespecting me. I told you she was a fucking problem. But, *nooo*. You thought I was being paranoid." I turn on my heels.

With a firm grasp on my arm, Marcel turns me back around. He takes a breath. "Now I'm askin' you nicely, aiight? You need to calm the fuck down and talk to me."

I yank my arm away. "Get your hands off of me. Don't tell me to calm down! Where the hell were you when that bitch was insulting me, huh? Probably somewhere stuffed in some coat closet with your goddamn dick shoved down in some trick's greedy throat."

Oh God!

Marika, girl, pull it together! What the hell is the matter with you?

I know I am making a scene but I am too goddamn pissed to care.

Marcel's nose flares. "Yo, I'ma act like I didn't hear that shit." He grabs my arm firmly and pulls me into a small conference room, then lets me go once the door is closed. He locks the door behind him.

"I know you're upset right now. But do you mind telling me what the fuck is going on? Since when you start showin ya muhfuckin' ass in public, huh?"

Before I can reign in my temper, I go off, cursing and screaming. Accusing him of wanting to be with that bitch. Calling him all kinds of son-of-a-bitches. I am wild with anger. "And now that crazy bitch is saying she's goddamn pregnant…by *you*!"

He scowls. "Are you fuckin' kidding me? And you believe that dumb shit?"

"You want that bitch, you can have her. I'm not tolerating this shit from her or any other bitch. And I'm not tolerating you fucking bitches behind my back!"

"Whoa, whoa. Hold up. Wait? You think I'm fucking *her*?"

I huff, folding my arms tightly over my chest. "Aren't you?"

His gaze narrows. "Hell no. I don't want her ass. I can't believe you'd ask me some shit like that. And I can't fuckin' believe you'd accuse me of creepin' on you. What the fuck, yo." He shakes his head in disbelief.

"Then why is that *bitch* telling me otherwise, huh?"

"Because she's fuckin' crazy! You said it yourself. And now she has you effen buggin." He shakes his head again, frustration etched over his handsome face. "And now you're acting just as fuckin' crazy as she is."

I snarl. "Oh, so now I'm the crazy one here? Well, mighty funny she seems to be making a whole lot of sense to me."

"Will you listen to yourself, yo. I mean really? Are you hearing yourself right now?"

Several tense seconds tick by as we eye each other before Marcel says, "I need you to hold it together. Why are you letting this chick get up in your head, blacking out, acting like some jealous lover?"

"Do I *need* to be *jealous*?"

"Are you effen kidding me right now?"

"Has she still been calling you?"

He blinks. "Excuse me?"

I tilt my head. "I asked has…that…*bitch*…called you?"

He takes a deep breath. "Yeah. A few times."

"And did *you* go see her behind my back?"

A look of surprise registers on his face. "Yeah. To get her to fall the fuck back; that's it."

"And you gave that bitch a check!" I crumble it in my hand, then throw it in his face.

He frowns. "I gave her that check to bounce, period."

I tsk. "Well, we see how well that worked out. Don't we?"

"I just wanted her gone. She told me if I came to see her and brought her a check, she'd fall back."

I give him a yeah-right-tell-me-anything look. Right now I am so drunk with disgust that all I am hearing in my ear is, "*I fucked him. I fucked him. He fucked me. He fucked me. We fucked. We fucked…I'm pregnant…I'm pregnant…*"

I give him an incredulous look. "And you believed her?"

He shrugs. "I didn't know what else to do, aiight. I wanted to."

"So you sneak off to see that *bitch* for some clandestine meeting, then expect me to believe you didn't run off to *fuck* her!"

He gives me a frustrated look. "Marika, c'mon now. What the fuck, man? No. I didn't fuck her. Don't turn this shit into more than it is."

I scoff. "'Don't turn this shit into more than what it is'? Oh, give me a damn break, Mar*Sell*. You've done a fine job of doing that on your own.

He scowls. "Yo, listen. That broad coming here was outta pocket, but you're fuckin' buggin' now. I—"

Before he can get the rest of his words out, I am up on him.

Slap!

I reach up and smack his face. It happens so quick that I catch him off guard.

His jaw tightens as his hand goes up to his cheek. "For real, though? We slapping now?"

"Oh God, Marcel......... I'm so sorry," I stammer. I go to reach for him, but he brushes past me and opens the conference room door. The door slaps into the wall as he heads toward the bank of elevators.

Oh God! This is not good.

I follow behind him, hot on his trail.

Marcel steps onto the elevator. Eyes blazing fire, he puts his arm out to block me from entering. He uses his other hand to push the button for his floor.

"My advice, take the stairs," he warns, glancing up at the elevator's security camera. His jaw tightens.

"Mar*Sell*, please. I'm sorry. Let's talk about this."

He nudges me back. "Yo, I'm not tryna hear that right now. You should have thought about *talking* before you put your muthafuckin' hands on me. Right now, I'm not tryna be responsible for what I might do. So step the fuck back."

My stomach drops to my feet.

Still glaring at me, his lips tighten. "I'll deal with *you* tonight."

I step back from the elevator allowing it to close, my heart sinking as Marcel's face disappears from view.

Ohmygod!

What the fuck have I done?

THIRTY-SIX

Marika

Nose flaring.

Jaws tight.

Marcel is pissed. No. He's...*furious.*

At me.

That bitch has caused this friction between us.

And I have allowed it.

I let her get to me.

Let her get inside my head.

Causing me to get bat-shit crazy and lash out at my man.

Slapping him.

Blaming him.

Holding him responsible for what that *bitch* is doing to us. When in fact he is not culpable. Neither of us is to blame.

She's the crazy, desperate one.

And, yet, *I* slapped *him.*

I am so, so, very sorry for what I've done. But I know an apology will not be enough.

I've crossed the line.

Marcel and I do not fight.

We do not argue.

We disagree.

We talk.

We make love.

We fuck.

Talk again.

Then fuck again, and again, and again.

Then talk some more.

Then fuck all over again.

We do not yell or scream or disrespect each other.

But in a blink of an eye, I have allowed this craziness with that... that desperate, emotionally unstable tramp to take me out of character and come at my husband all sideways and crazy.

The man I love.

The man I've always trusted and respected.

Nightmare. Definitely a bad fucking dream. Shit like this only happens on television. And in other couple's lives. Not in ours.

We're always so discreet.

Always so careful in whom we bring to our bed.

Until this shit...

"Marcel, I'm sorry," I whisper, crossing into the sitting area adjacent to our bedroom. It is all I can imagine to say with him sitting there barefoot and bare-chested in his underwear. Boxer briefs.

I fight to keep from staring at his muscular shoulders and pecs tapered down to rippling stomach ridges.

I blink back images of his hard body hovering over mine.

He has a drink in his hand. Rémy. The crystal decanter sits half-full on the table with its Harcourt stopper off, next to the remote for the surround sound.

"You're *sorry*?" He blows out a long breath.

"I was—"

He yanks up his hand, stopping me from taking a step toward him. My mouth clamps shut. He's not done.

"*We* brought that broad into our lives. *We* fucked her. And yeah, the pussy was good. Damn good…"

I flinch.

"But do you really think I'd let some random broad, whose only good for suckin' dick 'n' takin' it in the ass, come between us?"

I shake my head. "No. I didn't—"

"Then why the *fuck* would you?"

I blink in surprise. Marcel has never spoken to me in this manner. Never.

Then again, I'd never given him cause to.

His jaw clenches and a look of utter fury darkens his eyes.

"Take off your clothes."

"Marcel, baby—"

"I'm not asking."

With a swallow, my fingers fly up to the buttons of my blouse, quickly undoing them. I shrug out of my blouse, allowing it to flutter to the floor.

My stiffened nipples and dark-chocolate-colored areolas are visible through my ivory lace bra.

Marcel rakes his graze over my covered breasts, then sucks in a breath. The burning in his stare causes my nipples to pucker tighter. I am tempted to caress them.

But I know he wants them on display. Not played with.

"Can we at least talk about—?"

"The skirt."

I attempt to step out of my heels when he stops me. Tells me to leave them on.

I unfasten my skirt. Slide it down over my hips, the silk-blend material crumpling around my ankles.

"Take off your bra." There's a flicker of lust lighting his eyes despite his clipped tone.

"Baby, you have to believe—"

He narrows his gaze, cutting me off again. "You fucked up." Although his voice is even, ire blazes in his expression. "You understand that, right?"

I nod, eyes wide.

Hurt and disappoint flash in his eyes, then they become blatant flares of anger. He's never been *this* livid—with *me*, ever.

I shift uncomfortably and swallow, unhooking my bra. "Baby, let me—"

"I'm not tryna hear shit you have to say. Not right now." He reaches behind his back and retrieves a red silk scarf and a leather ball gag.

I choke back a groan as realization dawns. I am going to be gagged. And most likely blindfolded.

I swallow.

Marcel wants me to submit. He wants to have total control. I am to give my self sweetly over to him. Allow him free rein. There will be no pretending. Not tonight. There will be no exceptions. Not tonight. If I am to make this right between us, it will be Marcel's way. And I'll follow his rules. No questions asked. I will cede power, my will, over to him.

Our gazes lock. This unease between us, this temporary divide, is my doing. And. although Marcel won't stay mad for long, I'll need to ride out the storm.

And hope like hell I don't get swept up in it.

I swallow, heart racing.

No. Marcel won't use his anger to lash out at me. But he'll use it to make me never forget.

That he is my man.

That I have truly fucked up and crossed a very dangerous line.

And I'd better think long and hard before ever doing it again.

Despite the thick tension in the air, I grow wet with desire. And knowing.

Obedience. Power. Control.

For as long as Marcel wants it, I am willing to give it to him.

Until he has forgiven me...

He brings his drink to his lips, then takes one big gulp. He sets his glass down onto the table, and my mouth waters as he licks his tongue over his lips. I drink in the sight of him. Suddenly I want nothing more than to have my pussy where his tongue has been. Me melting on his tongue. Me coming all over his mouth.

The thought causes me to groan low.

"Can we please talk about this?"

"You slapped *me*," he seethes.

"I know," I whisper. "I'm—"

"You let some random piece of ass get you twisted outta pocket."

"I know. I—"

He doesn't let me finish. "Your ass is mine tonight, Marika."

My toes curl in my heels. My pulse quickens. Heat flashes through my ass cheeks.

The message is clear. He is going to fuck me until my ass burns, until tears spring from my eyes, and I am begging him for forgiveness. He's going to fuck me slow and deep until he drains me, wrings me out, and I pass out.

And then when I come to, he is going to fuck me endlessly all over again until I am losing my grip on my own sanity.

Knowing Marcel, if it is the last thing he does tonight, he is going to make me regret ever doubting him, ever questioning his love, ever second-guessing his commitment. Marcel is going to make me wish I'd never allowed jealousy and doubt to edge over me.

"I know," I mutter, feeling my knees buckle.

When he stands, his long scrumptious dick is rock-hard.

And my panties are sticking to my folds, my sopping wet pussy quivering, my heated flesh quaking with need.

THIRTY-SEVEN

Marika

Sweet delight. Blood boiling, body on fire, I surrender to Marcel. Give him what he's demanded of me.

Total submission.

Wicked need simmers as I give him complete control. Tonight there are no illusions. No smoke screens. Marcel is too pissed with me for me to toy with him.

And I won't.

So I submit.

Pussy juices trickle down my inner thighs as I knee-walk over to him. My pelvic muscles tighten at the sight of him.

I see why that bitch is after my husband.

Raw energy.

Burning fire.

Sexual hunger.

My nipples tighten. *God, yes!* The mouthwatering ache causes my body to shiver as I inhale, deep and slow. I can smell him.

Masculinity.

The clean scent of soap mixed with the musky heat of his skin. I breathe him in. Savor him as his gaze rolls over my body, settling on my breasts. I can practically see the drool gathering in the corners of his mouth as I inch closer to him. Yes, Marcel is upset with me. But his lust, his overwhelming desire for me, is softening his heart.

He scowls. "Hurry the fuck up, Marika."

Oops. Maybe not…

I swallow around a lump in my throat.

When I reach him, Marcel stops me from coming any closer. He stands up and my breath escapes in a long hiss at the sight of his hard dick straining and swelling against the fabric of his boxers. The head of his dick hangs out past the leg of his underwear, causing my lips to quiver at the sight of beads of precum covering its slit.

He's excited. The nasty fuck's turned on by all of this.

"Yeah, you like seeing that hard-ass dick, huh? Got my shit leakin'."

"Yes."

"*You* do that shit to me, Marika. *You*. Not some random broad."

"I know," I rasp out.

"Shut the fuck up." He roughly cups my head in his hands and grinds himself into my face. "I should choke the shit outta you." I open my mouth. Try to suck him in. My tongue flicks over his hanging dickhead, catching a droplet of his sweet nectar. But it isn't enough. I need more of him. Want all of him. My hands go up, try to hook my fingers into the waistband of his underwear to free his cock. I feel like I am going to die if I don't taste him…now.

Marcel backs away from me, depriving me, leaving my mouth wet and needy. "Nah, fuck that. Greedy ass. Put ya muthafuckin' hands down." He smacks my hands away. Then steps back, yanking his boxers down over his hips. "Is this what you want?" He glares at me as his thick, chocolate dick springs upward, pointing like a long, angry arrow.

My insides suddenly start to shake.

"Yes," I manage to say, fighting to keep from reaching out for it. My whole body vibrates with wicked need.

He shakes his dick at me, then steps forward and slaps me across the lips with it. My mouth snaps open and waters. I extend my tongue and Marcel slams his dick down against my tongue, then back across my opened mouth. I feel like I've just been slapped with an expandable baton.

He steps back from me, taunting me. "You don't get to put ya muthafuckin' hands on me, then think you gonna get rewarded with some of this good dick."

"I'm s-so—"

"Nah, shut the fuck up. I want you to watch what you missing out on."

He grabs his dick at the base, then bends forward and raises his gaze to meet mine before licking the crown of his cock and drawing himself deep into his mouth.

For the love of God…

My groan only emboldens him further to lovingly suck his dick in long, lascivious pulls.

I nearly cry out in sweet agony when he swallows seven, eight, nine inches of his own dick down into his throat. Everything inside of me explodes watching him tease me—no, no, *torture* me—like this.

Denying me his dick! Motherfuck him!

His head bobs up and down the length of his shaft, then his mouth suckles on the head, licking around his sticky crown every so often.

Oh, God, yes…

What a beautiful sight!

I moan my appreciation. Ache with jealous delight in having a man with a big, long dick. Still I envy his mouth, wishing it were my own mouth engulfing him, my own tongue laving him.

My cunt muscles twitch, then contract, hungry for the thick heat of his seed. My mouth droops open in waiting anticipation, hoping he'll be generous enough to share his cum with me. Instead he pulls his wet, shiny dick from out of his mouth and straightens himself, pulling his underwear back up over his hips; most of his dick is now exposed out from the top of his waistband, pressing along the ridges of his stomach.

I moan in protest, but he only scowls at me, squeezing his swollen cockhead. "This muhfuckin' dick is angry as fuck. It's ready to beat you the fuck up."

Yes, yes…beat me, daddy! Fuck my pussy up good…

Marcel leans down and exhales. His breath spreads over my throat, heating my skin and spreading over my breasts. "You disappoint me, Marika; real shit." He caresses my nipples. "I can't believe you let some unstable broad get all up in your head like that. I thought we were stronger than that."

He speaks so low and slow as he rolls my nipples between his fingers that I am struggling to concentrate on what he is saying. Besides, my mind is still on the imageries of him sucking his own dick, and the idea of him *beating* my pussy up.

"I—"

He twists my nipples. "Not one fuckin' word. Talking to me is what you should've been doing earlier instead of comin' at me all crazy." He plucks my nipples. "You don't get to say shit now."

"Marcel, baby…"

"You will speak when I'm ready to hear you," he whispers against my ear. Then murmurs something in French as he twists and pinches my nipples.

I groan as an agonizing heat swallows me whole. I reach between my thighs to soothe the ache pounding in my clit.

"Nah, fuck that, Marika. Get ya hands away from your pussy. That's *my* muthafuckin' pussy. You don't get to touch that shit. Ya ass gonna suffer."

Reluctantly, I abandon the wet space between my legs.

Then he tells me to place my hands behind my back and cross them at the wrists. *Sweet Jehovah.* I do as I am told. Allow him to bind my hands together with the scarf.

My toes curl. And then a groan gets caught in the back of my throat when Marcel pulls out a crop. A crop!

Oh, God!

I search my lust-hazed brain trying to recall when he'd gone into our toy chest and retrieved it, or if it had already been out in the open. I can't recall.

"What you did was fucked up. But you gonna learn tonight, baby."

My inner walls clench.

I will never resist him.

Never.

Marcel knows this.

His sexy lips curl as he runs the heel of his palm over the length of his straining bulge. I don't think I've ever seen his already big dick so thick—so, so, huge. Not like this.

"Marcel, if you'd just let me—"

His gaze on me darkens. "I told you to keep ya mouth shut, and you still running it, right?"

I shiver when the tip of the leather crop skims over my flesh.

"I'm gonna spread you over my knees and whip your ass raw, Marika…"

My pulse quickens. Arousal surges. Marcel has never whipped my…ass.

It is not a threat. It's a promise.

One he plans on keeping. Marcel is always a man of his word.

He swats my ass for emphasis.

Why had I ever doubted him?

"And then I'm gonna eat that sweet pussy…"

I moan low in my throat.

Marcel reaches between my legs, pats the crotch of my cum-sodden panties.

"Look at ya pussy all wet." He presses into the fabric with his fingers, then pinches my clit. "All this for me."

It isn't a question.

He already knows. I am always wet for him.

He brings his hand to his nose, sniffs, then licks his fingertips. And then…

"I'm gonna fuck you in ya ass. I love you, Marika. But tonight, I'ma split ya shit open. You're gonna learn to never put ya mutha-fuckin' hands on me."

I groan against the gag. "God, yes…"

My need for him swells. Hotter. Wetter.

My God, I wish he'd stop torturing me. Wish he'd dole out my punishment. And just fuck me already!

I can't take this anymore.

The heat is becoming so unbearable.

I cry out against the gag, "Oh, God! Just fuck me already. *Please*."

My breathing hitches when he reaches for my taut nipples and pinches them hard.

"You still talking shit, right?"

My cheeks flush and I bite down on my lip, shaking my head.

I swallow when I notice his dick twitch and start to swell again.

Despite everything, I know Marcel's desires for me are real. As are mine for him.

He walks over and grabs the ball gag, then stalks back over to me. "I got something for that shit. Open ya mouth."

Again, I do as I am told. Do whatever is necessary to make things right with my husband. I open my mouth. Allow him to push the ball into my mouth, fitting it between my teeth, then fasten the leather straps behind my head.

My eyes widen as Marcel taps the riding crop against his thigh. I swallow hard. Then gasp as he trails the edge of the crop over the hardened peaks of my breasts, causing them to become so painfully rigid that I think they'll snap open at any second.

"Tonight, I'ma make you wish you never put ya muthafuckin' hands on me, baby. I'ma make you wish you never doubted me or ever questioned what we have. And you know I'm a man of my word."

He slides the crop along the crack of my ass, causing it to brush the back of my pussy.

I moan, wind my hips.

Whap!

I grunt.

"Keep ya greedy-ass still. You disrespected me. You knew you had it coming. Punishment. I'ma redden that beautiful ass until it glows fire."

If I weren't already on my knees, I'm sure they'd have buckled at those words.

"I know—"

Whap!

I gasp as he smacks my ass again.

Lightheaded, tears spring from my eyes.

I know this is supposed to be punishment. But I love it. Love the sting. Love the burn. *Oh, God, yes...*

I gasp again and again when Marcel slides the crop between my pussy lips, over my clit, then into my slick heat. Then back over my clit.

The crop, oh, God, yes…so fucking barbaric, yet so unbelievably sensuous.

Whap!

I scream against the gag when the leather snaps into my ass, then moan when Marcel slides it back over the back of my cunt, before slipping its tip into me, fucking the mouth of my pussy before rubbing it over my clit again and again until I am delirious.

He lifts the tip to my mouth. Tells me to lick it clean. And I do. I stick the tip of my tongue out, my gaze set on his as I lick the leather, catching the sweet musk of my wetness.

"Yeah," he says huskily. "Lick your juices."

I lave my tongue over the leather, then just when I'm about to suck the crop into my mouth, Marcel pulls it away from me.

Damn him!

He sucks it into his own mouth, forcing a groan to spill out over the gag in my mouth. Then without warning, he snaps it over the side of my right breast, catching my nipple and areola with the flat edge.

I cry out.

Sharp pain followed by a burst of aching heat.

Oh, God, yes…yes…

He snaps the crop over my left breast and my nipple flares searing heat that bursts into flames. I close my eyes and swoon. I am not sure when I pass out, or how long I'd been out, but when my lids flutter open, the gag is off, but my hands are tied over my head and I am naked and spread for Marcel's unyielding pleasure.

I thrash my head when he strikes my cunt with a lash.

Tears flood my lids.

I feel…

Vulnerable.

Deliciously helpless.

And seconds later, Marcel's tongue, moist and greedy, gliding over my pussy lips.

"Oh God, *yes!*"

Marcel looks up at me. His eyes narrow and darken.

"Do you know how much I love you, Marika?" He reinforces the question by pinching my engorged clit. Fire flares through me, then dances in the pit of my pussy, sending me over the edge.

"Uh…*yessss*…"

"Do you not know that you are the only woman I've ever loved?" He pinches my left nipple, then the right one. "That I will ever love?"

I moan. "Baby, *pleeeease*. Let me…"

He scowls. "Let you what, Marika? Tell me some bullshit that I already know? How sorry you are? Nah. I'm not tryna hear that shit." He brings the lash across my labia, striking my clit, my slit, causing my cunt to flare open.

I arch into the sizzling heat. Blink through the tears.

"Uhhh, I am so—"

Slash!

More tears spring from my eyes.

"Marcel, *pleeeeease*…"

Slash!

"Please what, Marika?"

Slash!

Mewling like a wild bobcat, a molten river flows from my swollen breasts to my clit, then bursts out of my hot, overflowing slit. My pussy has become a wet fountain of sensations, spurting and pulsing. Tingling. Throbbing. Aching.

I groan and arch my spine.

"You're my fuckin' wife, yo. I'd never fuckin' disrespect you. Or play you."

Slash!

He lashes my pussy until fire explodes from my clit.

Then leans in. Cages my cunt in his mouth. Tongues it. Kisses it. Loves it. Sucks and suckles until I erupt into his mouth, then releases my clit with a wet, juicy sound.

"I'm not done with you," he rasps, reaching over and freeing my wrists. "Get on your hands and knees."

I glance at the clock. And almost scream. It's almost midnight. This marathon of torture has been going on for almost four hours. My head demands that I put a stop to this. That I tell him that he's made his point. But my body is screaming for more. It is burning for more.

I am defeated.

Sore and satiated, I quickly do as I am told.

Marcel slips a hand between my legs and spreads my knees apart. My pussy is exposed to him. All pink and wet and swollen and ready for him.

Whap!

The open-hand slap on my ass causes my body to catch fire. I yelp, arching my spine into the flames.

"Have I ever put my hands on you, Marika?"

Whap!

"N-noooo…"

Whap!

"You still doubt ya man?"

Whap!

"No, no, nooo, baby, never…I'm s-s-s—"

Whap!

"Get ya muthafuckin' face down in that mattress." *Whap!* "I'ma fuck you in ya ass now."

I try to scramble away. "Marcel, no…wait."

He catches me by the waist. Pins me down. "I told you. This ass is mine tonight."

Whap!

And then he is yanking me up off the bed, snatching a pair of panties from off the bed and ordering me to slip them on. My heart leaps. My pussy purrs. They are a pair of custom, lace, black vibrating thongs. The vibe fits into the pocket stitched directly in the gusset. He already has the wireless vibrator into its pocket.

I weave unsteadily as I attempt to step into the underwear. Marcel immediately grasps my arm, catching me before I fall. He helps me into the thong. Then orders me back on my knees. "I want ya ass out to the edge of the bed."

And then he is blindfolding me, and he surprisingly steps away. Leaving me. Making me wait. The anticipation, the waiting, slowly becoming more than I can bear.

Maddening silence…

THIRTY-EIGHT

Marcel

Two weeks later…

Real shit, I'm sitting here at my desk, completely fuckin' distracted by my thoughts. I have mad shit to do today, but my concentration is shot to hell. There's a pile of notes from Arianna of calls I need to return. E-mails to respond to. Contracts to look over.

But my brain is everywhere else but where it should be. Here handling business.

Even though shit's been quiet for the last two weeks, I'm still feeling some kinda way with how shit popped off between Marika and me over that Marisol-Ramona broad, or whatever the fuck her name is.

And, yeah, Marika and I talked shit out. And we've both apologized—her, for jumping to conclusions and not trusting me; and me, for not telling her about meeting up with that broad. I was able to see how it looked to her.

But still, she should have trusted me enough to know I'd never cheat on her. What the fuck for?

Hell, if she wanted to shut down threesomes, I'd be cool with it. I'm not gonna front like I wouldn't miss that shit, because I would. And I know she would as well. We both enjoy rocking in the sheets with the opposite and same sex…with each other.

I can't see myself creeping behind her back to chill with another muhfucka. And I can't see her doing that shit to me.

It wouldn't be right. And the shit just wouldn't be the same. I don't know. It's hard to explain the shit. I mean, Marika and.... damn. Our sex life is already fuckin'-unbelievably incredible when it's just her and me in the sheets. But when we pull another muh-fucka—chick or dude—up into the mix with us, that shit kicks our freak meter up another hundred notches.

Real talk, a muhfucka doesn't know what their partner will or won't do given the right time, space, and opportunity. And, on some real shit, I'm convinced there are more bicurious and bisexual muhfuckas out here, than not. Muhfuckas just not open about it with their partners. But that's never been our issue.

Nah, Marika and I push each other's sexual boundaries, and we've always fucked with no regrets. Well…up until this shit with that Marisol-Ramona chick. I regret that night ever happened. That was my dumb mistake.

One I'm glad didn't get any uglier than it did with Marika turning up.

Still, that shit kinda fucked me up. Marika and I have never beefed over no shit like pussy. Then again, we'd never encountered any shit like we had with that broad.

I mean, yeah. A few fan-email-radio stalkers here and there, but nothing major.

Anyone we've ever gotten between the sheets with has always known how to move. But that shit with Marisol-Ramona-or who-ever the fuck she is, I take full responsibility for.

I rub the side of my face.

Damn, I still can't believe Marika really fuckin' slapped me.

Yeah, I'm over it now, but man…listen, I was heated when that shit popped off. I couldn't look at her ass. I was so muthafuckin' pissed. Mostly at that fucked-up broad, mostly at myself for pushing up on her ass, then at Marika for buying into her bullshit, doubting me, doubting us. That shit had me hot.

Marika was outta pocket for not talking that shit out with me; feel me?

Putting my hands on her def never crossed my mind, but punching up holes in every muthafuckin' wall and knocking some random muhfucka out had.

I had to spin off on her ass before I said some shit I couldn't take back. But when she walked up in our bedroom that night tryna plead her case, I wasn't beat. I had something for her ass 'cause on some real shit—although I was pissed that she'd slapped me—that shit also turned me the fuck on.

But I wasn't about to tell her no shit like that.

Nah. I had to check her lil' ass so she'd know to not ever do that shit again.

I whipped her pussy and clit up real good with that lash, then got between her legs and ate her like a man starving at the last supper. Licking, sucking, suckling, feasting, slinking my tongue inside her, sliding it in and out and all over her enflamed pussy lips and clit, then I hurled her over the edge when I pushed the tip of my finger into her ass, letting her know that ass was mine. I was claiming that shit.

I'd never tried to put my dick in Marika's ass because it's big as fuck. And I never wanted to put her through that kinda pain. But all bets were off when she took it to my face.

I pushed my finger in further and she exploded into my mouth, fucking my face, riding my mouth like it was a dick. Yeah, I know the shit was supposed to be punishment, but the shit turned her on. And the more turned on she got, the more turned on I got.

Mad or not, Marika had me turnt up. She looked sexy as fuck

blindfolded, hands tied, and gagged, with her breasts and cunt all whelped up, her nipples tight, her clit engorged.

No lie. She became my canvas that night, lashings and lust, want and need. Hurt and disappointment all displayed across her body.

I struggled to tear my gaze away from her. I wanted to scoop her up in my arms and hold her, let her know that shit was aiight between us, but she had to catch heat first. All of it in every part of her body, crackling fire.

Marika gasped and shook. I had her spooked. Had her in a sexual frenzy. Had her on the verge of losing it. I had her right where I wanted her.

Vulnerable.

Begging me to fuck her.

Begging me to forgive her.

"Get on your fuckin' knees, yo."

I tied her hands behind her back, then watched as she did what she was told. I slapped her ass, then pulled open her cheeks and slid the handle of the lash into the back of her swollen pussy. She wasn't getting this dick until I was ready to give it to her. I handle-fucked her until she came all over and around it, her pussy muscles milking the leather. Then I pulled it out and sucked it into my mouth, sucking her juices off, depriving her of a taste. Taunting her.

Then I caught her completely by surprise when I pressed on the wireless remote to them lil' vibrating panties I had her slip on.

She moaned.

And then I snapped the leather across her ass, hard. Harder. Harder. She whimpered. Pressed the remote for the highest setting. She groaned. I lashed her again, then again. My dick throbbed. And, although I couldn't see her eyes behind her blindfold, I imagined her eyes stinging with tears, the way her ass cheeks stung. I lashed her again. Warned her to never put her hands on me. Scolded her as if she were some snot-nosed brat who'd stuck her filthy hands in the cookie jar. I lowered the vibrators setting to a low hum. The flogger landed against her flesh, again. And she fucked my head up by pumping her hips, jutting her ass out for more.

She wanted it.

Begged for it.

Greedy ass!

Real shit, I almost nutted on myself.

I tossed the lash aside and began licking her cheeks, licking her crack, licking her hole. And then I eased in back of her, slathering lube all over my dick.

"Facedown." I pushed her head down into the mattress. "Ass up." The palm of my hand landed on her ass.

I flipped the vibrator back on high, and she moaned. Loud. Rolled her hips. Wanting this dick. Wanting the lash. Wanting everything I had to give her.

I drizzled oil over her cheeks, down into her ass, then slid my finger over her hole, then dipped inside, knuckle deep. Pulled out. More oil. Slid back in. One finger, then two.

Pulled out. More oil. Pushed back in. One finger, two, then three.

I pressed wet kisses into her sweaty neck. "That's right. I'ma make you nut outcha ass. I'ma have ya ass crawling into work tomorrow." I slapped her ass again with my free hand.

"You ready for this dick…?"

She grunted. Rolled her hips. Pumped her pelvis. Fucked my fingers into her ass.

I pulled out, sucked my fingers. Savored her ass. Then leaned in and stuck my tongue inside, prepping her, readying her as I reached around and palmed her pussy, pressing the vibrator tight against her clit. She groaned low, then loudly. "Yeah, that's it," I murmured into her crack. "Cream in them panties."

My tongue withdrew. It was time. My aching dick was ready. Her pulsing, winking hole was talking to me, aroused and on fire. I added more lube, then pressed the head of my dick up against her hole, slapping it, sliding it up and down over it, then pressing it against her entrance.

"Let me in. Let me get this ass."

I heard her suck in her breath, then let it out in a long exhale. I pushed in. Pushed in some more. She grunted. I pushed in some more. Stretching past her tightness.

"Yeah, there you go. The head's in."

I kept still. Heard her breaths rush from her nose. Heard her gulp in deep breaths over her gag. I coaxed her to fuck herself back on this dick. Urged her to slurp it into her ass.

And she did.

I wanted to push in balls deep, but I knew that shit would've killed her. I was tryna teach her ass a lesson. Not gut her intestines open.

I pulled back, fucked her hole with the tip of my dick, then plunged about six inches in, then seven, pulled out to the head. Tip fucked her, then plunged back in, seven inches, eight inches. Nine inches.

She screamed.

My teeth grazed her shoulder.

"Yeah. That's right…squeeze that dick…yeah, there you go… get that dick."

She grunted into her gag.

"Yeah, that's right. Give me that ass cream…"

She whipped her head around, chancing a look at me. Her teeth gnashed. Drool pooled out of her mouth, soaked into the leather ball. She cried out against the gag, "Yes! Yes!"

I fucked her slowly, sensually. I stretched her over my dick. Alternated the vibrator's speeds, fast, slow, intermittently as I fucked into her ass with shallow thrusts until she melted all over my dick and I was growling and my dick was pulsing. And heated seeds of pleasure jutted out in thick ropes inside her, coating her asshole, flooding her.

Marika limped for three days afterward. Her asshole throbbing, her ass cheeks swollen, a reminder of the ass fucking and whipping she'd gotten.

A soft knock sounds at the door, jolting me from my thoughts. I look up to see Arianna, my assistant, standing in the doorway, holding two folders in her hand.

"What's up," I say, straightening my tie. I shift in my chair. Press my legs together.

My fuckin' dick's on rock.

Shit.

Arianna walks into my office, wearing a powder-blue dress that clings to her body.

I blink, tryna recall the last time she's come to work with her body on display, showing all this ass and breasts. Plump. Juicy. Ripe and ready to be plucked and fucked.

"These in the first folder need your signature," she says, handing me the folder. "And this one here has the schedule the promotions team worked on for Carlos."

"Oh, aiight. When's the promo tour?"

She smirks. "It's all in the folder. In two months. They're wrapping up the finishing touches on his video as we speak. And it should start running sometime in the next week or so."

"Oh, aiight. And what's up with the interview with *Elle* and *Vibe*?"

"Scheduling issues. But we're on it."

I eye her.

Her brows crinkle. "What?"

"Um, where you going"—I point at her dress—"showin' all ya *ass*ets?"

She grins. "I'm not showing *all* of my nothing. I felt like dressing up, that's all."

I raise a brow. "Yeah, aiight. Let me find out you prowling."

She sucks her teeth, putting her hands on her round hips. "Whatever. Sign those documents, please. And look over Carlos' tour schedule." She starts shaking her ass for the door, then stops. "Oh, and your one o'clock is in the conference room."

"Is his manager with him?"

She nods. "Yes. And oh-emm-gee. He's frickin' *f-i-n-e. Fine.*" She fans herself.

I furrow my brow, giving her a confused look. "Who?"

I already know whom she's talking about, though. Roderick Grimes. This new cat, with green eyes and a Bohemian, neo-soul vibe, we're bringing into the label. Dude is from Texas. Dallas, I believe. And he's mad talented. He could become the next Maxwell as long as he stays focused and doesn't get caught up in dumb shit.

"Mister Dreamy Eyes, himself. I heard him singing. Ooh, he sounds good." She flashes her hands up. "I can see it now. Dreamy Eyes and Carlos on tour. We can call it the Pretty Boy tour."

I laugh opening one of the folders she's given me. "Girl, outta here with that."

She heads for the door, then turns back to me. "By the way, I wonder if the myth is true."

I look up from the document. "What myth is that?"

She grins. "That *everything* grows *big* in Texas."

I shake my head.

She grins, waggles her fingers and shuts the door behind her.

I groan inwardly, swiveling back and forth in my chair, glancing down in my lap.

My dick is still on rock.

THIRTY-NINE

Marika

"Hey, baby, where you at?"

I smile. "Just finished having drinks with Jasmine," I say, glancing at the time. It's a little before eight o'clock. "I'm on my way home now."

I'd met Jasmine at Mr. Chow in Tribeca for drinks and appetizers. And instead of following my first mind and driving here or calling a car service, I decided to take a taxi since our penthouse isn't that far from here.

I throw my hand up and wave for an oncoming taxi. It speeds by. I roll my eyes.

"Oh, aiight." He tells me he's thinking about heading down to the studio for a few hours after the radio show tonight to check on one of the new artists recently signed to the label. "You aiight with that?"

"Well, umm," I say saucily. "I was hoping to get a lil' taste before bedtime."

"Oh, word?" he lowers his voice. "What you tryna get a taste of?"

I wave at another oncoming taxi and it slows down, pulling to the curb. "I want a taste of that thick chocolate."

"Oh, word? You want some of daddy's chocolate?"

"Mmmmmhmmm," I purr. "You know my pussy loves daddy's thick chocolate."

I can practically feel him grinning through the phone. "Damn, you getting my shit hard. You know I love it when you call me daddy."

"I know you do," I coo, opening the door, then ducking into the cab. I give the driver my address, swinging the door shut. I sit back in my seat as he starts forward.

"But I'm sayin'…as bad as I'd love to slide home 'n' give my baby a round of dick, I really need to get down to the studio for at least an hour or two. But I got you when I get home. Aiight, baby?"

I smile. "I'll be sure to leave my panties off," I whisper, eyeing the driver as he watches me through his rearview mirror. For a second, I think I see him smiling, before he averts his stare.

"Nah, keep them shit's on, baby. I wanna pull 'em to the side.'

I moan low in my throat. "Mmm. I love the sound of that."

I get so caught up in my phone conversation, which quickly turns into three minutes of heated phone sex, with Marcel that I am not even aware that we've arrived in front of my building until the cab driver prompts me.

"Ma'am? We're here."

"Listen, baby, Nina just gave me the signal. We're about to go on the air."

"Oh, okay," I say, digging into my purse for the fare, then leaning forward. I hand the driver a twenty. "I'm in front of the building now. Thank you," I murmur to the driver before opening the door and stepping out into the evening air. "Can't wait to listen."

"Cool, cool. I'll hit you up on my break. Love you, baby."

"Mmm. Love you, too." I end the call, swinging the cab door shut and dropping my phone into my purse, then hurrying toward my apartment building.

"Hey, *mami*, I've been waiting for you. Long time no see."

I whip my head around. *Ohmygod!* "Bitch, are you crazy? What the hell are you doing here?" I reach into my purse. "I'm calling the police and telling them you're stalking me."

She yanks my bag. "Oh I wouldn't do that if I were you."

"What the hell is—?"

I don't get the rest of my words out. Marisol-Ramona-Alexandria reaches in her jacket and flashes a gun. My heart lurches as she aims the barrel at me.

I open my mouth to scream, but she slowly shakes her head, cocking the gun back. "Yell, scream, or say the wrong thing, bitch, and I'll shoot you in your face."

My eyes widen.

"I promise you. Tonight, I'll show you crazy, *mami*. Try me if you dare. I will put a hole in your head, then in your chest. Then drag you over behind the dumpster and wait for the rats to eat your skin off." Her eyes are unblinking when she says this. Snatches of our sexual encounter come into full view in my mind's eye. Followed by glimpses of the harassing phone calls. Showing up at my hotel room in Atlantic City. Popping up at the restaurant. Coming to my workplace. The threats. The obsession.

I blink. And then realization sets in. That everything that has been happening over the last several weeks with this bitch was leading up to this very moment.

"H-how…did you know where I live?" I stammer out, taking a slight step back.

"Don't ask stupid questions. I've been following you."

"Look, Marisol or Ramona or whatever name you're going by—"

She cuts me off. "It's *Ramona*. But it's about to be Missus Mar*Sell* Kennedy real soon."

Dear God!

I sweep my eyes toward the street, looking for help. There's no one out. Not one passerby. All is quiet. And it looks like I'm shit out of luck.

I swallow. "Listen, to me. You don't have to—"

"Oh, yes I do." She yanks my arm. "Now, let's go. We're going to walk into your building like we are the best of friends, then go up to your place. But if you even sneeze wrong or act like you want to send out an SOS alert with your eyes to that stumpy little prick at the desk, I'll shoot him first, then you. And trust me, bitch, I know how to use this. I've already shot one dumb fuck. Don't make me do it again."

She pokes the barrel into my side.

Oh, God, no!

"Now let's go." She loops her arm through mine.

"Please, wait. Let's—"

"Bitch, I said not another word. And I mean it."

I hear the gun click.

My knees buckle.

"Make a sound. And it'll be your last." She tightens her grip on my arm and pulls me along. "Now smile for the cameras," she says as we walk through the sliding glass doors. As soon as we step into the building the doorman, who looks from me to Ramona, tipping his head and smiling, immediately greets us.

"Evening, Missus Kennedy."

My heart pounds in my ears. I dart my eyes from him to Ramona, hoping he'll be able to pick up that I'm in distress. "G-good evening, Sheldon."

His brow furrows. "Is everything okay? You look a little pale."

Right at this moment I am terrified of what she might do if I yell for him to call the police or try to break free; the look in her eye tells me she's willing to pull the trigger, at any cost. I can't risk it. I won't chance it.

Ramona digs her nails into my arm, causing me to flinch.

"N-no," I say. "I'm okay; just a little tired I guess, that's all."

He tells me he hopes I get some rest as I'm being ushered toward the elevator. I force a smile. And as the doors close, Ramona says, "Maybe I won't have to kill you after all."

The blood drains from my face. The vacant look in her eye tells me she's more dangerous than I could have ever imagined.

My phone chimes as we step off the elevator. It's a text message. The chime lets me know it's from Marcel. A knot swells in my throat.

Ramona blinks. "Oh, no, *puta*..." She gestures with her hand. "Hand it over. Slow and easy."

I swallow. "Ramona, please," I plea. "Let's talk this through."

"Oh, now this shitty bitch wants to talk," she says more so to herself than to me. "Fuck you. What happened to talking when I was calling you, huh? What happened when I came down to your office building to talk to you woman to woman, huh? Oh, wait. I know. You told me to stop calling you. You slapped me. Remember that? And now you wanna talk? Oh, no. I'm done talking. Now hand over your phone."

My stomach quakes. I feel as if I'm going to be sick, reaching down into my purse and pulling out my cell. I hand it to her.

"I bet it was my bae calling."

I cringe.

Moments later we are at my door. I purposefully fumble with my keys to hopefully buy myself a few extra seconds, glancing up at the camera in hopes that Sheldon picks up on something.

"Hurry up."

Hands shaking, I put the key in the lock, turn it, and open the door. The security alarm beeps as the door slams in back of me. Ramona pulls her gun out. Points it at me, then at the alarm on the wall. "Shut the alarm, and don't try any funny business, or you. Are. Dead."

She stands in back over me, staring over my shoulder. Any thoughts of pressing in the panic code quickly leave me. Defeated, with my fate in her hands, I deactivate the alarm, and pray that this night doesn't end in tragedy.

She's fidgety. Looking around. Waving her gun frantically. And it's all making me really nervous. Frightened.

She points her gun at me.

"Ramona, listen to me. You don't have to do this. You can leave now, and no one has to ever know you were here."

"I'm not going anywhere. I'm here to claim what's mine. And I'm not leaving until *my* man gets home."

I swallow. Blink.

"In the kitchen. Now." I do as I'm told. She follows me. Then goes to one of the kitchen chairs, pulling it out. "Sit."

I take a deep breath. Try to calm myself. "Why are you doing this?"

"Bitch!" She snatches the crystal vase, filled with fresh-cut, long-stemmed lilies, from off the table and throws it, fierce and angry. Water, flowers, and glass hit the wall, then shatter to the floor. "Don't ask me a bunch of questions. And don't play stupid. You know why I'm doing this, because *you* left me no other choice. You did this! Now sit down. Shut the fuck up. And let me think."

I swallow, hard. My whole body is shaking on the inside. My knees wobble as I move toward the chair and sit. And my heart drops further when she pulls out a roll of duct tape from the inside of her jacket.

"W-what are you going to do with me?"

She stares at me hard. "I should fuck you in your ass the way you fucked me. Should make you feel what you made me feel. You made my pussy all wet and juicy. Made me come all over Mar*Sell*'s big, thick, long dick, while you stretched open my ass. You did that to me, *puta*!"

"Is that what you want, to fuck me? Y-you can…" Desperation rips through me. "You can take my ass. My pussy. My—"

"Bitch, I'm not going to take your pussy, or your ass. I'm going to *take* your man. I'm going to ride his dick in front of you. I want you to see the chemistry between us. Mar*Sell* loves me. I saw it in his eyes that night. Felt it in his touch. Now arms behind your back, wrists together."

She rips away a long strip of tape from the roll with her teeth. Then walks behind me, wrapping the tape around my wrists. I choke back a scream lodged way in the back of my throat. She tears off another strip, then another, wrapping my wrists tightly behind my back.

Please, God…get me through this.

My mind starts scrambling for words that will appease her. But what can you say to someone who is clearly undone and is convinced that her reality is real, no matter how fucked up it is?

"Please. Ramona. Listen to me. I'm sure you think what you feel for my husband is real, but you have to understand it's not love. It may feel like it. But it's infatuation. You're a beautiful woman."

"You shut your filthy lying mouth!" she hisses. "Don't tell me what I feel! All you had to do was let him go, bitch! I'm so sick of you bitches taking my men. First it was that Dominican-looking bitch fucking Alex. Now it's *you* trying to keep me from being with Mar*Sell*. Just like that bitch knew Alex was my man. You know me and Mar*Sell* belong together so why couldn't you just leave him, like I asked you to?"

I fight back tears as my life with Marcel flashes before my eyes. "I love my husband. And he loves me. I know there's someone special out there for you. You're a beautiful woman, who—"

"Wants your life, *puta*!"

And then I'm hit in back of the head, and everything else becomes a blur.

FORTY

Marcel

"What's good, my freaky peeps…if you're just tuning in, this is ya boy Mar*Sell*, your host for one of the hottest talk shows in the Tri-state area, *Creepin' 'n' Freakin' After Dark*. And maaaan, listen. Tonight's segment has been straight fire. As you heard from our last caller, dude caught his wife rockin' in the sheets with his sister and he took it to his sister's head. Knocked her eye sockets in and broke her jaw. Now what his wife and sister did was def some real foul-ish. But him putting his hands on his sister 'n' beating her like she was some dude on the street…" I pause, shaking my head, then sigh. "Man, that was dead wrong. They both violated his trust. And they were both outta pocket. But I don't care how big her dildo was, or how much man-swag she had, at the end of the day, she's still a female. Ya thoughts?"

The phone lines are lit up.

"Go 'head, caller…you're on the air."

"Man, fuc—*bleep* that. I woulda beat *both* their asses that night; word to mother, yo. I'm out bustin' my ass workin' 'n' holdin' shit down 'n' you behind my back ridin' some rubber dic—*bleep*, tryna play me for some sucker…" Dude huffs into the phone. "Hell, nah. Both y'all's asses gettin' handled."

I shake my head. "So, you think it's aiight for a cat to put his hands on a woman? By the way, what's your name? And where you calling from?"

"Oh, my bad. This's Truth from East Orange. And, nah, I don't think it's cool for any man to put his hands on a woman. Real men, don't beat *real* women. He gets his girl cousins or sisters to stomp her ass. Feel me? But bitches who on some grimy shit, or them stud bitches swingin' dic—*bleeps* hell yeah. Fuc—*bleep* what ya heard, fam, I'ma equal opportunity ass whooper. You dickin' my girl like you a dude, then you gettin' that ass handled."

Oh, this muhfucka's thinking is real fucked up. "I heard that, play-boy. Thanks for calling in." I end the call. "Next caller. What's ya comment? You're on the air."

"Oh, hi. This Twinkie from Fairlawn..."

Twinkie? What the fuck? "Oh, aiight, Twinkie. What's ya comment, ma-ma?"

"Well, I wanna say, I understand the guy who caught his wife in bed with his sister being upset and doing what he did. He was shocked and felt disrespected. I know because the same thing happened to my husband."

I blink. Sit up in my seat. "Say, what? Ya hubby caught you in bed with his sister, too?"

"No, no. He caught me in bed with the same woman we'd had a threesome with."

I swallow. "Damn. How'd that happen?"

"What? The threesome? Or him catching us?"

"Both," I say, glancing over into the control room at Nina. She shakes her head, smiling.

"Well, the threesome was my husband's idea. He'd been asking for one for years, and I'd kept telling him no. But then, for my thirtieth birthday, we went to this sex club in New York and.... liked it. So when he asked me a few months later about doing a threesome with one of his coworkers, I said okay..."

"Damn, ma-ma." I adjust my headphones as I talk. "So it was good like that?"

"Yes," she says softly. "It made me curious for more. And I wanted to finally give my husband what he wanted."

"Oh, aiight. So then what happened? Don't hold back now, baby? Give us the nasty."

She chuckles, then lets out a heavy sigh. "Well, the *nasty* is, he brought his coworker home, who I knew and felt comfortable with, and the three of us"—she clears her throat—"well, we did what grown folks do behind closed doors. Afterward, she went her way, and my husband and I continued doing what we do."

Will she get to the fuckin' juicy shit already, damn! I sigh. "So what happened next?"

"I couldn't stop thinking about that night. And started questioning if I were a lesbian or not. I never had those kinds of feelings or thoughts before. But," she pauses, "I don't know. Something must have happened that night. It made me come alive or something. All I know is, I started seeing her behind my husband's back. And the one day that my husband decided to come home for lunch…" She pauses again, then sniffles. "He catches us."

"Oh, damn. What'd he do?"

"He cursed his coworker out and told her to get out. Then he stood there and watched her get dressed. Then when she left, he went off on me. Accusing me of always being a lesbian. He called me all types of undercover dykes and other dirty, hurtful names. And telling our two kids that I'm a whore."

"Damn." I shake my head. "That's crazy."

"I know. Now he wants a divorce. And he wants custody of our kids. My whole life is a mess."

Poor thing.

"I'm sorry to hear how things turned out for you. But like I always tell peeps, threesomes are nice fantasies, but they're not meant to be every couple's reality. Most peeps can't handle what might pop off afterward. All it takes is one person to disrupt your whole world…"

I shift in my seat. Relieved that things with that nutty-ass Ramona chick hadn't gotten much more crazy than her incessant phone calls and emails and idle threats. On some real shit, I'm just glad she finally got the hint. And we haven't heard anything else from her.

I take a deep breath, exhaling slowly. "Stay lifted, ma-ma. Next caller. You're on the air with ya boy, Mar*Sell*…"

"Yo, what's goodie, man? This Lance from Teaneck."

"Oh, aiight, playboy…what's on ya mind?"

"Man, listen. Me 'n' my girl had a threesome 'n' that shit was off the hook, fam. My girl's mad cool 'n' real open 'bout gettin' it in."

"Oh, aiight. Cool cool. That's what's up. So, what's the problem?"

He huffs. "Man, listen. Now she's pressing me for 'bout letting another muhfucka get down with us."

I lick my lips. "Oh, word? And you tryna bless her with that."

"Say what? Fuc—*bleep* outta here, man. I ain't with that gay-ass shit. Ain't no way I'm about to let another niggah run up in my girl. And I def ain't with touching up on no other muhfucka. What I look like tryna have another niggah's dic—*bleep* slapping up against mine?"

I shake my head. "Man, there's nothing *gay* about two cats who are comfortable in their sexualities making it pop in the sheets with a chick. You sound like you struggling with some other ish, man."

"Yo, what the fuc—*bleep* is you sayin', B? I know you not even tryna call me out on some slickness?"

"Check this. Why you gettin' defensive, playboy? No slickness here, fam. All I'm saying is, if you're not comfortable with sharing ya girl with another cat, then cool. Say that. But saying all that extra ish makes you sound homophobic."

"Yo, man, fuc—*bleep* you. Ain't shit homo about me, muhfucka. I'm all man."

I laugh. "Yeah. And there lies the second red flag of the night. A *real* man doesn't need to *say* he's all man, he just is. Just like a man who is secure in his manhood and in his sexuality doesn't need to associate having a threesome with another dude in the sheets with him 'n' his girl as some *gay-ass* ish. If it's not your thing, then it's not your thing."

"Yo, fuc—*bleep* you, niggah. Just because you riding that rainbow shit 'n' wanna be some gay activist, don't push that shit on me. Go suck a dic—*bleep*, muhfucka."

I laugh again. "Sounds like insecurity to me, bruh. But it's all good. Go handle ya demons, bruh. Next caller."

There's a silent pause.

"Caller, you there?"

"I'm here, *papi*. Oh, how I've missed you…"

I blink. "Yo, what the…? Listen, you've been told not to call here."

"Before you hang up, or try calling the police, you should know I'm here with this sexy piece of ass you chose over me. But let's see how sexy she is when I'm done carving all in her face…"

My heart drops. "Excuse me? What did you say?"

"You heard me. I'm here with this sweet pus—*bleep*—y, *puta!*

I hear muffled screaming.

Motherfuck! "Yo, let me speak to my wife!"

"Oh, she's not taking calls. She's tied up at the moment."

Oh, fuck!

My first thought is to snatch off these headphones and haul ass back to my crib, but my legs won't move. Something keeps me planted in my chair. Tells me to keep this broad on the phone for as long as I can.

I feel my whole muthafuckin' world crashing in around me.

"I love you, Mar*Sell*, baby…"

I blink.

"I've always loved you. From the moment I laid eyes on you eight years ago in *Vibe*, I fantasized about being with you. But I never thought it would happen. Then late one night when I was in my cell, I heard *you* on the radio. And I knew I had to have you. I fell in love with you that night, *papi*. I've played your voice over and over in my head, masturbating, bringing myself to pleasure. You always know the right things to say to get me so wet and juicy. You have no idea how many nights I laid awake in my bunk, playing with myself."

I blink again. *Cell? Bunk? What the fuck?*

Nina rushes over to my desk, and whispers, "I'll call the police."

I shake my head. "Look, Ramona, I'm beggin' you. Let me talk to my wife."

"Oh, now you wanna be nice. Now you wanna beg. Okay. I'll play nice, for now. Only because I love you."

I cringe.

"Here, and make it quick."

I hear what sounds like something being ripped off of flesh. Tape?

"M-mar*Sell*…"

"Marika, baby?" Real shit, hearing her voice brings fuckin' tears to my eyes. "Yo, baby, you okay? Did that crazy broad hurt you?"

"N-no. But she—"

"Now, now. Let's not get all mushy on me."

My heart is racing. I force myself to breath in. Then exhale. Fight to stay calm. "Just tell me what you want. And it's yours."

"I *want* you. But you made it clear that wasn't going to ever happen. Remember? You practically told me I wasn't shit to you. Even after having all your dic—*bleep* in me. You treated me like shit. You hurt me, Mar*Sell*. I'm so sick of you big-dic—*bleep* niggahs using me."

"I never used you…"

"Yes, you did! Just like that fuc—*bleep*—ing Alex did. I hate lying-ass, big-dick motherfuc—*bleep*—ers! Alex knew how much I loved him, too. And so do you. And you both fuc—*bleep*—ing shitted all over my heart!"

This broad sounds like she's soaring off of something. My brain starts scrambling for words to talk her down, before she does some reckless shit. "Listen, baby. Please. Whatever you're thinking, you don't have to do it."

"*Pendejo!* Now I'm your *baby*. What was I all those weeks ago when I begged you to be with me, huh? What was I when I told you how much I loved you? What was I when you refused my phone calls and blocked me from your life? What, you thought you could make love to me, fuc—*bleep* me in *mi coño*, then take it all away from me."

I swallow. "Listen. I was wrong. Okay? I shoulda never treated you like that."

She huffs. "Well, you did, motherfuc—*bleep*—er! Now I'm gonna hurt you. You broke my heart. And now I'm gonna break yours."

"Let's talk this out. I'm sorry. Let Marika go. Okay? I'll come to you, and we can go anywhere you want. Just you and me."

"Just the two of us?"

I nod my head as if she can see me. "Yes. You and me, baby."

"Don't play games with me."

"I'm not playing games. I got you. You 'n' me."

"And you'll leave this bitch?"

"Yes. I'll leave her. I'll do whatever you want. Just don't hurt her."

"Well, then I want you to tell the whole world out there listening about our night together. Tell them how much you love me. Then we can be together. Tell the world how you realized how you *never* loved this bitch until the night you fuc—*bleep*—ed me. You and your fuc—*beep*—ing wife want to keep what the two of you did to me a dirty secret. Well, tonight, I want you to tell them, Mar*Sell*. Tell them how your wife fuc—*bleep*—ed me in my ass, while I rode your dic—*bleep*. Tell them how this bitch ate my pus—*bleep*—sy while I sucked all over your long, black…" She moans.

"Listen to me…"

"No! You listen! Tell your listeners how you and this bitch took turns fuc—*bleep*—ing me and how much I loved it."

Nina gasps.

And, I, well, fuck. I practically shit on myself, fucking stunned that all this shit is unfolding over the air.

"Tell, them now, Mar*Sell*. Tell your precious listeners, *now!*"

I look over and give Nina a pained look. She stares blankly at the phone lines, then manages to look at me and nod.

I swallow hard. "That's right, my freaky peeps," I say slowly.

"No, goddamn you! Say it like you mean it! Give it to them how you love it. Real raw and juicy!"

I glance back over at Nina. She's still on the phone with the police. She rushes to my desk and slides me a note asking for my address and saying the police want me to keep this chick on the phone, which I planned on doing anyway. I quickly jot down my address, and slide the note back to her.

I take a deep breath, then go into script, for Marika.

"That's right, my freaky peeps. Y-y'all heard it here. Live 'n' direct. Ya boy 'n' his wife got it in w-with this beauty on the line 'n' wore her guts out. We brought her up to our hotel room, got between the sheets, and rocked her lights out, dug in all three holes…"

She moans. "Mmm. Tell them how good it was."

I swallow. Right now, all I give a fuck about is doing and saying whatever the fuck I gotta to keep this broad from hurting Marika. So I go into explicit detail, reliving that whole night over the air-waves.

"Tell them how much you love me," she pants into the phone.

I swallow back the vomit rising in the back of my throat. My jaw tightens. My nostrils flare and I suck in deep, steadying breaths, tryna keep my shit in control. "I…love you." I croak back a groan. "I love you, aiight?" I feel like acid is burning the back of my throat. "Now let Marika go. Please."

"See, bitch!" she yells. "I told you! He loves me! You hear that! Say it again, Mar*Sell*. Let this bitch hear it!" I say it again. "He loves *me*! Not you, you ass fucker! You hear that, Alex! Fuc—*bleep* you! I got me a real man now who loves me! Not some big-dick dog like you! I'm over you, Alex Maples!"

I frown, tryna figure out who the fuck she's babbling about.

"No man ever made me come the way you did, Mar*Sell*. Your dic—*bleep* is so big…"

I cringe, but let her keep talking.

"And you ate my pus—*bleep*—sy better than any man I've ever been with. Better than any dike bitch I let eat me when I was locked up. I never had a tongue make my whole body shake. But, you, baby…you gave it to me so good…"

I groan inwardly. *Yeah, too muthafuckin' good!*

"My last lover was good in bed, too. Damn good. But all he was good for was fuc—*bleep*—ing and sucking and using women. I thought he loved me, but that tall, black, chocolate niggah never meant me any good. All he did was use me. Run through my money. Played emotional games. He liked to mind fuc—*bleep* women. And that's why I shot his ass. Left him for dead…"

I blink. *Oh, fuck!*

Nina slides me another note. Tells me the police are at my building. I sigh, relieved, hoping they get to her before it escalates.

"But, you, baby…I'm not gonna shoot you. I'm gonna—"

"Listen to me," I quickly say. "I don't know who this dude is who screwed you over. And it's none of my business. But, obviously dude didn't deserve someone like you. All I care about is you not doing anything stupid 'n' crazy, yo."

"I'm NOT fuc—*bleep*—ing *crazy!* Stop calling me that shit."

"I'm not calling you crazy. I said I don't want you doing anything cray—"

"Don't say *that* word! Or I swear I'll do something you'll regret. Don't make me do it, baby. Okay?"

I can feel Nina staring into me as she hands me another note. I glance at it. The police want me to keep this broad calm. Want me to not saying anything that's going to push her to the edge.

These muhfuckas actin' like I don't already know this shit.

I nod my head, and keep talking. I tell this broad whatever it is she wants to hear. I start asking her shit that I don't give a fuck about. Like, where she was born. *Nuthouse.* What her favorite color is. *Institutional gray.* What her zodiac sign is. *Crazy.*

"I wanna get to know you," I lie, straining to keep my composure. "If we're gonna be together, baby, then we have to trust each other."

My stomach twists in knots. I feel like I'ma shit on myself fuckin' with this broad. But I know it's what I have to do. So I tell her whatever she wants to hear. Then I tell her I wanna speak to Marika.

"Why? What the hell you want to speak to this bitch for?"

"To tell her that it's me and you now, that it's over between us. But I want her to hear it from me."

"I promise you, *papi*. Don't cross me."

"I won't."

A few excruciating seconds go by before I hear Marika's strained voice.

My heart is pounding so hard that I can barely think straight. I do all I can do to keep from breaking down.

"Marika, baby…I love you."

Sniffles. "I love you, too. Always."

"I know, baby. Listen. I need you to hold on, aiight? I'm gonna get you outta this shit, aiight?"

"S-s-she has a—"

Pop!

A shot is fired.

Nina shrieks, every ounce of blood draining from her face.

"MARIKA!" I cry out, my voice choking off in a sob. Fear slashing through my heart as I leap from my seat, cupping my hands tightly over my headphones.

My blood freezes.

The gun goes off twice more. Then there's a deadly, crippling silence over the airwaves.

Six months later
Margarita Island, Venezuela…

Dead. Everything inside of me, everything I am, died the night Marika was found in a river of blood.

Shot in the head.

Dead.

Murdered.

Thirty-six years old.

By some unstable broad who had fuckin' delusions that she was in love with me. That she and I were meant to be together. When all *we*—Marika and I—did was fuck her. Love? Fuck outta here! That broad fell in love with the dick, real and silicone. Not me. But somehow she got it stuck in her raggedy-ass head that I was hers. And fucked my whole world up.

She shot Marika twice, then turned the gun on herself.

One night of a hard dick, and all-night fucking cost me the love of my life.

My soul mate.

My lover.

My best friend.

The woman I loved getting freaky with. Loved baring my naked soul to.

Gone.

I swallow back a wave of emotions, glancing out into the Caribbean Sea.

Burying Marika was probably the hardest thing besides having to identify her body that I've ever had to do. I'm still shaken by it.

Still haunted by it.

Still fucked up over it.

All I've felt is emptiness, nothing but overwhelming numbness.

That broad, Ramona Ramirez—with all of her fuckin' aliases: Marisol Rodriguez, Alexandria Maples, and whoever the fuck else—had done this shit before. Stalk a muhfucka. Get the dick 'n' get nutty over it. That Alexander Maples cat, the one she kept rattling on about over the radio. She'd shot him several times and left dude for dead, all because he wasn't checkin' for her romantically. Fuckin' craziness, yo. She was on the run for over three months before they snatched her ass up in Arizona, where she was stalking some other muhfucka. So how the fuck she only served three years for that shit is beyond me. Good behavior or some other shit.

I sigh, reaching over for my drink and taking a sip. I swallow, then lick my lips, setting the cool drink back up on the small table. I reach over and grab the coconut oil and slather the front of my body with it, stretching my hand over my limp dick, oiling it up. Here I am stretched out one of the world's most beautiful nude beaches in Venezuela...alone.

This shit's not a good feeling. But I needed to get away from the media, from the paparazzi, from the memories. I needed to get from under the scrutiny, and the gossip, and the speculation about Marika and my sex life.

"Were the two of you in an open marriage?"

"Is it true your wife was bisexual?"

"Did the two of you engage in the swingers' lifestyle?"

"Rumors have been floating around for years that you are also bisexual. Care to comment?"

Fuck outta here.

Like I'd told one reporter, "Marika and I loved each other, unconditionally. We held no secrets. And we had no inhibitions. Our public life is open for the public to pull apart. But our private life, how we got down behind closed doors, is not open for discussion. Never has been. And it never will be. Now respect the fact that I'm grieving the loss of my wife, and fall the fuck back."

And that ended that.

Will I ever publicly disclose being bisexual? Nah. For what? That shit's no one's business unless I'm tryna build a life with you. Otherwise that shit is on a need-to-know basis.

I close my eyes. Allow the blazing sun to beat across my naked body.

I miss you so fuckin' much, baby...

"Excuse me? *Hablas español?*"

I raise my head and slowly lift my shades up over my head, and use my hand to shield my eyes from the sun. My breath catches. There's a curvaceous beauty standing in front of me.

Her bronze skin glitters under the rays.

"Nah, I don't."

"Oh, okay. You mind if I take this chair?" she says, pointing to the beach chair beside me.

I allow my eyes to rake up and down her body. Butt-ass naked, titties melon-ripe 'n' juicy, hips real thick, waist nice 'n' tight... she's bad as fuck!

There's a mischievous glint in her eyes.

"Nah, you good. Do you."

I drop my shades back down over my eyes, then lean back allowing the sun to bake into my skin.

Where was I? Oh, right...my life. I know at some point I gotta get back to the States, back to my life. I now not only have my label to run, I've inherited Marika's publishing house. Yeah, I held shares in the company, but it was her baby. One I'll die trying to keep alive. For her.

Right now, thinking about that shit makes my heart ache. Since Marika's death—nah, murder, I've left the radio station. Although I enjoyed kicking it live on the radio, that night—with my whole world unraveling for all to hear—crushed me. The love and support from my million-plus listeners and from around the globe has been real heartfelt, but still too overwhelming. I'm not ready to hit the airwaves, maybe never.

"Is this your first time on Margarita Island?" the silky voice says, floating over to me.

I turn my head in her direction. "Nah. My second time."

Her gaze slides from my face to my chest, then down to my abs, before lowering to my dick. Her tongue glides over her lips.

"Are you here alone?"

"Yeah," I say, staring at those beautiful milk wagons of hers. My mind starts wandering, imagining sucking her nipples into my mouth, and gently grazing my teeth over them. And a part of me feels guilty for lusting. "You?"

"No. With my husband and another couple."

"Oh, aiight." I reach for my drink, and take two long sips, swallowing back my dirty thoughts. I haven't fucked in six months. Haven't had the desire, or the energy to. Fuck, I haven't even sucked my own dick, or jacked off. And the last time I tried it, my shit went limp.

This whole shit has left me impotent. Turned me into one big-ass noodle-dick muhfucka.

"I don't mean to be straightforward," Beautiful says. "But…"

I don't wanna straight up ig her. But all I wanna do is bake under the sun and be alone in my thoughts. I inhale. Then slowly turn my head back in her direction. I exhale. "Speak ya mind."

"You have a beautiful body, and are exceptionally well-endowed. How many inches is that beautiful piece of man meat?"

"Thirteen, hard." *Yeah, when the muhfucka could get hard.*

She gasps, sliding a hand along the column of her neck, then over her breast.

"Where are you from?" she wants to know.

Why the fuck I didn't I bring my iPad and earphones?

I tell her New York. She tells me she's originally from Atlanta, but has lived in Germany with her husband—who's British, for the past five years.

"Oh, aiight."

I take another sip of my drink, then set the glass back down. I feel the alcohol slowly heating my insides. It's been a minute since I've tossed back a drink. With all that's popped off, I was afraid I'd end up becoming a full-fledged drunk if I'd taken to the bottle like I'd wanted and drank my sorrows away.

I choke back my emotions, turning my head so that this beauty eyeing me doesn't see that I'm on the verge of tears. It's so fuckin' hard to live life knowing the one you thought you'd spend the rest of your life living, loving and enjoying it with is gone.

Sometimes I wake up in the middle of the night, gasping for air, feeling as if I'm being suffocated, as if the life is being sucked out of me.

Then there are times when I get so overwhelmed with grief that I break down and start crying, balling like a fuckin' baby, because I'm fuckin' hurting. Other times, I'm consumed with guilt. Re-playing that night over and over in my head. Blaming myself for

Marika's death. Wondering if there was something I could have done, or said—or maybe something I did or said that I shouldn't have—that would have saved her life.

Sixteen years, gone! I wish those bullets would have been for me, then I wouldn't be here suffering in loneliness and filled with so much pain. *Why'd she have to leave me here on this earth without the love of my life?*

Marika fuckin' loved me. All of me. Every fuckin' stretch of my naked flaws, she loved, and accepted...unconditionally. And she allowed me to be me. No judgment. No ridicule. She simply got it. She understood the kind of man I am.

We had no secrets.

We were able to express ourselves freely. Explore our sexualities openly. She delighted in keeping the heat turned up in the sheets. There were no inhibitions. That shit didn't exist for us.

Now what?

I don't know if I will ever find that kind of love again. Or ever have the kind of openness Marika and I shared with another woman. Not that I'm looking. It's too soon for me to even consider it. I'm still too broken. Still...

I stare out into the Caribbean Sea. Reflect on my life, with and without Marika.

For the first time in my life, I'm so fuckin' lonely.

Yeah, I can get pussy. Yeah, I can get neck. But I can't ever get back the one thing that has always mattered the most—Marika's love.

I take several deep breaths, then exhale. Somehow, I have to accept life as it is, trusting that everything happens for a reason; that this is where I'm supposed to be...today.

I close my eyes briefly, and when I reopen them, I can feel her eyes on me. I turn to her, catching the lust in her stare as her eyes roam my body. Something else flickers in her eyes, when she smiles, and says, "My husband and I saw you earlier laying out on the beach." Her voice is low and sexy. "And we've been eyeing you all week."

"Oh, word? What, y'all swingers or something?"

"No, not really. We try not to live our lives defined by labels. We're what you'd call, free-spirited."

"Oh, aiight. Uninhibited."

"Yes, exactly." She swipes a strand of hair from her face. "I wish more people were so."

I grin. "True. I feel you. So, y'all like to get it in."

It's a statement, not a question.

"Yes." She lowers her voice. "Every now and then, we like to let our hair down, while we're on vacation, and express ourselves sexually. We love beautiful people. Men *and* women with hot bodies and…delicious packages."

Code: We're special kind of freaks.

"Oh, word?"

I feel my dick slowly starting to stir.

The lust in her gaze is starting to awaken the beast.

I want some pussy. Nah, I *need* that shit. Some juicy pussy with a side order of wet mouth and tight neck, followed by a long, wet tongue sliding over this asshole.

I feel my balls starting to heat. "So, y'all tryna fuck," I boldly say, staring at her peaked nipples. My mouth starts to water.

"We'd definitely love to have you join us back at our villa for a night of *naughty* fun, if you're open to it."

I eye her, reaching for my dick and slowly stroking it. "You lick ass?"

She licks her lips. "Love it."

"You think you can handle this dick?"

She stares at it. Admires it. I can see the wheels in her head spinning with fantasies. "My husband is eight inches. What's five more inches? I'd love to *come* trying."

"Oh, aiight."

I glance down at my stretching dick, feel it coming alive.

True, I'm missing my wife. But I'm still a man. And I have needs. I have desires. And wants. And right now, my dick's come alive and I'm horny as fuck. And these balls are aching for release. I have six months of nut backed up in me.

A few moments pass between us.

I turn to her once more, inhaling her sweet scent. "Yo, ya man suck dick?"

She stares at me, unblinking. A sly smile slowly eases over her lips.

"Oh, that can definitely be arranged."

My dick rocks up, hard 'n' ready. And I take this as a sign.

I glance up at the bright, blue sky and smile, wiping a lone tear that slides down my face. Marika filled my life with so much joy. But, I have to move on. And there seems to be no better time than the present. Between the sheets, lost in the warmth of a tight, wet pussy...and a warm, juicy mouth.

ABOUT THE AUTHOR

Cairo is the author of *Ruthless, Retribution, Slippery When Wet, Big Booty, Man Swappers, Kitty-Kitty, Bang-Bang, Deep Throat Diva, Daddy Long Stroke, The Man Handler,* and *The Kat Trap.* His travels to Egypt inspired his pen name.

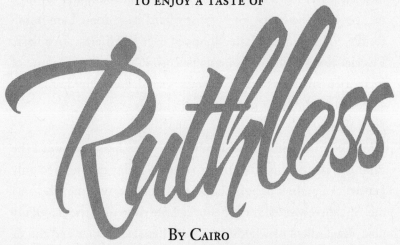

By Cairo

Available now from Strebor Books

Prologue

Remorse and guilt don't exist in an empty heart...

I wasn't born a killer.

And I hadn't initially planned on becoming one. I had hoped that if I had to murder anyone, Jasper would be first on my list. Not Felecia. Not my flesh and blood.

But here I am.

In the flesh.

A killer.

A murderer.

Still clutching the gun in my hand, I stare into Felecia's dead face. Her eyes wide and frozen in fear, her curled lashes still wet with tears, what's left of her bloody mouth is gaped open, front teeth cracked and knocked out, smoke still floating out of her lying dick suckers. I feel a surging rush of adrenaline pumping through me, yet I feel *nothing*—for her, for what I have done. I am numb to this, to her current state. Slumped over and lifeless. In a flash, Felecia, along with every mental snapshot—an entire lifetime of memories—of everything we've ever shared, gone. Her last breath snatched by the bitch she tried to do in. Me.

By choice.

I stare at the gun in my bloody hand, then look up toward the ceiling as if expecting the roof to open up at any moment, to only get struck by a bolt of lightning. This bitch betrayed me. She hurt me. She disrespected me. She fucked me over. And she *fucked* my man. Regardless of whether it's over between Jasper and me or not, this bitch fucked him, sucked him, while things with him were good—even if they were only in my own head. And the bitch continued fucking him on the sly—*after* shit between him and me went downhill.

So *I* killed her.

By choice.

Because I wanted her dead! Because she deserved to be dead! Because she ran her mouth and popped shit.

Sadly, I feel not one ounce of sorrow. No regret. No remorse. No guilt. Nothing. And no goddamn tears.

I'll admit. Killing this bitch wasn't my initial intention. No. I planned on confronting her, allowing her the chance to confess, to redeem herself—not that anything that came out of her cum trap was going to change the damage already done. She and I would never be close again. Then I was going to slip out of my heels and beat her ass real good. However, somewhere in the back corners of my mind, I knew it was a slight possibility that I would take it to her skull—not with my fist, with a bullet—if the bitch came at me sideways and crazy.

And she did.

The more she tried to lie and deny her way out of shit, the stronger the urge became. The more reckless she talked, the deeper my conviction became. Then the bitch had the audacity to tell me she was pregnant. The admission of who planted his nut in her became scribbled in the fear shown in her eyes. It was Jasper.

So, for that, I took her life. There was no blackout. There was no lack of judgment. There was no temporary moment of insanity. I didn't just get caught up in the moment. I was clear *and* in my right frame of mind when I reached in back of me and pulled out my 9mm, shoving it down into her motherfucking throat.

And I was fully cognizant of the look in her eyes when I pulled the trigger.

I am *still* very much aware of what I've done. *I've* murdered her.

And the scary thing is—standing here taking in the splattered blood on the walls and the loose teeth knocked out of her big-ass mouth—I know, deep down in the pit of my soul, I am very much certain, I'll have no problem doing it again, if I have to, *when* I have to…*if* I am forced to.

Bitch wanted to be me. Thought she was going to snatch my spot. I'm convinced she wanted me dead. Wished it. Hoped for it. Shit, the bitch admitted she didn't give a fuck. That she didn't care then. And damn sure didn't care now. I'm glad I didn't allow her up to the hospital to hover over my bed, secretly gloating that she'd had a hand in doing me in while I clung to my life, and sanity.

I glance over at the clock: 10:38 P.M. Then step away from her body. I walk into the bathroom and wash off the blood on the gun and my hands, carefully drying them. Then I wash my face, glancing up from the sink at the reflection staring back at me in the mirror. I don't like what I see.

I don't even know who I see.

The bitch staring back at me has my face, my complexion, my hazel eyes. But she is still a stranger to me. I don't like her.

I don't like me.

But this is who I am.

This is what I've become.

Thanks to Jasper.

Thanks to Felecia.

Thanks to every motherfucker who took his turn at fucking my throat raw.

I flip off the light and walk back out into my office over to my desk and pull out one of the burner phone's Lamar had given me, then place a call. "Who this?"

"Pasha."

"Oh, what's good? You still need that remodeling work done?"

"Yes. I'm ready for that paint job," I say, unlocking and opening my office door, then walking into the staff lounge, going over to the counter and pulling out the top drawer. I grab a steak knife, then shut the drawer. "And I need the carpet pulled up and tossed along with all the *dead* weight in the room."

"Oh, aiight."

He understands, clearly. She's dead. He's the only person I told about my meeting with her tonight here. The only person who I let know things might get ugly between us. He was the only person I let hear the extent of my rage toward her. And when I told him out of anger that I felt like killing her ass, he said, "Then maybe she should catch it. What she did was some real grimy shit. You didn't deserve that. So, whatever you decide, I'ma ride it out with you. Real shit, ma, I know that's ya fam 'n' all, but I think you should handle her."

He said it with no expression, no emotion. Then leaned into my ear and whispered, "I have a professional cleanup crew *in case…* things get bloody. I can get you a piece that won't ever trace back to you. You won't have to do anything except pull the trigger."

He walked me through it. Told me to make sure to turn off the security cameras just in case I decided to handle her—*permanently*, so no one would see her coming in if anyone were to ever ask to see any footage. Not that they would have reason to. But I needed to be three steps ahead. He told me to be sure to meet with her in my office, where it's soundproofed. Then handle my business.

"Right after you pop her top, hit me up and I'll handle everything else. I *specialize* in these kinds of jobs. Security work is my other gig." Without him saying more than that, it was evident at that very moment that there was a whole lot more to my armed-security stud. "You wanna rid ya'self of a poisonous snake before it has a chance to strike again, chop off its head."

The seed had been planted. Her slick mouth sealed her fate.

Hate me? Bitch, please!

There is no room in my life for snitches and snakes. Felecia really thought she'd reap some hefty reward by snaking me. Thought she had snatched her the door prize, along with a quick come-up by backstabbing me. Ha! I showed that bitch. She couldn't have possibly thought she'd get away with it. She almost did.

Almost.

But getting caught happens to the best of us. Eventually she would have to pay her dues. It was only a matter of time. And, tonight, her time had come.

It's over. When I walk out of here tonight, I will go home, grab a bottle of wine, run a bubble bath, then soak away any memory of tonight. Then I am going to pop two sleeping pills and sleep the rest of the night away free from any chance of being plagued with nightmares of what I've done. And, before the crack of dawn, I will wake up with a smile plastered on my face. Catch my flight to Los Angeles to spend the day with my son. Catch the red-eye flight back. Then Tuesday morning, bright and early, I will step up in my salon, facing the day with the same renewed purpose. To shut down *everyone* else who had a hand in hurting me.

And I will go on with my life as if nothing ever happened tonight. As if I hadn't laid eyes on this bitch in almost two weeks. I will pretend she never existed. As if, minutes ago, I'd never pulled the trigger, blowing a hole in the back of her head.

I grab a pair of latex gloves, then the toolbox from under the cabinet and take out a wrench and a pair of pliers, then place the toolbox back in its place.

"Oh, aiight. You still there?"

I walk back into my office. "Yes." He already knows where to park his trucks. Around the back of the building as we discussed. He knows to enter through the emergency exit door on the side of the building where the staff lounge is. I snap my fingers, suddenly remembering something. *Yes, that's exactly what I need.* A large bag of ice and a cooler. I pull out the key to my storage closet, unlocking it, then taking out what I need. One last piece to finish this bitch off...